PROMISED PASSION

She didn't need his help, Nareen told herself fiercely. She certainly didn't want it. Yet in spite of her silent protestations, Nareen knew that she lied. This man, this moment, were exactly what she wanted. And she had wanted them for what seemed a long, long time.

Her body shivered, her teeth still chattered, but within her rose a swelling urgency that drowned her physical discomfort in a surging tide of desire.

It ought to be so wrong. She was a runner. She and she alone ruled her emotions and her body. Her city was in danger and she carried information that her Master needed.

Yet none of that mattered. Not now.

Within this wagon, here in the wavering shadows cast by a guttering candle, there were just the two of them. A man and a woman. Together.

A DISTANT STAR

ANNE AVERY

LOVE SPELL BOOKS ◆ NEW YORK CITY

*To my mother, who cared enough to tell me
my first efforts at writing a book still needed a little work.
And to Jan Meriwether, who listened.*

LOVE SPELL®

June 2004

Published by

Dorchester Publishing Co., Inc.
200 Madison Avenue
New York, NY 10016

ISBN 0-505-52335-3

The name "Love Spell" and its logo are trademarks of Dorchester Publishing Co., Inc.

Printed in the United States of America.

Visit us on the web at www.dorchesterpub.com.

Prologue

The wind whipped through the open door with a cold wail, pushing the old man before it and stirring the flames of the meager coals burning in the rusted brazier. The man turned to shut the door, shoving against the heavy wood with his shoulder.

Though the papers and maps before him stirred in the sudden draft, the younger man seated at the table paid them no heed. His gaze was fixed instead on his visitor.

"It was a false lead," said the old man. He crossed to the table with a heavy, dragging gait. "That runner you hired has returned, but it wasn't worth the coin you paid. The man wasn't your brother."

For an instant the glittering candlelight reflected, hard and cold, in the icy blue of the younger man's eyes. His fist thumped down on the table, making the papers jump. "Damn a backward world like this!"

He rose abruptly and pushed back his chair. Its wooden legs screeched against the stone flagging. On his feet, he towered over his companion.

"I could have found that out myself two weeks ago if I'd simply transported in. But instead, because you insist we follow the Rediscovery Service's rules, we waste time and learn nothing." His fists clenched. "Do you still maintain the rules apply to us?"

The old man nodded, his mouth set in an obstinate line. "They're good rules, Jerrel. Too many problems have been caused by people using our technology on worlds that weren't ready for it. Do you want to see another war like the one on Argus two hundred years ago, when our people landed and announced they'd come to bring those farmers back into the Empire?"

"That was just bad luck," Jerrel snapped. "No one knew those primitive farmers possessed such deadly weapons."

"Exactly my point. You know as well as I do that the Service exists for the sole purpose of finding and covertly studying the lost worlds, getting to know the people and their societies *before* we make First Contact." Norvag glared at Jerrel, revealing the frustration of a long-standing argument neither had ever won.

"The Rediscovery Service has a high casualty rate, despite their caution. Your brother and his partner, Danet, knew the risks they faced. Breaking the Service's rules now could only endanger them both." Norvag paused, then said more calmly, "Besides, Santar wouldn't appreciate your breaking the law on his behalf and you know it."

Jerrel stiffened as though about to protest, then sighed and ran his fingers through the unruly curls of his short-cropped, chestnut-colored hair. "You're right, as usual. At least about my brother. He's always been too idealistic—never did have any sense when it came to the practicalities of life."

"Why don't we go back to Anweigh?" Norvag urged. "On any world the best place for information is always the largest city, and we promised Danet we'd wait for him there. If anyone can find Santar it's bound to be him. He's been here longer and knows the ways of this society better than you or I."

Jerrel shook his head. "Santar disappeared in Matcassen, not in Anweigh, and we're only a few days' travel from Matcassen now."

"But what if someone recognizes you, realizes you're Santar's brother?"

"How? By the fact that we have blue eyes? That's about the only thing the two of us ever had in common." There was a note of regret in Jerrel's voice. "Even if blue eyes are a rare trait on this damned planet, it's not enough for anyone to connect the two of us. And if someone does, then that someone has information about Santar that I want, too."

He stood lost in thought for an instant before his attention was caught by Norvag discreetly rubbing his hands together. Quickly he moved around the table to push a roughly made chair close to the fire.

"And you don't have much more sense than Santar, my friend. You could be using a thermal suit and a medical robot to help with your leg instead of suffering in this infernal cold." Though he spoke with stern disapproval, there was real affection in Jerrel's eyes. "Sit down, Norvag, and warm your hands."

Norvag hesitated, then gratefully settled into the chair and stretched his hands to the fitful blaze. "I'm not the man I was, it's true, and winter is hard on old bones." He grinned. "My first assignment for the Service was on a world colder than this and I never even noticed the weather. But that was over eighty years ago."

"Eighty years . . ." Jerrel murmured, staring into the flickering orange flames. When his companion said nothing, Jerrel glanced over at him, his brow creased in worry.

"You visited a dozen planets with the Rediscovery Service in the first sixty-five of those years, and how many more with me over the last fifteen, my friend? Yet Santar disappears on his first Service assignment on a world that seems a child's playground in comparison to some."

Norvag glanced up at the younger man. "Danger doesn't have to come dressed as a seventy-cubit Thersasian rock lizard to be dangerous, Jerrel. And if you've forgotten the singing spiders of Taursus IV, I haven't."

Jerrel's mouth lifted in a mirthless smile. "I haven't forgotten." He shrugged a massive shoulder. "But you and I survived both the rock lizards and the spiders. Santar's mission here was simple observation and recording. You saw his orders—study the society here and decide if the people could accept a First Contact, if they were ready to be brought back into the Empire. Pretty straightforward Service work, yet the computer on his scout ship lost track of him despite the communications link planted in his skull."

"And still you believe he's alive." Norvag shook his head slowly, doubtfully. "If Santar were wounded, unconscious—even dying—his ship's computer would have beamed him back up automatically. Unless a severe head injury damaged the com link."

"The computer records indicate only that the connection with the link was broken six months ago," Jerrel said fiercely, beginning to pace restlessly before the fire. "If it hadn't been a one-man ship, we might have . . . There are a dozen possible explanations for a failure!"

"Possible, perhaps, but none probable except that the link itself was damaged or destroyed. And that happens only if—"

"I would *know* if he were dead, Norvag."

"You haven't seen him since he entered the Service, and you've been half a galaxy away for most of that time."

"I was half a galaxy away, yet I knew we had to come. Knew even before Danet broke Service rules to tell us he'd disappeared." Jerrel halted his pacing abruptly. "He could have ordered the link to shut down."

Norvag snorted. "Even you, who seem to think some guardian force watches over you, have never considered shutting down your link. Why should Santar?"

Jerrel opened his mouth to protest but the words died unspoken. Slowly the angry tension drained out of him to be replaced by a dragging weariness. His face fell and his shoulders sagged. He shook his head hesitantly. "I don't know, Norvag. I just don't know."

At the pain in his friend's face, Norvag said soothingly, "Still, it is a possibility." He shifted

11

in his chair, easing his stiffened leg.

Jerrel laid his hand affectionately on his companion's shoulder. "You have many fine qualities, my friend, but you've never been very good at dissembling. I know you think Santar's dead."

He squeezed Norvag's shoulder gently, then let his hand drop. "I can't give up hope. Not yet. Besides you, he's the only person in this universe who matters to me."

Norvag studied the expression on Jerrel's face, then sighed and turned his gaze to the fire.

"If only you would be willing to accept the Triumvirate's ruling . . ."

Jerrel's head jerked up. "Admit my father was a traitor? Recognize the power of those three fat, corrupt—"

"They *are* the Triumvirate. And your father *did* refuse to support them in the war."

"That didn't make him a traitor."

"It did in the eyes of the Triumvirate, and of most of the other nobles. You and Santar are the last of the bn'Hadar family. Will you let your name—a name that has hundreds of years of history behind it—die out because of your father's mistakes?"

"He fought for what he believed in!"

"And that cost him his life and your inheritance."

Jerrel took a deep, steadying breath. "His life I regret. The inheritance means nothing."

"Without it, you've spent the last fifteen years roaming the galaxy with no home but your ship and no friend but me."

A muscle at the side of Jerrel's mouth jumped. "The life I live has made us both wealthy." He paused, then, eyes glittering dangerously, added,

"Adventurers, I think you called us once. It's as good a name as any. Better than mercenary or profiteer, which many have used. But if the life is no longer to your taste, you're free to go."

Jerrel waited, but Norvag said nothing, only sat staring into the dying fire with a fixed, stony expression.

"Why don't you try joining the Rediscovery Service again, Norvag?" Jerrel continued bitterly. "They're generous masters. Look at you! Sixty-five years of distinguished service and all you have to show for it is a pension you can't live on. That and a leg that can't be healed because they followed the non-revelation policy instead of rescuing you when you needed help. Just as they've refused to look for my brother."

"It was a risk I accepted when I joined the Service." Norvag got to his feet with an awkward lurch to confront the angry young man before him. "Whatever the price I paid, I at least knew I was doing work that mattered. Santar understood the importance of that, even if you never have."

When all the answer he got was a stony glare, Norvag sighed. "I agreed to join you because I didn't want my friend's son to throw away his life as his father had. But in fifteen years you've never listened to me. Not once. You won't listen to me now."

Limping heavily, Norvag crossed the room and jerked open the door. The icy wind rushed in, instantly banishing whatever warmth the fire had generated.

"Santar's dead, Jerrel, and you're on a fool's mission." When he received no reply, the old man shook his head regretfully, then silently left the room.

13

As he drew the door shut behind him, one last, frigid blast of winter air forced its way in. It swirled across the room, extinguishing the guttering candle, then wrapped around the room's sole occupant. Jerrel, gaze fixed on the closed door, suddenly shivered.

Chapter 1

The leagues flowed by under Nareen's running feet, slowly or swiftly as the terrain dictated, but always steadily. Even the biting winter wind had not delayed her.

It was her second day on the trail and she gloried in her continuing strength. Even the urgency of the message she bore could not dampen the pride that surged through her.

"Be proud of your work," Gravnar had told Nareen often as she struggled through her lessons. "No one can travel as swiftly or carry messages as accurately as a runner. Pride makes you run faster and longer, see and remember more. But pride is the only emotion you can afford. To observe, you must put aside everything else, every personal feeling. Emotions cloud your vision."

"But how can you see without feeling, too?" she had protested in those first grueling months of training.

15

"You must learn," had been the stern reply. "As a runner, your task is to carry the Master's messages, to remember everything you see and hear, and to report accurately. That is all. It should be enough."

It had never been enough. Not really. Even Nareen's memories of her bitter childhood and the recognition of her good fortune at being selected to train as a runner could not extinguish the independent spirit that burned within her.

That spirit had made it difficult for her to submit to the rigorous mental training every runner had to undergo. The arduous physical discipline she had accepted joyfully, grateful for the chance to dispel some of the energy that frequently led her into mischief. But only by dint of much hard work had Nareen learned to at least feign some semblance of the emotional uninvolvement required of a proper runner.

Even now, bearing an urgent plea for help for the city-state of Kalinden, the only real home she had ever had, Nareen knew she ought to be coldly intent on her mission. Instead, she couldn't help worrying. There was Gravnar and her friend Trizgar, who had been sent to warn the holdings along the border about the invading beastmen. If the savages came as far as they had the last time they'd crossed the border, if they were half as murderous and vicious as they had been then . . .

A stumbling misstep brought Nareen's thoughts up short. She glanced down at the jagged rock she'd tripped on. It would have been so easy to fall. With a mental shake she started to run again, this time with her mind on the uneven trail before her. Not concentrating on her work had often gotten her in trouble, but if it caused her to be injured now, there was no one else to carry the message for help to Matcassen.

Twilight was fading to darkness when Nareen finally saw the stone walls of Matcassen in the distance, looming black against the sky.

Nareen couldn't decide whether she felt more pride at completing her journey so quickly, or relief that she wouldn't have to spend another night slowly picking her way along the rugged trail by the light of the half-moon. It would be good to be warm again.

She stepped up her pace and soon found herself on a road that ran directly to the main gate. Nareen pulled her small, heavy-hafted dagger from her belt. As she passed the signal bells mounted by the side of the road, she struck them twice, sharply, with the butt of the dagger, in the universal signal that a runner was approaching. At this time of night the city gates would be closed to all except traveling Masters and runners. The signal bells were Nareen's guarantee of entry into the city.

The gate, however, didn't open. Nareen jerked to a stop, astonished. With the butt of her dagger she pounded on the heavy wood.

"Open up!" she shouted, ignoring the need to regain her breath after that last, long run. "I am a runner from Kalinden. Open to me immediately!"

A murmur of voices arose from behind the gate. A heated argument was conducted in whispers, but Nareen could distinguish no words. She pounded on the gate again.

"Fools! The penalty for delaying a runner is death! Your Master will not be pleased with your stupidity."

17

The whispering stopped. An iron bolt was drawn back and a heavy crossbar lifted. The massive gate swung open, just wide enough to let her slip through, then thudded shut behind her. A flare was thrust in her face.

"Idiots!" Nareen snapped, trying to see beyond the light. Her fingers curled around her dagger.

"Aye. It be a runner, Hasst," said the one who held the flare.

"Of course I'm a runner. Did I not say so? And take that flare from before my eyes." Anger surged through Nareen—at the slowness of the gatekeepers, at the unnecessary delay when she'd strained every fiber of her being to bring her urgent message to Matcassen as fast as was humanly possible.

"Oh, aye," said the speaker, hastily complying with her demand.

Nareen was surprised to see a number of armed men standing in the shadows beyond the two gatekeepers.

"What's this?" she demanded. "You greet me with soldiers?" Her gaze skimmed over the men, quickly taking in their number, armaments, and rather shabby dress.

"Beg pardon, runner," said the one addressed as Hasst, stepping forward with a clumsy bow. "Master's orders."

"To delay a runner?"

"No." The man paused uncomfortably. "Had t'be sure you *were* a runner."

"That's ridiculous! Who else would I be?"

Hasst and the man who held the flare glanced at each other, then at the men behind them, as if seeking an answer to Nareen's question.

"Robber, mebbe," Hasst offered at last.

18

"Absurd. No one would dare disguise himself as a runner." Nareen unobtrusively returned her dagger to its sheath at her waist.

"Week ago. Came right in, jus' like you. Tried to kill t'Master, he did, pretendin' he were deliverin' a message."

Nareen couldn't be certain, but she thought Hasst looked slightly paler. Her own blood drained from her face. The penalty for impersonating a runner was well-known, and horrible.

"Died this mornin'," Hasst's companion added wide-eyed. "Took him most of a week t'do it, too."

For a moment Nareen said nothing, too stunned by this unexpected news to react. Before she could recover, a tall form materialized from the shadows.

"What is the meaning of this?" the newcomer demanded. The guards stiffened at the peremptory tone.

"A runner, Captain," one said, saluting smartly by bringing his right fist up to thump his chest. "The gatekeepers have just let her in."

"A runner!" The one addressed as captain stepped forward into the light. His eyes glittered in their deeply shadowed sockets as he looked Nareen up and down. "How can you idiots be sure? Don't bother to answer," he added sharply, cutting off their excuses. "I see you haven't the slightest idea."

"Sir," said Nareen, defiantly meeting the man's gaze. "I am Nareen, Sixth Runner from Kalinden. I bear messages for your Master that cannot wait."

The man was unmoved by her demands. "Maybe you do. We'll see." He turned slightly and

19

pointed at two of the guards. "You. And you. Take this woman to Tork. He will decide if she is what she claims to be. Kill her if she tries anything."

Nareen bit back a sharp reply. She'd recognized the name Tork. At least they were taking her to the chief runner of Matcassen. There would be time enough to lodge her protest when she was brought before Master Lindaz.

The two guards wasted no time in leading her through the squalid streets. While her thoughts whirled with the gatekeeper's news, her mind carefully recorded the state of everything she saw, each building they passed and every turning.

The way hadn't changed from what she'd been taught by a Matcassen runner several years before, but the city was more noisome and run-down than she'd expected. Matcassen controlled vast holdings, including territories that had once been independent city-states with their own Masters. Yet none of that wealth seemed to have reached the people of the city.

Nareen knew that Gasperian, the present Master of Kalinden, and his ancestors were considered unusual in their willingness to share with their people the treasures in gold and silver wrenched at such cost from deep within the earth. But because of their historical generosity, Kalinden enjoyed a peace and prosperity known to few of the larger and far more powerful city-states that ruled the civilized areas of Errandane.

As her escort led her deeper into Matcassen, Nareen noted there were guards posted in the streets, something she had never seen in Kalinden, and guards at the Great Hall. Her companions were evidently known, for doors in the Hall quickly opened before them.

Instead of being taken to the main reception hall as was customary, Nareen was led to a small room off a side passage. Her escorts remained in the room, alertly poised on either side of the entrance. Before she had time to grow impatient, the door opened to admit a wiry man about her size dressed as she was in the tunic and special aard leather boots that identified a runner.

"Welcome, runner," he said, closing the door behind him and stepping forward. "I am Tork, Chief Runner for Master Lindaz."

"I am Nareen, Sixth Runner for Master Gasperian of Kalinden," Nareen said, rising from her chair to greet her visitor. "Your Master seems to have forgotten the courtesies due a runner, Tork."

Though there was little to be gained by her protest, it was a relief to Nareen to vent some of the frustration and anger she felt at the unnecessary delays. With Kalinden at risk, every minute was precious and not to be wasted.

The man flushed under his tan. "I regret your reception, Nareen of Kalinden. There is much to explain and little time. Please, sit down. I have ordered food to be brought. While we wait, you may give me your report."

Nareen drew herself up straighter. "My message is intended for Master Lindaz. It is urgent and should not be delayed," she protested.

"I will be the judge of that," Tork said. "You will give your report to me. Those are Master Lindaz' orders," he added as Nareen started to object.

Nareen had no choice. A runner, even a runner carrying a message as important as hers, was obligated to obey a Master's orders. And though she'd often rebelled against what she considered the many unnecessary rules and restrictions that dictated a runner's actions, Nareen knew she would gain nothing by disobeying now.

Swiftly, as she'd been trained to do, Nareen gave her detailed report, beginning with the beastmen's first incursion across the border. She included the required information on conditions in Kalinden, reviewed her observations of the crofts, herds, and state of the land she'd passed through, then, for Tork's benefit, listed the changes she'd observed in the path she'd taken. There was one small consolation, at least—much of her report was of little interest to Lindaz, anyway. His advisors and overseers would want the most recent information available on his holdings, but like any Master, Lindaz would pay scant attention to the mundane details of the daily operations in his territories.

At last she sat, waiting quietly for Tork to rouse from the listening trance. When he finally stirred, he turned first to the guards at the door, who had stood silently throughout Nareen's report.

"Leave us," he said. "You can see she is a runner, just as she claimed. Inform Master Lindaz she bears an urgent message for him and may be trusted."

Nareen waited until the guards had left the room before speaking. "It seems strange that Matcassen should greet a runner so discourteously," she said at last, sharply, relieved to vent her growing impatience.

Tork met her gaze, clearly nervous. "It was necessary. You must have been told of the attack on Master Lindaz. It was not the first. There have been problems in many of the holdings, and attacks against several of the advisors and scholars, as well."

"Why? Other than the beastmen, Kalinden has never had such problems."

"Gasperian is a wise and generous master. Kalinden is fortunate. You saw the conditions of the streets of Matcassen. Did that not tell you something?"

"I am a runner. I observe, I do not judge." Nareen knew that wasn't quite true. She was forever getting into trouble with her tendency to have opinions and express them plainly, but it was the proper reply expected of her and she did *try* to think and act as a runner ought.

Tork glanced at the door, then leaned forward conspiratorially. "That is what we are taught. But who sees more than a runner? Who knows more of what passes in the world than we do? If we . . ."

He was interrupted by a loud knock on the door. Tork had only enough time to sit back in his chair before the door swung open. A servant entered bearing Nareen's meal.

Neither spoke while the servant set the plate of food, two goblets, and pitchers of water and wine on the table. Only when the door had shut again and the servant's footsteps had disappeared down the stone passageway did Tork resume.

"Eat. You must be hungry. It will be a while before Lindaz will receive you, and five, perhaps six days of hard travel still lie before you."

Nareen was reaching for the pitcher of water, but her hand froze halfway. "What do you mean? It took me only two days from Kalinden."

"I know. This is information that must go to the Ruling Council of Errandane in Anweigh. Although Lindaz is required by law to send a runner, he will not. That leaves only you."

"I have to return to Kalinden. I can't go on to Anweigh!" Nareen thought of Gasperian and his advisors, of her friends anxiously waiting for her to return with word that help was on its way.

"There is no one else to send." Tork met Nareen's startled gaze. "There are only five runners in Matcassen. Master Lindaz does not like the expense of keeping us."

"That's impossible! For a city the size of Matcassen . . ."

"You can expect no help here, runner. Not to carry your message and not to aid Kalinden." Tork hesitated, then continued slowly, "Perhaps it's just as well. You cannot be unaware that we 'helped' Bayanar two years ago. That city now belongs to Matcassen."

"I had heard . . ." Nareen paused, then carefully poured water while she digested Tork's startling information. "Bayanar had been claimed by Matcassen for generations. Kalinden, never. Our situation is different. We are at peace with our neighbors, and the beastmen—"

"Are attacking Kalinden, not Matcassen."

"But the laws of Errandane—"

"The laws are what Master Lindaz says they are. Or perhaps I should say, what the Lady Xyanth says they are. Kalinden is better off without Matcassen's help."

"But there are no other cities close! Runners have been dispatched to Narlon and Pasmene, but neither city is half as powerful as Matcassen. Besides, it will take weeks for their troops to reach Kalinden. Anweigh is even more distant!"

Tork met Nareen's worried gaze directly. "Then Kalinden will have to stand alone."

*   *   *

"Lindaz is a fool!" The tall, golden-haired woman whirled to confront the man before her. "And you are, too, Gorvan. Santar is dead by his own hand."

"Lady, the attacks on Master Lindaz—"

"Could have come from any number of those who seek revenge against him. Lindaz doesn't need to conjure phantoms to explain them."

"But never before has anyone dared to act against the Master. You forced this Santar to reveal those strange tales and—" Gorvan immediately regretted his words.

Xyanth's hand with its claw-like nails came up as though to strike him. "Santar is dead, I tell you! I saw him die!"

"Lady Xyanth, please! I only meant . . ." Gorvan shrank back, wide-eyed, from the angry woman before him.

"You think I share Lindaz' fears? You grow more witless than he is!" Xyanth dropped her hand in disgust and turned to the fireplace. With the long iron poker she stabbed at the burning logs, watching them shatter under each swift thrust.

At last she turned back to the silent Gorvan, her thin mouth twisted in a sneer. "A beardless boy comes preaching of right and wrong and telling children's tales of rings that record everything and wagons that fly. Because of those wild tales, Lindaz now thinks he sees retribution on all sides."

"But the weapon this Santar showed us! And you said his body disappeared! Master Lindaz says he spoke of some mighty Service that—"

"My husband grows old and fat and fearful. You

tried that 'weapon.' No one could make it work, not even our most skilled weaponers. Santar was a trickster. Did I not have the ring which he said could remember and record everything that happened, just like a scribe only better? It wouldn't work for me, nor for you nor anyone else. Even Santar couldn't show us these 'records' it supposedly made. Just because he learned the beastmen's language doesn't mean the rest of his tales were true."

Though he was sweating with nervousness, Gorvan persisted. "But, Lady, dead bodies don't just disappear."

"Enough! Bring me that ring again. I will show you his stories were nothing more than fantasies."

"Bring you the ring, Lady?" Gorvan seemed honestly surprised. "But I don't have it. You do."

"I? I gave it to you."

"No, Lady. I distinctly remember—"

Xyanth tossed her head in irritation. "No matter. I have heard all of Santar I want, in any case. Wherever the ring is, it will do us no harm." Her pale green eyes grew suddenly cold and hard. "What interests me is the information you have brought."

Gorvan straightened, obviously relieved at the change in topic. "There isn't much. The captain of the guards tells me a runner has arrived from Kalinden bearing an urgent message. As the Master instructed, she was sent to Tork first."

"Any hint of the content of this message?"

"No, Lady."

"And you have had no word from the border?"

"None."

Xyanth considered the information, then said

softly, "Yet the arrival of this runner is promising, I think."

"Lady, is it wise to have dealings with the beastmen? They're dangerous and—"

"Silence! I've heard enough of your carping fears." Her eyes glittered. "As Lindaz grows more unsure and incapable of acting, *I* grow stronger. My plans are carefully drawn. I do not intend to let anyone stop me now."

"But, Lady, you rule as no other woman ever has. Surely—"

"It is not enough! I will not be content with Lindaz' crumbs, like some cur dog tossed a worthless bone. It was *I* who told him how he might have Bayanar, and *I* who showed him how the cities of Ravelatt and Warsen and Dansedich might be his, as well."

Though she did not speak loudly, Xyanth's voice quivered with anger. "My price for those cities was to be named co-ruler and heir. I have given Lindaz far more than he ever dreamed of, yet he puts me off with feeble excuses and paltry lies. I will not be bought with lies!"

Xyanth drew herself up proudly, glaring at Gorvan. Then she stalked across the floor to sit in the massive carved wood chair beside the fireplace.

For a few minutes there were no sounds in the room but the fire and the steady drumming of the Lady Xyanth's fingernails against the arms of her chair.

Gorvan shifted uncomfortably under his mistress's gaze but made no effort to break the silence. He watched as a grim smile of satisfaction slowly lit her face. The smile did nothing to calm his fears.

"But there are ways," she said at last, very

softly. Her eyes were unfocused yet glowing, as though she were looking inward to particularly pleasant thoughts. "It may be that Santar will prove far more useful dead than he ever was alive."

She studied Gorvan. The smile grew wider and she nodded.

"Yes," Xyanth said, "there are certainly ways."

The main reception hall was empty of all but a few advisors and scholars when Nareen was at last brought to stand before the Master's dais. Two armed guards kept her well back from the huge, empty chair that dominated the chamber. Tork had taken up his position to the side of the platform, where he could both see and hear everything that went on.

Lindaz, followed by more advisors and attendants, entered the hall from a small door behind the dais. He was dressed in robes of costly fabrics and wore a long over-vest of the richest fur. The fat hand wrapped around his staff of office sparkled with the jewels in his numerous rings. His girth was enormous, and he moved in a slow waddle that detracted considerably from his impressive appearance.

Nareen remained standing while the old man sat. As a runner, she knelt only before her Master and the Lord High Master of Anweigh.

"They say you come from Kalinden, runner," Lindaz said at last. His small, glittering eyes stared unblinking at Nareen.

"Yes, Master." She touched the fingers of her right hand to her forehead in the salute of all runners throughout Errandane. "I bear a message for you from my Master, Gasperian."

"Speak." Lindaz gestured impatiently.

In the clear, carrying voice she had been taught, Nareen gave her report. "Kalinden seeks help. The savages from the Troodon Mountains have attacked holdings on our northernmost borders. Many have died in the attacks, fields and herds have been destroyed. Though our warriors are even now fighting them, the power of the beastmen is well-known. Master Gasperian has sent me to claim your assistance under the Edict of Trassdeance."

"Absurd," Lindaz snapped. "The Edict gives him the right of help only if he is in danger. Kalinden is strong. The gods are my witness! I am already taxed almost to death to help support his troops for just such an emergency! They surely are not threatened by a few savages raiding some unimportant holdings."

Tork had warned her that Lindaz might object. "It has been half a hundred years since the beastmen last attacked, Master, yet the scars of those battles can still be seen on the walls of Kalinden. You will remember what Matcassen suffered. Together, we can easily vanquish the invaders. My Master calls on you by right of the Edict."

"Impossible! They told you at the gate about the attack against me?"

"They had to explain why they dared detain a runner."

"I was attacked, in my city!" Lindaz leaned forward, quivering with indignation. "I cannot risk troops to help anyone now."

"Is that what you wish me to tell Master Gasperian when I return?"

"That is what you will tell them in Anweigh."

Tork had been right, but Nareen found it difficult to believe a Master would so openly flaunt the laws of Errandane. Her voice rose.

"I have been traveling two days, Master Lindaz. It is your responsibility to send the message to Anweigh with a runner who is rested, just as I have carried it from Kalinden."

"Don't speak to me like that!" Lindaz glared. "I cannot risk a runner to carry someone else's message.

"The law dictates . . ." Nareen began indignantly, taking a step forward. She stopped as her two guards moved to block her path.

"Master Lindaz!" All heads turned as a golden-haired woman rose from her chair in the shadows at the side of the dais. "A word with you." She crossed to the Master's chair.

"Lady Xyanth." Lindaz acknowledged the woman only grudgingly.

Watching husband and wife, Nareen thought there could scarcely be a more oddly matched couple. Lindaz, grotesquely fat, seemed the epitome of self-indulgent deterioration. Xyanth, half her husband's age and radiantly fair, bent gracefully over him, whispering in his ear with an air of patient, pleading reason.

At last the Lady Xyanth stepped back. Lindaz, face drooping in a petulant pout, glared at Nareen.

"I must think more on your message, runner," he said grudgingly.

"Is that what I am to tell my Master?" Nareen asked.

"You are to go on to Anweigh!" Lindaz snapped. "Do as you are bid! Now get out of my sight."

Nareen would have protested further, but one of the guards grabbed her arm in a painful grip. She had no choice but to go with him.

The bed, at least, was comfortable, Nareen decided as she settled down for a few hours' sleep before she set out again.

She'd failed in her mission, and that failure weighed heavily. Kalinden would be able to stand alone, but at great cost. Yet there was no way she could force a Master to obey the law if he chose not to.

Although she was strong enough to continue to Anweigh, the two days she'd already spent on the trail would inevitably tell on her in the long journey ahead. And even if she made good time, Anweigh lay so far from Kalinden that troops might arrive too late to be of much help.

Nareen still wasn't completely sure she should go on. Kalinden needed to know it could look for no help from Matcassen. Nareen was the only person who could tell them that. Shouldn't she return, as was expected of her? Yet wasn't the chance of help from Anweigh, the capital and most powerful city in all Errandane, worth more than the certain knowledge that Matcassen would provide no help at all?

The worries and doubts chased each other through her thoughts until she finally slept.

Nareen had no idea how long she'd been asleep when she was brought awake by the muted sound of someone fumbling at the latch on her door. For a moment she froze, listening to the night.

It had to be past the hour of turning, the hour that marked the deepest dark of night, for Nareen could detect none of the noises usual to a Great

Hall. Whoever her visitor was, he had tried to make no noise, which didn't speak well of his intentions.

Every sense alert, Nareen carefully slid out from under her covers. Though clad only in her under-shift, she'd slept with her dagger as she'd been trained.

Holding the weapon waist high before her, she moved silently across the darkened room to the far side of the door. Although her heart raced and her muscles were taut with tension, dealing with an unknown intruder seemed preferable to the uncertainties that had plagued her dreams.

After a few minutes her visitor, evidently satis-fied that Nareen still slept, slid the latch all the way back and softly pushed the door open.

Only a little light entered from the torches mounted at great intervals along the walls, but it was enough for Nareen to detect the cloaked figure that slid into her room and moved toward the bed.

Chapter 2

"This is insane! Everyone here has told you—no man hunts drevon alone!" Norvag paced back and forth across the room in agitation, scarcely heeding the pain his jerking motion generated in his damaged leg.

"I'm taking Rakin and Borlat. They'll provide all the help I need," said Jerrel as he calmly added an additional packet of dried meat to the small bundle he would take with him.

"Wonderful. Two idiots—no, three!—alone on that damned mountain, chasing after drevon. For no reason except you're bored!"

Jerrel drew tight the leather lacings on his bundle. "It's still four or five days until that Merchant Baecknar arrives with his caravan. I can't sit around here all that time doing nothing."

"Better that than tumbling over a cliff or being gored by a drevon!" Norvag halted before Jerrel, hands on his hips, chin thrust out pugnaciously.

Jerrel grinned. "Sometimes you sound just like my mother."

"Well, sometimes you act just like your father! And that's no compliment!"

"I suspected it wasn't."

"Heedless madman, that's what he was. And you're the same! Think you're damned immortals. There were times in the past fifteen years when I know you got us into trouble just for the entertainment."

"Never!"

"What about when you signed us on with those murdering Sarden traders?"

"We made a very tidy profit out of that whole affair."

"And nearly got knifed for our pains! And don't forget that trip through the swamps of Darmek. Over a month fighting our way across that hell, and then I find we could have taken a raft around in no more than four days."

"But think of the country we saw, Norvag," Jerrel said, laughing.

"That nightmare of a place! And this hunt for drevon is just another piece of your madness! You've heard the tales of what they're like. You'll end up dead, and then there'll definitely be no chance of finding Santar, if he's alive. Have you thought of that?"

The grin disappeared from Jerrel's face. Despite his teasing, he knew his friend's worries were justified. He clapped the old man on the shoulder.

"I've thought of that, my friend," he said soberly. For an instant Jerrel wondered if he ought to reveal his true purpose, but immediately thought better of it. If Norvag was worried about a drevon hunt, he would be three times more concerned if he were informed of what Jerrel actually planned.

"At least take me with you," Norvag insisted. "I know I'm an old man, but I've still got some good leagues left in me."

"And I need those leagues for more important work," said Jerrel, touched by the old man's loyalty and courage. He felt a pang of guilt for all the times he'd taken those qualities for granted. "I need you here, in case Danet sends any word. By now he should have received the message we sent from Anweigh."

Jerrel picked up his bundle and threw it over his back, tying it into place with the thongs sewn to his leather jerkin. "I've been on more dangerous outings than a drevon hunt. Nothing's going to happen. Nothing at all."

Her visitor must be a man, Nareen decided, for he was much larger than she. After the dimly lit hallway he would be unable to see for a few seconds. And Nareen had the advantage of surprise. She shoved the door closed with her foot.

"Welcome, stranger," she said softly. Before he could locate her, she silently moved to the side.

The stranger chuckled. "So you heard me. I should have realized a runner would be prepared. That is good." When Nareen did not respond, he continued, "I mean you no harm. I am Danet, advisor to Master Lindaz." He paused. "May I light a candle?"

Nareen hesitated. "Go ahead. Slowly." Again she moved.

The man seemed to pull something from under his cloak, then knelt and placed whatever it was on the floor. Nareen heard the scratch of a firestick.

He must have brought his own candle. She turned her head slightly so she wouldn't be blinded by the sudden light.

The flaring candle, set in a silver holder, illuminated a curly-haired young man wrapped in a voluminous cloak. He rose, the candle in his hand, and turned to Nareen. She had moved. When he saw her dagger, he chuckled again.

"I see you are even better prepared than I expected. Except"—he paused to eye her appreciatively—"for your apparel. Perhaps you would like a little more time to dress?"

Suddenly aware that her undershift was her only garment, Nareen spoke more sharply than she intended. "I am not accustomed to unannounced visitors, advisor."

"No, of course not. I do apologize." Abruptly he turned his back on her. "Please don't mind me."

Nareen hastily pulled on her tunic while keeping a sharp eye on her visitor. "You may turn around."

Danet turned back to face her. "Decent again, mmm? Such a pity. I preferred your previous costume."

"I am a runner," Nareen snapped.

"True. But a woman as well, though your tunic may disguise that fact." At Nareen's indignant hiss, Danet smiled. "But you would rather be thought a runner, and I am constantly being told I should behave more like an advisor. To business, then, Nareen of Kalinden."

The smile disappeared. Danet reached into a pocket of his robes and pulled out a small leather pouch.

"You travel to Anweigh in a few hours. This pouch contains a ring which must go with you.

36

After you give your report to the Lord High Master and his advisors, you are to deliver this ring, in privacy, to a warrior named bn'Hadar."

"Indeed?" said Nareen. Though his visit to her room was certainly unorthodox, there was nothing unusual in Danet's request. Runners often carried small items such as signature rings and seals between the cities, either at the command of a Master or for a generous, but discreet, payment.

"Indeed." Danet's eyes seemed to twinkle in the flickering candlelight.

"And why should I do this, advisor?" Nareen demanded. She'd never been interested in the extra earnings available to a runner, and if Lindaz were the sender . . . Well, she'd rather be turned into a slimy hosnath than do a favor for *that* one!

"Why? Do runners ask why if the recompense is sufficient?"

There was no doubt about it—his eyes *did* twinkle. To Nareen's surprise, he was amused rather than angered by her truculence. That realization did much to soothe the irritation his command had generated. "And who," she asked, more calmly, "is sending the ring?"

"I am, of course!" Danet was openly grinning. "Am I not the one standing here?"

"Then Lindaz is not . . ." Nareen's question died away. It was, she knew, a totally inappropriate question for a runner to ask.

Sudden understanding flashed in Danet's expression. "No, Lindaz knows nothing of the ring, and I am counting on you to ensure that he continues to know nothing of it." He held out the small pouch.

Without hesitation Nareen took it and slipped it into the special pocket sewn into her tunic. Anything that would get back at Lindaz—even something so trivial as hiding the ring—was all right with her. She gave the runner's salute, fingertips to her forehead. "It shall be as you will it, advisor."

For the first time, Danet's expression grew somber. "No, runner, it is not as I *will* it. Let us just hope the gods are well disposed to us and that we are very lucky."

It was still dark when Tork rapped on Nareen's door to waken her. He was surprised to find her already dressed.

"You are eager," he said.

"I have my city to think of, Runner Tork," Nareen said with dignity. His approval warmed her.

"I brought you a light breakfast, water for your journey, and extra dried meat. It isn't much, but you'll need it."

Tork waited silently while Nareen consumed the fruit and bread that would be her last full meal for some time. When she finished, she collected her few belongings. He led her through the darkened passages of the Great Hall and along the streets of Matcassen, still empty and silent at this early hour.

They stopped at a small side gate. The gatekeeper was dozing in his hut but jerked awake at Tork's rough shaking. "Chief runner!" he exclaimed, frightened at being caught napping.

"Open the gate, fool, and be quick about it," Tork snapped.

Tork accompanied Nareen only to the worn stone steps outside the small gate. "He travels safest who travels most quickly," he said. His eyes were dark with concern as he spoke the traditional runner's farewell.

Nareen said nothing. She watched the slight but widening haze of gray visible on the horizon, grateful for the older runner's concern.

"You will take care?" he asked. "You're sure you *can* go on to Anweigh, runner?"

"Of course." Nareen drew herself up proudly. "I have scarcely tested my strength."

Tork nodded. "The path through the Gorob Mountains is relatively short but very dangerous. Take care, Nareen of Kalinden."

Nareen thought of her home and friends. "I shall, Runner Tork," she said. "Of that you may be very sure."

Nareen remembered her words late that afternoon as she carefully picked her way through the treacherous rocks on the almost invisible trail she had chosen. If the high pass from Kalinden to Matcassen was seldom traveled, this way through the Gorobs had almost been forgotten. Only a runner, rigorously taught to memorize every path, would know of this route along the sides of the rugged peaks that formed Errandane's western boundary.

It was fortunate that Tork had given her an extra supply of dried aard meat and a second flask of water. From what she knew of the path, there was little possibility of finding shelter and additional food until she was much closer to Anweigh. The meat, the flasks of water, her dagger, and the light but protective skin from a grackle's wing were all she carried in her runner's belt. It would have to be enough in the days ahead.

An icy wind blew almost constantly. The land was bleak, harsh, and forbidding. The steep cliffs and rugged slopes were formed of slick gray and reddish-brown stone that provided little opportunity for anything to grow except the coarse, tufted grass the drevon ate. Only occasionally did she see any habitations, and those solely in the valleys far below her.

Nareen stopped to eat a small piece of meat and to refill her flask from a stream. Though the path was far more difficult than any she had ever traveled except in training, she was pleased at her progress.

She leaned back against the rock, enjoying the brief rest. Something hard dug into her skin. It took a minute to realize the hard object wasn't a rock but the contents of the small pouch she carried tucked in the inner pocket of her tunic.

Suddenly curious to know more about what she carried, she pulled out the pouch. A ring, Danet had said. A ring for a warrior named bn'Hadar. An odd name, one that should make it relatively easy to find him even in Anweigh.

Nareen tugged open the pouch, expecting a signature ring, or possibly some bright jewel intended for a highborn lady.

The ring that glittered in her hand was unlike anything she had ever seen.

The central stone was enormous, square cut, and of a milky blue that rivaled the sweep of the sky above her. The band was of heavy, intricately wrought gold. Nareen turned the ring over in her hands, studying it.

Odd markings incised into the band looked like words, but they weren't in any language she recognized. A ridge of metal ran from front to back on the underside of the mounting. It seemed strange to have an edge like that where it might cut into the wearer's finger. Though she turned the ring over in her hands, she could see no useful purpose the ridge could serve.

Nareen shrugged and tucked the ring back in its pouch, then stuffed the pouch into her tunic pocket.

She would have liked to know something more about the ring, where the stone came from, and who this bn'Hadar was, but none of that really mattered. She was responsible only for delivering the ring. The chances of her ever learning more about it were slim indeed.

Nareen stopped once more at nightfall, ate another piece of meat from her small hoard, then, wrapped in the grackle skin, slept until moonrise in the slight shelter provided by some tumbled boulders. While the moon was up she made what speed she could, then slept again in the brief, dark hours before dawn.

Sometime during the night the wind dropped. It proved no blessing, for the next morning a heavy, bone-chilling fog drifted down from the heights to wrap around her, obliterating any sign of the trail. Nareen's progress the night before had necessarily been slow, but at least there had been the vague moonlight to show her the way. Now everything disappeared in a deceptive mist. Though she would lose time by waiting, she might lose everything, including her life, if she ventured forward.

41

With a resignation born of training, not nature, Nareen drew the grackle skin about her and settled back in the niche she had found to wait out the mist.

Damn the fog, Jerrel thought, vainly trying to peer through the enveloping mist. Perhaps Norvag had been right after all. Rakin and Borlat were back at camp, dressing the first drevon he had killed. He was alone on the mountainside in fog that blinded him. And somewhere not too far away was a wounded drevon that would do its best to kill him if it could find him.

It would have to be his luck, of course, to find drevon so far down the mountain. Though he'd brought his two companions along precisely because they wouldn't ask questions, he'd been forced to kill the first drevon so they wouldn't think anything was odd about their expedition. Then, to top it off, he'd come across the second drevon only a short distance from camp.

And there the luck—if you could call it that—had ended. His arrow had only wounded the animal, not killed it. Though the drevon had plunged off through the rocks in the first agony of its injury, Jerrel knew it wasn't hurt badly enough to have died—the limited amount of blood he had found proved that. And a wounded drevon always returned to attack its attacker, if it could. It was one of the few things he'd been told you could count on when dealing with the beasts.

Jerrel had tracked the creature, his only advantage the steady breeze that kept him downwind. But as he climbed higher, the breeze died and the fog moved in, turning the advantage over to the drevon, an animal that had been born to these rocky heights and had a superb sense of smell.

Jerrel debated the relative insanity of staying put, trying to go back and find the camp, or going ahead. Any way he ran a risk, either from the drevon or from the mountain itself. Once or twice the fog lifted slightly, but only for a moment. He still couldn't see more than an arm's length in front of his face.

Suddenly he heard the choking cough of a drevon. From afar, safely in camp and accompanied by stalwart men, Jerrel had thought the sound ludicrous. This close, knowing the animal was wounded and enraged, he had a hard time laughing.

Securely grasping his spear, Jerrel inched forward along the mist-shrouded trail. He would have felt a lot better if his main weapon had been a disrupter rather than the primitive implements he carried, but he'd promised Norvag . . .

Jerrel hadn't gone far when he heard a sound he hadn't expected, the cry of a frightened human being.

Jerrel rushed forward, only to slam into a gray stone outcropping he hadn't seen. Jerrel cursed. He wouldn't be much help to that other man, whoever he was, if he ended up breaking a leg out of stupidity. More cautiously, using his spear to probe before him, Jerrel pushed on.

Ahead, the drevon coughed again, then bellowed, a cry of mingled pain and rage that made Jerrel swallow hard. There was no further cry from the human.

A path he could scarcely see led Jerrel around a jumbled pile of enormous boulders, then disappeared. For an instant Jerrel froze, uncertain, before he realized the way now angled down the face of the mountain, rather than across.

The drevon coughed once again. This time the sound seemed to come from slightly below Jerrel's position. He moved forward cautiously. Was it only his imagination, or did the mist seem to thin a bit?

A few steps farther and it became clear the drevon was in some sort of open area almost directly below him. Jerrel could hear the animal shuffling and scuffing the earth, moving back and forth with nervous, angry energy. It apparently was unaware of Jerrel's presence—at least for the moment.

With such limited visibility, Jerrel had no choice. He had to know where the other man was before anything else. "Traveler!" he shouted. "Where are you?"

"Here! In a niche against the rock face!"

A boy, not a man! He couldn't expect much help from that direction.

"Can the drevon get to you?" Jerrel knew his voice would attract the drevon to him, but hoped the boy's voice would confuse the animal, make it unable to decide which target to choose.

"Not unless he pushes his head around a rock in front. But I can't move, either."

Jerrel could hear the thread of fear. "Don't try. Let me handle it." That sounded good, but what was he to do?

At that moment the fog shifted, giving him an almost clear view of the area below him. The drevon was in the center of a small, flat place created by chance when a slab of rock had fallen from the cliff above.

The animal lifted its massive head with the four wickedly sharp horns to stare at Jerrel's location, then shifted to glare at the boy's hiding place.

Jerrel could see his arrow still lodged in the beast's shoulder. The wound had bled enough that the thick, shaggy white hair all along the drevon's side was matted and red.

He had a clear shot, but this time he had to be sure he killed the beast. The best way was to get in close with his spear.

Somehow he had to reach the drevon without attracting its attention. The path twisted down between large boulders and would be difficult to negotiate in the mist. A steeply tilted slab of rock whose top was just below Jerrel provided a more direct, if dangerous, route.

"Traveler!" he shouted again. "I need your help."

No response. Jerrel could only hope that meant the boy was saving his breath for more important things.

"Keep the drevon's attention on you by talking. I'll move down under cover of the fog. When the fog lifts—if it does!—I'll kill the beast." The fog was moving down again, hiding the clearing below.

There was no sound for a moment; then the boy started singing. His voice was pure and strong and sweet. A pity it was wasted on the drevon.

From the sounds of the drevon's hooves on the stone, his plan was working. The boy seemed to be holding its attention.

Jerrel placed his quiver, bow, and hunting belt with his knife and food packet on the ground. They would slow him down dangerously. Then he slid over the rock before him, reaching with his foot for the fallen slab he'd seen. There. A little farther. He dropped down to the slab, flattening his body against the fog-slick stone so he wouldn't slip.

Jerrel rose into a low crouch, then carefully crept down the face of the slab. His hunter's boots made no sound, and the boy's song hid any slight noise his clothing might make.

For a moment it seemed the fog might lift again; then it came swirling back. Jerrel reached the bottom in mist so thick he could only grope blindly for the opening in the rocks he'd seen from above.

Though he couldn't see it, Jerrel could smell the drevon—its rank musk-and-blood scent hung heavy in the air. Balked of an easy target, it had grown impatient. With a bellow of rage it charged the boy's hiding place.

The shock of hitting solid rock stopped the drevon for only a moment. From the sounds, Jerrel thought it had fallen to its knees. It recovered quickly. He could hear the scuffle of its hooves as it retreated a few paces, then charged again.

At the first charge, the boy stopped singing. When the drevon retreated, he began again, even louder. Jerrel couldn't help smiling. This time the boy was singing a tavern song far too bawdy for one of his years.

Jerrel moved around the last rock and into the clearing, spear at the ready. The drevon was only an immense shadow in the mist. When it charged, its bulk seemed to fill the clearing.

The drevon hit the rock face with a force that shook the ground around it. Again it was driven to its knees. In that instant the fog lifted.

It was the biggest drevon Jerrel had ever seen. With a cry that echoed off the surrounding rock, he leaped forward to drive his spear home in that massive wall of flesh, home to the heart of the beast.

As Jerrel's spear cut through the thick hide, drove down through thick muscle and past enormous ribs, the drevon rose to its feet, pulling Jerrel up with it. The spear jerked out of Jerrel's grasp.

He staggered, then grabbed at the bloodied, matted hair, struggling to hold on. The drevon had become a raging storm of violence that flung Jerrel aside as though he were an insect.

He hit the rock, hard. The impact knocked the air from his chest in an explosive gasp. He tried to move but was too dazed.

The drevon twisted around, head down, then charged.

From the corner of his eye Jerrel saw a flash of movement, then heard a human cry. Roused by the cry, he rolled, not far, but enough so the drevon's horn caught his side and back rather than his chest. The pain was a galvanic charge. He rolled farther, onto his knees. His fingers wrapped around a fist-sized stone. With an effort he forced himself to his feet, still holding the stone.

The boy who had saved his life stood across the clearing from him.

Between them, the drevon trembled. Jerrel's spear thrust had weakened it, wounded it fatally. But it wasn't dying quickly. Again it bellowed, uncertain which of its opponents to charge first.

Without thinking and heedless of the pain, Jerrel threw the stone at the drevon's injured side with as much force as he could muster. The boy, at least, should have a chance at escape.

The drevon whirled toward Jerrel. But even as it lowered its head to charge, the boy leaped onto its neck. A knife glittered in his hand.

The drevon reared up and back, seeking to dislodge its burden. It bellowed, but the bellow changed to a choking, gurgling gasp as the boy, one fist tightly wrapped around a horn, leaned forward to bury his knife hilt-deep in the artery just below the juncture of the drevon's neck and jaw.

Bright red blood spurted, soaking boy and beast. The drevon, overbalanced by the boy's weight, toppled backward on top of him.

First its shoulder landed on the boy's leg, pinning him to the ground. The boy cried out, once. But he made no sound when the drevon's head fell back and the wickedly sharp horns pinned him to the rock.

The drevon shuddered twice, in spasms that shook its entire body. Then it lay still.

The boy didn't move at all.

Chapter 3

"You're a fool, Lindaz!" Xyanth paced back and forth in agitation. Her heavy brocaded gown swirled about her, rustling and whispering across the stone floor of the small room. "The beastmen's invasion of Kalinden gives us an opportunity to achieve what we have dreamed of for years, but instead you sit here whimpering that it's too dangerous to risk."

"Gasperian . . ." Lindaz' protest was interrupted by a harsh oath from Xyanth.

"Gasperian is a fool, as well, but for different reasons," she snapped. "He is content to sit as Master of Kalinden, trying to make stupid peasants happy when he might have ruled a far greater domain. He never had the vision you and I have built upon."

"We *have* done well together, Xyanth, haven't we?" Lindaz smirked. He picked up a jeweled wine goblet from the inlaid table beside his chair and drank deeply.

Xyanth stopped abruptly in front of him, head regally high, thin lips curled in disgust. Her eyes glittered.

"We? Look at you!" Xyanth pointed at Lindaz' belly. "You were a man once, but you've grown fat and timid and stupid. I thought we might build a power to challenge Anweigh. *I* might still do so, but you will remain forever cringing behind your guards and feeding your fat face."

"You don't understand." A muscle in Lindaz' cheek twitched and his lower lip quivered slightly.

Xyanth laughed.

Lindaz flinched at the sound but continued. "I'm more than twenty-five years older than you and my health isn't good. It's not!" he exclaimed when his companion snorted in disbelief. "What we did, what we were, is in the past. Matcassen is the most powerful city, short of Anweigh, in all Errandane. Isn't that enough?"

"You might now rule Anweigh had you listened to me. But you hesitated, just as you hesitate now, when Kalinden could be ours."

"I can't risk it. Not now."

"You mean you want to hide in Matcassen, stuffing yourself with food and pleasuring your fat body with disgusting indulgences."

"The attacks against my life—"

"Are unimportant and can be dealt with!" Xyanth leaned forward to stare into her husband's eyes. "*I* can deal with them, and Kalinden as well. Make me heir! Give me the right to lead troops against the beastmen. Think what I could achieve from that vantage!"

"You're a woman! You're not even strong enough to lift a battle sword!" Anger was coming to Lindaz' rescue. He started to rise from his chair, but the effort was too much. He fell back, fat jowls quivering.

Xyanth studied her husband. "That doesn't matter. Even if my physical strength isn't equal to a man's, my cunning is."

"Then use it to find out how this Santar plots against me. I'm your husband. Isn't my life worth more than your dreams of power?"

Before Xyanth could reply, there was a sharp knock on the chamber door. A guard entered and snapped to attention.

"Advisor Danet wishes to speak with you, Master."

"Let him pass," commanded Lindaz, relieved at the excuse to end his conversation with his wife.

"Master Lindaz," said Danet, entering the room. He crossed to stand before Lindaz' chair. "Lady Xyanth," he added, bowing low with a courtly sweep.

"Advisor." Xyanth gave a scarcely perceptible nod in recognition.

"I have come, Master," said Danet, turning his attention to Lindaz, "because I am concerned about some rumors I have heard."

"Rumors?" Lindaz frowned.

Xyanth bent forward, eyes fixed on the advisor.

"Yes, Master. Rumors that the beastmen will soon be invading Matcassen." Though his head was deferentially bent, Danet's attention was fixed on Lindaz. "Word of the runner's message has spread. There are those who say the beastmen

51

have been deliberately provoked, that their move into Kalinden is but a prelude to an even more deadly attack against Matcassen."

"Impossible!" Lindaz' exclamation was tinged with sudden nervous fear.

"Absurd." Contempt was the only discernible emotion in Xyanth's voice.

"Absurd, perhaps, but not impossible." Danet looked directly at Lindaz, then at Xyanth. "And even were it impossible, the rumors themselves—as well as the fears they engender—could be harmful."

Porcine eyes wide, Lindaz stared first at Danet, then at his wife. "I told you so! It's this Santar again! He—"

"You have been with us—what?—two months, advisor?" Xyanth interrupted smoothly. Her irritation was revealed only in her suddenly narrowed mouth. "You cannot yet appreciate our people's fear of the beastmen. There are many still living who remember the last time the savages invaded Matcassen. The rumors are natural, but groundless."

Danet lowered his gaze respectfully, grateful that Xyanth's sharp eyes were fixed on her husband and not on himself. "Perhaps you are right, Lady," he murmured. "My concern was that you be informed."

"We thank you." Xyanth's tone was clearly dismissive.

"Master Lindaz." Danet bowed low. "Lady Xyanth." He backed toward the door. Just before he turned to leave he glanced toward Xyanth. She was staring expressionlessly at her husband, who was swallowing a deep draught from his goblet.

Even from the doorway Danet could see Lindaz' hand shaking.

As he headed down the hall at the sedate pace expected of an advisor, Danet's thoughts raced. How could he use Lindaz' brief slip about Santar to gain more information? What would Jerrel say? What should he do next? It was a pity that that runner had already left the city.

The boy was dead. Jerrel cursed himself, cursed his failure of hand and eye when he shot the drevon the first time, cursed the fates that had brought the boy to this place.

Slowly he crossed the few feet of bloodied stone to where the boy lay, skirting the wide red pool that poured from the drevon's slashed throat.

The massive head of the drevon was twisted, snout skyward, pulled around by the boy's grip on one of its horns. Trapped between the double horns on either side of the beast's head, the boy lay pinned against the rock. One sharp horn had pierced his leather tunic. Blood was everywhere, with no way of determining which was the boy's, which the drevon's. Neither beast nor boy moved.

Jerrel knelt beside the child, studying him. He looked too young to have been on the mountain alone, too delicate. His skin was tanned, as though he'd spent a great deal of time outdoors, but the weather had not coarsened him. There was a faint hint of pink in the cheeks, of deeper rose in the lips, shades more suited to a girl than a boy who killed drevons. His features were regular and finely cut. Jerrel would have liked to have seen his eyes, hidden now behind the closed lids. His eyelashes were unusually thick and long, black like the heavy, straight hair cut in a chin-length crop.

With a sigh, Jerrel stood, wincing at the pain the movement caused him. Carefully he felt along his side and as far across his back as he could. The wound didn't seem to be serious, though it hurt badly. He didn't want to think what might have happened if the boy hadn't cried out when he did.

The boy. Unable to face the sight of that crumpled form, Jerrel studied the rocks around him. This was such a bleak, lonely spot for a grave.

Jerrel knelt again and reached to free the horn that had impaled the boy. To his surprise, it came out easily. Ignoring the pain of his own wounds, Jerrel grasped two horns, then slowly stood, muscles bulging, and dragged the heavy head off the boy. It wasn't enough, however. The boy's legs were still trapped under the drevon's massive shoulder.

Jerrel tried but found himself unable to shift the drevon further. He would have to pull the boy free. He moved to the child's head, took a firm grip on both arms, and tugged.

The boy moaned.

He lived! Jerrel almost dropped him in his surprise, but recovered himself and, giving one more heave, pulled him from beneath the drevon.

The boy moaned again.

He was so covered with blood it was hard for Jerrel to decide what to do first. He fumbled at the fastenings of the boy's belt. There was something familiar about that belt, but he was too intent on his task to pay attention to the nagging memory.

The belt came free, and Jerrel reached for the

lacings on the leather tunic. As with the belt, the congealing blood made the leather slick and hard to handle.

The boy looked so pale. Since that second moan Jerrel had heard no other sound. Had moving him injured him further? Suddenly desperate for reassurance that the boy still lived, Jerrel slipped his fingers between the half-open lacings to feel for a heartbeat.

He froze.

Hesitantly he slid his fingers farther under the edge of the tunic. There was no mistaking the soft, rounded mound which met his touch. This was no boy, but a woman.

The nagging memory crystallized. The belt. It was identical to the one worn by the runner he had hired. And the knife?

He rose and moved back to the drevon's head. Not a knife. A runner's dagger. Jerrel balanced the deadly weapon across his fingers. It was superbly crafted, the long, finely honed blade compensating for the unusually heavy haft.

Another moan jolted Jerrel from his thoughts. If the runner died, whatever message she bore would die with her. He wanted very much to know what might be so important that she would have chosen this path instead of the easier routes available.

And he wasn't forgetting that he owed her his life.

Kneeling once more, Jerrel used the dagger to cut the tunic lacings and slice open her undershift, then pushed the leather and cloth aside. Though the tunic had been slick with blood, the runner's skin beneath was smooth and white, unstained. Only one long red streak along her left side marred her flesh.

Jerrel explored the wound with a gentle finger. The drevon had only gouged her side. The wound would be painful, but not fatal. He ran his hands along her sides, across her chest and belly, down her slender legs. He was no medic, but he could detect no other injury.

Gently Jerrel lifted the runner's head and probed for any wound. All he could feel was her thick, heavy hair wrapping around his fingers.

Her eyelids fluttered. A soft sigh escaped her lips. Jerrel looked down into eyes of the most startling, vivid green he had ever seen.

For an instant her eyes darted back and forth as she struggled to full consciousness; then they widened slightly, focusing on Jerrel.

"The drevon!" She jerked in his hands, fighting to sit up, then fell back with a cry of pain.

"Lie still, runner," Jerrel said, restraining her. "The drevon is dead, and it is you who killed him. You saved my life."

"Dead!" Her eyes filled with remembered fear. Her lips firmed and she blinked, forcing the fear back.

Jerrel felt a renewed surge of admiration for the woman. "You've been hurt," he said, "though I don't think it's serious. Can you feel anything?"

For a moment she said nothing; then her hand fluttered toward her head. "It hurts here," she said. Her hand moved to her side. "And here."

Jerrel captured her hand in his. For an instant he found himself caught in wonder—it was such a tiny hand, so delicate. It barely spanned the palm of his own, yet it had been strong and sure enough to kill the huge drevon.

"Your head hurts because you hit it on the stone," he said. "And the drevon's horn sliced your side. The wound looks—and probably feels—far worse than it really is. I haven't been able to find any other injury."

Again she blinked, assessing his information. Her free hand fumbled with the tunic on her injured side, as though seeking something. She relaxed, then stiffened as her fingers touched the cut lacings.

"My tunic!" She struggled to sit up, gasping in pain.

"It's all right!" Jerrel pushed her back. "I had to see how badly you'd been injured."

His eyes fixed on her face, he deftly twitched her tunic back into place. Crimson darkened her cheeks. Her embarrassment was unexpected, and undoubtedly real.

Jerrel rocked back on his heels, then quickly undid the lacings of his own jerkin and handed them to her.

"Here. You can retie your tunic once you're back on your feet."

Without lacings or hunting belt, his jerkin and the simple wool shirt beneath it fell open, revealing the broad expanse of his chest. The air felt cold against his exposed flesh.

Jerrel tugged his shirt closed, noting how her eyes followed his movement. He couldn't help laughing.

"We're even now," he said, and was pleased to see the tentative smile that quivered on her lips. "If I help you, do you think you can stand?"

At her nod of assent, Jerrel leaned forward to slide his arms behind her, then pulled her to her feet. The motion wrenched a sharp cry from her.

She collapsed against him, head against his bare chest, hands grasping his jerkin.

"My hip. It's my right hip!" She trembled.

Without releasing her, Jerrel ran his hand across her hip, trying to detect what was wrong.

"It seems all right to me."

"I've twisted it. In my fall, probably."

Which meant she wouldn't be able to walk. Jerrel considered the possibilities. Without thinking, his hand rose to her head. Slowly, comfortingly, he stroked her hair. She was so small, so very delicate. Yet he could feel the strength in her body as she fought against her pain.

"I'll carry you back to my camp," he said at last. "From there we can get help."

"No!"

The vehemence of her protest startled him.

"I have a message that I must carry on." She pushed away from him, though she still gripped his clothes for balance.

"How?" It was clear from her stricken expression that she had no answer to his question.

When she didn't respond, Jerrel said, "I'm going to carry you over there, out of the wind." For the first time he realized the fog had lifted, driven out by a chilling breeze.

"I can walk, if you'll help me."

Jerrel started to protest, but changed his mind when he saw the firm set of her jaw and determined tilt of her chin. Careful not to touch her injured side, he shifted around so she could lean on him as she walked.

Walking wasn't the right word to describe their faltering progress, Jerrel quickly decided. Though she tried, she couldn't force her injured hip to move. All she could manage was to hop on her good leg, then drag the other while she clung to him for support.

She seemed unaware of her gaping tunic. Her lip bled from where she'd bitten it to keep from crying out. By the time they'd crossed to some rocks where Jerrel could prop her up, she was shaking all over.

"Wait here," Jerrel commanded, once he was sure she wasn't going to faint. "I'll get our things."

Jerrel collected his hunting belt, bow, and arrows first, then returned to the clearing to pick up her runner's belt. He started to fasten it around his waist, then had to smile—her waist was half the size of his. He settled for looping her belt over his and slid her dagger into the sheath with his hunting knife.

At her request, he also retrieved the grackle skin. When he saw the niche, he shuddered. The space was so small she must have felt the drevon's breath when it attacked.

While he'd fetched their things, she'd managed, somehow, to use his laces to refasten her tunic. Her effort was crude but effective. She was also considerably paler than when he'd left her. Though she tried to hide it, Jerrel could see she was trembling with the effort of remaining upright. He hated to think of the agony the trip back to his camp would cause her.

"All ready," he said, deliberately keeping his tone light.

"My message. I have to get my message to Anweigh," she said between clenched teeth. Her eyes had grown so large they seemed to consume her other features.

"I'll send a runner on," Jerrel said, thinking of

the runner he'd hired who was still in the village, undoubtedly enjoying doing absolutely nothing while continuing to collect the extortionate daily fee he was charging. "But we have to get help first."

"You? You have a runner?"

If she'd had the strength, Jerrel knew she would have laughed. Runners were for rich men, not hunters dressed in soiled and bloodstained clothes. There was a two-day growth of beard on his face and he hadn't bathed since he'd left Norvag. In her place, Jerrel decided, he would have laughed anyway.

"Yes, I have a runner," he said, unable to keep a slight smile from his face. "One smart enough not to try to ride a drevon."

She *did* laugh at that. But when he tried to lift her, she gave a choking cry, then fainted.

The way back to camp seemed far longer than it had on the way out. Once again Jerrel stopped to rest. The runner wasn't very big, but carrying her in his arms over the rocky trail was hard work. The muscles of his arms and back were beginning to ache from the strain.

Gently he laid her down in the shelter of some tumbled boulders, out of the chill wind. She'd shown no signs of regaining consciousness, but then he'd inadvertently jostled her a number of times as he struggled over the path. The rough handling was more than enough to keep her unconscious.

Freed of his burden, Jerrel straightened, then moved his arms back and forth, trying to ease some stiffness from his muscles. He wasn't that far from camp, but at the rate he was progressing, it would be another two hours or so before he reached it.

Sighing, he bent down again beside the runner. She was still pale, though the cut on her side had stopped bleeding.

Gently he tugged at the torn tunic and undershift, trying to adjust them so they provided a little more protection. As he did so, something small yet solid fell out of her clothes to roll on the ground.

Jerrel reached for the fallen object, a heavy gold ring. He was on the point of stuffing it in his pocket when something about the stone caught his eye.

He looked closer, then froze. It couldn't be. The light was poor and he was tired.

He turned the ring over and ran the tip of his finger along the underside of the stone's mounting, then peered more closely at the marks cut into the inside of the band. The marks, in the alphabet of Arcana, spelled out a name: Santar bn'Hadar.

It couldn't be, but it was. The ring he held was Santar's recorder ring.

Shaken, Jerrel glanced down at the runner, a sharp question on his lips. But that still, pale figure wasn't going to tell him anything right then.

Santar's ring. Jerrel closed his hand around the ring, so hard the edge of the stone dug into his palm. A dull pain settled in his chest, shoving out the hope that had resided there throughout his search.

Jerrel had seen the ring only once before, the last time he'd seen his brother. Santar had been excited and proud, anxious to show off the symbol of his new rank—the recorder ring given to all new Rediscovery Service Officers on the completion of their training.

The rings recorded everything the wearer saw, heard, felt, or smelled. The information thus gathered was used to generate tapes which would allow those who followed the first Rediscovery Team to learn the planet's languages and customs in a matter of hours through hypno training. No one except Rediscovery Officers were allowed to wear the rings.

Though he hadn't seen Santar since the graduation, Jerrel couldn't imagine his brother voluntarily removing his ring and giving it to someone else. And if he hadn't removed it himself, then . . .

No! He wouldn't let his imagination run away, Jerrel told himself firmly. Just because Santar would not willingly have removed the ring didn't mean he was dead. There were any number of possible explanations, and somehow he, Jerrel, would find out which was correct.

Again Jerrel glanced down at the unconscious runner. What did she know about the ring? About Santar? To whom was she taking the ring, and why? Who had sent it?

The runner gave no answer to his unspoken questions. Nor could she until she awakened, something that was likely to happen more quickly if he got her back to camp where she could be made warm and relatively comfortable.

His mouth set in a grim, determined line, Jerrel stuffed the ring into a pouch on his hunting belt. Placing one arm behind her shoulders, the other behind her knees, he picked her up, then stood.

The weariness of a few moments before had been driven from his body as if by magic. The sooner he got her back to camp, the sooner she would be able to answer some, at least, of the questions churning in his brain.

Restlessly Jerrel paced about the campsite, pausing every now and then to check on the runner where she lay wrapped in the warm, musky-smelling hide of the first drevon he'd killed.

It had been dark when he'd returned to find only Rakin in camp. Jerrel had been exhausted and his back muscles had begun to throb. Too tired to travel further, he had sent Rakin back to the inn for help.

When Borlat finally reappeared after an unsuccessful hunt for fedding, the nocturnal rodent many considered a great delicacy, Jerrel had sent him up the mountain to recover what he could of the drevon. Jerrel wanted no witnesses in camp when he questioned the runner about the ring.

Again Jerrel checked on the runner. With just her face peeking out of the shaggy drevon hide, she looked even smaller and more fragile than the day before. So pale was she, Jerrel wondered for an instant if her stillness was due to something more profound than sleep.

He knelt beside her and felt for the pulse at her throat. It was there, reassuringly strong and steady.

Instead of moving away, Jerrel leaned closer to brush back a strand of hair that had fallen across her cheek. He wished she would open her eyes, not just so he could ask about the ring but because he wanted to see if those hidden orbs really were as green as he remembered.

He thought of her facing the wounded drevon armed only with her dagger, and shook his head in wonder. He thought of her huddled in that too-shallow niche defiantly singing a bawdy tavern song, and couldn't help smiling.

Somehow, though he couldn't have said why, he was convinced she knew nothing about his brother. He knew relatively little about the customs of this world, but he did know runners were supposed to avoid personal involvement in anything connected with their work. Which meant this runner might know nothing more about the ring than who had given it to her, and to whom she was supposed to deliver it. And that was information he felt sure she wouldn't be willing to share.

She showed no sign of rousing any time soon. Despite the cold air and icy water, Jerrel decided he would take a bath in the stream. He wanted to wash some of the blood from his clothes and skin. Though it was absurd, he had an urge to present a more respectable appearance when the runner finally awoke.

Nareen blinked, startled by the brilliant blue of the sky. From somewhere in the bushes, a bird sang, defying the cold. She took a deep breath and immediately wrinkled her nose in disgust. Her bed had the rank and unmistakable smell of drevon.

Drevon! Memories flooded in. Of fear, of the enormous beast that had tried to kill her. Memories of pain, and of the tall stranger whose voice had sounded so pleasant in her ear. She remembered, too, the feel of his hands, the tickling warmth of the mat of hair that had softened the hard expanse of his chest, and the disturbing, tantalizing man-smell of him.

Nareen lay still, trying to identify her surroundings by sound. She could still hear the birds and, now that she concentrated, the soft murmuring of a stream not far away. There was the muted crackling of a small fire—even over the smell of the drevon hide Nareen could catch the tempting odor of meat cooking. But she could hear no footsteps, no voices.

Without thinking, Nareen tried to toss the hide off and sit up. She immediately fell back, gasping in sudden awareness of a hundred aching hurts. The back of her head ached. Her left side hurt—a lot. And her hip throbbed, reminding her of the excruciating pain that had lanced through her when the stranger had lifted her into his arms.

The numerous bodily torments could have been endured. But the injury to her hip was serious enough, Nareen knew, to make it impossible for her to go on to Anweigh.

She blinked, fighting back angry tears. What was she to do now? She remembered the stranger had said he would send a runner in her place, but she also remembered exactly how scruffy he'd looked. There'd been nothing to suggest he was rich enough to afford a trained runner.

Cautiously Nareen pushed the hide back and sat up. Her message had to be carried to Anweigh, whatever the cost.

And she mustn't forget the ring the advisor had entrusted to her. She slid a hand through the opening of her tunic and fumbled for the pouch. She froze as she located the pocket stitched to the tunic's inner seam. The pouch was there, but nothing was in it.

Desperately she probed further, until her fingers poked through the bottom of the pocket. The realization of what must have happened washed through her with a sickening sense of failure.

Nareen pulled the pouch—or what remained of it—from the torn pocket. The drevon's horn that had torn her tunic had also ripped a hole in both the pocket and the pouch. The ring must have fallen out somewhere back on the trail when she was unconscious.

Unless . . . No, she wouldn't even consider that possibility. The stranger who had rescued her might be nothing more than a poor hunter, but he wasn't a thief. Of that she was certain.

Nareen shifted position slightly, trying to ease the ache in her hip and side. The pain brought her back to an awareness of her surroundings.

She was cold, she realized suddenly, and hungry. The meat bubbling in a small pot over the fire smelled so *very* good. With that thought came shame that she could even think about eating after discovering the loss of the ring.

It also reminded her that the unknown hunter would be returning soon.

She was just trying to struggle to her feet when she heard footsteps and the sound of someone whistling. By the time the hunter finally walked around the thicket of junfeg bushes and into camp, Nareen was on her feet. She hoped it was just the effort of rising that suddenly made it so difficult for her to breathe.

Despite the cold, he had obviously bathed. Wet hair curled in thick ringlets around his finely shaped head. He'd removed his leather jerkin and his shirt. The soiled clothes, dripping water, dangled from his hand while he remained bare-chested. His soft leather leggings were soaked, as well. They clung to his legs, clearly defining the powerful swell of muscle in his calves and thighs. Only the soft hunters' boots he wore seemed to have escaped immersion.

He stopped, obviously startled at seeing her on her feet. A slight smile broke the stern lines of his face, and his strange-colored eyes warmed. As he came closer, Nareen could see droplets of water glistening in the hair on his chest.

Only one thought came through clearly: she had never before seen so magnificent a man, and never one in such a disturbing state of undress.

Jerrel couldn't help smiling in relief. Only a short time ago he'd wondered if she were even alive, and now, somehow, she'd managed to stand despite the injury to her hip.

Which wasn't to say she looked good. She looked, in fact, perfectly awful. She was still pale, and there was a tightness about her mouth that spoke of pain more forcefully than words ever could. Her hair was tousled and matted in places with dried blood. Her right arm and hand were frightening to behold, even though he knew it wasn't her blood that stained them. And there simply weren't words to describe the state of her tunic and leggings.

Yet neither that nor his unspoken questions about her possession of Santar's ring detracted from the admiration he felt. It couldn't have been easy for her to get to her feet, and it was clearly costing her an effort to remain standing. There might not be much of the little runner, but what there was, was all heart.

He crossed to her quickly. "You shouldn't have tried to stand without help," he chided, reaching out to touch her.

His fingers were icy cold, so why did his touch

make her suddenly feel so uncomfortably warm? Nareen glanced down to where he grasped her arm.

At the sight of her filthy arm under his still-damp fingers, she uttered a small, involuntary cry of disgust and shrank away. She'd been trained to think of her work, not herself, but she couldn't prevent the shame that rushed through her at the thought of the unappealing spectacle she must make.

He jerked back, concerned. "Did I hurt you?"

"No." Nareen wrapped her arms around herself, struggling to regain emotional control.

She was a runner. She ruled her emotions, not the other way around. There was no time for any consideration of her appearance, for shame and confusion at the nearness of a stranger. Her duty was the only thing that mattered.

"No," she said again. "You didn't hurt me. Forgive me, I . . ." She what?

She wanted him to go on touching her. She wanted to rest her head against his chest, as she had on the mountain, and to have his arms about her. She wanted to forget her failed mission, her loss of the ring, and to feel as safe, as protected, as she had felt then.

"I am concerned about the message I bear," she said, eyes fixed on the ground before her.

"You can't travel."

"No."

Jerrel studied her bent head for a moment, wishing he knew what thoughts were going through it. "Come," he said, gesturing to a large rock near the fire. "Ease your leg. You can sit on that rock there without straining your hip."

Jerrel made no offer to help as Nareen hobbled

to the rock, then cautiously lowered herself until she was half sitting, half leaning against it.

In order not to embarrass her by watching her halting progress, Jerrel made a show of laying his shirt and jerkin out to dry on rocks near the fire and then of pulling on the one clean shirt he'd brought. Strange how he hadn't noticed the cold while he was standing near her.

"I've made some stew," he said, collecting two crude wooden bowls and spoons from Rakin's pack. "It's not much, some drevon meat and a few spices, but at least it's warm. We can eat while we talk."

"You butchered the drevon?" Nareen exclaimed, startled. And here she'd been thinking he'd abandoned the drevon to rescue her.

"Hardly!" Jerrel shook his head, remembering the effort it had cost him just to carry her back. He knelt by the fire and began ladling the stew into the bowls. "This is another drevon I killed. My men took care of it while I kept hunting." His mouth twisted ruefully. "Though I might better have stayed in camp and sent them out, instead."

"I saw the wound across your back," Nareen admitted, gratefully accepting the fragrant, steaming bowl of stew he handed her. Despite the difficulty of getting to the rock she sat on, she'd watched while he set his clothes out to dry, watched the way he moved and the play of muscle under his skin.

"I wasn't thinking of my wound." Jerrel's gaze met hers directly. Her eyes, he realized, really were as green as he'd remembered. "I was thinking of you. You might have been killed. I should have brought down the beast the first time I had the chance."

69

For an instant Nareen felt the terror of the drevon creep back. But only for an instant. The understanding she saw in his eyes wrapped about her, driving out the fear.

"What do we do now?" she asked. She took a bite of the stew. It tasted as good as it smelled.

"I brought two men hunting with me. One I sent up the mountain to bring down the dead drevon. The other I sent back for help. A healer, a litter for you, and men to carry the litter. I told him to bring a runner, as well. They should be here soon." He paused, studying her expression. "You look as if you don't believe me."

What could she say? Nareen wondered. She glanced about the camp, noting the coarse, threadbare blankets the hunter and his men had used as beds, the few weapons, the simple garments he'd spread on the rocks. "How long until they arrive?" she asked at last.

"Two hours. Perhaps three."

"A real runner?"

"Yes."

She would have to hope he wasn't lying. And what could he gain by lying? Her hesitation, she saw, was making him smile.

"You don't believe I can produce a runner, do you? Perhaps if I introduced myself," he said, rising easily to his feet and making a formal bow. "Jerrel. Traveler and merchant. At your service."

"A merchant? But . . ."

"Not all merchants are old and fat or travel in great caravans with their aard wagons." He grinned. "Some of us find it more profitable to travel light. And what about you? I can't call you 'runner' all the time."

Nareen couldn't help smiling in return. "I am

70

Nareen, Merchant Jerrel. Nareen of Kalinden."

"Kalinden?" He was obviously surprised. "The path you were following comes from Matcassen, not Kalinden."

"True. But there were no runners available in Matcassen, so I had to go on." She hesitated. "I was carrying something else, a ring, but now it's gone. The drevon tore a hole in my pocket and the ring fell out. You didn't see it, did you?"

"A ring?" Jerrel said casually. The subject didn't seem to interest him. "What did it look like?"

Again she hesitated. Runners were forbidden to discuss the messages or the goods they carried with anyone. But then, runners weren't supposed to lose the things entrusted to their care, either.

"It was a man's ring, heavy gold with an unusual blue stone."

"Was it valuable?"

Exactly the sort of question a merchant would ask, but somehow Nareen didn't like hearing this man ask it. "I don't know. I only saw it once."

"Whose was it? Where were you taking it?"

He was asking a lot of questions, Nareen thought irritably. But perhaps that, too, was understandable. Information could be bought and sold as easily as goods.

"You know I can't tell you that."

Jerrel shrugged and returned his attention to the stew. "I can't help you. Sorry." She really didn't seem to know much about the ring. It would have helped to know the names of the person who sent it and the person for whom it was intended, but he was certain she would never voluntarily reveal that information.

Despite his disappointment, he couldn't repress a distinct sensation of relief. He wouldn't have liked to think that she was involved in his brother's disappearance.

Nareen studied the man across from her, puzzled. It wasn't completely unknown for a merchant to travel without a caravan, but it certainly wasn't common. Somehow, she couldn't picture this magnificent male as being involved in trade.

Nareen shook off the thought. It didn't matter. He could be a Master, for all she cared, so long as he helped her off this mountain and found someone to carry her message in her stead.

In the meantime, the damp clothes on the rock had given her an idea.

"Would you," she asked hesitantly, "have another clean shirt I could use? And soap? I'd like to wash before your men arrive." As a runner she had the right to claim whatever she needed, but given the meager supplies in camp she doubted Jerrel's ability to produce the requisite items.

"Forgive me! I didn't think . . ." He crossed to a small leather bag lying on top of one of the blankets. "Ah, here we are. Rakin won't mind." He flourished a rough wool shirt similar to the one he wore.

Jerrel picked up a piece of soap he'd left on the rock with his clothes, then offered shirt and soap to Nareen. "I should warn you, however, that the water is very cold."

"I don't mind, so long as I can be *clean*." She accepted the items and the hand that Jerrel extended to help her to her feet. She even, after a few painful steps, accepted the arm he offered to help her down to the stream.

"Be sure to stay on the bank," Jerrel warned as he helped her settle on a mossy ledge at the edge of the swiftly rushing water. "The rocks are slick and the water ice cold. You ought to be able to scoop up enough water to rinse off the worst. I'll arrange for you to have a proper bath later."

"Anything else?" Nareen inquired, her brows drawn together in irritation. The stream wasn't far from the camp, but it was far enough that the walk had strained both her hip and her patience.

"Be careful with that slash across your side. And call me when you're through. I'll come help you back to camp."

Nareen glared at the stream and didn't offer a comment, but she was already tugging at her tunic as Jerrel started back to camp.

Because of her hip, her boots and leggings were hard to remove. She ought at least to have asked Jerrel's help in removing her boots, Nareen thought as she struggled to pull one off, then the other.

Eventually, however, every article of clothing lay in a heap on the moss beside her. Nareen shivered a little as the cold air struck her exposed flesh, but it felt good to be free of the stiffened leather and filthy cloth. She would need her boots, and her leggings could be washed out, but she didn't want to touch the tunic ever again.

The water *was* cold, but it felt good to rinse her body. After a while, in fact, the water felt more refreshing than cold.

With her immediate needs attended to, Nareen dunked her leggings, then vigorously rubbed the lump of soap across them. It took a couple of rinsings, but they didn't look too bad, she decided, wringing them out at last. And moving was taking some of the stiffness out of her muscles. Which gave her an idea.

Jerrel was repacking his bundle when he heard her scream. Pausing only to snatch up his hunting knife, he thundered down the path to the stream. What could possibly . . . ?

He raced past the last huge rock, knife at the ready, and almost fell as he tried to stop abruptly on the slick, damp moss. His imagination had conjured a dozen possible explanations for Nareen's scream, but it hadn't prepared him for what he found.

Chapter 4

He could have handled thieves, Jerrel thought wildly. Even a drevon if he'd had to. But what did he do about the woman, hip deep in the swirling waters and completely naked, who clung to a rock in the middle of the stream, struggling to keep her balance?

Nareen's black hair lay plastered on her head, accenting the oval of her face and the graceful column of her neck. Though her face, throat, and forearms were tanned, the rest of her body was a pearly white. Even from several feet away Jerrel could see the faint blue tracings of veins that lay just below the surface of her translucent skin. Her small, high breasts had grown firm and pointed in the icy water.

Jerrel gasped, felt his heart start beating again. Relief that she was all right flooded through him, then anger that she should have frightened him so.

"What do you think you're doing?"

"I wanted to wash my hair," she said defiantly. A crimson flush darkened her already tanned face, then swept downward. She tried to bring her hands up to cover herself, but the current was so strong it almost knocked her over. She clutched at the rock again and blushed even more furiously.

"I told you—" Jerrel began, only to be interrupted.

"I know, but—"

"I thought you were being attacked!"

"The water's cold—"

"I told you it was!"

" . . . and I slipped."

Shouting like this was accomplishing nothing. Jerrel took two deep breaths. Then a third. Then he closed his eyes. It wasn't just the run down the path that was making his blood pound.

When Jerrel opened his eyes again, he fixed them firmly on a ratty bunch of junfeg bushes downstream on the opposite bank. His words, when he spoke, were carefully enunciated. "Have you finished washing your hair?"

"Yes." Nareen found it hard to keep her teeth from chattering. Her wound ached abominably and her hip was throbbing as the result of her having slipped on the polished rocks of the stream bed. It was the pain from that misstep which had caused Nareen to cry out. She tried again to stand without clinging to the rock. "I was just getting out."

"Indeed." The junfeg bushes, Jerrel decided, were the sorriest bit of shrubbery he had ever seen. He kept on staring at them.

"I don't need any help," said Nareen with dignity. One hand on the rock, she carefully slid her right leg forward a few inches, braced herself, then hopped. She was at least a couple of inches closer to the bank. Between the pain in her hip and the numbing drag of the icy water, Nareen wasn't sure she could repeat the maneuver. What kind of a fool was she even to have thought of bathing? And how had she gotten so far out? The rock hadn't seemed so far from the bank when she'd started.

Again she slid her leg forward, then hopped. And again.

But this time she didn't quite manage to regain her balance. Stones shifted under her feet and her hand slid across the glistening rock she was using for support. Nareen had time for one quick gasp before the insistent current caught at her body, tugging her under.

Jerrel heard Nareen's gasp and whirled about just in time to see her lose her balance. Without thinking, he dropped his knife and jumped, feet first, into the stream.

The current rolled her into his arms. He grabbed her, but the slick bottom stones proved his undoing. With Nareen firmly in his arms, Jerrel slipped and went under, too.

They were both gasping by the time Jerrel regained his footing and stood. Nareen's gasps held a sharp note that hinted at the pain inflicted by her tumbling.

Careful not to slip again, Jerrel made his way toward the bank and gently deposited his burden on the edge, her feet still dangling in the water. She leaned forward against the solid strength of him, clinging to the support he offered. Her breath came in whistling sobs compounded of hurt and humiliation.

Jerrel gently untangled her fingers and leaned away. With her injuries, she was a fool to have attempted to bathe in the stream. Yet it wasn't anger but concern that prompted him to push back the dripping tendrils of hair plastered across her brow, then cup his hands about her face, forcing her to open her eyes and look up at him.

"Are you all right?"

Nareen nodded, unable to speak. With her mouth open and her breath coming in short, quick pants, she found herself incapable of looking away from the brilliant blue eyes above her, trapped by some force she could not name and did not understand. She was aware of her pain, of her nakedness, of the biting cold air against her wet skin. Somehow, none of that mattered. In that moment all that mattered were his eyes, his hands about her face, and the comforting, massive strength of the man.

Though his gaze never wavered from hers, Jerrel was achingly aware of her, of her nearness. Black hair and green eyes. Ruby red lips, parted slightly. Translucent flesh and pink-tipped breasts that rose and fell with each breath she took. Her hands, so small and delicate, had moved to rest on his.

A man might drown in the stream, but he ran a greater risk in the green depths of the eyes that held his. Jerrel released her.

Heedless of the shifting rocks beneath his feet or the current plucking so demandingly at his legs, he moved a short distance downstream, then pulled himself up on the bank.

Without looking at her, he asked, "Can you get dressed?"

Her answer was an almost inaudible, "Yes."

"Call me when you're done." Jerrel stamped one foot, then the other, trying to force out the water that filled his boots. "It was my only dry shirt," he grumbled, "and my only damned pair of boots."

He turned and stalked back up the path toward camp.

Nareen had never been more glad to see strangers than she was to see the men who walked into camp a couple of hours later. The cold of the stream had been nothing compared with the frost that hung in the air between her and this hunter who disturbed her so. As he'd promised, Jerrel had helped her back to camp once she'd dressed, but he'd scarcely spoken since.

In the bustle of breaking up camp, Nareen was able to avoid Jerrel and concentrate on immediate concerns. Jerrel's men really had brought a runner with them, and it was a relief to pass her message to him. Though it galled her not to be able to continue, she'd done what she could to ensure that Anweigh was alerted to Kalinden's plight. With any luck, the runner would reach the capital in five or six days and troops would set out for Kalinden shortly thereafter.

Too much time. So much could happen in the long weeks before help arrived. If only Lindaz . . .

Nareen had learned long ago that it was futile to wish for what could not be. She ought to take what comfort she could from Tork's veiled warning about the danger of help from Matcassen.

She ought to, but she couldn't.

Once the runner had set out, Nareen relaxed

and permitted herself to be placed on the litter that had been brought for her. At first, despite telling herself she really didn't care about Jerrel's avoidance of her, Nareen found herself trying to keep track of the big man's movements. But as the day wore on and the inevitable jouncing began to aggravate her hip, she concentrated instead on a tight-lipped struggle not to expose her increasing pain by crying out.

Because the litter bearers could not move very fast, it was long past turning and into the early morning hours before the group reached the small inn that was their destination.

Nareen, exhausted, was only partially aware of the activity swirling about her. Despite having been wrapped in warm blankets, she was shaking with cold and close to tears with the pain. She was only vaguely aware of being shifted to a bed, of drinking something hot and soothing. She wasn't even sure if she dreamed of the blue-eyed man who leaned over her, gently adjusted the covers around her, then cradled her hand between his until she slept.

With his brother's recorder ring on the little finger of his left hand—it had been too small to fit any other finger—Jerrel sat in the massive wood chair by the fire in his room, studying the shadowed corners of the room, wondering.

Did he really want to activate the ring? Would it tell him what he had refused to believe for so long, that Santar was dead and that he, Jerrel, was totally alone in the universe? And if Santar was dead, did he want to know the manner and time of his dying?

Yes! Jerrel's lips thinned. Most emphatically

yes. There was no way he could bring Santar back, no vengeance he could claim, but he had to know.

Closing his eyes, Jerrel cued the com link planted inside his skull to connect with the neural transmitter within the ring. He wouldn't start at the end of the recording. He didn't want to know that. Not yet. But to understand whatever the last recording would tell him, he had to know something of what had come before.

Jerrel opened his eyes as he felt the recorder begin to function. The shadows of the room around him dissolved, then reshaped themselves into the crowded streets of a city. Matcassen. That was what the ring told him. Matcassen as seen through Santar's eyes.

Slowly, hesitantly, Jerrel released his mind fully to the ring's influence. Though he knew, in some part of his awareness, that he remained seated in a chair beside a still-flickering fire, though he knew the shadows about him retained their dominion of the room, Jerrel's senses told him otherwise. His eyes saw the people, most of them shabbily dressed, that swarmed around him in the marketplace. His ears heard the babble of voices, the shrill cries of the vendors, the confused chittering and lowing and squawking of the animals. His nose smelled the combined odors of unwashed bodies, frightened animals, and the pungent spices of the food being offered for sale, and wrinkled in distaste.

Jerrel walked the filthy, stinking back streets of Matcassen. He saw the dirty children, heard hungry babies squall, talked to the few timid, uncertain people who would stop for his questions. He felt the people jostling past and knew the pain of seeing them as Santar had seen them, the poorest of Errandane, the oppressed citizens of the powerful city of Matcassen.

Through the neural link, Jerrel knew Santar's doubts, felt his growing anger, and traced the tortured steps of his decision to confront the leaders of a city that could permit such misery. And even while Jerrel's mind was shouting, "No! Santar, no!" Jerrel's senses were leading him through Santar's days as his brother bribed, cajoled, and bullied his way into a meeting with the Master of Matcassen.

But even as his rational mind protested the actions it could not change, something in Jerrel knew pride at the decisiveness of the brother he had always thought so young and helpless.

It was foolish of Santar to reveal the existence of the Empire. More foolish still to think that vague threats and promises would move a man like Lindaz to act for the good of people he cared nothing about.

Worse, each time Santar betrayed a skill or ability that didn't exist on Errandane, each time he spoke of other worlds, he broke the non-intervention rules of the Rediscovery Service and the laws of the Empire.

As Jerrel shared his brother's actions through the impressions stored in the recorder ring, he knew Santar would fail, knew he was running risks he probably didn't understand. Yet something within Jerrel couldn't resist hoping.

But then Jerrel, through Santar, met the beautiful Lady Xyanth. As he felt his brother's confusion and shy eagerness, Jerrel knew there was no hope. He, Jerrel, had known women like Xyanth. But Santar never had and therein lay his doom. With fear and regret, Jerrel released himself wholly to the impressions flooding through him from the ring.

It is late at night in the Great Hall of Matcassen. The guard on his rounds outside calls softly to a companion. The sleeping chamber I have been given is luxuriously comfortable. I am planning my next steps, pleased with my day's work.

A knock, almost inaudible, sounds at the door. I open the door to find a hooded figure standing in the dark hallway outside. Before I can speak, the figure moves past me into the room, gesturing for me to shut the door.

When I turn back to my visitor, I am startled to find the Lady Xyanth before me. She has pushed her hood back, revealing her delicate features and the heavy mass of golden hair piled on top of her head. She smiles, almost timidly, and stretches her hand out to me. I cannot resist and quickly cross to her, murmuring confused words of welcome.

"I could not stay away," she says. "I had to come."

She seems shy, unsure of herself, and her uncertainty soothes me, making it easy to invite her to sit down, to offer her a glass of wine. She speaks, hesitantly, of her admiration for what I am attempting to do. She has tried to help their people, she says, but has achieved nothing and can only hope I will succeed where she has failed. I sit, awed by her beauty and confused by her words. Her admiration and trust are an even headier mixture than the strong, dark wine, and I have already drunk enough of that to make my head spin.

We talk. Suddenly, I'm not sure how, we are standing beside the huge bed and she is undressing before me, slowly, temptingly. She lies back on the bed, naked, and her waist-length golden hair fans across the pillows and over her full breasts. I can see her eyes glittering in the candlelight as she watches me watching her. I tremble, uncertain, afraid, yet aching with wanting her. She draws up her legs and spreads them wide. . . .

Enough!

Jerrel jerked forward in his chair. Despite the chill of the room, he was sweating. He wiped his brow and found his hands were trembling uncontrollably. With a curse he leaned forward, head bowed, elbows on his knees. He clenched his fists until the skin over his knuckles showed white in the firelight and the ring pinched his flesh.

Jerrel shook his head, trying to clear it of the images that had flooded his brain for the past hour.

Had Xyanth . . . ? Did Santar . . . ? Jerrel's mouth twisted in a grimace. Much as he disliked the thought of reactivating the recording, he had to know what had happened to his brother.

Again Jerrel cued the com link to the ring, but this time he ordered it to search only for the last few recorded minutes. Though it made it more difficult to understand the recording, Jerrel fought to maintain his awareness of the room about him. That awareness, at least, would provide some protection against what the ring might reveal.

I am tired, sated, and acutely conscious of the woman in the bed beside me. I turn to her, but before I can say anything she lightly lays a finger against my lips to silence me.

"Let me get you some wine," she says, her voice low and infinitely enticing. She rises from the bed and crosses to the table, seemingly unaware of her

nakedness, then returns with our half-filled goblets.

My eyes fixed on her, I take the goblet, smile, and sip. The wine seems oddly bitter but I am thirsty and drain the goblet, regardless. I reach to touch her but my vision is suddenly blurred, my head spinning.

I cry out but she only stands there beside the bed, watching me, and then the blackness reaches up, swallowing me . . . !

Slowly Jerrel straightened. The fire was almost dead and the room nearly as dark as the blackness that had swallowed Santar. Jerrel sighed and forced his still-clenched hands to open. He tugged the ring from his finger, then unfastened the heavy gold chain he wore around his neck and threaded it through the ring. For a moment the ring dangled on the chain, the gold of the band glinting with the reflected red light of the dying fire. The milky-blue recorder stone looked dull and lifeless.

Quickly Jerrel refastened the chain about his neck so the ring lay cold and hard against his skin, hidden beneath his shirt.

Jerrel awoke late after an unrefreshing sleep that had been disturbed by tormenting dreams of his brother. He chose clean clothes from his bag, grabbed the coarse length of cloth he'd been given as a towel, and headed for the walled-off courtyard that served as a bathing area for the male guests at the inn.

Stripping quickly in the brisk air, he emptied the contents of a large pitcher of water over his head. The shock of the icy shower was enough to clear his head of the last vestiges of sleep. He shivered, then quickly washed and doused himself once again, thinking longingly of the warm shower and heat dryer available to him on the ship. His habit of bathing daily, despite the cold, had been cause for much comment in the inn.

Once dressed and his dirty clothes handed over to the inn's laundress, Jerrel headed across the main courtyard toward Nareen's room. Despite the strong soporific she'd been given, she should be awake by now. Jerrel found himself suddenly eager to see her again.

Jerrel could hear the sounds of an argument long before he reached the runner's room. Surprised, he hurried forward and pushed open the door.

She was pale, but her pallor came from anger more than pain. She was standing in the center of the room, awkwardly balanced on her good leg, glaring at the equally angry and far more indignant man who stood before her, glaring back.

"I *will* have a bath, Healer Fane," she said fiercely, "and I *will* dress as befits a runner, in leggings, boots, and leather jerkin."

"And *I* say you will not!"

Jerrel stepped unnoticed into the room.

"I am Nareen of Kalinden, Sixth Runner for Master Gasperian. By the laws of Errandane, you *must* provide what I ask," insisted Nareen, drawing herself up proudly.

The gesture might have been more impressive if her hair hadn't been tousled and if she'd been dressed in something more than the shirt Jerrel had pulled from Rakin's pack. The shirt was rumpled and far too large. It covered her hands and fell almost to her knees. Her hands clutched a wadded mass of cloth that dragged on the ground and appeared to be a woman's gown. Her boots and leggings had been removed, exposing slender, shapely legs that reminded Jerrel all too clearly of how she'd looked without anything on at all.

Jerrel swallowed, ignoring the sudden warmth in the room, and stepped forward. "Is there a problem?" he asked.

The two combatants jumped, obviously startled by his unexpected appearance. At sight of him, Nareen's complexion seemed to darken slightly. She ran a hand through her hair in a vain and oddly feminine attempt to arrange it properly.

"This woman refuses to follow my orders," exclaimed Fane angrily, stepping forward. "She should spend the next few days quietly in bed. I've told her that trying to pull on boots and leggings will only aggravate the injury to her hip, and moving about will exhaust her." He huffed in indignation. "I have spent over thirty years of my life learning the healing arts, but all I get from her are insults!"

Jerrel struggled to suppress the smile that threatened to spread across his face. The healer reminded him very much of the tiny, pugnacious sgniths he had raised as a child.

"Your pardon, merchant," said Nareen very formally. "It is true I do not intend to follow the healer's orders, but I have *not* insulted him."

Jerrel's eyebrow quirked, but he said, very seriously, "I am sorry she has given you such trouble, healer. Perhaps if I might have a few words alone with her?"

Fane sniffed, eyed Nareen with ill-concealed disdain, and left the room.

"Shall we sit down, Nareen of Kalinden?" Jerrel asked, allowing his smile to break free at last. He extended his arm to her, which she accepted after a moment's hesitation.

The distance to the chairs Jerrel indicated was mercifully short. Nareen was already regretting her hasty defiance of the healer, but his smug superiority and immediate assumption that she would follow his instructions without question had irritated her from the first instant he opened his mouth.

Nareen tried, but couldn't quite repress a sigh of relief as she settled on the worn cushion of the chair. She started to sit back but found she was too short to do so without straining her hip. Before she could shift to a more comfortable position, Jerrel snatched the cushion from the other chair and placed it behind her.

"Is that better?"

Nareen nodded mutely. He had touched her for only an instant as he helped her settle against the extra cushion, but it had been enough to momentarily rob her of all power of speech.

"I am glad to see you up," he said, "but I suspect you are not yet as strong as you pretend."

Nareen started to protest, but something in his expression, in the understanding that warmed his eyes, made her stop. His smile widened, drawing her gaze to his mouth and the faint suggestion of a dimple at the left corner.

Her first thought as she'd roused from sleep was to wonder if he were still beside her. Her second, disappointment that he was not. Her third had been no thought at all but an uncharacteristic emotional confusion. Never before had any man occupied her thoughts, filled her awareness as this man did. Nareen found her reaction to him troubling, yet undeniably appealing.

Which was absurd. She was a runner, he a merchant, albeit unlike any other merchant she knew. They had met by chance under circumstances which inevitably brought them closer than would have been normal. But that was all. As soon as her hip was healed she would return to Kalinden. He had his life, as well, and only here in this place and for a very short while did it impinge on hers.

Yet ever since waking she'd thought of the handsome merchant, remembered the size and strength of him, the feel of his arms about her, the very smell of his skin. She'd grown tense worrying about how she might react when he eventually appeared. The healer's examination and their subsequent argument had been welcome for the momentary respite they brought her from her troublesome thoughts.

And now here he was beside her, placing cushions for her comfort and making her smile. He had bathed, shaved, and changed his rough hunter's garb for the long woolen gown and heavy over-robe commonly worn indoors in winter. A well-shaped foot shod in a closely fitted felt slipper peeked out from under the hem of his robe. The soft leather belt he wore was unadorned, but the hilt of the dagger thrust through a loop in the belt was crafted of silver and gold. Although the gown was loose, restrained only by bands at his wrists and the belt at his waist, it could only soften, not hide, the powerful lines of his body. The opening at the neck of the gown revealed the strong, clean lines of his throat and a hint of the curling chest hair Nareen remembered so clearly. She could see the glint of a heavy gold chain half hidden under his robe. He wore no other ornament, and his dark, curling hair was cropped unfashionably close to his head.

"Are you satisfied?"

The words brought Nareen's careful inspection to an abrupt end. "Satisfied?"

"That I am who I say I am. You didn't seem too sure the first time we met."

"Ah . . ." To her chagrin, Nareen felt her face grow warm. "I did not mean to doubt . . ."

"Understandable, under the circumstances."

"But not acceptable, after your hospitality." Nareen thought some of the sparkle drained from his eyes at her words.

"It's no more than what is due a runner, and the woman who saved my life," Jerrel said, thinking of the ring he'd taken from her. "You are an honored guest here, runner, until you're ready to continue your journey. But don't you think it would be better if you heeded this Fane's advice?"

"I can't lie around like a Lady, merchant. I wouldn't know how."

Jerrel smiled. "No, perhaps not." He paused. After reviewing the contents of the ring last night, he wanted to go on to Matcassen immediately. But he'd already made arrangements to be picked up by a merchant's caravan due through in the next few days. It might be better if he stuck to his original plan. Riding on one of the caravan's wagons would be far easier for both Norvag and Nareen and would maintain the cover he'd assumed of merchant and traveler.

"We await a caravan to take us to Matcassen," he said at last. "You're welcome to travel with us if you wish, runner."

"Nareen," Nareen prompted before she could think how inappropriate such familiarity would be from the Sixth Runner of Kalinden.

"Nareen." He bowed his head slightly in acquiescence. "Though an aard wagon will be far slower than you're accustomed to traveling, it will give you time to rest and recover. And Norvag and I would be more than happy to have your company," he added gallantly.

An aard wagon. Nareen thought of the huge wagons that were home and transportation for the itinerant merchants who traveled between the cities of Errandane. It would take days, perhaps weeks, for the slow-moving caravan to reach Matcassen. Days spent in the close quarters of the wagon with the man beside her. The thought was frightening, yet infinitely tempting at the same time.

"Thank you. You are very kind," was all Nareen said.

Chapter 5

The next three days spent in Jerrel's company were some of the most tormenting, disturbing days of Nareen's life.

Jerrel was gentle, sometimes funny, often sad and thoughtful. Occasionally he became irritable and restless for no reason Nareen could detect. He brought her meals, placed cushions for her comfort, escorted her on short walks around the inn, and helped while away the time by playing gonzat, an old board game at which they found themselves equally matched.

With him, Nareen found herself forgetting about Kalinden and the beastmen, the lost ring, her mission, even forgetting the runner carrying her message to Anweigh.

Jerrel occupied her thoughts, waking and sleeping. When he was near her, she was intensely, achingly aware of his presence. When he was

92

absent, she could think of little except when she might see him again.

And for those reasons Nareen anxiously awaited the arrival of the caravan and the opportunity to escape this man who was becoming almost an obsession with her. She liked her life the way it was and didn't need distractions—especially not distractions like Jerrel.

Fortunately, she didn't have long to wait. On the morning of her fourth day at the inn, Merchant Baecknar's caravan arrived in a tumult of noise and confusion that drew everyone to the courtyard.

From the window of her room Nareen watched as six of the huge, wooden aard wagons rumbled through the broad gates. Another forty or so wagons remained outside, drawn up in a long line that stretched for half a mile along the road.

As in all caravans, these wagons were gaily painted, box-like affairs, twice the height of a tall man, with huge spoked, wooden wheels. Four enormous aards were yoked to each wagon. The shaggy beasts were the only creatures strong enough to pull the wagons.

Watching the confusion in the inn courtyard below, Nareen thought of Jerrel. Once they joined the caravan, he and Norvag would be traveling in the men's guest wagon. Since she would be in the women's wagon, she might not even see him that much. And that would be for the best. Wouldn't it?

Nareen headed downstairs as quickly as her hip would allow. Out on the low stone steps of the inn's main entrance, the sounds and smells of men and beasts milling about enfolded her. She smiled, feeling the stir of excitement a caravan always roused in her, then moved off the steps and into the confusion.

A short, thickset man with bright red hair brushed past her, shouting something to someone on the far side of the courtyard. His accent smacked of the southern plains of Garnebi, but the smell that clung to him was compounded of aard and dekneb—the tangy, pungent spice that flavored much of the caravaners' food.

A towheaded child shouting gleeful taunts over his shoulder plowed into Nareen, throwing her off balance, then raced off with a second child in hot pursuit.

Nareen staggered and would have fallen but for the strong arm that suddenly wrapped around her waist and pulled her against a wall of bone and muscle she recognized immediately.

"Are you all right?"

Jerrel's words were softly spoken, but Nareen could hear each one clearly even in the surrounding din. They might have been alone for all the attention she was capable of paying to the commotion in the courtyard.

"Yes, of course I'm all right," she said sharply, pulling free. "I simply wasn't watching what I was doing." Her back where it had touched his broad chest felt suddenly unprotected and cold in the gray, winter day.

"So, will the caravan take us on?" she asked to hide her confusion.

"Norvag is out negotiating our passage now." Jerrel smiled, studying the commotion around them. "I don't think the innkeeper and his family have had this much excitement in months."

The left corner of his mouth quirked up more than the right when he smiled. Nareen had noticed that before. And as before, she had to repress a strong urge to touch a finger to his lips, to trace that lopsided curve. As she watched, the smile disappeared.

"They say it will take at least six days to reach Matcassen." Irritation sharpened his voice.

"Aards can move only so fast," Nareen said. "It may take even longer." She studied the low-hanging gray clouds on the horizon. "This road isn't a high road. A winter drizzle won't bother it, but it won't hold up well if those clouds drop a deluge."

Jerrel made a slight sound of disgust and shifted impatiently. His eyes went from the lowering clouds to the chaos in the courtyard. "You'd think there would be a faster way to get from one place to another. After all these years . . ."

His words trailed off. Shrugging off his irritation, he said, "We might as well find Norvag. With luck he's already got everything settled."

They dodged two laborers hauling a bale of junkle fibers, then barely avoided being hit by a young woman trundling a barrow heaped with fresh bread from the inn's kitchens toward the caravan's central kitchen wagon. Men and women bustled back and forth on their various errands, each intent on his or her particular task.

Children of all ages, some from the inn and surrounding holdings, some from the caravan, dodged in and out of the wagons and under the bellies of the passive aards.

The huge animals stood tranquilly munching on the hay heaped before them, ignoring the commotion around them. They were massive creatures, taller at the shoulder than most men. Their thick, reddish-brown hair fell almost to the knees of their short legs, making them seem larger still. With their powerful shoulders, thick necks, and heavy heads, they were intimidating beasts, despite their gentle dispositions.

It didn't take long to find Norvag, but what he had to say wasn't what Nareen wanted to hear.

"What do you mean there isn't any room in the women's wagon?" she demanded indignantly.

"Just that," Norvag said patiently. He was standing at the top of the steps to a wagon drawn up outside the inn gates. "There's no room in the women's guest wagon. I reserved space in the men's wagon for Rakin and Borlat and an entire wagon just for the three of us. We'll travel in far greater comfort than anyone else in the caravan except, perhaps, Merchant Baecknar himself."

"It's not comfort I'm worried about," Nareen snapped, eyeing what little she could see of the wagon's interior with misgivings. At least, not comfort in the sense Norvag meant. No matter how luxurious the wagon's fittings, there would be no comfort for her if she were forced to share the cramped interior with Jerrel for six days.

Right now Jerrel was inside the wagon, checking over the arrangements. From where she stood at the foot of the steps, Nareen could see he took up far too much room for her peace of mind.

Norvag grinned but said nothing. Nareen had the unwelcome feeling the old man knew exactly what she was thinking.

Six days enclosed in that cramped wagon with Jerrel . . . Nareen's mind veered away from the thought. There had to be some other solution. "What about some of the caravan families? Surely they have space for me."

"They might." Norvag nodded thoughtfully.

Nareen could see the sparkling mischief in the old man's eyes. That sparkle was all that was needed to set her into motion. "I'm going to find Baecknar. He's bound to know who can provide me accommodations," Nareen added over her shoulder as she limped up the line of wagons in search of the merchant.

Here along the road there was less confusion than in the enclosed area of the courtyard, but the people of the caravan were still busy, taking advantage of the stop to tend to repairs on the wagons or adjust the loads of raw materials and merchandise they carried.

The huge wagons provided both storage for goods and housing for the people who lived and died within the caravan's community. A very few of the wagons, such as the one Norvag had hired, were used to carry passengers as well as goods.

Nareen had few hopes of finding a wagon that would provide more space. Since a caravan earned its money by selling and trading the goods it carried, space was a commodity that couldn't be wasted on people. Only the work wagons, those devoted to the manufacture of leather goods or cloth or jewelry, had much room inside. But even those were crammed full of worktables or looms or other equipment.

It wasn't space Nareen was seeking, however. She needed distance, distance from the disturbing presence of a man she hardly knew.

It took Nareen nearly an hour to locate Merchant Baecknar, the man who led the caravan and who made the final decisions about the caravan "guests."

"Of course you can stay with a caravan family if you choose, runner," he said, his eyes glittering coldly, "but it will cost you. And I won't give any discount on the price your friends are paying to rent the guest wagon just because you do not travel with them."

"What do you mean it will cost me?" Nareen demanded indignantly. "I'm a runner of the city of Kalinden. By the laws of Errandane you're required to provide me passage."

"I'm required to provide passage to a runner on a mission," Baecknar agreed. "But you're limping and therefore cannot perform your duties. I've no doubt you already passed any message you carried to another runner. That means you're no longer on a mission and that I don't owe you free passage."

"I *demand* passage on your caravan, merchant!" It was only with difficulty that Nareen restrained herself from stamping her foot.

"You *have* passage, runner, in the most comfortable of my guest wagons. And it has cost you nothing." Baecknar shrugged in indifference, his gaze fixed on some activity near a wagon farther down the line. "If you insist on being lodged with a family—and our family wagons are already overcrowded—it will cost you."

"How much?" Nareen demanded in exasperation.

Baecknar considered the question. "One hundred credits in the coin of Anweigh."

"One hundred . . . You're mad! I doubt if Norvag paid you that for an entire wagon!"

The merchant's face was expressionless.

Nareen fumed. The sum he demanded was far too great. Mentally she reviewed her resources and the help she might reasonably expect from her friends. It didn't add up to half the amount Baecknar demanded.

"I'll give you ten," she said.

"Hah! You're in the mood for jests."

They haggled, but Baecknar wouldn't come down far enough, and Nareen couldn't come up enough for the two to reach any agreement.

Nareen retreated at last, angry and frustrated by her failure to obtain other quarters. As she plodded back to the wagon Norvag had hired, she considered her options.

She could always refuse any help at all and simply return to Matcassen by one of the easier paths—walking, if she had to. But the effort of hiking up and down the length of the caravan in search of Baecknar had already tired her. At this rate, it would take her longer to go on foot than to stay with the caravan.

She could ride on top of one of the wagons during the day and sleep on the ground at night, but she knew it would irritate her unbearably to think of everyone else sleeping comfortably in a warm wagon while she huddled in her grackle skin on the damp earth. It was one thing to endure such discomfort when she was on a mission, quite another to do so under circumstances like the present.

Or she could accept the comfortable bed and accommodations that Norvag had arranged for her and simply avoid Jerrel as much as she could. If she rode on top and entered the confined quarters of the wagon for the night only, she might be able to endure the six days before they reached Matcassen.

She *might* be able to endure . . . But thinking of Jerrel and of her response to him, Nareen wasn't so sure she could.

* * *

She should have slept on the ground wrapped
in her grackle skin, Nareen decided sourly that
evening, eyeing the interior of the guest wagon
with disfavor. It had been a mistake to enter the
wagon at all, but after hours spent in the winter
wind riding on top of another wagon, a comfortable bed had seemed too tempting to resist.

There were only three beds in the cramped interior: two narrow cubbyholes on each side above
the storage cabinets and one large bed at the front
over the big holds that were crammed with trade
goods.

Jerrel had already claimed the bed at the front.
It was the only one large enough for him. Norvag
had one of the cubbyholes, but because they were
set too high for the old man to get in easily, Jerrel
had pulled out the cubbyhole's pallet and was in
the process of arranging it on the floor.

He hadn't even bothered to look up when she'd
appeared in the doorway. Norvag had smiled, at
least, and indicated the one cubbyhole remaining.

"That one's yours," he said. "We decided not to
wait for you any longer."

Nareen nodded her understanding. She didn't
trust herself to say anything because her attention was suddenly—and involuntarily—focused
on Jerrel.

Or, more accurately, on his rump.

He'd been crouched, back turned toward her,
while he helped arrange the covers on Norvag's
pallet. The broad wall of his back under its leather jerkin was impressive but not overly disturbing
to her peace of mind.

But when he straightened his legs while still

bent over at the waist, he presented a totally unexpected view of the seat of his breeches tautly stretched over a firmly rounded and very male posterior.

For an instant Nareen stood transfixed, painfully aware of the heat rising in her throat and face. Then Jerrel straightened to his full height. The strain on the leather of his leggings eased, the hem of his tunic slid back down until it covered at least the upper three-quarters of his hips, and he started to turn toward her.

Before he could turn fully, Nareen slid past him, head down. "If you don't mind, I'm going to bed," she said, her voice sounding far more snappish than she'd intended.

It only needed an instant's observation to see that escaping into the relative privacy of the bed assigned her wasn't going to be quite so easy.

The cubbyhole was set high on the wall—her head didn't even reach the bottom of the opening. Access to it was provided by a series of notches carved in the wall which served as a sort of ladder and which, under normal circumstances, would have been very easy to climb. Unfortunately, her hip was still too stiff for her to manage the ascent easily.

Setting her jaw in determination, Nareen started to pull herself up by her hands.

She'd just reached the point where she could peer over the edge of the cubbyhole when a large, masculine hand was placed squarely over her rump.

"Here you go," Jerrel said cheerfully and gave a shove, propelling her abruptly, nose first, onto her pallet.

"You . . ." Nareen turned to glare at the pro-

101

vider of such undignified assistance, fully prepared to wage verbal battle. Her words died on her lips as she found herself staring directly into eyes that shone black and glittering in the dim candlelight.

"I thought you might need a little help," he said blandly, then turned away before Nareen could reply. He extinguished the candle behind him, leaving only one small stub burning in the wall bracket near his bed.

Nareen shifted on the pallet so she could poke her head out. She ought to drop the matter, but a tiny, irrational voice in her head kept screeching that his hand was indelibly imprinted on her behind.

From his pallet on the floor, Norvag said, "Sleep well."

The words startled Nareen. She'd forgotten the old man's existence. "And you," she said, forcing the words to come out courteously. The light was dim and Norvag was lying so his face was shadowed. For a moment, Nareen could have sworn he winked at her.

She couldn't be sure, and her attention wasn't on him, anyway. It was fixed on Jerrel where he stood at the side of his bed. The dim light of the flickering candle shone full on his face, highlighting the planes of brow and cheek and casting velvety shadows at the corner of his mouth and in the hollow of his throat.

He bent to tug off his boots, stooping so his face was hidden from her. The light glowed softly on the thick curls of his hair, instead.

Nareen was mesmerized by the way the muscles of his thighs knotted as he stood, first on one leg, then on the other; by the beauty of his hands as they grasped each boot; by the grace with which he swung up onto his bed.

He turned, then froze as he caught her eye. Somewhere in the recesses of her brain where some small trace of rational thought still struggled to function, Nareen knew she ought to draw back, ought to . . . But all she could do was gaze until he looked away and blew out the remaining candle, hiding her in the merciful dark.

Nareen sank back on her pallet, trembling. Control. She had to regain control of herself. She was a runner, after all, and had been trained to master her emotions, to ignore outside distractions.

Close your eyes, breathe deep, she told herself. Then exhale slowly. Concentrate, shut out all distractions, all thoughts, all external awareness, all . . .

In the dark, Nareen could hear Jerrel shift his position in his bed, then begin to remove his leather jerkin. Her eyes flew open and her breath caught in her throat. Had she ever really heard that soft, shushing sound of leather rubbing against leather before? It was such a slight sound, so unimportant, yet . . .

She could hear Jerrel pull his jerkin off, then his shirt. The darkness was so intense Nareen could not see even the cubbyhole's ceiling only inches above her, but in her mind's eye she watched as Jerrel tugged the coarse shirt over his head, imagining the way his muscles slid beneath his skin as he moved.

Nareen listened, and silently raged that even the slight sounds of his movements should so affect her that she was incapable of maintaining mastery of her thoughts, raged that his presence could so easily shatter the self-control she had struggled for so long to learn.

Yet even her anger was inadequate to repress the heated, aching need that her awareness of him had aroused. And that need was more frightening, and far more tempting, than anything she had ever known.

She squeezed her eyes shut, willing herself to concentrate, to block out these unwelcome, distracting thoughts and emotions.

He had six days ahead of him, Jerrel thought—or longer. And for at least some part of each day he would be confined in this wagon with *her*. He gritted his teeth and shifted uncomfortably.

It had been hard enough back at the inn to control his response to this infuriating, infinitely tempting female. Here in the confines of the wagon it would be nearly impossible. If he made another mistake as stupid as that of helping her onto her bed, he wasn't sure he would manage to restrain himself. Even the thought of that gesture, of the feel of that firm, rounded bottom . . .

Jerrel clawed at the coarse sheets, fighting to ignore his body's involuntary response. Alone with her like this . . .

No, not alone. A muscle in Jerrel's jaw twitched. There was always Norvag, who had been damned insulting over dinner.

His old friend hadn't said a word, hadn't raised an eyebrow, hadn't, by even the most casual gesture, indicated he was aware of Jerrel's restlessness. Not once had he mentioned the countless glances Jerrel had thrown at the wagon door or at the third, untouched, plate of food on the table that had been intended for Nareen.

Norvag hadn't said or done a thing, which meant the old man knew precisely what had caused Jerrel's restlessness and was deriving an unholy amusement from the knowledge.

Jerrel thrust his hands behind his head to avoid pounding them against the wall. Tomorrow he would walk rather than ride. That might work off some of the excess energy that was undoubtedly responsible for his restlessness. And he would take his meals alone, outside, rather than be confronted by a small, green-eyed, black-haired runner.

The sound of the rain thudding on the wagon's roof had provided a steady, nerve-grinding background of noise since near dawn. And dawn had been hours ago.

Nareen scowled, surreptitiously studying Jerrel as he idly shifted the playing pieces around the gonzat board on the table before him. She hadn't slept well the night before—and she knew whose fault that was.

Jerrel had tossed and turned for what seemed like hours, nearly driving her mad. Her dreams had provided no respite. They were filled with a tall, broad-shouldered, blue-eyed demon who tormented her unmercifully. In her sleep he had pursued her, plagued her, rousing a fire within her that not even the icy waters of a dream-conjured stream were sufficient to quench.

And she had awakened to find him standing by her cubbyhole, his gaze fixed on her face.

Nareen shifted uncomfortably on her seat. It wasn't her fault if her treacherous body had responded to him without her willing it. And she certainly had not intended to blush when he helped her out of the cubbyhole, or to stammer like a mindless idiot when he offered her a

105

steaming cup of rich, slightly bitter havik.

"Perhaps another game of gonzat?" Jerrel moved the pieces across the game board with an air of restless frustration.

"We just finished our sixth game." Keeping her voice calm to betray none of her tension was becoming increasingly difficult.

She shifted again on the hard, cramped bench jammed into the corner of the wagon's narrow central aisle. She couldn't endure much more of this.

"Norvag? A game?"

"You always beat me." Norvag seemed the only tranquil occupant of the wagon. With his chair—the only real chair in the wagon—tipped back against the wall and his stiff leg stretched into the aisle, the old man gave the impression of being thoroughly content with his lot.

Nareen knew he was also amused, and the knowledge irritated her. She'd spotted a twinkle in his eyes a couple of times, and once, when she and Jerrel had hotly debated the legality of a particular move in gonzat, she'd found him openly grinning at her. But what he found amusing about the situation she couldn't fathom.

She certainly wasn't finding it amusing. Her only consolation was that she'd conducted herself throughout with the dignity and restraint befitting a runner. At least she'd been able to salvage that much self-control from the riot of emotions within her.

Nareen stood abruptly, suddenly unable to tolerate another second trapped in the corner on a hard and narrow seat.

The minute she was on her feet, however, she remembered that escape wasn't going to be all that simple. The table was only a few inches in front of her, blocking the aisle and covered with the gonzat board and playing pieces. Jerrel, sitting hunched on a stool beside her, was setting up the pieces for another game. He effectively filled what little space was left at this end of the wagon, and Norvag, still propped back against the cupboards, occupied the remaining few feet in front of the door.

For an instant Nareen froze, daunted by the obstacle course between her and the freedom outside the wagon. But only for an instant. She'd faced a wounded drevon without flinching; she wasn't about to let herself be intimidated now.

"Excuse me," she said. "I'd like to get out if you don't mind." Her teacher, Gravnar, would have been proud of the calm courtesy with which she phrased her request.

Jerrel's head jerked up. "What?" He looked blank for a minute. "Oh! Of course." He rose hastily, almost tipping the table over when he knocked against it, then squeezed back against the cupboards.

But no amount of squeezing was going to reduce that sizable bulk to anything resembling a reasonably built male, Nareen thought, eyeing with disfavor the minuscule passage he'd created.

A small voice within her tried to explain that there really wasn't much else he could do, but Nareen wasn't in the mood to listen to small, interior voices. She wanted out of the wagon. Period.

"Thanks." She shoved on the table, trying to free up a little more space.

The wagon swayed slightly, throwing her off

balance. They'd been moving since shortly after dawn, but the motion was much more noticeable when she was standing than when she'd been seated.

Without meeting Jerrel's eyes, Nareen shifted so her back was to him, then cautiously started to edge past him. But even sucking in her stomach and standing on tiptoe didn't make her thin enough to slide out without touching him.

Her buttocks brushed against his legs. Nareen, after one quick intake of breath, straightened even more, thrust her hips out, and arched her back slightly in an effort to avoid him. She was almost free when the wagon lurched, throwing her back against him.

She might almost have fallen into a patch of stinging mozwort, so quickly did her body react to its contact along the length of Jerrel's muscular frame. She certainly jumped away from him just as quickly as if he *had* been mozwort. The difference was the intense tingling of her body was totally unlike any known reaction to the noxious plant.

"Rough ride sometimes," Norvag commented.

Nareen bristled, but the old man was innocently studying a stain on the ceiling above his head. She pulled at the hem of her tunic to straighten it, settled the cuffs of her shirt more comfortably about her wrists, then stepped around Norvag to open the door.

"Damn." One word, but it came from her heart.

Outside the rain was coming down in sheets that blurred the shape of the four huge aards pulling the wagon behind them. Nareen could barely discern the wagon's driver, huddled in his box.

"Still raining. I could tell from the sound of it hitting the roof."

Nareen whirled around, prepared to defend herself, but Norvag continued to study the fascinating stain.

Without meeting her eyes, he lowered his gaze and glanced out the door, pursed his lips, nodded slightly, and said, "Doesn't look like it's going to let up any time soon, either."

The wagon lurched slightly, forcing Nareen to grab hold of the door frame. In the corner Jerrel swayed, then resumed his seat on the stool. He appeared to be studying the gonzat board, but Nareen couldn't help noticing that his breathing seemed a little ragged, as though he'd been running.

She looked longingly over her shoulder at the rain-drenched fields just visible beyond the oozing mud of the road. She wanted out, out of the cramped wagon and away from its occupants. Especially from one occupant. But escape would exact a high price in physical discomfort, and she wasn't sure she was ready to pay that price.

Yet.

Chapter 6

By the following morning Nareen was ready to scream from frustration. She had passed, if possible, an even more restless night than the one before. There had been no letup in the downpour and no break in the dragging monotony of long hours spent crammed in the wagon with an old man who was far too casual about the matter, and a glowering hulk who was rapidly becoming downright impossible to tolerate.

Not, Nareen had to admit, that Jerrel had said much. But his studied attempts to avoid her—impossible in the limited space available—and the tension that seemed to radiate from him only exacerbated her already tightly strung nerves. Never had she been so intensely aware of anyone, and never had it been more difficult to assume the calm and patience required of every runner.

If only she had something to do. She'd cleaned

and sharpened her runner's dagger until she was in danger of wearing away the hardened metal. She'd refolded her grackle skin and carefully repacked it in her runner's belt—three times.

Another game of gonzat with Jerrel, which he hadn't suggested for several hours, was unthinkable. Being that close to him, bending her head over the board when he was only inches from her—she couldn't endure it again. Besides, his presence flustered her so that she'd lost the last sixteen games. Further humiliation was unnecessary.

When the caravan had stopped at mid-morning she thought she would have an opportunity to at least visit another wagon. But the stop was brief—just long enough to let off five of the passengers from the men's guest wagon and to load the trade goods their families had brought as payment—and no one had appeared outside any of the other wagons she could see through the driving rain.

Worse, the departure of the five passengers left empty bunks in the much larger men's wagon. With a vague smile that Nareen found absolutely infuriating, Norvag calmly announced that he was moving to the men's guest wagon to keep an eye on Jerrel's two hired men, Rakin and Borlat.

The old man pulled on a pair of the waxed leather boots he'd borrowed that provided some protection from the mud, wrapped himself in a woven cape, gathered his small bag of belongings, and departed. Just like that. Leaving her alone in the wagon with Jerrel.

For several minutes not a word was spoken. Jerrel had hardly looked up when Norvag left, his attention once more fixed on one of his endless games of gonzat.

Nareen stood halfway between the door and table, unwilling to venture out in the rain after Norvag and even more unwilling to get any closer to Jerrel than she had to.

"Well?" she demanded at last.

Jerrel's head came up. He let out a deep sigh, then squared his shoulders exactly as a man does who's preparing to face a dangerous opponent. "Well, what?"

"Aren't you going, too?"

"Going where?"

"To the men's guest wagon."

Slowly, and with great deliberation, Jerrel moved one of the playing pieces. "No."

Nareen shifted her weight impatiently. "You can't stay here."

Blue eyes met her gaze directly. For an instant Nareen thought he wasn't going to respond. Then: "Why not?"

Nareen opened her mouth, ready with a sharp retort, but no words came out. She'd been about to say that being this close to him was driving her mad, that, without Norvag as chaperon, sharing the wagon with him would be an intolerable torment.

But she couldn't say that. Not all the demons of Errandane would make her confess that she was so intensely aware of him, of every move he made, that it was impossible to endure his presence any longer.

"Because you can't," she said at last. "It wouldn't be right."

His gaze dropped to the playing board and he moved another piece. "I saw the beds in the guest wagon. The idea of sleeping curled into a ball so I can fit in a space half my size doesn't appeal. I paid for this wagon, and I intend to stay here." He paused for a moment. "You're welcome to stay, if you like. Or you can move to the women's guest wagon. The choice is yours."

Nareen stamped her foot, fully aware the gesture was exceedingly childish and petulant. "There isn't any space left in the wagon. And Baecknar said the other wagons are too crowded for me to stay in any of them."

Jerrel didn't respond. Instead, he slowly pushed his stool away from the table and stood up. It took him no more than one and a half steps to cover the distance dividing them.

Even though she didn't approve of cowardice, Nareen would dearly have liked to run. As far and as fast as her legs would take her, which would be considerable if it weren't for the fact that her hip was still too stiff to do much running. That and the fact the weather would have proved a severe hindrance.

Jerrel didn't say anything. He just stood there, only inches from her, with an odd expression on his face as if he were considering the same alternatives she was. Which was ridiculous.

And that worried her. If her imagination was conjuring up ideas like that, she must be even more out of control than she'd thought. Which meant running was a smarter alternative than it had first appeared.

She couldn't run, but she could put some distance between them, regardless of the miserable weather.

"I'm going for a walk," she said.

She was crazy to go out in weather like this, Jerrel thought, staring at the door Nareen had just shut behind her. She was crazy, and he was very, very glad she was gone.

The past two days had been hell. In comparison, the weeks he'd once spent struggling to escape the jungles of Dormat III seemed a pleasant little adventure. At least then he had only had to deal with three warring tribes that thought nothing of eating a stranger for dinner, several species of creatures with voracious appetites and very big teeth, and a dozen or so deadly poisonous plants. In retrospect, that little visit had been a snap.

He turned away from the door, suddenly restless. His eyes fell on the gonzat board. One hundred and seventeen games. More, actually, but he'd lost count at one hundred seventeen. It had seemed a better idea to concentrate on gonzat than to think about the tantalizing visions that had plagued him and that had centered around one small, irritable, and infinitely desirable runner.

With great deliberation Jerrel heaped the game pieces on the playing board. Taking care not to let a piece slide off, he carried the board to the wagon door, opened the door, and hurled both board and playing pieces out into the rain.

The pieces sank in the mud immediately. The board fell, face up, directly in the path of the following wagon.

Jerrel rather liked the sound the board made as it shattered under the hooves of a totally unconcerned aard.

Nareen was wet and cold and thoroughly irritated by the world in general and every member of the caravan in specific. The bales of junkle fiber she was stretched out on were hard and lumpy, and the protective canvas spread over the top wasn't doing much of a job of protecting either her or the bales.

After leaving Jerrel, she'd first sought refuge in the women's guest wagon. To her surprise, she'd met with vehement objections to her proposal that she be allowed to sleep on the floor. The women knew she had passage on Jerrel's wagon. They'd been extremely rude, and when Nareen had demanded they let her in because she was a runner returning from an official mission, they'd hooted and jeered.

"We're sleeping two and three to a bed," one of them had sneered, "and you have a wagon all to yourself. You and those two men, that is. Do you really expect us to let you in here when we're already too crowded?"

Nareen had retreated with all the dignity she could muster, which hadn't been much.

The residents of the other wagons had proved no more interested in having her, even if they'd been more polite. And Nareen had had to admit that there really wasn't any room available.

The small guest wagon had seemed crowded with just the three of them. Some of the family wagons were no larger, yet held eight or ten people. The children were usually stuffed into the sleeping cubbyholes while the adults occupied stools and benches in the narrow aisles. And almost everyone she saw, whether child or adult, was busy at some task.

Abandoning her search for space within a wagon, Nareen had slogged through the mud along the line of the slow-moving caravan, looking for a wagon where she could ride outside yet still be protected from the weather. The grackle skin she wore wrapped around her was proving to be almost useless against the insistent, drenching rain, and even her protective runner's boots were beginning to leak.

One of the drivers, ensconced in a shelter box scarcely large enough for him, gave her permission to ride on top under the canvas covering the bales strapped to the roof.

At the time, the offer had seemed ideal. Now, with the bales beneath her becoming harder by the minute and the canvas, weighted with rain, hanging within inches of her nose, Nareen wasn't so sure.

It was getting colder and she was hungry. She could always fetch something from the kitchen wagon, but that would mean going back out into the rain and the muck. And that prospect was even more daunting than the idea of staying in her uncomfortable, makeshift shelter.

The wagon lurched suddenly as it hit a rut. Nareen was thrown, hard, against the bales stacked beside her, then tossed back, even harder, when the wagon settled back into the track. An icy stream of water, driven under the canvas by the wagon's motion, ran down the bale that Nareen was propped against and into her collar.

Nareen yelped, then cursed. She drew the grackle skin closer around her, but that only served to plaster her wet clothes even tighter against her skin. She cursed again, using words her friends would have been shocked to learn she knew. A drop of water dripped from the canvas onto the tip of her nose; almost immediately another plopped into her left eye.

This time Nareen couldn't rouse the energy to

curse. She sighed, then settled back against the bale, trying in vain to find a softer spot. It was going to be a very long night.

With the table folded back in its cupboard, Jerrel needed exactly seven steps to cover the distance from the door to the end of the aisle. He knew, because he'd been pacing back and forth, seven steps each way, for what seemed like ages.

Norvag had reappeared at dinnertime with food enough for three on a covered tray. But although they'd waited until the spicy sauces congealed on the plates, Nareen hadn't appeared.

At first Norvag had denied any knowledge of the runner's whereabouts, but when pressed he'd confessed that she had tried, and failed, to find shelter in the women's guest wagon and in several of the private wagons.

When Norvag admitted that he didn't know where she'd finally ended up, Jerrel had leapt to his feet, ready to start a search for her. Only his old friend's reminder that Nareen could take care of herself and that she would scarcely appreciate being embarrassed by a search had convinced him not to rush out into the rain.

But now Jerrel was beginning to wish he'd followed his first inclination. The candles were slowly sinking into melted puddles of wax. Norvag had departed long ago, insisting he would rather stay in the larger men's wagon than spend another night sleeping on a pallet on the floor. And Nareen hadn't reappeared.

Perhaps his old friend was right. Perhaps she'd found another, completely comfortable place to stay. But what if she hadn't?

It was true she'd been restless and unreasonable, clearly dissatisfied with the only accommodations they'd been able to obtain. It was true that he'd found it less of a strain on his self-control not to have her in the wagon. And it was probably also true that she was far happier not to be trapped in the wagon with him.

But none of that made him feel any less concern over her absence or any more sure of what action he ought to take.

And so he paced.

Seven steps up, turn, seven steps back. Every once in a while Jerrel opened the door and thrust his head out to see if he could spot any sign of the missing runner. All he got for his pains was ice cold rain down his neck.

Another candle flickered and went out. Jerrel stopped in his pacing, noting for the first time how few candles were left burning. He hadn't realized how late it had become.

He was a fool, he told himself silently. Nareen was somewhere warm and dry, and undoubtedly quite pleased at not being forced to share the wagon with him one more night. If he had any sense he would go to bed as well. With luck, the skies might clear tomorrow and he could get out and walk and forget all this useless worrying.

The decision made, Jerrel extinguished all the candles but the one burning in its bracket on the wall beside his bed. He pulled off his boots, then his jerkin and shirt. The gold chain with Santar's ring Jerrel stuffed into a pocket of his jerkin before unlacing his leather breeches. There wasn't much need for modesty if he had the wagon to himself.

At that moment footsteps sounded on the wagon steps. Jerrel froze, uncertain how to react. It was undoubtedly Norvag, who had probably decided that a crowded guest wagon wasn't really where he wanted to spend the night. Then again . . .

Only five and a half steps were needed to cover the distance to the door this time. He jerked the door open.

"Oh!"

The faint exclamation came from the most bedraggled creature Jerrel had ever seen. It took him a moment to realize that the dripping, mud-caked specimen on the steps was Nareen, the respectable Sixth Runner from Kalinden.

"What in the devil . . . ?"

"I fell. G-getting off the wagon." Nareen's teeth chattered so hard her words were almost indistinguishable. "Those b-bales . . . I got stiff and my hip . . . The m-mud is awful. It's still raining . . ."

The words penetrated Jerrel's brain at last, jarring him into action. "For God's sake, what are you doing just standing there?" he demanded, pulling her into the wagon and slamming the door behind her.

"Take off your clothes. Everything," he commanded, forestalling her inevitable protest. "Just leave them on the floor and I'll hang them out in the rain. That will at least wash out the mud."

He frowned, noting how pale she looked even in the dim candlelight. Her eyes, usually so brilliantly green, showed as huge, shadowed orbs under the dripping tendrils of hair plastered across her face. She was shivering uncontrollably.

"Here," he muttered, pulling the muddy grackle

skin from around her and tossing it on the floor. "You have to get out of those clothes, get warm." He unfastened her runner's belt and hung it on a hook beside the door, then bent and while she leaned against him pulled off first one mud-caked boot, then the other.

Nareen fumbled at the lacings on her jerkin, but her hands trembled so much she could scarcely grip the leather ties.

"Let me do it." Jerrel batted her hands away and jerked the lacings open, then tugged the sodden garment off her shoulders. "You're a fool, you know that?" he demanded. Worry tightened his voice. She was so pale, so cold. . . . "Whatever possessed you?"

"I d-didn't w-want . . ."

Jerrel could actually hear her teeth clicking as she shivered. He jerked at the knotted strings at the throat and wrists of her shirt.

"I c-can t-take off m-my . . ." Nareen tried to twist away from him, to no avail.

"You can hardly stand." Jerrel slipped one sleeve over her hand, then the other. "The sooner you're out of these wet clothes, the better. You might as well stop fighting me about it." He grabbed the hem of her shirt and pulled the garment over her head.

His hand against her cold flesh was like a flame against a block of ice, incapable of melting the ice but sufficient to turn the blood that seemed frozen in her veins into liquid once more.

Beware! a voice within her cried. But Nareen was too drugged by cold to pay heed. Jerrel would care for her. Jerrel would make her warm again. And she was so very cold. Without realizing what she did, Nareen sagged against him. He was so warm. So strong and comforting. She was safe here, with him. Safe.

Vaguely Nareen wondered about that word. What was it she had to fear? *Yourself!* the small voice cried. But that was absurd. There were no dangers, only the cold and rain outside. Inside, with Jerrel, there was warmth and his comforting presence.

It felt so good to feel the broad expanse of his chest against her cheek, her breast. Nareen clung to him, running her hands along the hard line of muscle on his side, across the silken smoothness of his skin.

Jerrel gasped, then pushed her back. She was cold and wet and dazed, yet the touch of her icy hands on his body had roused a fire within him that he doubted even the rain could quench. And he had no intention of going out in that downpour.

And yet . . . Jerrel sucked in his breath.

She was so delicate. Strong and supple, superbly conditioned, but still so delicate. So desirable.

Her breasts were small, the skin above them translucent. Even in the dim light cast by the one remaining candle he could see the faint blue tracings of veins beneath the surface. With the cold, her nipples had tightened, as though demanding his touch.

He forced his gaze away. It was the cold that drew them taut, and that angered him. It should be his touch, his mouth . . .

"Undo the fastenings on your leggings," he commanded hoarsely, turning from her. "I'll find something for you to dry off with."

His gaze desperately roamed the small wagon. He wanted to spin around, to watch her undo the leather lacings at each side of her waist, to watch as she slid the damp leather down her hips, her thighs . . .

Curse her, that she could so easily undermine his self-control. Without thinking, Jerrel threw aside the covers on her bed and pulled the coarse sheet free. It would have to serve. At least it would be large enough to wrap around her and hide her body from his sight.

The sheet in his hand, Jerrel turned back toward Nareen, determined to ignore her nakedness. He would simply fling the sheet around her, then bundle her into her cubbyhole, under the covers where she would be safely out of his sight.

She was fumbling with the lacings and accomplishing exactly nothing. Her fingers trembled, her body shook, and a heavy hank of dripping hair had fallen across her face, obscuring her vision.

With an exclamation of dismay, Jerrel crossed to her and immediately wrapped the sheet about her, drawing her against him so that she might absorb the heat of his body. What kind of lustful fool was he, not to realize that while he indulged in fantasies she was continuing to suffer?

"I d-don't w-want . . ." she objected, trying to push away.

"I'm not concerned with what you want," Jerrel snapped. "I'm concerned about making sure you don't get sick."

With one hand he fumbled at the ties of her leggings. The wet leather was difficult to pull free, and the sheet further hampered his efforts. But he wasn't about to remove the sheet in order to see what he was doing. Nareen needed the warmth and protection the sheet provided, he tried to assure himself, knowing that was only part of the truth.

If freeing the laces was difficult, sliding the wet leather leggings down Nareen's legs was even more so. And not just because the leather clung to her damp skin or the sheet got in his way.

Jerrel was sweating by the time he finally got Nareen's leggings off. Briskly he began to rub the sheet across her shoulders, along her back and down her arms, all the while holding her firmly pressed against his chest so that the heat of his body might warm hers.

He tried to keep his mind focused on his task, but the feel of the lithe body beneath his hands threatened to undermine his good intentions. He wasn't even sure who was warming whom, for with each passing second, with each stroke of his hand, his own body temperature rose higher.

She didn't need his help, Nareen told herself fiercely. She certainly didn't want it. Yet in spite of her silent protestations, Nareen knew that she lied. This man, this moment were exactly what she wanted. And she had wanted them for what seemed a long, long time.

Her body shivered, her teeth still chattered, but within her rose a swelling urgency that drowned her physical discomfort in a surging tide of desire.

It ought to be so wrong. She was a runner. She and she alone ruled her emotions and her body. Her city was in danger and she carried information that her Master needed.

Yet none of that mattered. Not now.

Within this wagon, here in the wavering shadows cast by a guttering candle, there were just the two of them. A man and a woman. Together.

123

Nareen shifted in Jerrel's arms, clinging even more closely to his warmth and strength.

Together. Such a tempting word, yet so strange to one who had been cast in the streets as a child, to one whose very work demanded an emotional reserve that ought to keep her at a distance from those around her.

Together. A few sounds, strung like beads on a string, that created a word capable of touching her heart, her very soul.

Nareen rubbed her cheek across the broad plane of Jerrel's chest, ran the palm of her hand down the ridge of muscle at the side of his belly.

Jerrel gasped. The muscles beneath her hand quivered.

A small sigh—of satisfaction, of need—escaped her lips. Nareen nuzzled the masculine swell of his breast. The small, hard tip of his nipple rubbed against her cheek. Unthinking, she turned her head to run her tongue across that enticing nubbin of flesh and was rewarded for her effort with Jerrel's shuddering intake of breath.

"Don't . . ." His hands clamped down on her shoulders and he tried to push her away. "You don't know . . ."

But she *did* know. She knew, suddenly, exactly what she wanted. Knew that she had the power to claim her prize—to demand it, in fact. And she knew that it would be impossible for Jerrel to deny it to her.

The cold that had wracked her body only a short time before was a thing of the past. It had burned away in the fire rising within her, burned away with her doubts and fears and uncertainties.

"Nareen!" The name was torn from Jerrel's throat. It was a protest—and a plea.

But neither protest nor plea was answered. The creature he held had been transformed from a dazed and shivering waif into a demanding, tempting woman, and he could no more resist her than he could resist the inexorable wave of desire sweeping through him.

"Nareen." He scarcely breathed her name this time, yet Nareen heard. Heard and understood.

She tugged at the sheet around her, pulling it free, then letting it fall, unheeded, at their feet. For an instant she pulled back from Jerrel, looking up into the shadowed face so close above her, seeking an answer for a question she could not put into words.

And the answer was there in the glittering intensity of his eyes, in his half-parted lips.

Neither spoke. With a sigh that was half release, half an admission of defeat, Jerrel lowered his head and brought his lips crushing down on hers.

There was nothing cold about her now. She burned with a heat that almost frightened him but that he could not resist, like a fire that beckoned to a weary traveler at the end of a fruitless journey.

It felt so good to hold her, so right. As if all the pain and loneliness of those years spent between the stars or fighting for survival on some hostile planet had never been. Here, with this woman, Jerrel knew he could warm his soul at the flames of her desire and put aside his struggles in the act of lying with her.

Wrenching his mouth from hers, Jerrel stooped and picked Nareen up in his arms. He stood there for a moment, gazing upon her greedily. But only for a moment. Then he crossed to his bed at the end of the wagon and lifted her into it.

The light from the dying candle shone full on her face. In that instant, any doubt he might have had vanished. She wanted him, needed him. And in that wanting, that needing, was everything he had dreamed of but never had, everything he had longed for and never possessed.

The flame of the candle sputtered, then flared again brightly.

"Come to me," Nareen whispered, stretching out her arms to him. "I want you."

Without taking his eyes from her, Jerrel swung up into the bed beside her and gathered her against him. He had no words for her, but then he needed none—she understood everything he could not say.

The flame of the candle wavered and sank, flared once, then died, plunging them into darkness. It didn't matter. They had no more need for light than for words, for the flame that burned between them was sufficient for even the darkest night.

Chapter 7

Those long, dark hours of passion and discovery hadn't been a dream, after all. They'd been real, as real as the man lying beside her. Nareen shifted slightly so she could gaze on Jerrel's face.

He was still asleep. In the pale gray light filtering through the small windows at each side of the wagon he looked younger, vulnerable.

Nareen's heart squeezed within her. The night had brought a thousand lessons, lessons in the way her body responded when touched just so, in the ease with which her slightest caress could rouse a quivering response from the powerful male she had thought almost invulnerable, lessons in the ecstasy that was possible between a man and a woman.

Their first coupling had been the frenzied joining of two people caught in the heat of the moment, the fire within one rising to meet the fire of the other in a conflagration capable of driving back the edges of the cold, black night.

But as the hours lengthened, that first firestorm of need had tempered to a steady blaze capable of warming the soul as well as the body. Then it was not just the coupling that mattered—it was the sharing, the mutual exploration, the simple act of touching and of being touched.

To Nareen's delight and wonder, Jerrel had seemed to find the same pleasure in a gentle caress, a hesitant kiss, as she did. Even the brush of her fingertips along his arm or across the ridged muscles of his stomach was sufficient to draw a quivering response from him.

In the way he reached for her, in the gentle protectiveness with which he drew her into the circle of his arms, he had revealed a vulnerability, an uncertainty that was strangely at variance with the armor of impervious self-sufficiency he had always displayed before.

What power had brought them together? Nareen wondered. She had thought herself contented, independent. She had thought the hurts of the past had faded long before, or been buried deeply enough that they had lost the power to wound. She had thought that in her work she had found everything she needed in life—friends, position, security, a reason to exist, a purpose to guide her days.

If sometimes the restraints of her work had galled, if she had chafed under the need to distance herself from those around her, from the messages she was required to carry, then that was only to be expected. Life came with no guarantees or promises. And what she had was far more than she'd ever imagined possible when she was a child on the docks of Margash.

But not until last night, when she'd found herself in Jerrel's arms, had Nareen wondered if there might be more, if life might hold riches she had never dreamed of.

Nareen studied Jerrel's features, memorizing each line, every curve. Her finger itched to trace the hollow of his cheek, the strong ridge of his jaw. Her gaze followed the arc of his mouth, the sensual swell of his lower lip.

Obedient to an inner urging, Nareen dropped her head and gently, hesitantly, ran the tip of her tongue along his lips. Her touch was whisper-light, yet it was enough. Jerrel stirred. His lips parted, inviting her in, and his warm breath mingled with hers.

Nareen pulled back. She wanted to touch and be touched, to hold and be held, to give love and to receive that love in return. But first she wanted to gaze into Jerrel's eyes as he awoke, to look through those strange blue windows into his very soul and see some part, at least, of the uncertainty and the wonder that were hers this morning.

Jerrel's eyelids fluttered, then opened. His eyes were the blue of a summer morning, intensely clear and bright. As he came to full awareness, his gaze fixed on her and he smiled. Nareen watched, fascinated, as each pupil expanded, swallowing up the iris until only a narrow blue rim remained.

"You didn't slip away in the night." His voice was scarcely more than a whisper.

Nareen shook her head. So he had feared it was all a dream, too. "No."

Jerrel's smile widened. One corner crooked up more than the other, creating a slight dimple. He brought his hand up and gently ran one finger along the side of her face.

"I'm glad you didn't," he said, very softly.

Nareen's heart soared. In his eyes, his touch, was all the assurance she needed. She bent her head once again to taste the heady elixir of his kisses.

His mouth was warm and welcoming. His tongue met her searching thrust, met and parried and sought its own sweet welcome. Nareen broke free to trail kisses across Jerrel's cheek and jaw and down his throat. His coarse, dark beard rasped against her lips and tongue. The heat of his skin, the very smell of him tantalized her, driving her further.

Slowly Nareen eased her body down the length of his. Jerrel tried to hold her, drag her back, but the gentle brush of her tongue across the palm of his hand, a nip at the base of his throat, the slight catch of the skin of her bare breast against his heated flesh were enough to reduce him to trembling acquiescence. For an instant Nareen broke off her tormenting progress to glory in his increasingly ragged breathing, in the racing pulse she could see so clearly at the base of his jaw. Then, her hunger too great to tolerate further delay, she returned to the tempting task before her.

The broad bulk of his shoulders and chest, the flat plain of his tautly muscled belly were like a vast continent awaiting her exploration, drawing her onward. Nareen lavished her kisses along the hard curve of his breast, across the arch of his ribs, down the slight dip between the muscles of his stomach and side. And with each kiss, each hot sweep of her tongue against his skin, she exulted in her conquest, her triumph.

Yet conqueror was equally conquered, for in Jerrel's ready response to her domination lay her victory, and her downfall. She nipped at the small, hard peak of his nipple and her own nipples hardened in response. She ran her hands across his stomach and felt her stomach muscles contract. She lightly brushed her fingers through the dark, curly hair of his groin and could not keep from crying out at the hungry spasm that seized her, threatening to tip her into shuddering ecstasy before she was ready.

Like every conqueror before her, Nareen ventured too far. Softly, ever so delicately, she ran the tip of one trembling finger up the side of his engorged shaft. Jerrel gasped. His head rocked back in the pillow and his body arched, straining toward her, toward her touch.

Emboldened, Nareen brushed the palm of her hand along the silken length of him. She barely touched him, yet the heat of him, the hungry need she'd roused, was sufficient to incite rebellion against her sensual rule.

With a harsh cry, Jerrel rolled her onto her back, pinning her to the bed with his massive body. It was then that Nareen learned what it is to suffer the revenge of the conquered. For every tormenting kiss she'd given him, he doubled her penalty, tripled it. His hands, his mouth, his tongue returned tenfold the exquisite torture she'd inflicted on him, until Nareen writhed beneath him, consumed by her need, her longing for the release that was in his power to grant her.

No, that was wrong. Even in this haze of heat and searing sensation, Nareen knew she was no supplicant and Jerrel was not her master. Here, now, they were equals. A man and a woman sharing not only their bodies, but themselves. Finding in each other not only physical release, but the courage to be vulnerable, even if only for a little while.

Those thoughts were torn from her as Jerrel poised himself between her legs, then thrust forward to claim her. Nareen's eager, exultant cry matched his choked gasp. She arched upward, forcing him deeper within her.

Together they moved in an urgent, insistent rhythm that shut out all thought, all awareness of anything save each other and the mounting inferno between them. Just before those raging fires could consume Nareen utterly, they flashed over into a brilliant, crimson ecstasy of pure sensation and precious release. A moment later, Jerrel collapsed, trembling in the throes of his own deliverance.

Nareen had no idea how long they lay there, their limbs tangled together, their bodies limp, replete. Eventually Jerrel shifted to lie beside her. Without speaking, he slid his arm under her head and pulled her against him.

Slowly the aching heat within Nareen receded, leaving in its wake a sweet lassitude that weighted her limbs and tempted her with sleep. Heavy-eyed, she turned her head on the pillow and met Jerrel's steady gaze. She smiled, ever so softly, then laid her palm against his cheek in a gesture of . . . what? She was too sleepy to think clearly.

It didn't matter. Whatever she was trying to say, Jerrel understood. He turned his head to brush a warm kiss in the center of her palm, then drew her even more tightly against him.

Trailing his hand down her body, he reached for the covers tangled about her hips, then gently drew them up around her shoulders and tucked them in.

The last thing Nareen was aware of before she drifted back into sleep was the soft caress of his fingers along the side of her face, the gentle brush of his lips at her temple, just where her pulse beat below the skin.

Cautiously Jerrel slid out of Nareen's arms, then out of bed. Let her sleep a little longer. It was still early and there was more than enough time to rouse her and tidy the wagon before Norvag appeared for breakfast.

For a moment he stood beside the bed, watching her sleep. What was it about this runner, this woman, that drew him to her? Why, of all the women he had known in his life, was she the only one capable of piercing the armor he'd placed around his emotions, around his very soul?

Was it her fiery response to his slightest touch? Was it the proud spirit that had made her his equal in their loving, capable both of giving and of receiving, of accepting what he offered and of making her demands of him in return? Or was it something else, something not so easily linked to lovemaking and nothing more?

Carefully Jerrel tucked the covers in around Nareen. The night had been unlike any he had ever known. Gentler at times. Sweeter. Yet there had been little gentleness in his taking of her and no false modesty in her response to him.

They had crossed the hours of the night like a fiery comet arcing across the heavens, wrapped in the heat of their passage until they'd faded at last into the infinite, welcoming darkness. Whatever the future held, this night would stay with him for the rest of his life.

Here, on this forgotten world, with this proud and passionate woman, by chance he had found a hope for the peace he hadn't realized he'd sought through all his wanderings. Yet even if she were free of the responsibilities that bound her, how could he ask her to leave behind the only world she'd ever known to join him, a man who knew a hundred worlds but could call not one of them home?

The steady drumming of the rain on the roof was his only answer.

At last Jerrel turned away from the bed and began to dress. As he slid his jerkin on, the chain he'd removed from around his neck the night before slid out of his pocket and onto the floor.

Jerrel stooped to retrieve the chain, then paused. The ring he'd strung on the chain—Santar's ring—glinted dully in the gray light. He'd forgotten.

Slowly Jerrel rose to his feet, the chain dangling from his fingers. Here was his answer.

He had come to Errandane to find his brother. To that end he hadn't hesitated to steal a ring carried by the woman who had saved his life. He hadn't even blinked when he'd lied to her. And if he had to do it over again, he would do the same, with no more hesitation than the first time.

Once he found Santar, what then? If he were free, would he take Nareen with him? Could he?

It wasn't that the rule of non-intervention would stop him. But did he have the right to take her from the only home she knew and thrust her into a universe containing thousands of worlds, none of them like hers?

He knew he couldn't stay with her. However great his love for her might become, it would inevitably be tarnished by his frustration with a world where he would have to live a lie for the rest of his life. He would have to hide what he knew, who he was. He could never talk of his home world, of his family, of the things he'd done, the places he'd been. He would disappear behind the mask he would be forced to assume.

So what remained? Jerrel's hand closed around the ring and chain. He glanced back at a still sleeping Nareen.

Four days, he thought. That was what remained. Four days with her, to share as they wished. Together.

His hand clenched until the ring dug into his flesh. Four days, knowing there would not be a fifth.

Jerrel forced his hand to open. If only he could ask her why she'd been carrying the ring and for whom it had been intended. But he couldn't, and she wouldn't answer if he did.

Slowly, with great deliberation, he stuffed the ring and chain into a hidden pouch on the inside of his belt.

Four days would have to be enough.

Strange how the rain and the cramped quarters had ceased to matter, Nareen thought. The first two days had been unendurable torture, these last two like the sweetest honey, rich and gone too soon.

Even the weather after three and a half days of sodden gloom had changed to match her sunny

mood. Sometime during the afternoon the caravan had passed through the last of the rain. Neither she nor Jerrel noticed. They'd had no need
of the sun to warm them.

This evening, for the first time, they'd dined
alone. Norvag had chosen to take his meal outside with the other travelers but he'd left in his
place two bottles of zafa he'd purchased at a holding they'd passed that morning.

"It's good," he'd said, offering the bottles to
Jerrel. "Rather like a sweet Altarean wine, only
smoother."

"Altarean . . . ?" Nareen had stumbled over the
word. "What's that?"

"Uh . . ." Norvag had looked flustered, then
glanced over at a suddenly scowling Jerrel. "It
doesn't matter."

And he'd been right. It hadn't mattered, because
the zafa was as good as promised.

Nareen took another sip from her wooden goblet, savoring the taste of sun and sweet fruit, then
looked up to find Jerrel studying her. Was it the
zafa, or the eager light in Jerrel's eyes, or some
heady mixture of both that made her head spin
so? she wondered.

Nareen watched, fascinated, as the color of
Jerrel's eyes subtly changed from light blue to the
darker, richer blue of a deep, calm lake. Slowly the
slight, lopsided smile that lifted the corner of his
mouth faded, and his lips, so sensually full, parted
slightly. The tip of his tongue darted out briefly,
then disappeared, leaving behind a slight film of
moisture that stirred in Nareen a sudden desire to
know again the feel and heat and taste of him.

Then his lips compressed and he frowned slightly, as though an unpleasant thought had struck

him, and he looked away, leaving her feeling oddly bereft.

Jerrel rose to his feet. He picked up the zafa bottle and both goblets in one hand and carefully edged around the table, then turned and stretched out his hand to her.

"Come with me," he said softly.

Without hesitation, Nareen placed her hand in his and slid around the table to stand beside him. His hand was so warm, so comfortingly strong.

"Come." He drew her to the door. "We'll leave the candles burning to light our way back."

Most of the caravan wagons were dark, their occupants already asleep. From somewhere off to the side Nareen heard an aard snort and the soft, soothing voice of the man set to guard the beasts for the night. Farther up the line several people were grouped about a small fire. The sound of their voices came to her as a low murmur.

The night was surprisingly warm and the soft breeze brought the sweet scent of dead grass and damp earth.

"The moon hasn't risen yet," said Jerrel, "but the stars will give us enough light to find our way. Are you cold?"

Nareen shook her head, forgetting he couldn't see her clearly in the dark since their eyes hadn't had time to adjust.

"I'll keep you warm," he said, his voice suddenly low and husky. He wrapped an arm around her shoulders and drew her against him. "And I still have the zafa. We won't suffer."

Jerrel led her away from the wagons. They went slowly, carefully picking their way across the clumpy grass as their eyes adjusted to the dark. It would have been easier for Nareen to walk without Jerrel's arm about her, but she made no effort to free herself.

"This is far enough," Jerrel said at last, stopping beside a mass of rocks that showed vaguely gray in the dim starlight.

He bent to set the bottle of zafa and the goblets on the ground, then, before Nareen realized what he intended, put a hand on either side of her waist and swung her up on top of one of the larger, flatter rocks.

Without thinking, Nareen put her hands over his to steady herself. Seated on the rock, she looked down into Jerrel's upturned face but all she could see was the planes of brow and cheek and jaw painted pale silver and his eyes, black and glittering in the starlight, looking up into hers.

For an instant, inexplicable fear surged through her. It was as though he were wearing a mask, a protective covering of starlight and dark that shielded him from her.

But that was foolish. Nareen shook her head to dispel the unwelcome thought. There was nothing secretive about his hold on her, nothing secretive in the way he'd held her to him as they'd crossed the winter grassland.

Jerrel released her, slowly, reluctantly, his hands sliding from under hers, down her waist and along her hips until his fingertips brushed the cold, hard, gritty rock beneath her.

Sitting there above him, with her face in shadow and her slender body drenched in starlight, the little runner looked like one of the mythical spirits of his own world, a being formed of mist and magic, insubstantial yet all too temptingly real to mere mortal senses.

Her hair, those silken strands he so delighted in wrapping around his fingers, shone in the pale light. Her form was revealed as much through shadow as through the vague sheen on the leather of her tunic and leggings that highlighted the line of her shoulders, of her body, of her slender legs. Jerrel's gaze slid along the curve of her thigh, over her bent knee, down her leg, then back up again.

What sort of magic had she wrought on him these past two days? What unknown means had she employed that he had so easily put aside all his doubts and fears and guilt? Here, away from the confines of the wagon and with the cool night air between them, he ought to be freed from some, at least, of the fascination she held for him.

But he wasn't.

His hand ached with the memory of the yielding firmness of the muscles of her thigh, the soft, responsive swell of her breasts. His fingers rested against cold stone, yet they tingled with the remembered warmth of her skin.

Jerrel took a deep, steadying breath, then stooped to retrieve the zafa. Silently he handed Nareen both goblets to hold while he refilled them. Although the pale light reflected dimly from the lip of the bottle, the dark wood of the goblets made it almost impossible to see where he was pouring.

Without thinking, he wrapped his hands around hers, then immediately wished he had not. The heat between them seemed sufficient to char even the seasoned wood of the goblets.

No flames burst forth, and he succeeded in pouring the zafa without spilling any. With great care Jerrel balanced both his full cup and the bottle of zafa on the rock, then placed a hand on the rock near Nareen and vaulted up to sit beside her.

Picking up his goblet, Jerrel extended it toward Nareen, intending to touch the rim of her goblet in a silent toast. But instead of raising her cup in response, Nareen wrapped both her hands around it and bowed her head slightly in acknowledgment.

Hastily Jerrel did the same, silently cursing himself. It was just such simple mistakes that revealed their different origins.

And that thought was an unpleasant reminder that he didn't belong here, that this woman, this moment in the starlight, had no part in his search for his brother. They were diversions—tempting diversions, but diversions nonetheless.

Jerrel kept his gaze firmly fixed on the goblet he held, trying, and failing, to push down his intense awareness of Nareen beside him.

Nareen shifted her position, leaning back to prop herself up with one elbow. Her face, bathed in silver starlight, was lifted to the glittering vault of the sky above them.

"I've sometimes wondered," she murmured without glancing at him, "about what's out there. If there are other worlds, other people. What they're like." She lifted her goblet to gesture toward a particularly bright cluster of stars. "There might be whole worlds in just that little space. Worlds with men and women and children and . . ." Her voice trailed off.

Jerrel couldn't interpret the expression on her face. She shook her head, as though bemused by her fantasies, then took a drink of zafa.

"What makes you think there's any world but this one?" Jerrel asked cautiously. The information that Danet and Santar had already gathered indicated that Errandane, like most of the worlds lost in the Empire's breakup, possessed tales of people on other planets. But her words seemed to spring from something other than mere legend.

She shook her head again. Jerrel could have sworn he heard the silken rustle as the strands of hair brushed against one another.

"I don't know," she admitted. "Fantasies from childhood, perhaps. Sometimes, when I was in Margash, I used to imagine other places, other lives. I guess I've never forgotten that."

"You've mentioned Margash before," Jerrel said. He hesitated. Was it only his imagination, or had the expression on her face darkened in the pale starlight? When she didn't respond, he added, "How is it that you're now from Kalinden?"

"I . . ." Nareen stopped, uncertain. She seldom spoke of her childhood, but suddenly she wanted to explain, to share some of herself with this man, this stranger. For that was what he was, a stranger, despite the intimacy of the past two days.

And yet . . .

She glanced over at Jerrel to discover his gaze firmly fixed on her. Her breath caught in her throat. Just the sight of him was enough to send the blood racing through her veins.

"I was a child in Margash," she said at last, forcing herself to look away. "I was taken to Kalinden when I was about five years old."

"What caused your parents to move to Kalinden?"

"I . . . I have no parents. They're dead . . . At least, I hope they are."

141

The last words were spoken so low Jerrel had to strain to hear them.

"You hope they are?"

Nareen's head came up and she fixed her gaze firmly on the sparkling points of light above her. Jerrel could see her jaw clench and the movement of her throat as she swallowed convulsively.

"I wouldn't like to think they simply abandoned me," she said at last. "I spent a year—I think it was a year—struggling to survive around the docks in Margash. I can't bear the thought that I might have been deliberately abandoned to that misery."

"But you said you were only five!" Jerrel protested, appalled. He'd been in enough port cities on enough planets to know the horror of life on the docks.

"I wasn't always alone, but sometimes it might have been better if I had been. Then I wouldn't . . ." Nareen's voice caught. She paused, forcing some measure of calm into her words. "There were packs of children like me. Sometimes I lived with them. Once an old woman fed me for a while. She didn't have much but she shared that little with me. She was taken away by the authorities, along with a lot of others like us who had sought shelter in an abandoned building near the docks. I escaped. I never knew what happened to her."

She shifted slightly on the rock beside him, turning her head away from him, and took a sip from her goblet.

"How did you come to be a runner for Kalinden?" Jerrel asked softly. He longed to take Nareen in his arms, to kiss away the remembered hurts that made her voice quiver so.

For a moment he thought she wasn't going to answer. She drank again, draining the cup, then held out the goblet for him to refill.

"I tried to rob a man there on the docks. A wealthy man, from the looks of him, and a stranger who might not have known how to protect himself." She studied the contents of her goblet.

"I'd learned some of the skills of a thief, but not enough. The man caught me. He was Gravnar, the Chief Runner for Kalinden, traveling on official business for the Master. He caught me, since he was much quicker than I'd expected, and threatened to drag me before the authorities." She took yet another sip of zafa.

"I don't know why he didn't, and he's never explained. But instead of having me arrested he took me back to his lodgings. He had another child, a boy, that he was taking into training to be a runner. The boy had been indentured into Kalinden's service by his parents, who were merchants in the town. Originally Gravnar had no such plans for me—thieving orphans aren't trained as runners—but he has a kind heart and I proved intelligent and quick." She sighed, then gazed back up at the stars.

"He gave me a chance, and Kalinden gave me a home," she said, almost whispering. "I owe them everything. Everything," she added fiercely, sitting up abruptly. "And now, when I should be seeking help, I sit on a rock drinking zafa and talking. Talk, talk, talk, and my city in danger."

Nareen started to rise, but the rock's surface was uneven and she had drunk too much zafa. She slipped and would have fallen if Jerrel had not reached out to catch her.

The zafa splashed across the rock. Her goblet rolled to the ground and she slid, unresisting, into the strong hold of two arms that wrapped around her, drawing her into the safety of their embrace.

She was so small compared to his bulk, Jerrel thought, holding her against him. So small, yet so desirable. She easily fit in his arms, folded naturally against his body as if she belonged there, as if she had always belonged there. Jerrel drew her even tighter against him. Her face was turned to him and he could see a tear glittering on her cheek in the dim starlight.

Without thinking, Jerrel bent his head and gently kissed the tear away. The droplet was warm, salty against his lips. His tongue flicked out to capture it.

She moaned. Her lips quivered, her body arched toward him, and Jerrel could resist no longer.

Chapter 8

The night, the cold, the hard rock beneath them dissolved and faded from Jerrel's consciousness. It didn't matter. He needed neither the earth beneath him nor the sky above when this woman was in his arms. For now, at least, she was his universe, a universe deep enough and wide enough to hide even his doubts and guilts, where even his restless, lonely soul might find peace.

He kissed her cheek, her brows, the thick, dark lashes of her eyelids. She moaned, protesting, demanding. Her hands slid up across his chest, along his throat, behind his neck. He gasped, even as he kissed the pounding vein in her temple—she had only brushed against his skin, yet it was sufficient to send a sudden, aching tremor through his body.

Her fingers tangled in his thick curls. Her hands were small, yet he was helpless against them as she pulled his head down, his mouth onto hers.

She tasted of sweet zafa. And of some rich, honeyed essence that was hers and hers alone. He ran the tip of his tongue along the swell of her lower lip, across the sharp, perfect line of her teeth.

She released her indrawn breath in one tremulous exhalation that flowed over his lips, drying them yet leaving them even more achingly sensitive than before.

Jerrel groaned and brought his mouth crushing down on hers once more. His hand slid up her back and behind her head, supporting her, preventing her from escaping him and his rising need for her.

And while he gathered her closer, she, too, made her demands and wrapped him in the bonds of her arms as though she would never release him. Never. And that only served to inflame him more.

She stiffened suddenly, then pushed away from him, evading his kisses. Even in the dark he could see that her eyes had grown large and round.

"Come with me," she said, suddenly eager, almost laughing. Her hands clutched at his jerkin. "That's the answer, you know. You must come with me to Kalinden."

"To Kalinden?" Jerrel gaped, disoriented by the sudden shift in affairs. His heart hammered inside his chest and the blood pounded through his veins so he could scarcely think.

"Of course! Don't you see? You're a merchant and you said you had business in Matcassen. But you could find things to trade for in Kalinden. Things far finer than Matcassen can offer. And you're a warrior! My city has need of warriors like you, big and strong and brave. They would pay you well. I know they would!"

"Nareen, I . . ."

"Don't you see?" She cupped her hands around his face, as though the contact would somehow transfer her sudden enthusiasm to him. "We can be together. And you can help Kalinden, help my friends."

Even in the dim starlight Jerrel could see her eager smile.

"It hurts so much to think of parting, yet I couldn't . . . But it doesn't matter, does it?" She laughed, low and deep in her throat, happy. "You can come with me. Kalinden needs you." Her hands slid along his jaw, behind his head. She drew closer to him, her lips only inches from his. "I need you."

Her words were scarcely a whisper, yet Jerrel heard them. And wished he had not.

He ought to speak, ought to tell her that he could give her nothing, because he had nothing to give. Ought to tell her that he was not what she thought him, that he had come this way for a purpose, and that his purpose did not, could not, include her. Ought to tell her that he would leave her, sooner or later, regardless of what lay between them.

Ought to, but he couldn't.

Not because she was kissing him, or because he ached with his need of her. He couldn't tell her because he was afraid. Because he didn't want to leave her, but must. Because there was no future for them. Not here in her world, not out there in his.

She had transferred her attention from his mouth and was planting small, eager kisses at the base of his throat. Her lips burned against his flesh.

"Nareen, I . . ."

"Don't say no," she whispered, then ran the tip of her tongue along the corded line of muscle at the side of his neck, up to the small hollow at the base of his jaw, where she kissed him once again. Her hand released its hold on his hair, then slid around to lie against his cheek, forcing his head around and down to meet hers. "Don't say anything. Not yet."

"Nareen . . ." But his protest faltered, then died. She felt so good in his arms, so right. There were too many empty years ahead for him to deny the sweet promise of the night before them.

"I will not go with you to Kalinden. I *can't*." Jerrel stood with his back to the wall inside the wagon, arms folded across his chest, adamantly refusing to meet Nareen's stricken gaze. He was unhappily aware of the message his position conveyed. He was also grateful for the symbolic protection of the stout wood behind him.

Nareen was standing several feet from him at the opposite end of the wagon, but her dismay and disbelief struck him in an almost palpable wave.

For the past two days he'd resisted all her arguments and blandishments in favor of his accompanying her to Kalinden. But this was their last night on the road. Tomorrow they would arrive in Matcassen, and he could not put off this confrontation any longer.

"Kalinden needs you," Nareen pleaded. "Surely you can put aside—"

"I can't, and I won't." Jerrel's words cut like shards of brittle glass. "Nor will I explain my reasons. Whatever the danger to your city, it has nothing to do with me."

"But it has everything to do with me!" Nareen exclaimed. "Does that count for nothing?"

Jerrel shifted uncomfortably. Rather than face her directly, he glared at the floor. A dozen times he had considered temporarily putting aside his search for Santar so he could help Nareen as she asked. And a dozen times he had pushed aside the temptation not to let her go.

Santar needed him. It was as simple as that. His conviction that his brother was still alive had brought him to Errandane. With the recorder ring's evidence, he was more sure than ever that he was right to continue his search. His personal desires would have to be put aside.

Especially if those desires were impossible to fulfill. He couldn't have Nareen. His rational mind knew it, even if his heart did not.

"I will stay in Matcassen," Jerrel said at last, firmly. He forced his head up so he could meet Nareen's anguished gaze squarely. "You will have to go on to Kalinden. Alone."

The huge wagons of the caravan rolled past her, the lumbering aards paying no more attention to the bitter wind whipping up the hillside than they had to the mud or rain three days before.

Nareen stood shivering, her gaze fixed on the walled city spread across the plain before her. She was dimly aware of the wagons passing, of the few individuals who paused, uncertain whether or not to approach her. They invariably chose to go on, ducking their heads or tugging their hoods down tighter against the sharp blasts of winter.

It didn't matter. She had nothing to say to them or they to her. The journey was over. From here she would go on alone, on foot. Kalinden was only three and a half days away, even at the slower pace that was all she could manage.

Alone.

The word had a hollow, empty sound. It was a word she ought to know well after all these years. Strange, how little time she'd needed to thrust it from her consciousness.

But she hadn't forgotten it. And just as well. Those few, brief moments when she'd thought there was a chance for more had been nothing but a delusion fueled by too much zafa and the intoxicating heat of passion. And any fool knew that zafa and passion were dangerous tricksters.

Nareen shrugged, then settled the grackle skin more closely about her. Her arguments, her pleas, had availed her nothing. Jerrel had been adamant. He could not—or would not—accompany her to Kalinden.

It might have been easier if only he'd been willing to explain his reasons for refusing her. Nareen blinked, fighting back a tear. It was the wind, of course, cutting at her with razor teeth. She must move off this hill soon, go on to Matcassen.

Her gaze searched the line of wagons making its way down the hill and across the plain. He was there, somewhere, with the first wagons, but at this distance she couldn't pick him out of the figures plodding beside the caravan.

Nareen's fist clenched around the grackle skin, pulling it tight across her shoulders. He cared. Of that she was certain. She had seen it in his eyes, heard it in his voice, felt it in his touch. But there had been shadows between them, and he would not lighten them by sharing with her. He had chosen his path, and he did not want her there beside him.

Nareen sighed. It didn't matter. She wouldn't have accompanied him on his path because she had her own that she couldn't abandon. Though he had cared for her, he had not cared enough to join her, and that was all she needed to know.

Her path. She looked once more along the road that led to the gates of Matcassen, then on toward Kalinden. *This* was her path, and she had best be traveling it.

The room the inn had provided was slightly larger than the wagon—fifteen paces from side to side—but it still felt cramped and confining to Jerrel. For an instant he longed for an excuse to escape, like the drevon hunt . . .

That thought brought him up short. He stopped his pacing to scowl at the room's drab brown walls and the narrow bed . . .

No, he wouldn't think about that, either.

With a muttered curse he crossed the room to pull back the faded fabric covering one window and peer out into the busy street below. It was early evening, yet the traffic in the street didn't appear to have diminished since they'd arrived several hours before.

He'd had no choice. His only reason for being on this benighted planet was to find Santar. No distractions, however appealing, could interfere with that.

Perhaps if he could have explained it all to Nareen, if he could have made her understand . . .

The worn curtain ripped under the strain of his grip. Jerrel stared down at the remnant he held, then flung it from him in disgust.

There was nothing he could have said that would have soothed the pain he'd caused. One day he would forget the anger and bewilderment and hurt that had shimmered in Nareen's brilliant green eyes last night when she finally understood. She hadn't begged or cried. She'd thrown back her shoulders, lifted her chin ever so slightly, and said, very quietly, "I see." Then she'd turned and left the wagon in dignified silence. He hadn't seen her since.

He would never see her again.

"You can always go to Kalinden."

Jerrel swung around, startled. He hadn't heard Norvag enter the room.

"Once you find Santar . . . once you know . . ." Norvag's words trailed off. He made no effort to move away from the door he'd shut behind him.

"No." Jerrel almost choked on the single syllable. The word hung in the air between them, heavy with unspoken meaning.

"I thought it just a physical attraction, a way of passing the time, a . . ." Norvag paused. To Jerrel, he looked older, more tired. His shoulders drooped. "I was wrong, wasn't I?"

Jerrel turned back to brace a hand on the frame above the window. He stared sightlessly out at the street below. "It doesn't matter."

"She's intelligent. She could adapt—"

"To what? To a technology she can't even conceive of? To a life spent moving from one world to another, without any place to call home, without knowing what dangers she'll face from one day to the next?" Jerrel thumped his fist against the wall, making the window rattle in its frame.

"You could stay here . . ."

Jerrel laughed, but there was no humor in the harsh sound. "And live a lie for the rest of my life? Pretending to be someone I'm not. Hiding who and what I am, always wondering when I'll make a mistake, when I'll say something I shouldn't." He laughed again. The sound grated on his nerves. "You can't even get a decent hot bath on this damned world!"

But if it meant he could be with her . . .

Jerrel straightened, then turned back to his friend, his face set and grim. "No, Norvag, I won't spend the rest of my life on this world, and I can't ask her to come with me. We came to find Santar, and I intend to do just that. Once I know he's safe . . ." He stopped. A muscle twitched in his jaw. "I heard there's a good market for Denebian caphir beans these days. Deneb isn't all that far away . . ."

A knock at the door interrupted him. After a quick glance at Jerrel, Norvag cautiously opened the door to admit a heavyset, balding man.

"Borlat! You're back sooner than I expected."

"Didn't get in." Borlat stood twisting a much-battered leather cap in his hands and stared resolutely at the opposite wall.

"What do you mean you didn't get in? Your instructions were to take that message to Advisor Danet. What did you do with it?" Norvag demanded.

"Ain't there."

"Who? Advisor Danet? Where is he?"

"Out. Inspectin' some village or sumpin'. Won't be back two, three days." Borlat shifted from one foot to the other, obviously uncomfortable under Norvag's questioning.

"Who told you that?"

"Guard."

"What guard? Damn it, man, speak up!"

"Guard at t'Hall. T'Great Hall. Said this Danet fellow went off with some soldiers and 'nother advisor t'find out what was goin' on in this village, see?"

It was clear, even to Borlat, that his listeners did *not* see. He swallowed convulsively, then tried again. "Fellow from t'village tried t'kill t'Master, so t'Master—Master Lindaz—was goin' t'kill everyone in t'village, see? But this Danet talks 'im into waitin' an' findin' out more." Borlat looked at Norvag and Jerrel hopefully. "Y'see?"

To his satisfaction, it was evident they did. Pleased at his success, Borlat dug a crumpled, sealed letter out of his pocket, handed it to Norvag with much relief, and scuttled from the room.

"The man's a fool." Norvag tossed the letter on a nearby table in disgust.

"He has his uses." Jerrel shrugged, then frowned. "Now what? Following Danet to this village will draw too much attention. I could use the com links—" He held up a hand to stop Norvag's sputtering protest. "But I won't. There's no way of telling what he'll be doing when we link, and it wouldn't help his position to go into a communication freeze-up in the middle of an important discussion. It also might be downright dangerous."

Norvag eyed Jerrel doubtfully, then settled into a chair at one side of the table. "We have no choice. We'll wait."

Jerrel shook his head. "I've waited too long and accomplished nothing." He shifted restlessly, then once more turned to gaze, unseeing, out the window. "There is one other avenue open." He paused. When Norvag said nothing, he continued, "I'm going to seek an interview with this Lady Xyanth."

"La . . . No!" Norvag thumped his fist on the table. "Absolutely not! You're bigger than Santar, and almost ten years older. But anyone who knows Santar will know you're his brother. There are your blue eyes, to start with, and—"

Jerrel turned back to face his friend. "It could be to our advantage if she recognizes me. The ring gave no hint that Santar ever told anyone about me, but it might shake her up, make her reveal important information if she thinks I know something about him. It's worth a try, and better than sitting in this damned room going mad from doing nothing."

Before Norvag could reply, a second knock, this time much louder, sounded at the door, and a voice called from out in the hall, "It's Rakin, sir. I'm back."

Without waiting for permission, the second of Jerrel's two hired escorts pushed open the door and walked in. Rakin was tall, almost as tall as Jerrel, and thin. His sharp-featured face betrayed an intelligence that had been lacking in his companion.

"Here to make my report," he said, nodding first to Jerrel, then to Norvag.

Norvag's eyebrows rose. "You're back sooner than I expected. I take it you had no difficulty in learning the latest news."

Rakin shook his head. "There's only one bit of news worth knowing. Matcassen sent troops to Kalinden six days ago with Lady Xyanth at their head. They're to help Kalinden fight the beastmen invading from the north." He paused to allow Jerrel and Norvag their exclamations of surprise, then continued, "The force that left isn't as large as you'd expect, but Master Lindaz has had several attacks on his life lately. According to some reports, he didn't want to release any troops, even if there was an official call for help from Kalinden. Lady Xyanth seems to have persuaded him otherwise." One eyebrow rose slightly. "Some say the Lady has other plans in mind than just helping a neighbor."

Rakin had little else to add to his report and was quickly dismissed, leaving Jerrel and Norvag alone in the room.

"It would seem that Nareen may rest easy, after all," Norvag said, thoughtfully drumming his fingers on the table. "And with Xyanth gone, we really have no option but to wait here until Danet returns." He looked relieved.

Jerrel smiled, but without humor. "Oh, no, my friend. *You* will wait. *I* am going on to Kalinden."

"It is *not* all good news. Do you understand nothing I say?" The man leaned across the table toward Nareen, as though he hoped to convince her by sheer force of will.

"I understand enough, Runner Tork. Matcassen has gone to the help of Kalinden. My city no longer stands alone against the beastmen." Nareen placed her hands on the table before her, forcing them to unclench.

She ought to feel something—joy, relief, hope. Tork's report of the Matcassen expedition to Kalinden was good news, despite his veiled hints about the Lady Xyanth's motives. But somehow Nareen found it difficult to feel any great enthusiasm. If only . . .

"Threats can come from within, as well as from without."

Nareen raised her eyes to meet Tork's. Something in that direct gaze roused her from her indifference. "What do you mean?"

Tork hesitated, as though considering the wisdom of saying more. He glanced nervously over his shoulder at the closed door behind them, then said, "There are rumors that the beastmen are not acting alone. That they were paid to invade Kalinden."

"Paid?" Nareen stiffened in her chair, all indifference forgotten. "Who would pay them? What fool would deal with such murdering animals?"

Anger flooded her. Every child in Errandane knew what atrocities the beastmen were capable of. If anyone, for any reason, had dared incite their incursion into Kalinden . . .

"Well?" she demanded. "You cannot leave me with half a story, Runner Tork. Who is said to have paid them to invade Kalinden?"

There was no mistaking the fear in Tork's eyes. His determination to make her listen to his warnings had obviously led him to say far more than he'd planned. But he was committed. With a nervous glance to either side, as though he expected to find spies hidden behind the chairs, he croaked, "The Lady Xyanth."

"The Lady . . ."

Tork almost leaped across the table in his attempt to silence Nareen. "Not so loud," he hissed. "If her spies ever learned I had so much as hinted . . ." When he saw that Nareen understood, he took his hand from her mouth and sat back down.

"Do you have proof?" This time Nareen whispered, too, leaning across the table closer to Tork.

He shook his head. "Those who have proof are either in her pay—or dead." A muscle at the side of his mouth twitched. "But I have heard and observed, and I have drawn my own conclusions. Didn't I tell you the last time you were here that there are none who can learn more about what goes on than we do? Then listen."

Quickly Tork recounted his observations, detailing the facts he knew and clearly stating the deductions he'd made from the information he'd gleaned. In response to Nareen's occasional questions he would pause in his narrative to explain some of the inner workings of Lindaz' court and of his relationship with his wife.

At first Nareen struggled to discount Tork's story, trying to maintain the emotional distance required of a runner. But she didn't struggle long. He was a runner, too, trained to observe dispassionately and to remember accurately. He would not have risen to be Chief Runner for a city of Matcassen's importance if he had not been very good at his work. And his words had the frightening ring of truth.

At last Tork sat back. His face was gray, as though the recital had drained all his energy, and he suddenly looked older than he had an hour before.

Nareen's eyes dropped. Rage boiled within her, rage that anyone should have betrayed her city for their own ends, rage that creatures like Lindaz and Xyanth should exist, let alone wield the power they did.

And coupled with that rage was fear, not for herself, but for the people of Kalinden. Without proof, how could she convince anyone as Tork had convinced her? Who would believe so wild a story?

At last she raised her head to meet Tork's worried gaze. "What am I to do?" she asked.

Nareen rose early with the intention of leaving immediately for Kalinden, but official duties delayed her.

Matcassen's chief herdsman, a hulking, soft-voiced man, demanded she carry a detailed message to his counterpart in Kalinden. Given her urgent need to return home as quickly as possible, Nareen found it almost impossible to maintain her listening trance as the big man droned on about a hoof disease that had afflicted the aard herds of both Matcassen and Kalinden and for which he'd discovered a singularly unpleasant-sounding remedy.

Three advisors sent official messages to Xyanth and the advisors accompanying her. Nareen almost blurted out a refusal before she realized the opportunity being presented her. Even if the messages themselves had little value, delivering them would give her access to Xyanth and her court.

The thought that she was betraying her solemn oath as a runner never to use the information she carried for the gain of herself or others did not deter her. When it came to the safety of her city and its people, the people who had offered a home to a homeless orphan, she would betray any number of oaths.

Nareen's last task before leaving the Great Hall was to leave a written message for the advisor Danet. She had waited, hoping he would return so she might explain in person the loss of the ring he had entrusted to her, but she could wait no longer.

The words were hard to write. It had been difficult enough, given her injury, to pass the message she carried to a replacement. But injuries were always a possibility and there was no shame in handing the task to another. Losing the ring was another matter.

She gave the note to an attendant with firm instructions for its delivery, then checked her runner's belt once more to be sure everything was in order.

Mentally she reviewed the path she planned to follow. It would take a little longer—four days, perhaps—but be easier to travel. For her people's sake, she wanted to be completely fit when she arrived in Kalinden.

Four days.

Alone.

Nareen shut her eyes, willing the hurt to go away. She breathed deeply, focusing her thoughts on the path ahead.

Alone.

Her eyes flew open. Enough! Once on the trail, with Kalinden ahead of her and the memory of Jerrel falling farther and farther behind, the hurting would end. It had to.

The main steps to the Great Hall were usually crowded with people, but after the last attack against Lindaz the guards had received orders to let only those with clearly stated business into the Hall. The decree had not been well received. Angry merchants and travelers swarmed about the guards ringing the base of the steps, demanding entry.

Intent only on making her way through the

crowd, Nareen was startled to hear her name called. She paused, scanning the sea of faces before her, until her attention was caught by a man waving from the far edge of the steps.

"Norvag!" She changed her direction and pushed past an irate guard arguing with a cluster of equally irate tradesmen, then stopped in front of Norvag. "What are you doing here?"

Nareen couldn't help but glance around her, looking for one other face in the crowd. She tried to ignore the sharp stab of disappointment that lanced through her when she didn't find a pair of blue eyes staring back at her.

"I was hoping you hadn't left yet." Norvag seemed pleased to see her, yet embarrassed, as well. "The guard wouldn't give me any information. They're not letting much of anyone in the Hall."

"No." Nareen wasn't sure what to say. Norvag had been kind to her and she liked him, but he wasn't the one she wanted to see. "I must be going—I have messages for Kalinden. Was there something you wanted?"

"Jerrel . . . I . . ." Norvag swallowed uncomfortably. "Jerrel is now going to Kalinden, as well. I thought you might take him with you."

Chapter 9

"Take him ... !" At Norvag's words, Nareen stopped short. Keeping her face carefully expressionless, she said, "He's decided to help Kalinden? He'll help us fight the beastmen?"

Despite Nareen's outward calm, hope flared within her. Had he reconsidered? Had he realized that what lay between them was something more than just a few days' entertainment on a wearying journey? Had he ... ?

"I don't know. But if you talk to him ..." Norvag took her arm, tugging her, unresisting, along the crowded street. "He's determined to go. I thought, perhaps—"

Nareen stopped dead in her tracks, jerking her arm free of Norvag's grip. "He didn't send you to find me." The small, brief hope crumbled and faded away.

"No, but ..."

"I have my duty, Norvag, and messages to carry. I cannot let myself be delayed. Tell him to follow the main road—it's his best chance to find another caravan."

The thought of the caravan, of the close, intimate quarters of the wagon, stabbed at her.

Ignoring Norvag's protests, Nareen started walking swiftly, forcing her way past people without thought to common courtesies. Beside her, Norvag struggled to keep pace, at times almost hopping on his one good leg in his effort to follow her through the crowded streets.

"If you would talk to him . . ."

"I did."

"He has a reason for what he does, you know."

"As do I. My city is at risk and I must return. If he isn't coming to Kalinden to help fight the beastmen, there's no reason for me to delay my journey on his behalf."

Nareen careened off a stumpy, broad-backed man pushing a cart stacked with crude pottery. He turned to curse her in a thick coastal accent, but she was already past him and didn't care. She wanted to run, but without an escort she couldn't force her way through the streets any faster than she already was.

Yet no matter how fast she ran, she wouldn't be able to put this hurting behind her. Jerrel hadn't wanted to accompany her. He hadn't even wanted to join her after his own task was completed. He hadn't wanted *her*, and that was all that mattered.

"At least talk to him. For a few minutes, no more." This time Norvag grabbed her arm with both hands. Ignoring her attempts to free herself, he dragged Nareen through the crowds, then down a side street.

The old man might not be able to move very fast, but he wasn't weak. Nareen couldn't break free of his grip. Despite her protests, she soon found herself climbing a wide, dark interior stairway to the second floor of an inn not far from the main thoroughfare. They stopped in front of a door halfway down the heavily shadowed hall.

Norvag knocked twice. He was about to knock again when the door was jerked open abruptly.

Jerrel was big, much bigger than most men on Errandane. In the cramped wagon he'd seemed enormous. But never had he seemed as threatening as he did standing in the doorway with the light from the windows behind him casting his powerful figure into relief. Even in the dark hallway Nareen could clearly discern the angry scowl upon his face.

She wanted to run, to turn and flee like any coward, but she couldn't. Despite the scowl, despite the menacing stance, the mere sight of him was sufficient to make her breath catch in her throat and her heart start pounding in her chest as though it would break free of her imprisoning body.

In that moment, Nareen knew she was lost.

"We'll rest here for a few hours." Nareen waved toward a shadowed thicket at one side of the path. She and Jerrel had left Matcassen early that morning. Though they'd maintained a steady pace, they hadn't traveled as far as she'd hoped. "The bushes will provide shelter and the stream has good water. When the half-moon comes up, we'll go on."

"Running? In the dark?" Jerrel's disbelief came

through clearly even though his voice was harsh with his uneven panting.

"We won't go any faster than we've been traveling, but at this slow pace we can't stop often or we'll never reach Kalinden." Nareen shrugged, even though she knew Jerrel couldn't see the gesture clearly in the dark. At least he could hear the indifference in her voice. He need never know what it cost her to keep up that protective facade.

Jerrel said something, but Nareen couldn't make out what it was. He'd used a lot of unfamiliar words during the course of the day, especially during the last few hours. Most of those words had sounded suspiciously like curses of one form or another. The man seemed to have a rather extensive vocabulary in that respect, but she hadn't asked for clarification.

Nareen unfastened the water jug from her belt. At least they could be sure of good water on this path and so didn't need to carry the weight of extra jugs. Even so, the clear, cold water of the stream would be welcome. It had been a long day. After a week and a half of inactivity she wasn't completely ready for an extended run and was more tired than she ought to be.

Behind her, Jerrel released a weary sigh and, from the sounds, collapsed on the ground. Nareen grinned to herself in the dark. She might be tired, but Jerrel, a man strong enough to lift her with one hand, was exhausted. That knowledge gave her an odd sense of satisfaction—and of power.

She emptied the jug's contents on the ground, then refilled it from the stream. After a few quick sips to quench her thirst, but without drinking enough to weight her stomach, Nareen rose and carried the jug to where Jerrel lay stretched out along the path, his head propped against a rock.

"Here," she said, squatting down beside him and extending the jug. "Don't take very much. It's cold and you're not. But it will help."

Jerrel opened his eyes wearily, then forced himself into a sitting position and took the water from her. "Thanks." He was still panting fairly heavily.

"Take a sip and warm it in your mouth first," Nareen warned. "You don't want that cold water to hit your stomach when you're still this hot."

"What I want is a good, strong ale. Or three." He sighed but did as she instructed, then handed the jug back to her. "If I'd had any idea what traveling with you would mean, I'd never have let Norvag talk me into this. I must be getting as crazy as he is."

In the dark and drooping with tiredness, Jerrel seemed a good deal less threatening than he had that morning. Nareen settled into a cross-legged position on the ground beside him.

"I wanted to ask," she said curiously, "what did you mean when you were talking about transporting through the ship? There are no ships around here and the nearest port is almost three weeks away, even for the strongest runner."

"I said that?" With a groan, Jerrel leaned back against the rock he'd chosen for a pillow and closed his eyes. "Forget I said that. It was a joke."

"A joke?"

"Yeah." He didn't bother to open his eyes. "Now can we go to sleep? I have a horrible feeling you're going to wake me up about two days before I'm going to be ready."

Nareen chuckled, then rose to her feet. "You'd better wrap up in that blanket you brought. You don't want your muscles to stiffen because of the cold. And the dead leaves under the bushes will keep you warmer and make a softer bed than the path."

Jerrel made no effort to move until he was sure Nareen had settled down herself. Then he slowly came back up into a sitting position.

A joke. It was a joke, all right. On him.

He'd planned on transporting back up to his ship, then down to an empty field or open space near Kalinden. The whole process would have taken a couple of seconds. No one would have noticed him, any more than they'd noticed his and Norvag's arrival near Anweigh what seemed an age ago.

Instead, Norvag had upset all his plans by showing up with that damned, annoying, irresistible, tormenting woman in tow. One look at Nareen's face had convinced him she was no happier about the arrangement than he was. Yet somehow Jerrel had found himself incapable of saying no to Norvag's outrageous suggestion that he accompany her to Kalinden.

Jerrel sighed, then stretched out his legs and began massaging the muscles of his thighs and calves. They were beginning to cramp from the cold.

This was crazy. He'd carried more than half his weight in supplies and weapons on a forced march through one of the most deadly jungles in the galaxy, and endured days with little water and no food as he and a companion fought their way over a rugged range of mountains that had claimed more than a few explorers' lives. He'd even spent a month as a slave at the oars in the huge galleys of Zakeb IV before Norvag had been able to stage a diversion and give him a chance to escape.

None of those adventures had been as physically exhausting as one day spent trying to keep up with a fleet-footed Errandane runner half his size. And only getting taken as a slave on Zakeb IV had been stupider.

Jerrel sighed again, then slowly rose to his feet. Logic and common sense had played no part in his decision to travel with Nareen. He'd growled and grumbled and protested, but in the end he'd given in to Norvag's proposal. All for the chance to spend four more days with a woman who had scarcely spoken to him since they'd left Matcassen.

And about all he'd seen of her since then were her heels.

"I told you to keep warm, not to let your muscles get cold." Nareen stood in the moonlight, hands on hips, glaring at the shadowy form of Jerrel propped against a rock.

"They didn't get cold. They got stiff," Jerrel snapped. He tried to force his right leg to straighten, then groaned. Stiff didn't go far enough to describe the state his legs were in.

"I said you weren't fit enough to travel with me. But you insisted."

"*Norvag* insisted. And I was too dumb to say no." Jerrel straightened his left leg, with the same results. "I'll have you know I could carry *two* of you from Matcassen to Kalinden without breaking into a heavy sweat."

"But you can't *run* that distance. There's a difference. You weigh too much."

"What do you mean I weigh too much?" Jerrel

started to rise to his feet in indignation, then immediately thought better of it.

"Too much muscle. You're built for power and endurance, not speed." Nareen was tapping her foot against the ground in impatience. "There's a reason most runners are about my size. I told you—"

"Then you don't need to tell me again!" Jerrel bent to massage the calf of his right leg. He winced as the overworked muscles protested against his prodding fingers. "If you want to do something useful, come work on my other leg."

For an instant, Nareen hesitated. She didn't want to touch him, didn't even want to get close. But the sooner they were on the trail again, the sooner they would reach Kalinden and she would be free of him.

With a grumble of disgust she knelt beside him and wrapped her hands around the calf of his left leg. She might have to help him but she didn't have to like it. Her fingers dug deep into the swell of muscle.

"Ow! What are you trying to do, cripple me even more?" Jerrel's leg jerked but he was too stiff to break free of her grasp.

"It's a technique all runners learn when they first enter training. It hurts, but it's effective." She pulled his leg back to her, pushed the soft leather top of his boot even further down around his ankle, and began working her fingers up the line of bone and flesh to the back of his knee, then down again.

"I hope you're right about its being effective," Jerrel grumbled, turning his attention back to his right leg, "because you're sure right about it hurting."

"You complain more than a suckling child," Nareen jeered, but she kept her head down and her attention on her task.

After a few minutes, Jerrel asked hesitantly, "Would you mind working on my other leg, too? Whatever you're doing, it seems to be helping."

In the pale light of the half-moon Nareen found it impossible to read any expression on his face. She couldn't hear any hint of mockery in his voice. Without speaking, she shifted her position so that she knelt between his legs and began working on the other calf.

As she worked, Nareen found her tension draining away. There was no risk in touching him like this. Under other circumstances, the moonlight and the soft murmurings of the nearby stream might have been considered romantic. But the night was cold, though still, and Jerrel, rather than whispering passionate words of love, was grunting every now and then as her fingers probed an especially stiff spot in his muscles. Hardly conducive to an impassioned interlude.

Nareen moved her hands up Jerrel's right leg, past his knee to his thigh. Even with both hands she couldn't circle his leg—the muscles were too massive, too powerful.

Her fingers probed the curves of his thigh, searching for the key points where her fingers could do the most good. It wasn't easy to find the right spots because his muscles were naturally rock-hard from years of exercise and the soft leather of his leggings shifted under her touch.

As she worked, Nareen kept her head down and her eyes on her task. In the moonlight her hands shone pale silver against the dark leather of Jerrel's clothing. Her ministrations would be far more effective if only he weren't wearing the leggings. The warmth of her hands rubbing against his skin . . .

Nareen froze.

"I'd like to learn the trick of this someday." Jerrel's voice had an odd catch in it.

He shifted slightly, then leaned forward so that his face was only inches from hers. Nareen could feel the heat of his body, could almost imagine his breath against her cheek. She stiffened, then bent to tend the thigh of his other leg, carefully ignoring him.

"Any runner can teach you," she said. Her fingers were trembling. To disguise her weakness, she dug deep into the major muscle at the back of his thigh, making him flinch.

"I hope they'd be a little more gentle."

Nareen could hear the humor, but beneath that was something else, something . . . Regret, perhaps? Was he pleading with her? She moved her hands higher, kneading his muscles with the tips of her fingers, the heels of her hands.

"It isn't a gentle process," she said with a grunt as she tried to force the stiffened muscle to ease. Still she did not look up.

For a moment Jerrel said nothing, then, very softly, "No. I don't suppose it is."

But it could be! Nareen longed to cry, *Oh, it could be!* Instead, she bit down on her lower lip, then moved her hands higher.

Jerrel's hands suddenly covered hers, pressing them against his thigh. Was it her imagination, or was his hand trembling? She couldn't tell. He pressed down harder, making it impossible for her to move, then pulled her hands free, forcing her around so she faced him.

Nareen tried to free herself—to no avail. Her head came up, and for the first time since she'd begun massaging his legs she looked directly at him.

His face was shadowed but his eyes glittered dangerously. His voice had an unexpectedly hoarse, choked note. "I thank you for your help," he said, "but I think I can manage now."

By the early morning of the third day both Nareen and Jerrel were moving easily. The steady exercise had finally worked out the last soreness.

Jerrel had settled into a steady pace that was faster than he'd ever run for so long a journey but that was still clearly slower than Nareen would normally have traveled. Though he no longer had to struggle as hard to keep up, she moved ahead of him with an easy grace that allowed her to bound over obstacles and up rocky hillsides as though they scarcely existed. When they stopped to rest she recovered faster than he did, and she needed far less water or food.

Even more amazing was her awareness of everything around them and her ability to remember clearly what they'd passed. Where he saw a muddied path, she saw the passage of six aards and one aard calf, accompanied by their herdsman. The clump of scraggly, low-growing trees they'd run past in a matter of minutes was nothing more than scraggly trees to him. Nareen had noted that bark from two of the trees had been stripped only a few days before, which meant that someone in a nearby holding had given birth recently, and that the mother was not well and needed medicinal baths the midwife would prepare from the dried bark.

For the first time Jerrel began to appreciate the valuable role a runner played in a world that possessed neither fast animals to carry riders and messages, nor technical means of communication. Nareen, and others like her, not only had to be superb athletes capable of remembering, word for word, any message they carried, they also had to be intelligent, observant, fully knowledgeable about the world around them, and totally trustworthy, as well. Even the most highly trained Imperial soldiers on Arcana would be incapable of carrying out the tasks Nareen accepted so calmly as part of her work.

Jerrel paused at the base of a trail snaking up the side of a steep hill and shook his head in wonder, watching Nareen spring from rock to rock, seemingly without effort. He could run up the hill, he could even jog up slowly with a heavy pack on his back, but he would never manage it as easily as she did.

As he started up the hill after her, Jerrel had to admit he was glad they were only a few hours away from Kalinden. The strenuous exercise of running almost continuously for three days may have forced him to concentrate more on the trail than on the woman who led him, but it hadn't been enough to erase his need for her.

It also hadn't been enough to make him change his mind. He wanted her, needed her, more than he'd ever wanted or needed a woman in his life. And, despite her hurt and anger at his refusal to join Kalinden's fight against the beastmen, he knew she still wanted him. But wanting and needing weren't enough to bridge the gulf that yawned between them and their two very different lives, different worlds. When they reached Kalinden . . .

"Don't come any farther!" The words were little more than a whisper, but there was no mistaking the urgent command they carried.

Jerrel jerked to a halt, uncertain who had spoken. His attention had been so fixed on the path that he hadn't noticed Nareen scrambling back down the trail toward him.

She stopped only a few feet above him. "Don't ask questions and don't talk. Just follow me." Her voice hadn't risen in volume, but the tension that vibrated in the words was enough to make him do as she asked.

Without another word, Nareen spun about and started back. This time, however, she climbed the rugged rocks at the side of the trail, carefully working her way upward. Within just a few minutes they were well above the trail and half-hidden in the jumbled boulders.

Jerrel had just about caught up with Nareen when she froze, her attention caught by something she'd heard or seen on the section of the trail that was now below them. She cocked her head, evidently listening intently, then dropped to the ground and scuttled behind a low wall of rock, motioning Jerrel to do likewise.

Instantly complying, Jerrel crouched behind a massive, rounded boulder that would shield him from any curious eyes on the trail, then wormed his way across to Nareen's side.

She turned her head toward him, her finger over her mouth to remind him not to speak. The warning was unnecessary. Whatever she had seen or heard was serious enough to make her eyes go round with fear and her jaws clench in rage.

The hairs at the back of Jerrel's neck rose. He moved closer so they were only inches apart and silently mouthed a question, "What is it?"

At that instant voices—harsh, guttural voices—rose from somewhere on the trail beneath their vantage point. A stone, undoubtedly dislodged by a clumsy foot, clattered against other stones as it rolled down the hill.

Nareen leaned closer, putting her mouth next to his ear. "Beastmen," she said. "And we're less than four hours away from Kalinden."

Chapter 10

More voices rose from below them. Jerrel glanced at Nareen. Her fear was still there but it was under control, just as it had been once before, when she'd faced an enraged and murderous drevon to save the life of a man she'd never met.

This time, however, it wasn't just raw courage that drove her. In her eyes, in the set of her jaw and the tension in the muscles of her neck and shoulders, was an anger that burned deep and fierce.

She motioned him to stay put, then cautiously slid forward until she could peer over an outcropping of rock.

Ignoring Nareen's command to stay where he was and careful to make as little sound as possible, Jerrel slid forward until he, too, could peer around the protective rocks to see who—or what—was passing below.

Jerrel's gut tightened and he blinked.

Beastman was a far more appropriate term than he had realized. Only from a distance would the creatures below ever be mistaken for humans.

They were massive, at least as tall as he was and weighing a good two or three stone more. Their powerful arms were shorter than a man's but far more muscular and ended in broad, three-fingered, clawed hands that looked capable of crushing small stones. In contrast, their legs were proportionately longer than a man's would be, which made them look thinner, even though they weren't. The beastmen's torsos were short and massive, topped by huge heads set on thick necks. Such bulk on top of the long legs gave them the appearance of a nircka bird, though Jerrel seriously doubted they were as gentle, or half as good to eat, as a nircka.

Their heads were huge. Two eyes set close together high on their foreheads were protected on both sides by bony ridges that joined just above the eye sockets, then ran across the top of their skulls. So far as Jerrel could tell from above, they had no noses. Their mouths were large, almost stretching from one side of their face to the other, and filled with unpleasantly sharp-looking teeth.

They wore no clothes, but from the appearance of their hair-roughened, dark-brown skin, they didn't need any. Vests or belts slung across their chests seemed to be used more to carry supplies and weapons—primarily knives and crude spears, so far as Jerrel could tell—than as protection or adornment. Which must have made it easier to bathe—if they ever bothered, Jerrel thought in disgust. Their stench reached all the way to his and Nareen's perch over a hundred feet above them.

It was clear the beastmen were some of the original inhabitants of Errandane and not brigands driven off from human settlements, as he'd first supposed. They must have been formidable opponents to the first human settlers. And now that those settlers' descendants had lost all knowledge of the advanced weaponry their ancestors brought with them, the beastmen would be even more dangerous.

Thirty-six of them, Jerrel counted, not including the ten or so that must have passed before he got his first view of them. They moved slowly and seemed rather clumsy, but probably made up in strength and endurance whatever they lacked in speed.

As the last sounds of the beastmen died away, Jerrel rose to his knees and would have stood if Nareen had not jerked on his arm and pulled him back down. Jerrel started to protest—he'd forgotten her presence entirely, so absorbed had he been in studying the beastmen—when she put her finger to her mouth again and hissed at him for silence.

Several minutes passed without a sound. Jerrel was growing stiff and impatient. He was on the point of getting up, regardless of what Nareen thought, when her head came up suddenly, as though she'd heard something. Jerrel strained but could hear nothing and was about to say so when he caught it, too—the almost imperceptible sound of bare feet against stone.

One beastman, then a second, came into view below. Both were moving far more quietly and cautiously than the group that had gone before. Both held long and very lethal-looking spears in addition to knives and shorter spears like those their companions had carried.

Out of the corner of his eye Jerrel caught a flash, as of sun on steel. It took him a minute to realize there were other beastmen—three or four, at least—spread out lower down on the hillside and moving with the same caution. At that distance, their dark skin blended with the rocks so they became hard to see.

And if they were on the hill below . . . Jerrel shifted so he could look up at the hill above them. He couldn't see anything. A huge, overhanging rock blocked all view up the hill—as it must block any view of their hiding place for anyone, or anything, above them. For the first time he realized how carefully Nareen must have chosen their hiding place. And she'd only had a few minutes to find any cover at all.

Nareen caught his glance and clearly understood its meaning. "It's all right," she mouthed, then motioned for him to keep down.

Obediently Jerrel lowered his head and returned his attention to what little he could see below. The beastmen he'd spotted earlier had moved out of sight. So far as he could tell, none had taken their places.

Silently he cursed himself. He should have been more alert. It was fine to rely on someone else who knew the countryside better than he did, but that didn't relieve him of the need to be vigilant as well.

After what seemed an eternity, Nareen released a soft sigh and slowly rose to a sitting position. "There won't be any more. At least not until we reach Kalinden."

"How can you be so sure?" Jerrel's words were

sharper than he'd intended.

"There were about fifty beasts in that group. They won't form groups any larger than that, and no group will hunt anywhere near another group." Disgust was clearly mixed with anger in her voice, disgust and something else Jerrel couldn't identify. Loathing? From the color of her complexion, she'd been close to being sick.

"What were they hunting?"

"You didn't see?" Nareen looked at him in disbelief.

"See what?"

"The blood. On their hides, their hands."

"But they weren't carrying hunting weapons. And I didn't see any of them carrying any game . . ." Jerrel's voice died away.

"You don't know, do you?" Nareen's voice died away. She swallowed. Hard. "They were hunting people."

Jerrel paused on the rocky hilltop, his gaze sweeping the windblown heights of the mountains before him. They were called the Troodons, he knew, thanks to the information gathered by Santar and Danet and passed to him via their ships' computers. And they were the home of the beastmen. At least, that was what he'd learned from Nareen. He hadn't wanted to display his ignorance by asking too many questions.

Beneath the looming mass of the mountains, perched on a rocky promontory like a brooding bird of prey, was Kalinden. The city was smaller than Matcassen, but its walls were higher and thicker.

The beastmen would have a hard time overcoming Kalinden's defenses, Jerrel decided, studying the city's position. But Kalinden wasn't impregnable, and if the beastmen's depredations on the surrounding countryside were prolonged . . .

He shuddered. After their encounter with the hunting group that morning, Nareen had followed the beastmen's trail back to the holding they'd raided. Or rather, what was left of the holding—a few walls and the remnants of the corrals.

The marauders had slaughtered everyone and everything they found, hacking their victims unmercifully long after they were dead.

In his years of roaming the galaxy, Jerrel had come upon similar scenes of destruction, but never any more senseless. Without speaking, he and Nareen had set about burying the family of five, wrapping the mutilated bodies in what scraps of blankets or sheets they could find and laying them, one by one, in the shallow graves which were all they could scratch out of the holding's frozen ground.

At first, he tried to persuade Nareen to leave the sad task to him, to no avail. She hadn't spoken, but in the blazing green fire of her eyes, in the whiteness of her face, he read her anger—and her resolve for vengeance.

Only once did Nareen break her silence. As she knelt to place the blanket-wrapped body of the smallest child, a boy of about seven, in its grave, Jerrel heard her murmur, "If she truly is responsible for this, then she will pay for it. I swear."

The task of filling in the graves and then covering them with stones was accomplished quickly. As he rose from placing the last stone, Jerrel said, very quietly, without expecting an answer, "I wonder who they were."

"The family of Nacintor the weaver. He was originally from the city of Narlon, but when he married Jamila he inherited her family's holding, so they settled here. Their firstborn, Jamilita, would have been eighteen next year, old enough to be offered in marriage." Nareen's words were flat, emotionless. Her eyes were fixed on the five mounds of rock in front of her.

"You knew them?"

She shook her head. "I never met them, but I knew them as a runner knows everyone on every holding ruled by their city. They were of Kalinden. They were my people."

Her voice died away and she turned from him, her gaze fixed on the mountains rising on the horizon. The wind picked up strands of her black hair, blowing them across her face and into her eyes, but she paid no attention.

Jerrel said nothing. He wanted to go to her, to comfort her, but he had no words to offer that would not sound as hollow and cold as the winter wind about them.

Her people. Such simple words to carry such depth of meaning. Nareen had never met this weaver and his family, yet she knew them. Their deaths mattered because they were her people. She, an abandoned orphan, had found a home, a place where she belonged in a world where everyone had a name and a history, where the loss of one could touch the whole.

Strange, the tricks life played. Jerrel's mouth twisted in a wry grimace. He, who had begun life as the cherished first son of a noble and powerful house on a planet that ruled an empire, had no world, no home, no family. His brother was missing and possibly dead, and the only man he could truly call a friend was too old to accompany him on his travels much longer. Jerrel glanced down at the rock-covered graves. When death caught up to him, it would probably be on some forgotten planet whose name he scarcely knew. There would be no one to mourn his passing, no one to say, *This was Jerrel bn'Hadar—I knew him*. Perhaps no one even to dig his grave.

Jerrel stirred, suddenly angry at himself. He'd never been given to morbid thoughts and now was not the time to start. Crossing to Nareen, he gently touched her arm. "We should go. There is nothing more we can do here."

At his touch Nareen sighed, then blinked as her eyes focused on the world in front of her. She nodded, once, then settled her runner's belt comfortably about her waist and headed for the path that would take them to Kalinden.

Now, with the vast gray bulk of Kalinden looming above them at last, Nareen began to run more swiftly. The grim determination emanating from her was almost physical. Jerrel knew she'd almost forgotten his presence, did not realize he'd paused and that she was leaving him behind. Shaking off his thoughts, Jerrel sprinted down the trail in pursuit.

Could it be possible . . . ? How could anyone . . . ? Would the Lady Xyanth really . . . ? The questions had churned in Nareen's brain, around and around and around, until the words were like a chant, matching the beat of her rapid footfalls on the trail.

If a hunting group of beastmen had worked their way south of Kalinden, what destruction had they wrought on the holdings to the north and west that were closer to the border and even more vulnerable? When she'd left Kalinden for Matcassen with Master Gasperian's plea for help, other runners had been setting out to warn the small crofters and the people of the holdings of the danger. By now, if all had gone well, those people should have gathered in the small villages or around the fortified gold and silver mines where they would have more protection. Many, undoubtedly, would have moved into Kalinden itself, seeking the even greater protection of the city's walls.

Behind her she heard Jerrel's heavy tread, matching her stride for stride. For a warrior and a man of his size, he'd held up well under the demands of their journey.

For the thousandth time she wondered what it was that had brought him to Kalinden, after all. It wasn't her, of that she was certain, although the fire that had flamed between them in the caravan wagon still burned fiercely.

But just as she had avoided him, choosing instead to concentrate on the trail ahead of them, he had avoided her. Since that first night when she'd made the mistake of trying to help ease his stiff muscles, he'd said little. During their few, brief pauses to sleep, he'd chosen to make his bed at some distance from hers, and when they stopped to eat he kept his attention focused on the dried fruit and meat that constituted their only fare.

Whatever his reasons, she reminded herself yet once again, they didn't matter. He had made his choice, she had made hers. Now, after seeing firsthand the threat the beastmen posed, there was no going back. Her city needed her; her people needed her. Jerrel did not. And that was all that mattered.

The first of the signal bells was just ahead. Nareen pulled her runner's dagger from her belt, then shifted it in her hand so she could strike the bell with the heavy haft as she passed. Without breaking her stride, she swung, giving the bell a far harder blow than was really necessary.

The bell rang loudly, its clear, metallic tones echoing and re-echoing on the surrounding hills. "A runner comes," its ringing said. "Open the gates and make way. A runner comes!"

Close behind Nareen, Jerrel winced as the sound assaulted his ears. The signal system made sense, allowing the gatekeepers to verify who was approaching and be ready to open for a messenger without wasting time, but it was hard on the ears of anyone unfortunate enough to be near a struck bell.

Even as he ran, Jerrel studied the steep approach to the city. Whoever had originally built the fortifications had chosen well. Where Matcassen and Anweigh had been built on broad plains with wide roads leading to their gates—clear indications of their roles as trading centers—Kalinden was remote and difficult of access, a perfect outpost for a land bordering on territory held by the enemy. No enemy could approach without being seen in advance. Not even the beastmen. And those savage creatures would have a hard time felling the massive stone walls that now towered above them at the top of the cliff.

Six bells, and at every one Nareen seemed to go faster, despite the steep path. Heads poked over the battlements, checking to see who rang the signal bells so loudly. The cries of the guards came clearly to their ears. "It is the Sixth Runner!" "The runner Nareen has returned, and someone with her!" "Open the gates! Be ready!"

As Nareen and Jerrel crossed the last few hundred yards of open space at the top of the cliff, a door opened in the main gates, large enough to admit one person at a time and no more. Nareen sailed through the opening easily. Jerrel had to duck, which threw his stride off. By the time he recovered, Nareen was already well away from the gates and racing across the cobblestoned plaza. In front of her ran three guards whose task it was to open a path for her through the streets.

"Make way!" they shouted. "Make way for a runner!"

Jerrel had time to gather nothing more than a blurred impression of what seemed like hundreds of people milling about the plaza with a contingent of armed soldiers arrayed near the gates, before he dashed off to catch up with Nareen and her escort. They obviously weren't going to wait for him, and he had no desire to try and fight his way alone to the Great Hall through Kalinden's crowded streets.

As they got deeper into the city their pace slowed. Even though the throngs of people were quick to move to each side of the narrow streets when they heard the escorts' cries, it still wasn't possible to progress at anything faster than a jog trot.

Though he could tell that Nareen was irritated by the necessary delay, Jerrel was grateful for the chance it gave him to recover his breath a little and to look about him.

His first and most vivid impression was that Kalinden was far more colorful than the drab, dirty Matcassen. Brilliantly colored pennants hung above a number of the shop doors, their color and design an indication of what was sold within. Potted flowers and bright curtains showed in the windows of rooms on the second and third floors of the narrow buildings, providing a vivid contrast to the gray stone and dark timbers of the buildings themselves. The people in the streets seemed to prefer bright hues for their clothes, as well, for even those garbed in the coarsest of brown homespun wore a bright scarf or woven belt.

It was, thought Jerrel, as though they were determined to counteract the gray harshness of the land around them with their own bright display. Having himself come from a world that reveled in color, he could appreciate their outlook. Given the threat that hung over them, it seemed an almost forced display of optimism.

The Great Hall lay in what appeared to be the exact center of the city, a massive building of gray stone to match the solid walls that protected the city itself. Jerrel had no time for more than a quick appraisal of the outside of the structure, but he noted the high, narrow windows and solidly built doors. It appeared the Hall was intended as a fortress as much as a seat of government.

Their escorts' warning cries assured their entrance into the Hall. Once inside, the group came to a halt. A man dressed in robes that indicated some sort of official function greeted Nareen and exchanged words with her that Jerrel couldn't hear above the babble around them, then scuttled off into the crowd.

The three men who had escorted them snapped to attention, then departed. Jerrel, still panting, stepped to Nareen's side. She paid him not the slightest attention.

187

Seemingly oblivious to her surroundings and to him, she straightened, closed her eyes, then brought her hands to her face so that her fingers pressed against her forehead, thumbs pointing outward. She took a deep breath, held it, then slowly released it before repeating the process.

By the time the official returned to gesture her forward, her breathing had stilled and all expression had been washed from her face.

Jerrel had seen similar techniques to control the body and focus the mind used on a dozen worlds. He himself had tried to learn to do it a number of times but had always been too impatient to master the process.

Nareen and the official crossed the main entranceway and passed through wide double doors standing open at the far side. Jerrel followed them into a huge, two-storied chamber that clearly served as the main hall. At the far end a massive carved wood chair dominated the room from a raised dais.

The chair was occupied by a man engaged in conversation with several heavily armed men clustered around him. At Nareen's appearance, the group on the dais broke apart, leaving the seated man alone.

Uncertain what was expected of him but anxious to hear every word of Nareen's report, Jerrel followed her into the hall. No one tried to stop him. It seemed the reception granted to runners was extended to anyone who accompanied them.

As Nareen passed through the crowd, murmuring conversations broke out in her wake. When she came to a halt at the foot of the dais, all conversation stopped and the hall fell quiet.

"Master Gasperian." Her face still calm and

expressionless, Nareen touched the fingers of her right hand to her forehead, then sank to one knee on the carpeted steps leading up to the dais. "I bring messages to you and to Kalinden."

"Sixth Runner." Gasperian's voice was deep and carried well in the cavernous hall.

From his position slightly behind Nareen and to one side of the steps, Jerrel could see Gasperian's eyes, black and shadowed in their deep sockets, studying the motionless runner. The Master of Kalinden was a man well past middle age, thin but still strong and fit. His shoulder-length black hair was heavily streaked with gray, as was his closely trimmed beard. Though he was an imposing presence, he was of no more than average height. Unlike much of his court, who were dressed in colorful robes of woven fabric, Gasperian wore a long, sleeveless leather coat over leather leggings and a plain, full-sleeved, collarless shirt that were much like Jerrel's own clothes. A highly serviceable-looking knife with a haft of worked gold was tucked into the Master's wide leather belt. On the second finger of his right hand he wore a massive gold ring that seemed, so far as Jerrel could see, to be his only badge of office.

After a pause, Gasperian spoke again, the disapproval clear in his voice. "You were expected at least nine days ago, runner. We feared you had met with an accident or been attacked. Were it not for the arrival of the Lady Xyanth and her troops, we would not even have known that you reached Matcassen." Gasperian let his words hang heavy in the air, then said, "Explain yourself."

Nareen's face was impassive. "I reached Matcassen, Master, in only two days. But Master

189

Lindaz refused to send help to Kalinden. At his instructions, I left Matcassen for Anweigh in an effort to seek assistance."

"Refused . . . Impossible! The Edict of Trassdeance requires . . ." Gasperian stopped, then regained control of himself with an effort. "Master Lindaz has not refused his help, as is evidenced by his sending his own Lady at the head of his troops. And I cannot believe that he would consider sending you to Anweigh when the law requires he send a Matcassen runner."

Nareen said nothing and did not move, but Jerrel thought he detected a slight flush on her cheeks.

"If you carried a message to Anweigh, Sixth Runner, how does it come about that you are already returned to Kalinden?" Gasperian spoke slowly, never taking his dark, glittering gaze off Nareen.

"I did not reach Anweigh, Master." In a few words Nareen recounted the tale of her encounter with the drevon, her injury, and return to Matcassen on Merchant Baecknar's caravan. She gestured toward Jerrel without looking away from the silent Gasperian. "This man, who is called Jerrel, saved my life, provided a runner to carry my message on to Anweigh, and bought passage for me on the caravan since I was scarcely able to walk, let alone run."

Gasperian turned his head slightly to study Jerrel. A good ruler, Jerrel thought as he met the man's black-eyed gaze. Intelligent, strong. Probably just and generous, but inflexible, and rigid in his adherence to rules.

"If you have served a Kalinden runner, sir, we thank you," said Gasperian formally. He turned his attention back to Nareen. "However, none of this excuses you from your responsibilities, runner. But we will speak of this later. What news do you bring, and what messages?"

At Gasperian's words, an old man dressed in a plain woven tunic, shirt, and leggings vaguely resembling a runner's costume stepped forward. He looked to be shorter than Nareen. Despite his years, he had the lean, wiry build of a runner. As Nareen started to speak, his eyes glazed over. Throughout her report he remained staring straight ahead and unmoving.

"I carry a message for herdsman Porza which can wait until later, and messages for the Lady Xyanth. The message from Master Lindaz, or, rather, the report of his words, I prefer to leave for a more private report, Master, as well as information that cannot be shared here." Nareen's voice carried clearly through the hall, though she had not moved and seemed to make no effort to speak very loudly. "But I have news that must be known by all."

In the same precise way that she had reported her journey, Nareen told of seeing the beastmen and of the devastation at Nacintor the weaver's holding. To Jerrel's surprise, she also mentioned the evidence of a birth in another holding, and provided other information about the conditions of the land through which they'd traveled.

When she'd finished, Nareen rose to her feet. The old man on the dais slowly roused from his listening trance, then quietly stepped back.

"You don't seem to have noticed much on your journeying, runner," Gasperian said.

Jerrel found it impossible to detect any emotion in the man's voice. He glanced at Nareen and was surprised to find an obvious, angry flush creeping up her throat.

"I observed much, but it will be of little use if the beastmen pass through. What value is it to know of the condition of the high pastures if there will be no aards to graze them, and no herdsmen to care?"

A number of listeners reacted to the defiance in Nareen's voice with gasps or exclamations of surprise. Gasperian's only reaction was a small, humorless smile.

"You are right, of course," he said. He rose. "Come. You may give me the rest of your report in private."

Closely followed by the old man who had come forward during Nareen's recital, Gasperian crossed the dais and disappeared through a small door to one side.

Nareen turned to Jerrel. "Wait for me," she said, then spun back and dashed up the dais steps and after the two men.

Jerrel studied the people around him. With the departure of Gasperian, they were beginning to mill about, gathering into groups for low-voiced, urgent conversation. Without appearing to pay any attention to his surroundings he strained for any word, any scrap of information that might be of use in his search for his brother.

But even as he began aimlessly circulating through the crowd, Jerrel knew he wasn't staying in the hall with the hope of finding a clue to Santar's whereabouts.

She had said, "Wait for me," and he would wait.

Chapter 11

As Nareen followed Gasperian and her old teacher, Gravnar, to the Master's private chambers, she struggled to force down her anger and regain the calm, impersonal demeanor required of a runner.

Somehow she had to convince Gasperian not to dismiss Tork's warnings about Xyanth. And that wasn't going to be easy since the Master clearly believed she was lying about Lindaz' refusal to aid Kalinden.

Gravnar was holding open the door to the Master's chambers. As she entered, Nareen caught sight of the somber expression on her old teacher's face before he turned to shut the door behind them. For an instant she felt like a student again, dreading the inevitable lecture on letting her emotions run away with her.

But only for an instant. This was not the classroom, and she was not reporting on the state of the aard pastures.

Gasperian seated himself in a heavily carved chair placed at one side of a massive table loaded with papers, maps, and official documents. He said nothing for a moment, and his dark eyes gave nothing away as he studied Nareen where she stood before him.

"Your accusation that Master Lindaz refused to send troops to aid us, refused even to send a messenger to Anweigh, is a serious one, runner," Gasperian said at last. "Worse, the first part of your charge is refuted by the fact that he *did* send troops."

"I do not accuse, Master," Nareen said with dignity. "I merely report. If you like, I will repeat Master Lindaz' words so you may judge for yourself." At Gasperian's nod of consent, Nareen repeated, word for word, Lindaz' statements from her brief interview with him.

Gasperian frowned, clearly weighing Nareen's report against the proof of Xyanth's presence. "You said you had more information."

Nareen, uncertain how best to convey Tork's warning, hesitated. Once again the doubts that had plagued her throughout the three days' travel from Matcassen rose up before her. Tork might be wrong, or using her for purposes of his own. But the man had been afraid and he hadn't provided his information willingly. Why, after so many years of staying in their own rocky wastelands, had the beastmen come marauding again? And, always, there was the memory of Nacintor the weaver and his family . . .

"Sixth Runner?" Gasperian's left eyebrow had risen in cold inquiry.

"Your pardon, Master." With a quick glance at Gravnar, Nareen dropped into the reporting trance and gave her two silent listeners Tork's words of warning.

But even as she roused from the trance, Nareen realized it was not enough. They were only words, and words could not convey the emotions of the man himself as he broke his runner's oath, betrayed everything he represented, and spoke of fears and guesses and conclusions drawn from sparse information.

In her mind's eye she could see Tork's gestures and expressions, hear the tension and uncertainty in his voice, feel his determination. It was these intangibles, these all-too-human emotions that had, she realized now, convinced her he spoke the truth. And she could convey none of that to Gasperian and Gravnar. They heard the words, and the words alone. There was nothing else for them and so they would not, could not believe.

As the silence lengthened, Nareen felt weighted by her failure. Yet what could she do? As she watched Gasperian's impassive face, anger grew within her. She was a runner, and a good one. She had been trained to observe, and she was not a fool. Why couldn't they, at least this once, put aside their traditional conceptions of what a runner ought to be and listen to her?

At last Gasperian spoke, but his words caught Nareen by surprise.

"This man who accompanied you, this Jerrel." Gasperian stumbled over the unfamiliar name. "What is he to you?"

"Master?"

"I have followed you since you were in training, sixth runner," Gasperian continued coldly, "just as I follow all candidates for runner. I know your strengths." He paused, his eyes fixed on Nareen's face. "And your weaknesses."

Though she tried to maintain the calm, detached expression appropriate to a runner, Nareen could feel an angry flush begin to color her cheeks, just as it had in the reception hall.

"You tend to let your emotions influence you too much. As now, when you cannot repress your anger that I have not reacted to your information in the way you think I ought."

Nareen's color flared higher.

"Kalinden is at risk. I do not need to tell you that. My need for information—information I can *trust*—is greater than ever. I would not like to lose the services of one of my most promising runners."

Hope soared within Nareen, only to be crushed an instant later at the next hard words. "I do not know what made you think I might believe such wild tales of another Master and his Lady. It is inconceivable that *anyone* should ever consider dealing with the beastmen, especially anyone of their rank. I do not know what made you disregard your responsibilities as a runner so that you should delay so long in returning to your city. Nor do I know who this Jerrel is or what he is to you."

He paused, as though to give her a chance to respond. When Nareen said nothing, he continued, "I do not know these things, and I do not care. I care only that the people who serve me, and thus serve Kalinden, fulfill their responsibilities as required. If I find that I can no longer rely upon you to act, to think, as a runner should, I will have no hesitation in removing you from your duties. Do I make myself clear?"

As Gasperian spoke, Nareen's anger rose until she could barely choke down a protest. She managed a quick nod, but looking into those cold, dark eyes that were studying her with such harsh indifference, Nareen knew he'd believed nothing of what she'd said.

"You may go." With that, Gasperian turned his attention to the papers stacked beside him on the table, not even bothering to acknowledge her departing bow.

Gravnar followed Nareen out of the room but made no effort to speak until they were out of earshot of the guards posted in the passageway.

"You did not handle that well," he said at last. He didn't look at Nareen and his voice was the flat, uninflected voice of a well-trained runner.

"He didn't believe me!"

Gravnar's eyebrows rose slightly, an expression which, in Nareen's experience, constituted a major display of emotion. "Did you expect him to?"

"I told the truth! I reported what I heard, accurately and without interpretation! I brought information he needs, that he *must* listen to!" Nareen was making no effort to control her anger and indignation.

"Even I, who know and respect Runner Tork, have a hard time believing you." Gravnar glanced at the people passing in the hallway. "But we will not speak of that here. You are undoubtedly tired and hungry. I have food and wine in my quarters. We will talk while you eat; then you can rest."

Nareen shook her head. "I have a message for herdsman Porza, others for the Lady Xyanth from her advisors. And I asked Jerrel to wait for me. I can't just leave him."

The old runner's face revealed nothing, but Nareen sensed a question behind that expressionless glance. "Then find him and bring him with you. As for your messages, Porza can wait. I happen to know that the Lady Xyanth will be joining Master Gasperian shortly to discuss strategies, so she will not be able to receive you for several hours. You have time to eat. I will expect you."

Without another word, Gravnar left Nareen. Repressing an urge to follow after her teacher, Nareen returned to the main reception hall in search of Jerrel.

Even though Jerrel was taller than average and should have been easy to spot, it took Nareen several minutes to find him in the crowd. As she searched, she couldn't help but be aware of the stares that followed her. Clearly, word of her report on the beastmen's incursion and of her private interview with Gasperian had spread. One or two individuals would have approached her had she not pointedly ignored them and pushed on through the milling mass of people. She wasn't in the mood to discuss the information she'd brought with anyone, regardless of who they were or what their rank was.

Nareen found Jerrel leaning against a pillar along the far wall, seemingly lost in thought. From the vague, almost sleepy expression on his face, she suspected he was eavesdropping on the conversation of three merchants near him.

Even with the dust and dirt of three days' hard travel on him, he was magnificent. He was standing on one leg, his booted feet crossed at the ankle, while casually propping his shoulder against the pillar. His arms were crossed over his chest, a pose that accented the powerful muscles of his arms and torso despite the coarse shirt and leather jerkin. The blanket he'd brought was looped over one shoulder and across his back like a poor man's pack, and he carried no weapons, except his big, deadly knife in its sheath on his belt. He hadn't shaved since they'd left Matcassen and his beard was growing in thick and dark.

Yet despite the grime, despite the rough clothes and poor equipment, he looked more a man than any of the well-dressed, well-equipped soldiers in the room. Nareen couldn't help wondering how that beard would feel if he were to kiss her. Rough. Rough yet . . .

She shook her head. It was not the time or place to indulge in daydreams. Especially daydreams like that. Whatever had brought him to Kalinden had nothing to do with her, and whatever had once been between them had been left far behind in a caravan wagon on a hill above Matcassen.

Nareen moved toward him. Jerrel glanced up. At sight of her his eyes widened, flashing a brilliant blue, and the edges of his mouth lifted in a smile. He straightened, took a half step forward, hands outstretched, then froze. The smile faded, the light in his eyes dimmed. By the time Nareen stopped in front of him his features had shaped themselves into a carefully polite yet neutral mask.

"Gravnar has offered us a meal," she said, keeping her voice as carefully neutral as his expression. "I thought that might be easier than your trying to find an inn immediately. After that . . ."

Her voice trailed away. After that, he would be gone. If he remained in Kalinden, there was always the chance they might meet on the street. She hoped they wouldn't. Wounds, especially wounds of the heart, healed better if they were left alone.

Nareen led Jerrel out of the reception hall and toward the wing where the Master's advisors, physicians, and senior runners were housed. As chief runner and now instructor to the runners in training, Gravnar merited larger and more comfortable quarters than most who lived within the Great Hall.

"There are basins of water, soap, and drying cloths over there," Gravnar said when they entered, gesturing to the articles neatly laid out on a bench at the far side of the room. "When you have finished, come and eat. I am old, but I haven't forgotten the hunger that twists one's belly after several days on the trail."

Though he welcomed the chance to wash off some of his grime, Jerrel found it difficult to concentrate on his task with Nareen standing only inches from him. For a moment, when she had come to him in the reception hall, he'd thought he detected a softness in her expression that hadn't been there since they'd parted that night on the caravan. But he'd been mistaken, and just as well.

As he finished drying his hands, Jerrel glanced over to find Nareen watching him. She revealed neither interest in him nor impatience at his slowness but stood patiently waiting for him to finish, as if she were merely observing the courtesies appropriate to a visitor.

Like him, she'd washed her face and neck and hands, leaving the dust in her hair and on her clothes until later. She hadn't been quite as careful with the drying cloth, however, for moisture still glistened at the base of her throat, where she'd left the collar of her shirt unfastened.

"Are you finished?" she asked.

"Yes, but you're not." Unable to resist the temptation, Jerrel gently dabbed at the wetness with his drying cloth, then immediately regretted it. Even through the thick fabric he could feel the warmth of her. And that roused memories that were best forgotten. Memories of how soft her skin was, of how white it was across her shoulders, her breasts, of . . .

Her quick intake of breath and the sudden tightening of her lips told him he had transgressed, and that she was not as unaware of him as she'd wanted him to believe.

Without speaking, Nareen turned and crossed to where Gravnar waited for them. Jerrel carefully folded the cloth, willing his pulse to slow, his hand to stop trembling.

He had his memories, but she had hers, too. Memories of how he'd rejected her pleas to help defend her people; memories of how he'd offered no explanation for his decision, made no apologies for his actions.

Memories such as those were better left alone. In time, they might fade, their hurt become less sharp. Or they might not. But there was nothing he could do about that. He tossed the cloth on the bench beside the basin, heedless of how untidily it fell, and turned to join the two waiting for him.

"There is bread and cheese, enough spiced quetnie meat for half a dozen people, and some fruit," Gravnar said as they took their seats around the table. "I have water and wine, or zafa, if you would prefer."

"I find I do not care for zafa," said Nareen carefully, her attention on the block of hard, white cheese she was cutting.

"But I thought it was one of your favorite drinks!" For the first time Gravnar's reserve cracked.

"Tastes change." She extended a piece of cheese to Jerrel. "Some cheese?" Her self-control, at least, wasn't dented.

"Thank you." Jerrel accepted the cheese with what dignity he could muster. With luck, she wouldn't have noticed the flush under his tan.

No one spoke again until the meal was finished. Jerrel pushed his plate back and took a sip of the dry red wine he, too, had chosen in preference to the zafa. The meal had been simple but satisfying. He hadn't realized how hungry he was.

"I thank you, Runner Gravnar," he said, trying not to watch Nareen's attempts to lick off the sticky juice that had run down her fingers from the mani fruit she'd been eating. He was grateful when she gave up the effort and went to wash her hands.

Gravnar nodded his acknowledgment of Jerrel's thanks. The man seemed almost human now, the expressionless mask of a runner having been replaced with a more normal expression of polite curiosity. Jerrel suspected the two cups of wine Gravnar had drunk were only partly responsible. The rest of the explanation seemed to lie in an almost fatherly affection for Nareen that Gravnar seemed at pains to keep hidden.

"I would not have thought it possible for a man of your size to be able to keep up with a runner like Nareen," Gravnar said, leaning back in his chair to study Jerrel.

Jerrel grinned. "It wasn't easy. And she did have to slow down a time or two."

"You did well," Nareen said, returning to her seat. She kept her head down, avoiding looking his way.

Now that Nareen was relaxing, Jerrel could see that the weariness from three days' hard travel was beginning to drag at her. He had to admit he was beginning to feel the effects, as well. The surge of energy caused by the excitement of their arrival was ebbing away, and a bath and bed, not necessarily in that order, sounded very inviting.

But he couldn't rest yet. He had to find a place to stay, find out where the Matcassen troops were billeted and when they were expected to leave. And somehow, some way, he had to find and speak to the Lady Xyanth.

"So what now?" Gravnar's steady gaze moved from Nareen to Jerrel and back again.

Nareen sighed. "I told you. I have a message for herdsman Porza." She frowned. "And several for the Lady Xyanth."

Jerrel jumped, then tried to cover his reaction by shifting his position. It seemed there was a chance that one part of his problem, at least, might be resolved very easily.

"I don't mean the messages," Gravnar said.

Nareen met Gravnar's gaze squarely, then glanced over at Jerrel. Her chin rose slightly. "I will do whatever is necessary, whatever I can to fight the beastmen . . . or any other enemy of Kalinden."

Gravnar turned to Jerrel. "And you? The business of a stranger such as yourself is not usually

203

any concern of mine, but since you came with Nareen . . ."

Nareen interrupted, her words suddenly clipped and sharp. "His business, as you say, teacher, is no concern of ours. He is not here for Kalinden's sake." She choked, then added, "Nor for mine."

"I . . ." The words died before Jerrel could speak them. What could he say?

And yet, suddenly, he wanted to explain, wanted at least to soften the hurt in those green eyes.

The days on the trail from Matcassen had drawn Nareen and him closer somehow. They hadn't made love, hadn't even kissed, but barriers between them that he'd never known existed had crumbled a little. He wanted to reach across those barriers where he could, so that her memories of him wouldn't be so harsh and bitter.

Before he could say anything more, he was distracted by a peremptory knocking on the door.

"Enter," Gravnar called.

The door opened to admit a teenage boy, one of the many who served as messengers in the Hall. "Your pardon, teacher," he said, bowing low. "The Master requests your presence in the reception hall."

Gravnar's brow furrowed slightly, as though in annoyance. Jerrel could see no other reaction to the summons.

"Very well." Gravnar nodded curtly. He rose to his feet, then said to Jerrel, "You may stay here tonight, if you wish. Nareen will show you the bed I reserve for visitors." He glanced over at Nareen, a speculative gleam in his eye, then turned and followed the messenger out of the room. The door shut behind him with a solid thump.

Gravnar's departure left a heavy silence hanging over the two still seated at the table. After a moment, Nareen said quietly, "You were about to say something before the messenger knocked."

Jerrel swallowed. It was strangely frightening to think of trusting another with something so deeply personal. "I wanted to explain . . . I . . ." He hesitated. "I'm searching for my brother, Santar, who disappeared some months ago."

Slowly Jerrel twirled his cup of wine between his fingers. As the wine swirled in the cup, the surface of the deep red liquid alternately showed almost black with shadow, then silver with reflected light. Black, white. Yes, no. Speak or be silent.

"I have reason to believe that the Lady Xyanth knows something of his disappearance. That she might, in fact, be responsible for it," he said at last. "A friend in Matcassen has been searching for information. I was to meet with him, but he was forced to leave the city before we got there. I left Norvag to wait for him and I came to Kalinden in the hope that I might somehow . . ."

He set the cup on the table and met Nareen's puzzled gaze directly. "I never meant to hurt you. I'd heard rumors of someone resembling Santar being seen near that inn, so we came to see if . . . He's my brother, the only member of my family left. I can't . . . He must come first. Don't you see?"

A brother. Nareen blinked at the pain and uncertainty she saw in Jerrel's eyes, heard in his voice. Somehow she knew that in those few words he'd revealed more to her than he'd intended, revealed a weakness, a vulnerability that she suspected he'd spent years hiding from the world. And he had revealed it because he wanted her to understand, and to forgive.

A brother. Nareen drew in a deep breath. What would it be like to have a brother? Someone you were tied to—*belonged* to—and who belonged to you?

In Kalinden she'd found a home, friends, a place for herself. And yet . . . Gravnar was as close to being her father as anyone could be, but he was not her father. The other runners were her friends and companions, but they were not brothers or sisters to her.

They were runners, which meant they were reserved, did not readily reveal their feelings—often did not *allow* themselves to feel, to laugh or love or hate. They were trained to avoid such strong emotions, to repress and ignore them until, eventually, they almost didn't exist. She was the only one who still had to struggle to control her passions, to fight not to laugh out loud or shout with anger.

And she fared no better with friends who weren't runners for she was inevitably constrained by their expectations of what a runner ought to be and how she ought to behave.

Yet for them, and for Kalinden, she would give her life itself if that were asked of her. Even if Jerrel had asked her, there in the caravan, to come with him to Matcassen, she would have refused. Kalinden and its people needed her and had first claim on her loyalty, just as Jerrel's brother, Santar, had first claim on his.

Nareen nodded. Yes, she saw. Saw and understood and forgave. It wasn't enough to drive out the hurt, but it was enough.

Which raised another question. If Jerrel was going to have any dealings with the Lady Xyanth he needed to know what kind of woman she was. Which meant he needed to know about Tork's suspicions and warnings.

For a moment Nareen hesitated, weighing her obligation as a runner not to speak of the information Tork had entrusted to her versus Jerrel's need to know. Jerrel's need won out. It didn't take her long to tell him what she had learned in Matcassen.

At last Nareen pushed back her chair and stood. "My report to herdsman Porza will not take long," she said. "And then we will find the Lady Xyanth."

The Matcassen soldiers guarding the Lady Xyanth's chambers wouldn't let them enter, so Nareen and Jerrel were forced to wait in the passageway. Though she would greatly have preferred to pace up and down the corridor as Jerrel was doing, Nareen controlled herself and instead stood quietly against the wall opposite the guards, to all outward appearances cool and detached.

The delay seemed endless. Nareen's weariness was once again beginning to creep up on her when Xyanth finally appeared at the end of the hall, a small army of advisors, guards, and servants in her wake.

She swept forward, her regal bearing and dark, brocaded robes sufficient to proclaim her rank. As she progressed along the corridor, she alternately passed through the golden bars of sunlight cast by the tall, narrow windows of the hall, into the shadows between the windows, and out again.

In the light, the gold embroidery of her garments winked and flashed with almost unbearable brightness. In the shadows, and with her dark garments, she seemed to disappear. Only her pale skin and fair hair showed clearly, as though she were a disembodied spirit come to haunt the ancient hallways of Kalinden.

Nareen blinked, startled by Xyanth's rapid change from glittering radiance to somber, shadowed wraith and back again. She moved to stand in front of the doors the guards had thrown open, scarcely noticing when Jerrel took a position a little behind her and to the side.

Xyanth stopped a foot in front of Nareen, but she did not acknowledge Nareen's salute, nor the guards who had snapped to attention and saluted by thumping their right fists against their left shoulders, nor the bows of her advisors, who quickly withdrew.

Her attention was wholly focused on Jerrel. Her expression, which had been tense, slowly relaxed. She did not smile, but Nareen, watching her, could see the pupils of her eyes expand until they shone like two black, glittering gems.

The woman was beautiful. Her thick blonde hair fell around her shoulders in a cascade of gold, softening and partially hiding her finely sculpted features. The sun streaming through the window behind her created a radiant nimbus that seemed a natural extension of so delicate and ethereal a creature.

She turned her gaze from Jerrel to Nareen—reluctantly, it seemed to Nareen. "You are the runner who first brought word of the beastmen, are you not?"

The woman's voice was soft and low, yet Nareen thought she detected a hint of steel beneath the velvet notes. "Yes, my Lady," she replied.

"Did you go to Anweigh, then?"

"No, my Lady."

Xyanth nodded, but her gaze turned back to Jerrel. Clearly the reasons for Nareen's failure to reach Anweigh did not interest her.

"And you?" This time the voice was pure velvet.

Jerrel smiled, very slightly, and bowed deeply. "My name is Jerrel, my Lady. I seek a word with you."

Xyanth's gaze slid slowly along the length of Jerrel's body, then back up to his face. She smiled, too, and nodded slightly.

Nareen, watching her, thought Xyanth made a mistake in smiling. Her ethereal aura disappeared as though it had never been, and something feral and vaguely predatory took its place.

Jerrel seemed oblivious to the change. His smile broadened almost imperceptibly. Nareen forced down a sudden sharp stab of anger—and another emotion she refused to admit might be jealousy.

"Come." Xyanth swept past them and into the room.

Two women servants appeared. As Xyanth stood passively, her eyes fixed on Jerrel, a slight smile on her perfect lips, the servants quickly unfastened and removed her heavy robe of state. Beneath the robe Xyanth wore a gown of some sheer fabric that only barely disguised her slender, full-breasted body.

To her fury, Nareen blushed. Despite the gown's fullness she could clearly see the dark aureoles of Xyanth's nipples and the curve of her waist and hips.

Such exposure didn't seem to bother Xyanth,

however. She turned slightly to accept a goblet of wine from a bowing servant, then glanced back over her shoulder at Jerrel as she sipped. When one of the women returned with a heavy, fur-trimmed velvet robe, Xyanth let the woman slip it over her shoulders, slowly, then fasten it in front. And all the while she kept her black-gem eyes fixed on Jerrel.

This is how she did it, Jerrel thought, watching Xyanth's performance unblinkingly, the slight smile fixed on his lips. It would have been so easy with a naïve, idealistic young man like Santar. So very, very easy. The golden-haired witch might be the wife of a ruler of Errandane, she might have the face and body of a guardian spirit of the gods, but she had the soul of the most scheming and unscrupulous of courtesans. Even he, who had known a dozen such on other worlds, could feel the heat rising in his veins.

Decently robed at last, Xyanth seated herself in an ornately carved chair. "Well, warrior?" she said, looking at Jerrel over the rim of her goblet. "Or should I call you that?"

"As a title, it will do as well as any, Lady. But perhaps it would be well to hear the runner's messages first." He inclined his head in Nareen's direction but kept his eyes fixed on Xyanth.

"Mmm." Xyanth turned to a rigidly erect Nareen. "Well?" The steel was back in her voice, without any touch of velvet.

"There was another attack against your husband's life, my Lady." Nareen's eyes were fixed on a spot slightly above and to the right of Xyanth's shoulder. She was afraid if she looked directly at the woman, or at Jerrel, she would lose all control.

"I take it he survived?" A slightly raised eyebrow was Xyanth's only concession to emotion.

"He did. The attacker is dead, and several of your advisors and guards are seeking further information." Protocol required that she wait for one of Xyanth's runners to be present to hear her message, but Nareen had no intention of waiting. Without giving Xyanth a chance to ask questions—something she didn't seem inclined to do, in any case—Nareen repeated the three messages from Xyanth's advisors. All three dealt with the attack on Lindaz and its aftermath.

As Nareen spoke, Jerrel listened, once again amazed at her capacity to remember so much and convey it so accurately. The three advisors might as well have been in the room themselves, dictating. On his world, where recording machines and com links were so readily available, he knew of no one capable of doing what Nareen did so effortlessly.

The messages were quickly delivered. Nareen, still without looking directly at Xyanth, paused and drew a quick breath. "That is all, my Lady."

Xyanth eyed her without interest for a moment, then shrugged. "Very well. You may go." She turned back to Jerrel, a slight smile once more upon her lips.

Out of the corner of his eye, Jerrel watched Nareen leave. Her face was set, her bearing erect, and she walked with a quick, proud dignity. She was, he could tell, extremely angry. The little runner clearly didn't approve of the Lady Xyanth.

At a gesture from Xyanth, one of the servants brought a chair for Jerrel—smaller and lower than Xyanth's, Jerrel noted wryly—and a second goblet filled with wine. That done, the servants withdrew, leaving their Lady staring speculatively at her guest.

"You are not from Kalinden," she said at last.

"That is true." Jerrel took a sip of the wine, which was sweeter than he normally drank. He had no intention of saying anything he didn't have to, even lies. Women like the cold-eyed goddess before him preferred challenges to easy conquests.

"Nor have you brought any weapons."

Jerrel took another sip. "You cannot know that."

His reply obviously amused her. "Oh, but I can, warrior. Your clothes are stained, as from a long, hard journey, yet there are no marks where a sword or spear would have rubbed. There have been no caravans in this city for several weeks—news of the beastmen has spread and no merchants want to risk the journey for whatever small profit they might earn—so you must have arrived on foot. You do not look to me like the kind of man who would use a pack animal, warrior. Therefore, you have no weapons."

Whatever else she was, the woman was no fool. Jerrel shrugged. "Weapons are easily acquired."

Xyanth eyed him from beneath thick lashes. With one finger she rubbed the rim of her goblet. The long fingernail looked like a small but very deadly dagger. She dipped her finger in the wine, then brought it to her mouth and slowly licked off the sweet liquid.

The gesture was not unlike Nareen's earlier, when she had tried to lick away the sticky juice from the fruit she'd been eating. But unlike Nareen, Xyanth knew exactly what she did and what effect it would have. She watched him watching her, and smiled again.

"It is true that weapons can be acquired, but to what purpose, warrior?"

Jerrel forced down a sudden surge of eagerness. The vague plan that he'd formed as he'd paced the hall waiting for Xyanth might just work, after all. It was, at least, a start.

"To aid those in need of a strong arm, my Lady. Assuming that those in need would be willing to show their gratitude for that service." Jerrel kept his face as carefully expressionless as a runner's and reminded himself of a saying from his own world: *When things come more easily than expected, it is time for wise men to be cautious.* With this woman, it would be wise to be very cautious indeed.

"And what form does this gratitude take, warrior?"

"It can take many forms, Lady." Jerrel let his eyes stray from Xyanth's face. Not far, but far enough. "All of which can be discussed later."

He rose and placed his goblet on the table near her chair. The movement brought him closer to her so that he was almost, but not quite, looming over her.

"My thanks for the wine," he said. Then he straightened, turned, and walked from the room without a backward glance.

Chapter 12

The hot, moist air of the Great Hall's bathing chamber wrapped soothingly around Jerrel. After a few hours of sleep in the bed Gravnar had offered him, he had risen to find the old man had left him a simple meal and instructions for finding his way to the bath.

He'd washed his hair and scrubbed the worst of the dirt and grime off in the outer room, and now he sat on a stone shelf that ran the width of the chamber itself, lazily dipping his cloth in the basin before him, then letting the warm, herb-scented water run over his naked body.

An attendant entered carrying a pan filled with fire-heated stones. He set it on a small stand in the corner of the chamber, then poured a ladle-ful of water over the stones. Instantly a cloud of steam arose so dense it almost hid the attendant.

Jerrel sighed in contentment, stretched, then leaned back against the stone wall. Errandane might be a primitive world, but it had its good points and this steam bath was one of them.

He watched as the water ran off his body, across the shelf, then down a drain set in the fitted stones of the floor. Some skills, at least, such as a knowledge of basic plumbing, seemed to have survived the centuries that had passed since the first settlers arrived from whatever world they'd been born on. The Great Hall, for example, had running water in rooms throughout the building.

Other skills, such as a runner's phenomenal powers of memory and observation, had obviously been developed to meet the challenges of this world. The people of Errandane had adapted, just as humans across the galaxy had adapted to the worlds they lived on.

Adaptability. It had always been humankind's chief talent. There were races that were far more intelligent than humans, or stronger, or longer lived, or that possessed mental skills beyond even the most advanced of humanity's machines.

But none of those races—not one—had proved to be as adaptable as humans. Taken from the world they knew, they struggled to function. Some managed to survive, others died, often quickly. None thrived except humans.

So why not ask Nareen to adapt? She was intelligent and trained as few others were to observe, to learn, and to keep on learning. Surely, if he was careful in explaining . . . There was so much he could offer her.

Jerrel retrieved the bathing cloth from the basin, then slowly ran it down his right leg, wringing out the water so it flowed in tiny rivulets along his thigh, his knee, his lower leg. By the time he reached his ankle he was squeezing the cloth so hard his knuckles gleamed white and his hand trembled.

Offer her what? A home? Children? A comfortable life lived with honor among friends? Was that the life he would choose himself, if he could?

Abruptly Jerrel flung the cloth from him. It hit the side of the basin, causing the contents to slop over the side.

He was wasting his time—indulging in ridiculous daydreams when he ought to be searching for his brother.

Jerrel sat up, swinging around and leaning forward so his hands grasped the edge of the shelf on either side of him and his legs dangled over the side. His shoulders tensed and he peered forward as though he might read some answer in the thick gray steam that filled the room.

A drop of water, condensed from the steam filling the room, dripped from the ceiling onto his nose. Jerrel brushed the offending drop away in irritation.

Though he had come to Kalinden in search of information about Santar, it wasn't his brother who occupied his thoughts, waking and sleeping. Somehow, by some sort of indefinable magic, Nareen had insinuated herself into his mind until she was almost a physical presence beside him.

Yet even if Santar were alive and safe, Jerrel felt himself a fool to indulge in this senseless obsession for a woman he couldn't have. There was nothing he could offer Nareen, no security, no home, no future. Nothing but his love . . .

Jerrel's head came up abruptly. His thoughts churned. Love? Where had that notion sprung from? It was absurd. Ridiculous! He didn't have a place in his life for love. An outcast like him ought not waste even a second on such fantasies.

And yet . . .

Images of Nareen came unbidden. Images of her laughing, or bathed in starlight, or lying beneath him, her lips swollen from his kisses, her skin flushed with the fever that consumed them both.

Mental images and nothing more, but in spite of himself Jerrel found his body responding. The realization that he could so easily react to mere memories angered him.

Enough! Such fantasies weren't love, and he had better things to do with his time than indulge in them. With an oath, he slid off the stone shelf. A dousing with cold water ought to get his mind back on track.

The attendant had pointed out the stone basin in one corner. It took a couple of fumbling tries for Jerrel to figure out how the crude faucet worked, but as soon as he pulled the right lever, ice cold water gushed into the basin from a pipe set in the wall.

Jerrel picked up the big ladle that hung on a hook at one side of the basin, filled it with the icy water, then tipped the ladle's contents over his head.

The shock of the cold water hitting his skin failed in its purpose. It was as if he had just plunged back into the stream by the hunting camp, as if in the next instant Nareen would again be swept into his arms, naked and shivering and tormentingly desirable.

217

And from that memory his mind leaped to another, then another. Once more he saw her springing onto the drevon's neck, risking her life to save his. Once more she led him up the mountain to safety instead of into the lances of the hunting beastmen, then worked, pale and silent, in the cold winter wind to bury people she knew, yet had never met.

With the memories came a sense of her pride, her capacity for loyalty, her willingness to put others before herself, to give, and then give more, yet never demand so much as an expression of thanks in return.

Once more Jerrel doused himself with the icy water. This time the shock jarred him back to reality. And the reality, he realized, was that he was thoroughly, hopelessly, stupidly in love with a woman whose life he could never share.

"He said no."

Nareen looked at her old teacher with dismay. In that one word was the destruction of all the plans she'd thought out so carefully before falling asleep last night. "He won't send a Kalinden runner with the Matcassen troops?"

Gravnar shook his head. "He won't send *you*. There's a difference."

"But he will send someone, someone who can be alert for any signs that Tork's information was right."

"He's sending Lainak."

"Lai . . . !" Nareen planted both hands on Gravnar's desk and leaned forward, as if poised to spring. "That idiot! He can't even—"

"Lainak has completed his training. And though he's not the most brilliant runner I've ever trained, he's done well." Gravnar frowned at Nareen's intemperate display of emotion.

"He's a stodgy, unimaginative drudge who couldn't spot a drevon unless it jumped out and attacked him."

"He is serious about his assignments and he has worked hard to become a runner."

"It took him almost a year longer than anyone else to learn the basic techniques of control!"

"At least he learned them. I can think of one runner who seems never to have learned them at all!"

Though Gravnar's voice hadn't risen, the look in his eyes made Nareen bite back the retort she'd been about to utter. After a brief struggle to restrain her anger, she said, more calmly, "It would seem that Master Gasperian does not believe Tork's warnings."

"Even you, runner, with your overdeveloped and highly inappropriate imagination, will admit that it's rather farfetched." Gravnar paused, as if to measure the effect of his words. "In the long run, Matcassen loses as much as Kalinden if the beastmen are free once again."

"But if Tork's information is correct? Can we afford to risk letting her into our city with armed troops without making perfectly sure that Tork is mistaken?" Nareen took three quick steps away from the desk, trying to gather her arguments, then turned back to face Gravnar.

Somehow she had to convince him of the wisdom of her plan. The old runner cared for her, she knew, but he was a runner to the very core of his being. That meant he would not let his emotions or his affection for her interfere with his duty. If Master Gasperian had decided not to trust the warnings she'd brought, if he had decided that she was to remain in Matcassen while a blind fool like Lainak accompanied Xyanth's troops, then it would take a great deal of convincing to get Gravnar to help her.

"If I could be assigned to the Lady Xyanth," Nareen continued, keeping her voice steady and without inflection, "I might be able to gather more information, find out who visits her, perhaps learn what they say. If she hasn't incited the beastmen, if she has no plans to take advantage of the situation for Matcassen's benefit, then we can accept her help and turn all our energies to fighting our true enemies. But if Tork is right . . ."

Nareen paused. Even now, when she'd had several days to think about Tork's accusations, she had a hard time putting the implications of the warnings into words. "If Tork is right, then we must do what we can to defend ourselves against enemies from within as well as from without."

"I understand all that, and so does Master Gasperian." Gravnar's lips thinned, as though he wanted to say more and could not. He would not, Nareen knew, no matter what his personal opinions. He placed a hand flat on the desk, then pushed himself erect.

"The decision has been made, Sixth Runner," he said formally. "Lainak will accompany the Lady Xyanth and you will stay in Kalinden to serve where and when you are needed, as Master Gasperian sees fit."

Nareen opened her mouth to protest, but Gravnar interrupted her. "That is all. The matter is closed." Without giving Nareen a chance to respond, he turned and left the room.

* * *

"Aye, sir, it's a fine sword. None better. Not the Master hisself has a finer. Ain't that so, missus?" The weaponer—a massive, heavily muscled man well past his prime who looked as if he'd learned his trade as a soldier—turned to the plump lady at his side for confirmation.

"Aye, sir. Raif's right. There's none better. None, even if it's I as says so." The plump lady dropped a quick curtsy in Jerrel's direction and blushed. "'Deed, sir, if you was wantin' finer yuh'd have tuh look—"

"What the missus, means, sir, is yuh couldn't find finer, not if yuh was tuh go tuh Anweigh, yuh couldn't. No, sir—"

"I'm sure your lady is right, weaponer." Jerrel weighed the gleaming length of honed steel in his hand, but it wasn't the sword he was thinking of.

The man's words had stirred surprising memories—of his studies when he was a child and his tutor had insisted he learn the old foundation languages.

Missus. An ancient term identifying a wife, a woman who had become the property of her husband. It was a title of respect, he remembered, signifying the existence of a bond between the man and the woman that was supposed to endure for the rest of their lives.

He hefted the sword, feeling its balance, letting it settle into his palm.

Strange how the old words cropped up on worlds far distant in time and space from the world of the language's origin. Missus Nareen. Jerrel frowned. That didn't sound right. Nareen Missus. No, not that way, either. And yet . . .

221

"If it's heavier yuh want, I could make yuh one tuh size," the weaponer was saying, watching Jerrel's frown.

"What?" Jerrel glanced over at the man, uncertain for a moment what he was talking about. "Oh, no. This will be fine, I think." He set the sword on the scarred table that served as counter in the small shop. "How much?"

The man named a price that Jerrel was sure was far beyond the weapon's true value, but he didn't quibble. He wasn't in the mood to waste time even if Errandane, like most human-inhabited worlds, did honor the ancient traditions of haggling. He did, however, insist that a fine, tooled-leather sheath be included in the purchase price.

The weaponer, scarcely able to suppress his pleasure at having contracted so advantageous a sale, disappeared with his wife into the workroom at the back of the shop to give the sword one final sharpening and polishing.

While he waited, Jerrel stepped to the doorway opening onto the street. Like many such primitive cities on other worlds, Kalinden's narrow streets were identified by the merchants or craftsmen who occupied them. It hadn't been difficult for Jerrel to find his way from the Great Hall to the Street of the Weaponers.

Unlike the streets where the sellers of food or household goods were to be found, the Street of the Weaponers was almost wholly filled by grim-faced men who were clearly there for a purpose, and not a pleasant purpose at that.

From open shops up and down the street there rose a deafening clangor as metalsmiths, many stripped to the waist because of the heat pouring from their glowing furnaces, labored to make the knives and swords and spear points that would be needed in the battles to come. Boys, some of them scarcely in their teens, pumped the huge bellows that fanned the flames. Assistants scurried about on errands or labored hunched over their tables, intent on whatever task they'd been assigned.

Above the din swirled the sounds of a hundred conversations, rumors of attacks by the beastmen, discussions of the value of spears over bow and arrow when dealing with the creatures, news of those who had died or been injured in recent encounters with the savages.

Beastmen or Calnites or rebels. Spears or dead-beamers or disrupters. The names of the enemies and the weapons might change from world to world, but the sounds of war never did. In the days and weeks to come, Jerrel knew, some of the eager, determined men he watched today would die. And still the Street of the Weaponers would be filled and noisy.

Jerrel's attention was caught by the sight of a short, black-haired, green-eyed woman pushing her way through the crowd. Jerrel cursed and would have stepped back into the dark shop behind him, but he was too late. Nareen had spotted him.

It would be so much easier if he never had to see her again. Then he might forget that moment of madness there in the bathing chamber. Yet he couldn't deny the honey-sweet curl of pleasure that stirred within him at sight of her. Nareen moved with a proud confidence that easily opened a way for her through the crowds. As he watched her approach, Jerrel was aware of an odd, tugging sensation in his chest, as if he'd been running and couldn't quite catch his breath.

223

"You got an earlier start than I expected," she said, coming to a halt before him, hands on hips.

"And what had you expected?" Jerrel decided to ignore the accusatory tone.

"That you'd sleep for another couple of hours, at least. Anyone else would have."

"I had things to do."

Nareen looked at the purposeful commotion around her, then back at Jerrel. "Such as buy weapons now that you've convinced the Lady Xyanth to take you on as a hired soldier."

"I haven't . . ." He stopped. This green-eyed creature never failed to astound him. Did she have spies in the Matcassen camp? "Nothing is decided yet. How did you know we discussed it?"

She shrugged. "Given what you told me about your search for your brother, isn't it the logical thing for you to do?"

There was no response to that, but Jerrel was saved from having to say anything by the reappearance of the weaponer. "Here yuh are, sir." He stopped when he saw Nareen, a guilt-stricken expression on his face. "Sixth Runner!"

"Weaponer Daet."

Jerrel couldn't be completely sure, but he thought the edge of Nareen's mouth quivered, ever so slightly. Clearly, the price of the sword would have been lower had she been present. She said nothing, however, while he strapped on the sword and took his leave of the weaponer, who was all too glad to see him go.

Nareen fell into step beside him. "Where are you going next?"

"I want a couple of good spears, a bow and a supply of steel-tipped arrows, dried food, a pack," he said, keeping his attention fixed on

NAME: _____

ADDRESS: _____

_____

_____

TELEPHONE: _____

E-MAIL: _____

____ I want to pay by credit card.

__ Visa   __ MasterCard   __ Discover

Account Number: _____

Expiration date: _____

SIGNATURE: _____

*Send this form, along with $2.00 shipping
and handling for your FREE books, to:*

Love Spell Romance Book Club
20 Academy Street
Norwalk, CT 06850-4032

*Or fax (must include credit card
information!) to: 610.995.9274.
You can also sign up on the Web
at www.dorchesterpub.com.*

Offer open to residents of the U.S. and
Canada only. Canadian residents, please
call 1.800.481.9191 for pricing information.

If under 18, a parent or guardian must sign. Terms, prices and conditions
subject to change. Subscription subject to acceptance. Dorchester
Publishing reserves the right to reject any order or cancel any subscription.

maneuvering through the crowd.

Nareen said nothing but her thoughts raced. The half-formed plan she'd started out with was beginning to take on firmer dimensions.

For the next two hours she helped Jerrel bargain for the equipment he wanted and made arrangements to store the purchases until they were called for.

Everywhere they went the talk was of raids by the beastmen. Jerrel was selecting from among several spears at one stall when a man with a battered face and heavily bandaged arm approached them.

"If you're that close to the beasts, stranger," he said, gesturing to the spears with his good hand, "you'd do better to run than try to fight with those."

Before Jerrel could respond, the shop owner appeared. At sight of the injured man, he exclaimed, "Opar! We didn't expect you back so soon! What happened? Your injuries! You're not . . . ?"

"Nay, old friend," said the one addressed as Opar, a tired, grim smile on his face. "I'm well enough. Better'n most." He settled onto a battered stool and hooked a thumb in Jerrel's direction. "Was tellin' the warrior, here, that if he has to use your weapons, he'd be better off runnin'. The beasts are vicious and far too strong for us to fight up close."

"Tell us more, soldier," said Nareen quietly. "Where did you encounter the beastmen? How many of you were there? How many of them?"

"They were near the village of Golrash. A huntin' party. Big one. We drove 'em off but lost half our men, either dead or wounded. Master Gasperian said we had ought to come to Kalinden, get more arms, more men. He sent troops to replace us, but they don't know the area."

He scowled and shook his head. "What's brought the beasts back? They've killed many of us, but we've killed them, too. Why are they riskin' a fight now?"

Opar looked at Nareen as though he expected her to provide the answers to his questions. She shook her head helplessly.

"What about your wounds, old friend?" the spearmaker said, pointing to Opar's bandaged arm and battered face.

"They'll heal," Opar grunted, raising his arm as if to prove his statement. "There's a new healer in the village. Come just before the beastmen. He's young, but good. Got medicines and herbs I never heard of, but they work." His cut and swollen features twisted with a pain that wasn't completely physical. "Can't bring back the dead, though. No healer can."

Since it was clear that Opar had come to see the spearmaker, Nareen retreated to the street while Jerrel quickly completed his transaction.

How many dead? she wondered, watching Jerrel choose two spears. How many injured? She could find out the numbers easily enough by checking with whatever runner had brought the original message of the attack, but numbers gave no hint of the human suffering and grief behind them.

As she watched Jerrel pay for his spears, her jaw set with renewed determination. Her plan would work. It had to.

They spent another hour going from shop to shop as Jerrel carefully selected his weapons. Once he was sure he had everything he might need, he suggested stopping for a meal.

Nareen chose a stall near the end of the Street of the Weaponers where they could get small loaves of coarse, flavorful bread stuffed with slices of roast aard. Food in hand, she settled on a pile of paving stones that had been dumped beside the blank wall of a building. The location was neither comfortable nor particularly clean, but it was enough to the side of the traffic on the street that they were unlikely to be overheard, and no one would be able to eavesdrop on them from behind.

As she nibbled at the simple yet tasty meal, Nareen turned over in her mind exactly what she was going to say. Her plan would work. If only she could get Jerrel to agree.

Out of the corner of her eye, she watched as he devoured his own bread and meat. She waited until he took a bite big enough to keep him from responding immediately, then said, "I'm going with you."

Jerrel choked, tried to swallow, then choked again.

"You want information from Xyanth, and so do I. With two pairs of eyes and ears open, we're bound to learn more than either of us could working alone." She paused for a moment, but Jerrel's protests were too muffled by bread and meat to be intelligible. She continued, "I know the territory, you don't. On the other hand, the Matcassen soldiers might talk to you more freely than they would to me. It's an ideal arrangement."

"No!" Jerrel was able to speak at last. "Absolutely not!" The thought of Nareen being trapped in an encounter between the soldiers and the beastmen horrified him.

"You can't say I'd hold you up, because you know *that's* not true, and—"

"Never! I would no more take a woman into battle—"

"I'm a runner! And if you think—"

"I've heard a runner from Kalinden has already been assigned—"

"A blind, bumbling fool incapable of thinking for himself—"

"And you've been forbidden to go—"

Nareen threw the remainder of her meal on the ground in disgust. She couldn't help noting that Jerrel was squeezing his food so hard the bread was crumbling beneath his fingers. The sight provided at least a small measure of satisfaction.

Let him go hungry. He deserved it if he was going to be so unreasonable. It was one thing for him to refuse to accompany her to Kalinden, quite another to deny her now.

She sprang to her feet and glared down at him. The pile of stones gave her a small additional height advantage.

"You owe me, merchant!" she stormed. "I brought you here, even though I shouldn't have. I didn't ask for explanations or promises or payment. I brought you because you asked and because of what had been between us. Well, now I want some payment. You can't tell me no."

His jaw set like a rock that had endured the storms of centuries, Jerrel rose to his feet. Though he stood on the ground and she had the advantage of the height provided by the pile of stones, he towered over her.

"I can and I will tell you no," he said between clenched teeth. "No."

"Give me one good reason why not." Determined not to be cowed by Jerrel's forbidding appearance, Nareen set her fists on her hips, elbows akimbo, and glared up at him.

"I don't need to give you any reasons. I'm not taking you with me."

"I demand—"

"Demand all you want, runner. You're not going with me." With that, Jerrel turned and stalked off, leaving an enraged Nareen perched on the rock pile, spluttering.

"I've received word of your messenger Mek, my Lady." Gorvan bowed slightly but kept a nervous eye on the woman seated in the chair before him.

"What do you mean you've received word *of* Mek? The man was due back two days ago. Where is he? What did he say?" Xyanth tapped an impatient foot on the floor.

"He didn't say anything, my Lady. He's dead."

"Dead! How can he be . . . ? What happened?"

"Some people from one of the villages close to the border brought his body in. They said . . ." Gorvan choked, tried again. "They said his body had been nailed to a tree. He was . . . I saw him. He was horribly mutilated."

"Damn the man!" Xyanth pounded a clenched fist on the arm of her chair. Her delicate features twisted in rage. "Couldn't he follow orders? He was told—*I* told him!—exactly which path to take, how to wear that chain so he would be recognized as my emissary. Were those instructions so impossible to follow? Now look!"

"My Lady." From long experience, Gorvan knew he had to distract her now, before she could work herself into a temper that it would take hours to calm down from. Not, he thought miserably, that the rest of his information was going to make her any happier. "The tree Mek was nailed to was at the head of the trail you told him to take."

"What?" Xyanth's head came up abruptly.

"I made the villagers describe it to me precisely, my Lady. There can be no mistake." Gorvan started to wring his hands, but stopped. The nervous habit enraged her. He didn't need to make matters worse and draw her fury on him.

"And the chain? Ah . . ." Xyanth's lips thinned until they almost disappeared. "Of course. He was robbed for that chain and hung there so people would think . . ."

"No, my Lady." If only she'd listened, Gorvan thought. Even through his fear he felt the satisfaction of knowing he'd been right. If only she'd heeded the warnings. There was a reason for calling those savages beastmen. But it was too late now. Mek proved that. "No one took the chain. It was knotted around Mek's throat. He'd been strangled with it. But the villagers couldn't tell if that was before or after the beastmen had clawed him so his flesh hung in strips from his body."

Xyanth sat, both hands wrapped around the carved wood arms of the chair, shoulders hunched, face pale, staring up at him with eyes grown suddenly very wide. "Strangled? With the chain that identified him as my messenger?"

"Yes, my Lady. Strangled—and badly clawed."

"Strangled." The word was little more than a whisper.

Xyanth rose from her chair without looking at Gorvan, then crossed to a nearby table that held a tray with a bottle of wine and two goblets. She filled one of the goblets and raised it to her lips. As she drank, her hand trembled.

*   *   *

The Matcassen troops, accompanied by a sizable contingent from Kalinden, assembled in the huge open plaza in front of the city's main gate a day and half later. Though the troops themselves were optimistic and the citizens turned out to cheer their departure, Jerrel couldn't shake his sense of foreboding.

He'd only seen the beastmen once, but it was enough to convince him that this unwieldy and heavily laden army was unprepared to handle the challenges ahead. He'd expected the troops to be armed with bows and arrows and throwing spears that would allow them to fight from a distance. Instead, most of the men carried swords or short spears, weapons which required them to confront the enemy at close range, where the beasts could use their greater size and strength to advantage.

There were too many men for them to be able to move quickly. Worse, the large number of pack animals loaded with tents and provisions would slow them down even further. The pack animals—hairy, long-necked beasts that stood about half the height of a man—were sullen, evil-tempered creatures given to vociferous protests at their burdens and the commotion around them. With them along, there would be no hope of sneaking up on the beastmen and taking them by surprise.

Disgusted, Jerrel forced his way through the milling crowd of men and animals to Xyanth's palanquin. The tent-like box, mounted on poles that would be carried by four men, was heavily curtained to protect the passenger from the dirt and cold and wind. For now, the curtains had been drawn back to allow Xyanth a clear view of what was going on around her.

Jerrel recognized four of the Matcassen advisors grouped about the palanquin. None of them looked pleased with the proceedings.

Xyanth herself looked beautiful but vexed. Her delicate features were drawn into as close an approximation of a scowl as she probably allowed herself in public. She was swathed in thick furs and leaned back against pillows that had been arranged for her comfort. When she caught sight of Jerrel, the edges of her mouth lifted in a faint smile that held no warmth.

"So, warrior, you've decided to come, have you?"

"My Lady, with you as this expedition's leader, how could I not?" Jerrel bowed slightly.

"We have yet to discuss your payment." Without taking her eyes off him, Xyanth drew her furs more closely about her. Her voice was low, rich with unspoken promises.

"I look forward to our discussion." Jerrel smiled, as though he would have said more if her advisors hadn't been present, bowed again, then turned to leave.

"Wait!"

Jerrel turned around, pleased that she had called him back. He'd expected she would. "My Lady?"

Her voice was sharper this time, as if she were irritated at herself for calling him back. "Come to my tent this evening after we've made camp. We can talk then."

Jerrel bowed again, then strode off into the crowd. More than once he'd needed to play a role, act the part of someone he wasn't. But never had he found it so distasteful. He could only hope it would pay off.

The small army finally filed through Kalinden's main gate—later than planned but in some semblance, at least, of order. Jerrel found himself somewhere in the middle of the plodding mass of soldiers, but as they crested a high hill about five miles beyond the city, he stopped to let the army pass him.

From the vantage of a mass of boulders at one side of the main road, he could look down on Kalinden. At that distance the city appeared shrunk to insignificance, dwarfed by the rugged country that surrounded it. He could see the Great Hall, crouched in the center of the city like a spider in its web, and the buildings clustering along the web-like network of streets. The massive city walls seemed to have shrunk to little more than ridges in the rock.

Somewhere in that maze of buildings Nareen was going about her work for the day. How long, he wondered, would it be before she forgave him? Would she ever?

Those were questions he'd never have the answers to. Whether or not he managed in the next few days to obtain a clue to Santar's whereabouts, he had no intention of returning to Kalinden. Or to Nareen.

Jerrel's hand clenched around his spear. He'd made his choice, and if he regretted it in the future, so be it.

It was well past dark when the army finally camped for the night. Jerrel presented himself at Xyanth's tent, as ordered, but was turned away. The Lady was tired, said the guard, and did not wish to be disturbed.

233

By the second day the army settled into a routine and made better time. Jerrel drifted through the ranks, talking to the Matcassen soldiers in hopes of learning something about Santar. He heard nothing of his brother, but he did catch snippets of speculation that Nareen might at least have found interesting, if not the actual proof she sought.

One of the soldiers he met—a lean, dark-bearded guardsman named Pardraik assigned to Xyanth's personal guard—seemed to share Nareen's doubts about Matcassen's presence on Kalinden territory.

"It's odd, I tell you, warrior. Not that we're here, but that we're led by the Lady Xyanth and not by a man who knows how to fight these creatures." Pardraik thumped the ground with his spear in emphasis. "By rights, Master Lindaz ought to be leading us, but he's cowering back in his Great Hall and sending others out to do his work." He spat on the ground in disgust. "It's that woman. Everyone says it, though few say it so plain. Lindaz' Lady hasn't been good for Matcassen. She won't be good for Kalinden."

"Why do you continue to serve her?" Jerrel asked.

Pardraik looked surprised by the question. "It's my duty. Why else, warrior? A Matcassen guardsman wouldn't shame his city by refusing to follow orders."

That night Xyanth sent for Jerrel, but he had little opportunity to be alone with her. Advisors, messengers, and her guards interrupted constantly. At last he withdrew, making little effort to hide his disgust. He could only hope that Xyanth would attribute his displeasure to his suffering from a frustrated desire for her.

When he returned to the camp he'd made, Jerrel was startled to find Pardraik hunched over a small fire, morosely studying the flames.

The guardsman didn't refer directly to Jerrel's visit to Xyanth's tent, but as they shared a simple meal he said, "Remember, warrior, there are more man-eating creatures around here than just the mountain cats. You should be careful."

The third day they passed two villages, both filled to overflowing with refugees from the surrounding holdings. Though he tried to remind himself that his only purpose in coming on the expedition was to gather information about Santar, Jerrel couldn't repress a rising anger at the devastation and suffering created by the beastmen. If Xyanth really was responsible for rousing the murderous creatures, then she had much to answer for.

It was late afternoon and Jerrel had paused at one side of the road to take a drink from his water jug when he glanced up to see Pardraik striding toward him. Beside him, head high, walked Nareen.

Chapter 13

Repressing a curse, Jerrel screwed the top back on the jug, then hung the jug on his belt. One thing he hadn't expected was that Nareen would somehow follow them.

As Nareen and Pardraik came to a halt in front of him, Nareen turned to the guardsman and said, "Thank you. I will seek out your Lady and tell her of my assignment to the Matcassen troops as soon as I have spoken with this warrior."

Pardraik nodded in acknowledgment. He glanced at Jerrel. His right eyebrow quirked upward in amusement, but he didn't say anything. A moment later he was gone, mingling with the men trudging past.

Nareen watched the guardsman go with regret. She hadn't expected Jerrel to be pleased with her sudden appearance, but she also hadn't expected him to scowl quite so fiercely. When he grabbed her elbow to pull her farther away from the road, she tried to break loose—to no avail.

"So you're now assigned to the Matcassen troops, are you?" Jerrel's voice was threateningly low.

"That's right." Nareen wrenched her arm free of his grip at last.

"You're lying." A grim smile replaced the scowl; the muscles of his jaw were taut with tension.

Nareen thought of denying his accusation but changed her mind when she looked into his eyes. It wasn't anger that flashed in those blue depths, it was concern.

"Do you have any idea how dangerous it is to be here?" he demanded. "We haven't met any beastmen yet, but we might at any moment."

"I crossed the path of a hunting group at midday. And if it comes to that, I'm probably far better at avoiding the beasts than you are at fighting them!"

"That's not the point!"

"The point is that we both have a reason to be here." Nareen controlled her anger with difficulty. She still hadn't forgiven Jerrel for refusing to let her come with him from the start, but that wasn't what was important now. "I need information that might help protect Kalinden; you want information on your brother. And both of us are seeking that information from the same source."

She paused, trying to gauge his response to her words. His jaw was still firmly set, but she thought he was less tense than a moment before. "We have to work together. There's no time for you to play the noble, protective male."

"What do you mean?" There was no mistaking the indignation in Jerrel's voice.

"Just what I said. We can't—"

At that moment a member of Xyanth's personal guard came running up. If he was surprised to see a Kalinden runner with Jerrel, he didn't show it. "Your pardon, warrior. The Lady Xyanth wishes to speak with you."

"Now?" Jerrel snapped.

"How fortunate," Nareen said smoothly, before he could say more. "I was just on my way to report to her. Lead the way and we'll follow."

The guard didn't seem to have any doubts about Jerrel's instant obedience to the summons. He whirled around and began trotting back up the road toward where Xyanth rode at the head of the army. Nareen followed in the guard's wake, but Jerrel, refusing to come running at Xyanth's bidding, opted instead for a comfortable strolling pace.

Jerrel was still a ways behind her when the guard Nareen was following finally stopped before a cluster of people in the middle of the road.

Nareen couldn't help but frown at the ornate palanquin and the number of attendants around Xyanth. But she made sure none of her distaste showed on her face when she was presented after a few minutes' delay.

"My Lady," she said, saluting Xyanth as was proper. "I carry no messages, but Master Gasperian has sent me to you. He says I am to travel with you, that you might find it useful to have a second runner with you who knows these trails well." The lies came far more easily than she'd expected.

"How thoughtful of Gasperian." Xyanth stood beside the open palanquin eyeing Nareen with a frown. "You seem to travel quite a lot, runner. I wouldn't have thought—"

Whatever else she had been about to say was cut short when Jerrel strolled up.

For an instant Xyanth's eyes flicked suspiciously from Nareen to Jerrel and back again. But when Jerrel gave Nareen the merest nod in greeting, Xyanth's tension eased. Waving Nareen away, she concentrated on Jerrel. "You don't seem to move very quickly, warrior."

"You had urgent need of me, my Lady? Your guardsman made no mention of that fact." Jerrel bowed, keeping his eyes fixed on Xyanth's.

Though she had clearly been dismissed, Nareen didn't leave but moved slightly to the side so she could hear and see the exchange between Jerrel and Xyanth. She couldn't repress a slight smile of satisfaction at Xyanth's irritation with Jerrel's response. The woman obviously didn't care to have anyone think she might be overeager to talk to the warrior she'd hired.

"I'm afraid I've forgotten why I called you," Xyanth said with every appearance of bored disdain. "Perhaps I will remember later."

"I hope so, my Lady," Jerrel responded, bowing again. "This evening, perhaps?"

"Perhaps. Who knows?" Xyanth turned and held out a hand for one of her attendants to help her into the palanquin. It was an effective dismissal.

As unobtrusively as possible, Nareen slipped away from Xyanth's group and into the mass of soldiers still marching past.

If Jerrel visited Xyanth's tent this evening, there was a good chance Xyanth would dismiss some of her guards. That might, Nareen decided, provide the opportunity she needed to get close enough

239

to the tent so she could eavesdrop on Xyanth's conversations.

Not that she wanted to spy on Jerrel, Nareen added to herself hastily, but there was always the chance that she could convince him to steer the conversation onto topics that might be more useful to her purposes. It was worth a try.

But Jerrel refused to be convinced by her arguments. "I'm not about to spend my limited time with that witch in trying to get her to talk about her political plots and schemes," he snapped. "If you want to talk to someone, try Pardraik. He's got as many suspicions as you and better opportunities, perhaps, to do your spying for you."

It wasn't difficult to find Pardraik, even in the disordered ranks of the Matcassen troops. The guardsman proved an intelligent and entertaining companion, but although Nareen was convinced he knew far more than he was willing to say, she failed to learn anything she could use.

"There are some who say Matcassen has come to fight more than beastmen," Nareen said conversationally after a few minutes.

"I've heard that," Pardraik said noncommittally.

"Would you attack Kalinden, guardsman?" Nareen took care to ask the question in an offhand manner.

Pardraik glanced down at her. The gleam in his dark eyes showed clearly he understood the drift of her questions.

"A soldier does what he's told," he said at last. "But there's no one I know planning on doing more than fighting beastmen."

Nareen didn't say anything for a few minutes, then, "Strange how rumors start, isn't it, guardsman? You never know where they come from, but sometimes there's more truth to them than one would dream."

"Such as?"

"Oh, rumors of Matcassen's intentions, that sort of thing. I've even heard rumors that Matcassen has had dealings with the beastmen. The rumors say that's why the creatures have moved down across the border and are attacking us now."

"Lies!" Pardraik stopped in the road, heedless of those around them. His hand clenched around his spear until the knuckles turned white. "No one would deal with the beastmen. No one!"

The guardsman's reaction startled Nareen. There was far more passion in the denial than she would have expected, and she read doubt in the dark eyes, in the way his jaw moved. It was as if his anger responded to an inner uncertainty that he could not bring himself to face.

Jerrel had been right, Nareen grudgingly admitted to herself. Pardraik knew, or at least suspected, something. With time she might be able to convince him to help her, but it would be difficult. His loyalty to Matcassen and his sense of duty would prevent him from spying on Xyanth unless he was convinced she had somehow betrayed Matcassen. He had his doubts about her, but doubts weren't certainties. Pardraik wasn't the kind of man to act unless he was very, very sure.

While camp was set up that night, Nareen strolled about with every appearance of aimlessness. A quick scan of Xyanth's tents showed the woman was too well-guarded for Nareen to sneak up and eavesdrop. She could only hope Jerrel's visit would be enough of a distraction so she could get closer.

At least the tent itself would provide a good hiding place. Besides the outer tent, there was an inner lining of heavy draperies that created an additional barrier against the cold. If she could get close enough to slide under the edge of the outer tent, she could hide between the two walls, unseen either by patrolling guards or the tent's occupants.

Nareen avoided approaching Jerrel but kept close enough so she knew when Xyanth summoned him. As she'd hoped, the guards who would normally have been posted around the tent were dismissed, leaving only a couple of men to patrol the area. Since no one had been allowed to set up camp anywhere near Xyanth's tent, it was fairly easy to sneak up to the back of the tent in the dark, then slide under the heavy canvas.

Though Nareen tried to make as little noise as possible, the canvas rustled as she brushed against it, and pebbles grated under her feet. Worse, her heart was pounding so hard she feared it could be heard even by the passing guards.

For a minute Nareen remained frozen, tensed against the possible need to run. But there was no outcry, only the soft murmur of voices from inside the tent and the vague sound of the guard's footsteps as he patrolled outside.

Gradually Nareen's heartbeat slowed and the indistinct murmur sorted itself into two voices, Jerrel's and Xyanth's. Taking care to make no noise, Nareen slowly worked her way around the tent until she could hear what was being said without straining.

" . . . several days more. I don't think I can tolerate this dirt and boredom much longer." Xyanth's voice was sharp with discontent.

"The trail of an army is not a suitable place for a Lady such as yourself. Why don't you return to Matcassen and leave the fighting to your soldiers?" Jerrel's voice dropped, heavy with unspoken meaning. "I would be more than happy to accompany you and your guards."

"Indeed?"

Nareen found her fists clenching at the sultry nuances Xyanth managed to convey in that one word. She forced herself to relax and concentrate.

Jerrel didn't respond, and a moment later Xyanth added, "You still have not told me what it is that brings you here, warrior."

"Would you believe me if I said it was yourself, fair Lady?"

Nareen almost snorted in disgust. The man was a consummate actor when he wanted to be. She'd have to remember that in the future.

Xyanth laughed, low in her throat. "You flatter me, warrior, and I distrust all flatterers."

"Ah, Lady . . ."

Whatever Jerrel had intended to say was cut short by a sudden commotion at the front of the tent. Nareen could discern nothing except the strident sound of voices raised in heated argument. A moment later she could hear the sound of the tent flap being thrown back.

"Your pardon, Lady . . ." a guard said.

"I gave orders I was not to be disturbed." Xyanth was almost snarling.

"Yes, my Lady. But Advisor Gorvan insists you see him, my Lady. He has Guardsman Kel with him."

"Guardsman . . ." Xyanth cut short whatever

243

she was about to say. "Very well, bring them in."

Judging by the sounds, Xyanth must have risen to her feet. Anger was clearly discernible in the woman's voice, but Nareen thought she detected another emotion, as well. Eagerness, perhaps? Or could it be fear?

"You will have to forgive me, warrior," Xyanth said. Though her anger seemed under control, her words lacked the sultry promise that had been there only a few minutes before.

"Of course, my Lady."

To Nareen, it sounded as if Jerrel were repressing his own anger at the interruption. It seemed he wasn't destined to learn what he wanted tonight, either.

She listened to the confusing sounds of people moving about in the tent, trying to sort out what was happening. Then she heard the tent flap drawn back into place and the steps of the guards moving away from the tent.

"Well?" Xyanth's voice was tight with repressed anger. "How dare you appear before me in this disreputable condition, guardsman? Where are the rest of the men I sent with you?"

"My Lady, Guardsmen Kel has only just returned to camp—alone. I thought you should hear what he had to say immediately."

Nareen didn't recognize the voice. Assuming this was Advisor Gorvan, there was an odd note of hesitant fear in his words, as if he didn't trust Xyanth to listen to him, despite his rank.

"My Lady," said a second, less educated voice. "You have to believe me when I say we tried to carry out your bidding. Truly we tried. But those beasts, those monsters, they—"

The man was pleading, obviously desperate and, it seemed, exhausted and frightened. At his reference to beasts, Nareen tensed and placed her ear against the tapestry wall that hid her from the tent's occupants. She doubted the three on the other side of the tapestry would notice even if it moved.

"Stop this sniveling and tell me what you've come to say," Xyanth snapped.

"We couldn't talk to them, my Lady. We tried, I swear we tried, but we ran into a hunting party of the creatures before we even reached their caves. They slaughtered us, my Lady, as if they didn't know who we were." The man was almost sobbing.

"You carried the chain that identified you as my emissaries?"

"Yes, my Lady. It was no use. They didn't care. I'd swear they knew what it meant, that you'd sent us, but they didn't care."

For a moment there was no sound from within the tent except the ragged breathing of the guardsman. Then Xyanth, her voice carefully controlled, said, "Very well, guardsman. That will be all."

"My Lady, please . . . The beasts are our enemies. They'll kill us the same as they will the people of Kalinden. Please—"

"That's enough, guardsman! You may go."

Something in Xyanth's voice seemed to bring the man back to an awareness of where he was. "Yes, my Lady," he mumbled, then shuffled out of the tent.

Neither Xyanth nor Gorvan spoke until the sound of the guardsman's footsteps had died away, then Xyanth said coldly, "Kill him, Gorvan.

Do it yourself and make sure no one sees you. That man is a danger to us now."

"Didn't you listen to him? Don't you understand?" Gorvan's voice was shrill, as if he were verging on panic. "You have to stop this insanity! Those creatures aren't helping us gain control of Kalinden, they're killing our people. They have no honor, no—"

"Enough!" Xyanth's voice cut like ice. "It's too late for us to turn back now."

"Us! My Lady, I told you from the beginning—"

"Quiet, you fool! Do as you're told. Now."

For a moment, Nareen though Gorvan would try to press further, but at last he, too, mumbled, "Yes, my Lady," and left the tent.

Nareen's thoughts whirled. Tork had been right—Xyanth was responsible for starting the beastmen on their murderous rampage. But even though Nareen had risked everything to obtain the proof she now held, she realized for the first time that she hadn't believed Tork. Not really. It had seemed so impossible.

But it wasn't impossible. Gasperian and his advisors would have to believe her now.

From inside the tent, Nareen heard the chattering chink of metal against metal, as if an unsteady hand were trying to pour a drink. Then Xyanth spoke to herself, so low Nareen could scarcely hear the words. This time there was no anger and no arrogance in Xyanth's voice, only the fear that came from confronting a horrible truth that could no longer be avoided.

"The beasts have betrayed me again." Xyanth's voice was unsteady. "By all that's holy, what do I do now?"

With that, Nareen carefully lifted the edge of

the canvas, checked to make sure there were no guards near, then slid out of the tent and disappeared into the darkness beyond.

So Nareen had returned to Kalinden. Jerrel sat hunched at the side of the small fire morosely poking at the glowing pieces of wood with a stick.

What was so urgent that she couldn't have remained a little while longer to tell him personally, instead of relaying her message through Pardraik?

After he'd left Xyanth's tent he'd walked around the camp, trying to control his frustration and anger at being balked once again in his effort to find out what Xyanth knew about Santar. He'd only been gone an hour or so. What was it Nareen had learned that was so urgent she couldn't delay that long?

Jerrel threw another small piece of wood on the fire. He was being unreasonable and he knew it. It was better this way. Once she was back in Kalinden, Nareen would be out of danger. And if anyone could take care of herself on the trail, it was she. She'd proved that on the journey from Matcassen.

Besides, this way there was no uncomfortable parting between them. He wasn't forced to say anything he would regret or didn't mean. Now he could just put her out of his mind and get on with the search for Santar without worrying about her safety, or her undeniable ability to thoroughly distract him.

Jerrel leaned back against the massive rock behind him, the rock he'd carefully chosen both to reflect the heat of his small fire and to prevent any unexpected attacks from behind.

Santar. He'd come on this insane expedition in the hopes of learning something about his brother. But what had he accomplished so far? Absolutely nothing.

Was there, he wondered, any hint, any clue that he'd missed in the recording in his brother's ring? Jerrel frowned. It was far too risky to read the ring here in camp. And yet that ring was the only link he had to a brother he hadn't seen for years.

Jerrel glanced around. There was no one near. He'd taken care to find a site a little distant from the rest; before he finally went to bed, he would move his pallet again.

Satisfied he would not be observed—he didn't care to find his throat slit some night because someone wanted a gold ring—he took off his belt and pulled the ring, still on its chain, from the belt's hidden compartment.

It was such a simple ring with its plain gold setting and massive recorder stone. Jerrel turned it over in his fingers. Locked in the micro-circuits buried in the stone was his brother's life as he'd experienced it in those last months and days.

Yet, oddly, it wasn't of Santar that the ring reminded him, but Nareen. To whom had she been carrying it? Who had sent it, and for what purpose?

Nareen. Like an incantation to summon a beneficent spirit, her name conjured a dancing, shifting image of her features in the flames. A burning stick crumbled in a shower of sparks and he could hear her laughter. Like the sparks, the laughter soon faded and she was gone, faded into the night, into the dark at the edge of his fire.

Gone. It was better so—wasn't it?

All about him the camp was still, with only the occasional footsteps of a patrolling guard or the crackle of the fire to break the stillness. Jerrel leaned back against the cold, hard stone. Above him, the night sky was alive with the radiance of the stars.

What if he were to tell her who and what he was? Give her a chance to decide for herself if she could accept his way of life? He could offer her the stars. She had more than enough courage to face such a challenge.

Somehow, looking up at those distant lights with the night wrapped still and cold about him, he felt suddenly cast adrift, spun outward from the planet as though no longer bound to the earth or to any earthly thing, tossed into the void without an anchor, without a hope of rescue.

Where was she? Was she safe? Was she thinking of him? Cursing him? With each step she took away from him, was she putting him farther and farther behind her, emotionally as well as physically? Or would she, somehow, see his image in the night, just as he was seeing hers?

Jerrel's gaze dropped to the ring he held. It was only a lump of metal and stone and microcircuitry. There was nothing magical about it, nothing secret. It wasn't even hers, and yet, somehow, it seemed a link to her and to what they'd shared.

Slowly Jerrel slid the chain over his head, then tucked it under his shirt. The ring was all he had of her—all he ever would have. The ring and his memories.

"My Lady." Jerrel ducked his head in a slight bow so that Xyanth wouldn't see the anger that he knew glittered in his eyes. He'd spent a useless day mingling with the troops, trying to obtain some hint of Santar, and had been on the verge of sleep when one of her guards had come to fetch him. The abrupt summons had meant he'd been forced to douse his fire and come almost at a run, like a trained pet called by its master.

However much it might serve his purpose to have her want him, tonight he was in no mood for the games she played. He forced his anger down. He had to take advantage of his opportunities when they arose, regardless of his feelings.

Behind him he heard the servants dropping the tent flap into place, then the retreating footsteps of both servants and guards. Xyanth's command that she be left alone was convenient, at least.

"Warrior."

Strange how she could invest one word with such silken promises, such tempting visions. Tempting, at least, for others. Jerrel straightened.

"My guards tell me your little friend the runner left camp yesterday. Without even consulting me!" She crossed the tent to him. The hem of her gown rustled on the heavy carpets covering the tent floor.

Jerrel glanced around him at the small but richly furnished tent. Large, inviting cushions were heaped at one side, intended, no doubt, to serve both as bed and seating. Heavy curtains hung on all sides, blocking out the cold night air and disguising the space so it seemed more a private chamber than a tent in the middle of an armed camp. A small folding table had been set up beside the cushions. It bore a tray with two goblets and a bottle of wine, already opened. Small, intricately cut metal lanterns hung from the tent poles at all four corners. The candles burning inside cast a softly flickering yellow glow about the tent.

How many men had been needed to carry such furnishings from Kalinden? he wondered in disgust. How many men who might, instead, have carried arms or food or medical supplies?

Nareen would scorn such comforts when those around her had none. Though at the proper time, in a gown such as Xyanth wore—soft, silken, almost transparent . . .

He jerked himself from his thoughts, then shrugged in seeming indifference. "So they tell me."

"And you don't care?" One perfect eyebrow rose.

"She served her purpose." Nareen, he felt sure, would understand and forgive his feigned callousness. Even though she'd never know, and he'd never have the chance to tell her.

Xyanth laughed, obviously convinced she knew exactly what he was referring to. "You are cruel, warrior. The little runner has left without even tending to her duty." The idea seemed to please her. "Come," she said, gesturing to the cushions, "I grow weary of all this talk of war and fighting. Let us share some wine and talk of things that are of more interest."

Jerrel chose a cushion farther away from Xyanth than the one she indicated. She made no comment, but handed him a cup of wine. As he bowed his head over the cup in the traditional Errandane toast, he couldn't help wishing he had some Narregian soul dust. Just a pinch of the potent drug—strictly illegal on four hundred and seventeen worlds and rigidly controlled even on its own world of manufacture—would be sufficient to wrest everything she knew about Santar from her.

"The beastmen do not concern you?" he asked. How was he to turn the conversation to his search for Santar?

"Those savages!" Xyanth's eyes flashed. Her hand clenched around her cup. She took a quick swallow of the strong wine. "I can manage them. I *will* manage them!"

Were there, Jerrel wondered, shadows in her eyes? Shadows of doubt, or of fear? And did her hand tremble, ever so slightly? In the flickering candlelight he couldn't be sure. Were Nareen's suspicions true after all?

"And how will you do that, my Lady?" He took a sip of wine. "Manage" was an odd choice of words when referring to the creatures he'd seen on the trail from Matcassen—creatures capable of the destruction they'd passed since leaving Kalinden.

"They can't . . ." Xyanth stopped, biting back her words with an effort. She smiled, but her smile was strained, artificial. "It doesn't matter." She leaned back against a cushion so that she was half sitting, half reclining, and took another, more cautious, swallow of wine. "Come, warrior. Why should we waste our time with such things? Let us talk of more interesting matters."

"Such as?"

"Nothing occurs to you?"

It was amazing how quickly the woman's moods could switch. Now she was coy, offering without promising, alluring yet distant. "What do you suggest?"

"Hmmm." Xyanth shifted on the cushions, leaning on one elbow to move closer to him, turning her head so her hair fell forward in a golden curtain that half hid her face. "Tell me, what brought you here? I've been curious. You're not like any other itinerant warrior I've ever met."

"You've met many?"

"A few." She said it slowly, with an emphasis that carried far more meaning than the words themselves revealed. ."But I'm asking the questions. Why are you here?"

Jerrel set his cup on the carpet and leaned forward, too, propped on one elbow. It might be a mistake, but he had decided how he would deal with her.

"I've come in search of my brother," he said. "He disappeared a few months ago. In Matcassen. His name was Santar." Did her brows contract in a sudden frown? He couldn't be sure with that mass of hair shadowing her features.

"Indeed."

"He looked like me. Blue eyes, curly hair. Smaller, though, and slender."

Xyanth shrugged. "The blue eyes are unusual. But as for the rest . . . There are thousands such."

"True, my Lady," Jerrel said softly, leaning even closer to her. "But none, so far as I know, that you have bedded lately."

Xyanth gasped. Her eyes grew wide and her mouth gaped. For an instant she stared at Jerrel in mingled fury and fear; then her lips curled back in a snarl. "You snake!" she hissed, then lunged at him, her fingers with their long, sharp nails curved to claw his face.

Jerrel was quicker. He threw himself across her, pinning her to the cushions with the weight of his body. With one hand he covered her mouth, with the other he held one wrist, leaving her to flail helplessly with her free hand.

"It's not that easy, my Lady," he said, ignoring her efforts to claw his back—the heavy leather tunic he wore was more than enough protection against such feeble weapons as her fingernails. "I know you seduced my brother, and I know he was fool enough to have told you his wild daydreams. What I don't know—and what you're going to tell me—is where he is now."

There was nothing beautiful about Xyanth now. Her face was crimson with rage. Hate poured from her eyes.

"There's no use in thinking you can scream. You sent your guards away, remember? Before you could call for help, I'd crush your throat. Do you understand?"

He had no intention of hurting her, but she couldn't know that and fear was his only weapon against her now. He had to make use of whatever time was available to scare her into revealing the information he wanted. Then he would leave her bound and gagged for the servants to find her in the morning. In the dark it would be easy for him to transport up to the ship and from there to wherever he needed to go.

"Do you understand?" he insisted, his voice a harsh, menacing whisper.

If his hand hadn't been over her mouth, Xyanth might have snarled. As it was, her eyes were sufficiently eloquent to express her fury and hate. Reluctantly, she nodded. Jerrel slid his hand from her mouth but remained poised in case she ignored his warning and began screaming.

"Beast! Maggot-infested aard dung! Slime-rotted worm! You stinking—"

Jerrel clamped his hand over her mouth again. "Such language accomplishes nothing, you know. I'd suggest you save your energy for telling me what happened to Santar." He gave her a few moments to calm down, then cautiously slid his hand off her mouth. This time she said nothing, just remained glaring at him with undisguised hatred.

"Now, what about my brother?"

"He was a fool! An idealistic nit without sense!"

"Indeed." Jerrel forced down a surge of anger. It was one thing for him to call Santar an idealistic fool, quite another to hear such an epithet from the lips of this scheming witch. "That doesn't concern me now. I want to know what happened to him."

"What should you care?" Xyanth spat out the words as if they were poison. "He was insane as well as a fool."

"Was he? Do you make a habit of bedding madmen, my Lady?"

"Why, you . . . !" The rest of the exclamation was cut off as Jerrel wrapped his fingers around Xyanth's throat.

"Come, now. Have you forgotten my warning about not screaming?" He tightened his grip slightly, enough to convince Xyanth of his intentions. Slowly she relaxed under him. Though her eyes never left his, Jerrel knew that behind those black windows her mind was spinning, trying to contrive a way out for herself and suitable revenge against him.

"All right," Xyanth said at last. "I'll tell you what I can, but it isn't much." She waited until Jerrel relaxed his hold, then continued, "It's true I bedded this brother of yours. But that's all. I know nothing of his disappearance, if, as you say, he disappeared."

"I don't believe you."

"He was pretty. I wanted him. I rather liked his blue eyes." She paused, her own eyes glittering. "I don't think I much care for blue eyes now."

Her voice was sharp with loathing, but low enough that Jerrel further relaxed his grip.

"I went to him one night," she continued. "Once. That was all."

She shifted under him. The movement was provocative, but her expression gave no hint she was aware of it.

"And that's all?"

In spite of being pinned against the cushions, Xyanth managed a fair approximation of a shrug. "All that mattered. Afterwards, we had some wine." Her lips curled in a sneer. "Like so many fool men, once he was sated he simply passed out. I left his room, and that was the last I saw of him."

Jerrel relaxed even more, then moved to take some of his weight onto his arms and off her. She might be telling the truth. Though the recorder showed that Santar, in his last moments of consciousness, thought she'd drugged him, there was no proof of that. She might simply have left him, and it might be someone else entirely who was responsible for Santar's disappearance.

But he didn't believe it.

Jerrel looked down at her beautiful face, at the mass of golden hair spread across the cushions. Once again she shifted under him, the motion even more blatant than before.

No. She knew far more than she'd admitted. Her beauty was only a mask, a way of disguising the soul-deep corruption beneath.

"I don't believe you. You—"

She twisted beneath him, abruptly and violently. Suddenly a searing pain shot through his side, then another. Without thinking, Jerrel rolled to the edge of the cushions, away from her attack. A knife! She had a knife!

Once freed of his weight, Xyanth started screeching, "Guards! Guards!" all the while stabbing at him with the stiletto.

Ignoring the pain in his side and the heat of his blood on his skin, Jerrel twisted to grab Xyanth's hand that held the knife. He slammed her hand down on the cushions, his grip on her wrist cruelly tight, while struggling to clamp his other hand over her mouth and stifle her screams.

He was too late. Another instant more and the tent was filled by armed guards. Jerrel swung around, but before he could get to his feet the guards fell upon him, dragging him away from a screaming, biting Xyanth. He lunged, shaking loose the guard who held his right arm, then twisted back, almost dislodging the man who had grabbed his tunic from the back. An instant later, he froze, the sharp point of a well-honed sword at his throat.

"Don't struggle, warrior. I'd hate to be the one responsible for your death."

Jerrel looked up to find Pardraik holding the sword. Strong hands on his arms and shoulders forced Jerrel down, and as he sank to his knees, Pardraik unwaveringly held the sword tip against his throat. It was clear that no chance for escape would be offered, regardless of the guardsman's doubts about the woman he served.

"You are as great a fool as your brother." The

words dripped with hate-filled venom. Xyanth, her gown torn and her hair in wild disarray, moved to stand before Jerrel. She still held the blood-stained stiletto in her hand.

A guard hovered protectively to the side and slightly in front of her, sword drawn. She stepped forward, but when the guard nervously moved closer as well, she impatiently gestured him away.

"He's dead, you know," she said. The corner of her mouth lifted in satisfaction. She raised the stiletto so it was directly in front of his eyes. "Just as you will be."

She smiled again, then slowly, consideringly, placed the point of the dagger against his throat on the opposite side from where Pardraik continued to hold his sword.

Jerrel kept his gaze fixed on Xyanth, as though oblivious to her threat. He could feel the prick of the sharp dagger as she pressed it deeper into his skin, but not so deeply that she cut him.

"A shame I'll have to ask my guards to kill you quickly," she said. "I might have enjoyed watching you die. A man your size . . . It probably takes a long time." She smiled again. Her eyes glittered in the light, hard and cold. "A very long time."

The stiletto flashed. Jerrel, steeled for whatever she might do, felt a hot burning as the dagger sliced the skin of his throat, then the sudden warm flow of his own blood. He continued to stare at her, unflinching.

Xyanth leaned forward to study her handiwork. "Tsk, tsk. Such a shame. You bleed so easily."

She stepped back, then snarled to the guards, "Get him out of here. I don't care how, but I want you to kill him. Now." She turned away, carefully straightening the sleeve of her gown.

"Afterwards," she added, her voice suddenly calm, "you can throw him out for the scavengers."

Chapter 14

The walls of Kalinden had never looked so inviting to Nareen. It had taken her less than a day to return, running as fast as she could and traveling through the night, but in that time she'd encountered three hunting groups of beastmen, two small and one large. All three groups had obviously suffered losses—many of the beasts were limping and their weapons were battered—but none were retreating.

The holdings she'd passed were deserted, though only four had been attacked. The inhabitants of the rest had clearly moved into the larger villages or to Kalinden itself for protection. Twice she'd stopped at walled villages, and both times the information was the same—the villages were packed to overflowing and had several times been forced to repel attacks by the beastmen.

None of it would make good hearing in

Kalinden. That is, if anyone would be willing to listen to her. Throughout her journey the same questions had circled through her head. What if they didn't listen to her? What if they didn't believe her? How could she convince them that she wasn't lying, or demented, or a fool?

And through that endless litany had twined her worries for Jerrel. What would happen to him? For all his strength and knowledge, he seemed to understand very little about the beastmen. Would he find the information he sought? Would he return to Kalinden afterwards? Would she ever see him again? Would she . . . ?

Since she wasn't on an official mission and didn't want to draw attention by arriving at the Great Hall with an escort, Nareen decided not to use the signal bells. That meant a delay at the gate until she identified herself and the bars across the small gate could be lowered to let her in. The guards were more cautious than usual, which made her glad she didn't have any beastmen right behind her.

The streets of the city were even more crowded than before. People scurried about on their individual missions, their faces grim. Whether they were dressed in the bright colors of a city dweller or the simple homespun of a crofter, they all seemed driven by a tension that almost vibrated in the air, as if it were a physical presence.

Many of the passersby carried the marks of an encounter with the beastmen—a bandaged head or broken arm or stiff gait. In the eyes of these people Nareen read pain, grief, horror, and an abiding anger that would mark them for the rest of their lives.

Around the Great Hall, that anger had found a

verbal outlet. People were clustered on the broad stone steps or in the plaza before the Hall, their conversations heated. Every now and then voices rose above the din, sharp and urgent.

As Nareen slowly pushed her way through the crowd, scraps of conversation drifted to her.

" . . . raids near the villages of Mesnar and Salgna. They say twenty died . . ."

"When are the other cities going to send troops? After all, Matcassen . . ."

" . . . attacks against the border garrison . . ."

"At least Matcassen has come to our aid, and though they say Master Lindaz is ill . . ."

" . . . my son dead, my daughter and wife injured . . ."

"Thank the gods for Matcassen . . ."

Nareen's heart sank. With everyone grateful for the presence of Matcassen soldiers in Kalinden territory, how was she to convince Gasperian that those same troops—or their leader, at least—were as great a threat as the beastmen?

The entrance of the Hall was even more crowded than the steps outside. Nareen ventured into the main reception hall only to discover that Gasperian, after hearing the reports of refugees from outlying holdings, had withdrawn with his advisors. No one she asked seemed to know where Gravnar had gone, so she decided to wait for him outside his own room. The choice was wise, for the old man appeared, walking alone and deep in thought, only a few minutes later.

At sight of Nareen, he stopped. For an instant, an expression almost of joy illuminated his face. But only for an instant. He frowned; then his runner's training reasserted itself, erasing all trace of human emotion from his features. He hurried forward.

"Sixth Runner." In that simple title, Gravnar managed to pack a hundred questions, most of them disapproving.

Nareen heard, and understood each one. "Teacher," she said. All her doubts returned. If Gravnar—a man who had rescued her from Margash, trained her, and who was as close to a father as she would ever know—could be so coldly unwelcoming, what would her reception be from others? Then she reminded herself of that brief flash of emotion he'd allowed to show and took heart. "I need to speak with you. I need your help."

Again a hint of emotion showed in Gravnar's expression, but this time it was composed of doubt and disapproval. "I don't know what help I can—or should—provide a runner who deliberately disobeys her orders and abandons her post."

"Please, teacher. If you would only listen . . ." Her words were heavy with urgency and worry, and Nareen knew as soon as she said them that she'd made a mistake. Allowing her feelings to color her words would only harm her case.

With an effort she added, more calmly, "I didn't ignore your orders out of caprice. You know I didn't. And I've gained information that is vital to Kalinden's safety. If you would only give me some of your time, listen to what I have to say . . ."

For a moment Gravnar said nothing, just stood and studied Nareen. Then he nodded, once. "Very well. I'll listen, but I make no promises."

With a relief she couldn't keep from appearing on her face, Nareen followed her old teacher into his room, then waited while he closed the door and took a seat at the table. The same table, she thought with a pang, where she and Gravnar and Jerrel had shared a meal. She could almost see Jerrel there, feel his presence.

Almost. But imagination and wishful thinking weren't what was needed now. She forced down her memories and turned her attention back to Gravnar.

Quickly Nareen recounted the substance of the conversation she'd overheard in Xyanth's tent, carefully omitting any mention of the manner in which she obtained the information.

For what seemed a long, long while, Gravnar said nothing, just sat and stared at Nareen. "I'm not an advisor, nor have I ever tried to be," he said at last, his voice completely uninflected. "I will take you to Gasperian so that he and his advisors may hear and judge your words."

"Teacher, I . . ." Nareen began, hope surging within her.

Gravnar held up his hand. "I don't do this for you, Sixth Runner, or because I believe the information you bear."

Nareen's hopes plummeted.

"I do it because you are . . ." He paused and his jaw moved slightly, as though he were struggling to keep his voice under control. " . . . or were a runner. A runner I chose and trained and for whom I am responsible. I do it because I am a runner, too, not an advisor. My role doesn't allow me to judge the validity of what you say. That is for others who are more fit than I to decide whether or not to believe this wild tale you carry."

Gravnar rose from the table and, without another glance at Nareen, left the room. After a moment's hesitation, Nareen followed him.

He didn't believe her. He'd known her since she was a child, taught her the skills of a runner, praised her when she did well in her studies, chastised her when she didn't, and defended her against those who disapproved of her—and still he didn't believe her.

Nareen made no effort to speak as she followed Gravnar to Gasperian's quarters. The knowledge that the Chief Runner no longer trusted her was like a knife stabbing to her very core, then twisting inside her. He was her friend, her teacher—all the family she'd ever had. And yet that wasn't enough to overcome his training as a runner. Even if it meant risking Kalinden's safety, he would not—could not—put aside the prejudices and strictures imposed by a lifetime spent performing as best he could the role that life had assigned him.

Was she being a fool, even if she was right about the threat from Matcassen? Was she risking too much for too little hope of success? When this was all over, whatever happened, would she find herself without friends and position, without honor? What could she possibly gain?

If only Jerrel were here so she could talk to him, share with him. He, at least, would believe her. Even if all he did was hold her, if she could see him, touch him, talk to him, perhaps somehow . . .

She forced that thought down. Jerrel wasn't here. Whatever his feelings for her—and she knew they ran deeper than he was willing to admit—they didn't matter. In his eyes his brother came first, just as Kalinden and the safety of its people must come before her need for him.

As they must come before any other consideration, including her own self-interest. Whatever the personal cost, she would do whatever was necessary to protect her city, her people—her home.

Nareen glanced at Gravnar, who was walking with bent head and stooped shoulders, as if he'd aged several years since she'd last seen him. For the first time she realized that the price might be far higher than she'd ever suspected.

They were admitted almost immediately to Gasperian's private quarters. Gasperian and his senior advisor, an old man named Dorflon, were seated at a table studying several maps spread out before them. Two other advisors, Jelnik and Tisnerl, stood behind the seated men, looking over their shoulders.

At sight of Tisnerl, Nareen's hopes lifted. He was the youngest of the advisors and noted for his unconventional approaches to problems. Of them all, he was the one most likely to believe her report, and to be willing to act on it.

Gravnar came to a halt before the table and bowed. "Master," he said, "Sixth Runner Nareen has returned. She bears no message but has information she feels you and your advisors should hear."

Gasperian's gaze fixed on Nareen. He frowned. "So you decided to return to your duties, Sixth Runner?"

Nareen hesitated. This was going to be even more difficult than she'd feared. "I have information I think you should hear, Master."

"You think I should hear! By the gods, is it not enough that I have to deal with these marauding beastmen? Must I now be subjected to runners who fancy themselves in the role of advisors?" Gasperian thumped the table. "You deserted your post and disobeyed your orders! I'll have no—"

"Perhaps, Master, it would be well to listen, at least, to what the runner has to say." Tisnerl leaned forward, studying Nareen.

"You can always listen to her in the hallway, Tisnerl," Dorflon grumped. He sat hunched in his heavy robes, glaring at the two runners standing before the table. "You're the only one who wasted any time considering that preposterous tale she brought us the last time."

"I don't think it's preposterous, and I do think it's worth our while to hear her report." Tisnerl's voice was low, unruffled by his senior's disapproval.

For a moment no one spoke. Four pairs of eyes studied Nareen from the other side of the table while Gravnar stood staring straight ahead, as if willing himself to ignore whatever happened. At last Gasperian nodded curtly. "Go ahead, but be quick about it."

"Thank you, Master." Suddenly, now that she was here, the words came easily. "You know of Chief Runner Tork's warning. I accompanied the Matcassen troops to see if I could obtain proof, or at least more information, so that we could be prepared in case of need." Quickly she recounted the soldiers' rumors and the conversation she overheard.

Throughout, she was intensely aware of Tisnerl standing behind Gasperian's chair, his gaze fixed on her face. She'd needed only one glance at the cold or openly hostile expressions on the faces of Gasperian, Dorflon, and Jelnik to know she had little hope of convincing them that her information was accurate. Though she faced Gasperian, as was proper, it was to Tisnerl she spoke, for him she shaped her words so that he would understand. He alone, of them all, had not yet judged and condemned her.

When she'd finished she stood silent, waiting.

At last, Gasperian spoke. "That is the most preposterous pack of lies I have ever heard."

Nareen's head jerked up and her eyes flashed. "I'm not lying!"

Gasperian's eyes flashed, too, dark and dangerous. "Such things are impossible! I cannot—will not—believe them!"

"They seem improbable, to be sure, but they are not impossible." Tisnerl's voice was low and calm, soothing. "If the Lady Xyanth's true intentions are disguised by our need, it is well that we are warned to be alert."

"Ridiculous!" Dorflon snorted, settling even farther into his robes so that he seemed to have no neck. "Outrageous! The Edict of Trassdeance requires that Matcassen assist us, and they have done so. We need no impudent runner to heap calumny on an act of goodwill."

"I agree." Jelnik spoke with an air of distaste, as though it offended his senses even to listen to such charges. "And we shouldn't neglect to consider the Sixth Runner's motives. Isn't that stranger who contracted as warrior with the Lady Xyanth the same man this runner brought from Matcassen?"

"That's true." Gasperian glanced at Jelnik, standing behind Dorflon's chair, then at Dorflon, before turning his attention back to Nareen. "This stranger, this Jerrel I believe you said his name was, seems rather too involved in these affairs, runner." He ignored Nareen's gasp of indignation and continued, "You didn't return from Matcassen when and as you should have, and you tell us you were traveling with him. Were you lovers? You allowed him to accompany you here—something no runner I ever knew would permit—and then you defied my orders and left Kalinden, quite possibly with the intention of rejoining him. Now you return, without the man and bearing tales that even the most credulous child would reject. I begin to wonder why this is so, and I do not like where my suspicions lead me."

"I've told you what happened in Matcassen," Nareen protested, "and explained how I was delayed. Jerrel offered me help, a means of travel when I couldn't travel on my own. And while it's true we became lovers—" The words caught in Nareen's throat, choking her. She paused, then said in a tight voice, "We are not lovers now, and have not been since before the traders' caravan reached Matcassen. I brought him here because he wanted to come for personal reasons and because I was still unable to travel as fast as I normally would have. And as for my disobeying orders and joining the Matcassen troops—I would have done that whether or not Jerrel was among them."

She was saying too much, she knew, arguing too heatedly. Neither action was appropriate to a runner, and that would be held against her. Yet she couldn't—wouldn't—stop. There was no one else to speak in her defense. Gravnar had stood throughout her recital, staring straight ahead. He hadn't even gone into the listening trance, as though he thought her information of so little value that it wasn't worth remembering. And now this!

"You accuse me of not following my orders to remain in Kalinden. Of that I am guilty. I admit it. But I'm guilty of nothing else. Your accusations only hide the importance of the information I bring you."

Nareen drew herself up to her full height and faced Gasperian squarely. "Judge me if you will. Punish me if you must. But I beg you to believe me when I say I'm neither lying nor acting out of a jealous self-interest. Tork was right to warn us. The Lady Xyanth has ties with the beastmen, and the Matcassen troops are not in Kalinden simply on some noble expedition. They're here to conquer us once we're too weak or blind to fight against them. If you ignore Tork's warnings, if you reject the information I bring you, then you will all be responsible for whatever evil befalls us!"

Nareen stopped, quivering with anger. She'd gone too far but she wouldn't retract one word, even if she could. Fools! How was it possible to be so blind?

"Are you quite through?" Gasperian's voice rang like cold, hard steel and his lips were white with repressed anger. When Nareen said nothing, he rose abruptly. "You are confined to your quarters until I have decided what punishment is sufficient for your insubordination and your lies. You have disgraced yourself and your profession and me, and you have seriously attacked the honor of Kalinden."

Without taking his eyes off her, he called, "Guards!" When they appeared he snapped, "Take this woman to her quarters and lock her in; then post someone outside the door so she doesn't escape. You are not to talk with her and you are not to allow anyone else to talk with her. Do you understand?"

The guards saluted smartly, then grabbed Nareen unceremoniously by either arm. As she turned to go with them, Nareen caught sight of Gravnar.

For the first time since they'd entered the room, he was looking directly at her. For the first time in all the years she'd known him, his emotions were written clearly on his face. Doubt, uncertainty . . . and pain. His mouth worked, as though he would call out to her, but no sound emerged. Nareen stiffened, then jerked one arm free of her captor's grip so she could go to him.

Before she could break free entirely, Gravnar glanced at Gasperian, a questioning frown on his face, then back at her. He took a deep breath and shut his eyes. When he reopened them, they were nothing more than dark bits of glass, revealing nothing of the emotions that lay behind. He straightened his shoulders, then deliberately turned from her.

The guard regained his grip on her arm, muttering, "Come along, runner. Ain't got all day."

The sound of the door shutting behind them echoed in the corridor, hollow and somehow very final. The sound was repeated a few minutes later when the door to her chamber was shut firmly behind her. Only this time there was the added heavy note of the key being turned in the lock and of the footsteps of only one guard walking away.

For a moment Nareen remained standing, staring blankly at the closed door. She was locked in, disgraced. Formal censure was certain, dismissal from her post a strong possibility. Gravnar had turned from her, shamed and hurt by her actions. Gasperian was enraged by what he saw as the dishonor she'd brought on him.

And for all that, she'd gained nothing. Advisor Tisnerl might have heeded her warnings, but what could he do? He was the youngest advisor in Matcassen, and though he was respected, his influence was limited. Why should he risk his own standing for the sake of a runner in disgrace?

Slowly Nareen sank to the cold stone floor in front of the fireplace. Disgraced.

What would she do if she couldn't be a runner for Kalinden? Where would she go? Ever since Gravnar had taken her out of Margash she'd wanted to be like him. She, an orphan, had longed for the dignity and respect that accompanied the position of runner for a Master. More, she had wanted to belong, to a place, to its people.

Now she'd thrown it all away in a futile attempt to protect her beloved city and its people from those who intended them harm.

A tear slid down her cheek. Nareen blinked, then wiped it away with an angry swipe. She hadn't cried since Margash. She wouldn't cry now.

If only Jerrel were here. If only she could be sure he were safe. If only . . .

Another tear fell, and then another, and another until they streamed down her cheeks. Nareen dropped her head upon her knees, curled into a small, huddled lump, and sobbed, once more an orphan cast out into a world that didn't want her.

*   *   *

Jerrel shifted so the rock he leaned against didn't cut so sharply into his shoulder. His side hurt where Xyanth had knifed him, but the wounds, which were minor, had stopped bleeding long ago. The cut on his neck had crusted over as well. Every time he moved his head he could feel it, sharp and stinging.

He'd been fortunate not to be killed immediately, as Xyanth had ordered. Instead, his execution had been delayed until morning because, as an expressionless Pardraik had explained, they didn't want any dead bodies around to draw the carrion eaters during the night.

The delay gave him a chance, at least, of escaping. But as the hours wore on, Jerrel was beginning to wonder just how much of a chance it was. The guards had been too enthusiastic—the coarse ropes which bound him were tied so tightly his hands and feet were beginning to swell painfully. He'd tried several times to cut the ropes by rubbing them against the rocks, but even the slightest movement brought his guard to instant alertness.

Worse, his muscles were beginning to grow numb with the cold and his cramped position. Even if he could get free, he wouldn't have much hope of escape if he was too stiff to move.

Jerrel closed his eyes and leaned his head back against the rock, silently cursing his stupidity. If only he'd been more cautious. He should have had the intelligence to check that Xyanth had no weapons hidden in the cushions. Instead, he'd blithely assumed that if she'd had a dagger she would have carried it on her body. He'd been fooled by the fact that the gown she wore was

273

too revealing for her to have concealed even a sharp pin, let alone a dagger.

Of course, there was another way out. All he had to do was mentally key his com link and order his ship to beam him up. If he couldn't get free of the ropes before dawn, then he would escape that way.

It would be so easy. But it would mean that his chances of learning anything about Santar would plummet from poor to absolutely none. The tale of his disappearance would be certain to rouse suspicion, if not outright fear. If he reappeared, Xyanth would undoubtedly command her guards to kill him on sight. They wouldn't have any qualms about leaving a dead body for the scavengers the second time around.

If only Nareen were still here. With her knowledge and quick intelligence she'd be able to get him free, or at least create a distraction that would give him the time he needed to cut his bonds. She might even have been able to glean the information he needed to find Santar, if only he hadn't been too proud to ask.

At the thought, his eyes flew open. Had it come to this, that he was relying on a woman to rescue him from his troubles?

Jerrel angrily shook his head. He'd botched this search for Santar, first to last. Wishing someone else would solve his problems for him accomplished exactly nothing. If he couldn't . . .

At that instant the guard abruptly leaped to his feet and stood staring, wide-eyed, into the dark at the far side of camp. From the distance came the cries of men, the sharp clang of sword against sword, and a deeper, harsher sound Jerrel couldn't identify.

Whatever the disturbance, Jerrel intended to take advantage of it. With the guard's attention fixed on the disturbance and not on him, he strained at the cords binding his hands and feet, trying to pull free. He could feel the warm, sticky flow of his blood where the coarse rope lacerated his skin, but despite his efforts he couldn't loosen his bonds by even a fraction of an inch.

A scream rang out, followed by excited shouts and the sound of running footsteps. Jerrel twisted around, trying to peer into the darkness beyond the small campfire. Whatever was rousing the soldiers was far more serious than a fight between a couple of drunken louts.

The guard snatched up the sword he'd left lying on the ground. He took two hesitant steps toward the sounds of battle, then stopped and turned to peer at Jerrel, clearly uncertain of where his duty lay.

Another scream rang out, this one shrill and immediately silenced. The guard spun around, sword raised against the unseen invaders. There was no one there. With a curse, he swung back, then ran toward Jerrel.

Jerrel tensed, ready to lash out with his bound legs, as the guard came to a halt in front of him. For an instant the man wavered, then, teeth bared in fear and determination, he swung his heavy sword over his head.

"To arms! To arms!" The panicked cry was accompanied by swift footsteps. Suddenly a boy, scarcely old enough to have earned the right to be a soldier, leaped out of the dark onto a low, flat rock at one side of the fire.

In the wavering light cast by the flames, Jerrel could see the whites of the boy's eyes, his gaping mouth, and the stream of dark blood that stained half his face. In one hand the boy held a sword whose tip and edge were almost black from the blood that dyed it.

For an instant the boy remained frozen, disoriented by the sudden transition from dark to light. Then he sprang off the rock toward Jerrel and the guard, wild-eyed, sword raised for battle. "The beastmen!" he cried. "The beastmen have attacked and there are hundreds of them!"

Chapter 15

Nareen paced restlessly. For two days she'd been held in her room. Besides the guards who brought her meals in the morning and at night, the only other person she'd seen during that time had been Advisor Tisnerl.

He'd come to her room that first evening, long after the guard removed her untouched meal. Taking a seat at the table, he said, "Please. I would like to hear for myself the message from Chief Runner Tork. Master Gasperian told us something of your report, but I need to know the specifics."

Nareen repeated Tork's warning word for word, just as she had for Gasperian several days before. Tisnerl sat silently through the recital, then made her repeat the conversation she'd overheard between Gorvan and Xyanth. After she finished, Tisnerl stared at the table, frowning. Then he rose to his feet, thanked her, and went away.

She hadn't seen him since, and her hopes that he might be able to make Gasperian heed her warnings had faded through the long hours of waiting and pacing.

Over and over again she reviewed Tork's warning, what she'd learned, what she knew. Each time she came to the same conclusion: she'd had no choice but to make the decisions she'd made, take the risks she'd taken.

And it had all been for nothing.

At the same time, inextricably mingled with her worries for Kalinden were her tormenting concerns for Jerrel. Where was he? Did he think of her? Had he found some trace of his brother? Was he safe?

She thought she might endure the rest if only she could be sure he was safe. But that was possible only if she rejoined the Matcassen troops.

And to accomplish that, she would have to be free.

Nareen came to a halt in the middle of the room. A plan, or at least its crude outlines, began to take shape in her mind. Slowly she pivoted on one heel, studying the room about her.

She still retained her runner's belt with its dagger and small supply of dried meat. Her morning meal of fruit and bread was on the table, untouched. She nodded to herself.

It might work. But if she failed . . .

If she failed, there was little more she could lose. It was worth a try, at least.

The darkness outside her small window told Nareen it was near the time for a guard to deliver her meal. She reviewed her preparations. The single candle burned on the table, giving her just enough light to see by. Yes, she was ready.

From out in the hall she could hear the muffled footsteps of someone approaching her door, then a few unintelligible words as the guards talked briefly. There seemed to be no one else in the hallway.

With her heart pounding in her chest so hard she almost feared the guards could hear it, Nareen grabbed the makeshift weapon and climbed on the chair she had placed beside the door.

Vaguely she could discern the retreating footsteps of the day guard. Relieved of his duties, he was undoubtedly headed back for the barracks, grateful the day was ended and he could have a good meal and a rest. The night guard fumbled with the door lock.

Silently she hefted her weapon—her runner's dagger with the blade wrapped in strips torn from her sheets. It had surprised her when the guards who first locked her in didn't take it from her. Perhaps they expected she would make no effort at escape, or they were so accustomed to seeing a dagger on a runner's belt that they hadn't realized it could be used against them.

Either way, their oversight was greatly in her favor. The dagger's weighted haft provided the perfect means for knocking someone unconscious without seriously hurting him. The strips of sheeting protected her hands from the blade itself, which she now grasped in order to gain the leverage she needed.

The door opened slowly. Nareen tensed and raised the wrapped dagger. Enough light came from the torchlit hallway to cast a long, dark shadow of the guard into the room. Behind the shadow came the man himself, carrying the tray with her meal.

Nareen swung. The haft made a dull thump as it connected with the guard's skull. The man collapsed without a sound, but the tray and the plates made far more noise when they hit the stone floor than Nareen had bargained for.

Silently cursing herself for not having made provision for the tray, Nareen sprang to the floor, then quickly thrust her head out the door to see if anyone had heard. There was no one in the hall and no heads peering out of any of the other doors. Luck seemed to be on her side once more.

She shut the door, careful not to make any more noise, then grabbed the long strips of sheeting she'd already prepared and bound and gagged the guard. He was, she noted with relief, still breathing comfortably, but it would be a while before he would awake.

Nareen unwrapped her dagger and thrust it in her belt, then pulled the door open just enough so she could slide through. A quick scan of the hallway showed no one about.

Satisfied, Nareen shut the door behind her, locked it, pocketed the key, then dashed down the hallway and disappeared into the shadows of the back stairway.

By mid-afternoon the next day, Nareen still hadn't thought of a good explanation for her departure from the army or for her subsequent return. She was counting on the fact that few people ever thought to question a runner, to protect her from questions which might be better left unanswered.

She estimated it would take her another half day to reach where the army ought to be camped if they'd kept to their previous rate of progress. Her estimate was wrong.

As she crested a hill, Nareen could suddenly see the army's camp laid out before her.

Or rather, what was left of it.

Of all the tents, only one remained. The rest were charred black spots on the ground. From this distance she could see a number of men moving about slowly. Most clustered around several small fires near the remaining tent. But they were only a handful compared to the force she'd left only a few days before. To one side of the camp she could see long rows of rock-covered mounds, identical to the mounds she and Jerrel had left at the ruined holding of Nacintor the weaver.

It needed only an instant for Nareen to take in the wreckage before her; then she was flying down the trail. As she ran, her feet beat a rapid two-note counterpoint to the name that repeated itself in her mind: *Jerrel, Jerrel, Jerrel.* All else was forgotten in her fear for him.

Not far from what remained of the camp, a dispirited guard didn't even bother to raise his spear in recognition of her approach. Nareen skidded to a halt before him.

"What happened?" she demanded, noting the man's bandaged head and bloodstained clothing.

"Beastmen," he mumbled, then brightened at a sudden thought. "Be there new troops behind you, runner?"

"No, I'm alone." Ignoring his obvious disappointment, she said, "When did this happen? How many were killed?"

"Two nights ago. More'n a hundred of 'em attacked us. Two, three huntin' groups, they say. I dunno. As for the dead . . ." He looked back over his shoulder toward camp, then shook his head. He turned back to Nareen. "You'd best ask in camp. There's a healer come to help us, and they say wagons are comin' from a village down the road."

"Have you seen a warrior, a stranger with blue eyes in camp?" Nareen briefly described Jerrel, but the man only shook his head again. He hadn't seen or heard of anyone matching Jerrel's description. "What about the Lady Xyanth and her guards? Where are they?"

That question roused the first real sign of emotion in the guard. He straightened angrily, then turned his head and spat. "They're safe enough," he said at last, his lips twisted in a sneer. "She ran away first thing, with all her guards around her. They say she's stayin' in the village, nice and safe."

There was nothing more she could learn from the guard. Nareen thanked him briefly, then quickly covered the remaining distance to the camp.

Once within the boundaries of the camp, Nareen slowed to a walk, stunned by the ruin around her. There were no bodies to be seen, but dull brown stains on the ground and broken, discarded weapons spoke eloquently of the battle that had raged there so short a time before.

Though the camp had been little more than a temporary bivouac, the soldiers, like all their kind, had carried personal items to remind them of family and friends. Scattered among the weapons and the charred remains of campfires were trinkets, medallions, and carved wood images in the likeness of a wife or child. It was these human items, discarded and ignored as if they had no more value than a shattered arrow or a broken sword, that tore at Nareen. These weren't mere soldiers who had fought and died here, but fathers and husbands and sons. It didn't matter whether they'd been from Matcassen or Kalinden. They'd been men fighting for their homes, their families, for what they believed in.

And the woman who had set this carnage in motion now cowered safely behind the walls of a village, unwilling even to come out to bury those who had died because of her.

Rage twisted in Nareen's stomach like an animal gnawing at her vitals. Somehow she would find a way to make Xyanth pay for what she had done. It was a promise.

But first she had an even more urgent need, to find Jerrel and assure herself he was all right. Ignoring the men sorting through the ruins in search of usable weapons, she headed toward the one tent left standing.

As she approached, Nareen realized that every man she could see had been seriously injured in the fighting. A number were strong enough to stand, but far more sat listlessly on the hard ground, huddled around the fires for warmth, or lay on makeshift beds, too seriously injured even to sit up.

Nareen scanned the men's faces, unsure whether she wanted to see Jerrel's among them or not. He wasn't there, at any rate. She pushed down the spark of hope that flared within her. His absence meant absolutely nothing.

Several of the men pressed forward, anxious to

hear her news. When they realized there were no troops behind her, that she knew nothing of any help that might be on its way, they slumped back into the dispirited anger that hung like a pall over the camp.

Nareen entered the tent, which was crowded with the most seriously wounded. A young man who was stooped over to tend one of the injured glanced up, then rose to his feet to greet her.

As he crossed to her, Nareen was aware of a slight tug of recognition, as though, somehow, she ought to know him. He was young, tall, and slender with curly, shoulder-length brown hair. His features were delicate, but there was a masculine strength in the way he carried his head, in the firm line of his mouth, that suggested that the impression of delicacy was not to be trusted. Dark brown, almost black eyes looked directly into hers, as if he were determined to see into her very soul. He wore a shapeless brown robe with a crudely woven belt knotted at the waist, and a pair of soft leather boots that had seen a lot of service.

"Welcome, runner," he said. His voice was low and gentle, but there was a hint of steel beneath the surface. "You bring us news?" He answered his own question a second later. "Ah, no. I see that you do not. In what way, then, may I serve you?"

"You're not from the Matcassen forces," Nareen blurted out. It was a statement, not a question, yet she couldn't force down the certainty that she knew this man. As a runner, she didn't easily forget someone once she'd met them, but where had she met him before?

"No." He smiled, amused by her abruptness. "I

am an itinerant healer. I was staying in the village of Elsin when the Lady Xyanth and her guards took refuge there. As soon as I heard the news of the attack, I came here to offer what assistance I could."

Was it only her imagination, or did she detect a note of distaste, almost of loathing, when he mentioned Xyanth? "I'm sure your services are much appreciated, healer," Nareen said politely. For once, it seemed, her memory was playing her false. She knew no itinerant healer who resembled this man.

"Yes," he said quietly, looking around him at the wounded filling the tent. "I am needed here."

I am needed here. They were simple words, yet Nareen thought she detected a deeper meaning behind them. It didn't matter. She had more pressing matters to think about.

At that moment a hand lifted the tent flap and a man, his arm in a sling, limped into the tent.

"Guardsman Pardraik!" Nareen exclaimed.

"Sixth Runner!" A bitter smile flashed across Pardraik's face. He greeted her with a mocking salute. "Welcome to the Matcassen camp."

"But why are you here? A man at the edge of camp said the Lady Xyanth and her guards were safe in Elsin."

A shadow passed across Pardraik's features. "Most of the guards are with her, as they are required to be, but a few of us chose to stay and fight. You are now speaking to the commander of the camp."

"You! But then the rest . . ." Sudden fear assailed Nareen. If this was all there was of the camp, and if Jerrel wasn't here, then . . .

"No, no," Pardraik said soothingly. "It's not so

285

bad as it seems. Those who remain in camp are, like me, too badly injured to be of much use in a fight." His voice dropped. "It's true a number of good men died in that first night's attack. We buried them yesterday." He paused.

For an instant fear assailed Nareen. Where was Jerrel?

"As for the rest," Pardraik continued, clearly understanding her need, "they left yesterday morning to pursue the beastmen. Jerrel was among a small group from Kalinden that was headed farther west to check on the village of Aignil."

Hope soared, almost choking Nareen with relief. Jerrel survived the attack. He wasn't dead or wounded—he was alive! But she wanted more than that. She wanted assurances, promises that he was safe.

The healer, who had been silent since Pardraik's entrance, asked, "Jerrel? There was a man named Jerrel?"

Nareen ignored the healer's question. "Then he was all right? He wasn't injured?" When Pardraik didn't answer, she grabbed the sleeve of his tunic. "What is it that you're not telling me?"

Pardraik hesitated, then said reluctantly, "He received a few cuts in the fighting, but before that he attacked the Lady Xyanth. We were under orders to execute him. If it hadn't been for the attack by the beastmen, we would have had to carry out those orders."

Nareen slowly released Pardraik's sleeve. "Execute him?"

"This Jerrel," the healer insisted, "who is he?"

"That's right." Pardraik's grimace was almost a sneer, but it was directed at himself, not at her. "I am a guardsman of Matcassen and bound to obey orders."

"Which way did they go?"

"They kept to the main trail that leads to the border, then were going to cut across to Aignil. By now, who knows where they might be?" Pardraik caught Nareen's arm. "You can't follow them. It would be far too dangerous."

Nareen brushed his hand off. "I'll be back." She lifted the tent flap.

"Runner . . ."

"This Jerrel . . . ?"

But Nareen was already headed to the trail that Jerrel had taken with the remaining troops.

Even when the troops left the main trail it was easy to follow them, there were so many. Nareen, alert for any sign of beastmen, jogged steadily on. She wasn't pushing herself since she didn't know what might lie ahead, but she also wasn't taking any more time to rest than she had to.

Just where she'd expected, Nareen found tracks showing that six men had split off from the larger body of troops. As she followed the smaller group's trail, her emotions veered between relief that Jerrel was no longer with the men who were actively pursuing the beastmen, and fear that he was now more vulnerable to surprise attack. Her one consolation was that, because she could travel so much faster than a band of heavily armed men, she was now only a few hours behind them.

The sun was beginning to slide toward the far peaks and Nareen was debating the wisdom of continuing in the dark, despite the risk, when she encountered the first signs of beastmen.

As she knelt in the path to study the beastmen's tracks, a sick feeling of despair washed over her. Beastmen couldn't smell, but they had uncanny vision and, once on the trail of humans, they were known to be untiring hunters. They were perfectly capable of tracking Jerrel and his companions in all but the darkest night.

The tracks showed that there were eight of the creatures, not counting the two to four that would be ranging on the hillside above and below the main group. And Jerrel didn't know they were behind him.

All thought of finding a safe place for the night vanished. Even though she had no weapon besides her runner's dagger, and her training had equipped her more to evade danger than to confront it head-on, Nareen didn't hesitate. She started running.

Twenty minutes later Nareen came across the first beastmen—four of them, dead on the trail. They had been killed at fairly long range by a volley of arrows.

That improved the odds, at least. Now there would be no more than eight against six. So long as their arrows held out, Jerrel and his companions would be able to keep the beastmen at a distance. But only so long as they had arrows. Once those were gone, the beastmen would move in with spears, knives, swords, and their own clumsy bows and arrows. Their weapons were crude, but in hand-to-hand combat the beastmen's greater size and weight gave them the advantage over their better-armed human opponents.

Moving as cautiously but as quickly as she could, Nareen pushed on. About a quarter of a mile further there was another beastman dead in the trail, then another. It was clear the humans had chosen to flee in the hope of reaching safety in Aignil rather than hole up in the rocks where they would eventually be overrun.

But then, as she had known they inevitably must, the men's arrows had run out. The next beastman Nareen encountered had been killed by a spear. That left perhaps five beastmen against six humans. In close combat, the advantage was on the side of the beastmen.

Somewhere, not too far ahead on the trail, the humans would have to take a stand and face the beastmen. They couldn't outrun the creatures, and they couldn't compete with the beasts' better night vision.

The sun was almost gone and there was, at most, a half hour of light left. Nareen quickly scanned the rocky hillside. If she could get above the trail, she might be able to provide some help to the six men, even if only by throwing rocks to distract the beastmen.

For an instant, fear—not for herself, but for the men ahead—held her frozen, uncertain. Yet it wasn't six men she was trying to help, it was five nameless, faceless human beings—and Jerrel.

Jerrel. The name was like an incantation against evil, driving out her fear. If the best she could do to save him was to throw rocks, then she would throw a hundred rocks, a thousand if need be.

Nareen scrambled up the hillside, then turned and ran parallel to the trail, heedless of her own safety. A couple of minutes more and she could hear the dim echo of the sounds of battle.

The six men had turned to face their pursuers at a point where the trail widened at the base of a steep rock cliff that provided a protective wall behind them. It hadn't been enough. Four men and two beastmen lay dead, their bodies tangled where they'd fallen.

A sob, compounded of fear and relief, burst from Nareen. Jerrel was one of the two men still standing.

His back to the cliff wall, he was defending himself as best he could against two howling beastmen. But he wouldn't be able to withstand their onslaught for long. Even from this distance Nareen could clearly see the broken shaft of an arrow protruding from his thigh. His left arm hung useless, and blood soaked his jerkin on that side.

Heedless of his injuries, teeth bared, head defiantly high, he wielded his sword with deadly efficiency, parrying the clumsy but powerful thrusts of a spear from one of the creatures and the rain of blows from the sword of the other.

The second man faced only one beastman, sword to sword, but his wounds and the beast's greater physical strength were quickly wearing him down. He couldn't hold out much longer.

Nareen dashed forward, then vaulted onto a rock that provided a better view of the struggle below her. Snatching up a small stone, she flung it at the back of the single beastman. Then she grabbed another stone and threw it with as much force as she could muster at the beast with the spear.

Both rocks struck home, but the beasts barely flinched. Nareen grabbed two more stones and threw them, then two more.

The fifth stone hit the spear carrier just behind the ear with sufficient force that the beast turned with a roar to confront this new and unexpected enemy. The diversion was enough to give Jerrel his opportunity. He lunged, driving his sword deep into the creature's gut, then swung around so the dying beast fell in the path of its enraged partner, making it stumble.

Elated at her success, Nareen turned, ready to throw another rock at the third beast. She was too late. The beast raised its sword in both hands and brought it down with frightening power. The man cried out, sagged to his knees, then crumpled into a heap on the ground and was still.

For an instant, horror held Nareen frozen. Her mind numb at the viciousness of the attack, she watched helplessly as the beast tugged its blood-stained sword free of its victim's body, then swung about, ready to attack Jerrel.

Nareen shouted, a shrill cry that was almost a scream, then pulled her dagger from her belt and raced forward.

Jerrel, alerted by her cry, twisted around just in time to avoid the beastman's charge. The distraction allowed the second beast to move in. Jerrel saw his danger too late. He pivoted, but the creature's sword had already drawn blood as it sliced across his right side.

Staggered by the blow, Jerrel faltered, then pressed forward.

In that second, Nareen launched herself at the back of the first beastman. The creature's stench was overpowering, almost making her gag, and its rough hide scraped the skin of her hands so that she bled.

It spun around, trying to dislodge her. Nareen clung grimly, fighting not to lose her hold. It clawed at her, its long, sharp nails raking across her hair and cheek. She scrabbled for a firmer grip. It ducked its upper body, striving to throw her over its head.

The movement was the beast's undoing.

Nareen was thrown forward, higher on its shoulders where she could reach around in front of it. With a cry of triumph she drove her runner's dagger deep into the creature's throat, under the jaw where it was most vulnerable.

She jerked the dagger free, then plunged it in again. The second stroke was unnecessary. The creature was already dead as it started to fall.

Nareen leaped free, her dagger still in her hand, and desperately looked toward Jerrel.

With only one enemy to deal with, Jerrel had pressed his advantage. As Nareen watched, he lunged forward under the beastman's clumsy guard and drove his sword into the creature's belly, up to the hilt.

The beast roared in rage and pain, then took two staggering steps toward Jerrel, claws scrabbling vainly at empty air, before collapsing.

Jerrel stood, swaying slightly and staring down at the creature as though incapable of comprehending that he had won.

Thrusting her dagger into her belt, Nareen skirted the body of the beastman at her feet, then crossed to Jerrel. As she came to a stop beside him, he dazedly turned toward her.

Gradually his eyes lost their glazed expression and focused on her. The edge of his mouth quirked in a slight, lopsided smile.

"It seems . . . I owe you my life . . . again, little runner." His words came in short gasps, as if the effort of speaking was almost more than he could manage. He raised his right hand to gently brush a strand of hair out of her eyes. "You have . . ." He swayed, but grabbed hold of Nareen's shoulder to steady himself. "You have . . . a strange taste . . . in riding beasts."

He started to topple forward. With a cry of dismay, Nareen wrapped her arms about him in an effort to break his fall. Half staggering under his greater weight, she eased him to the ground, then knelt beside him.

His eyes were closed, his breathing unsteady, shallow, and labored. Desperately Nareen shook him, willing him to rouse. "Jerrel. Jerrel!" He gasped, but still his eyes remained shut.

Fear that Jerrel was dying flooded through Nareen. As the black emotional waters raged in her mind, they ripped free a truth she hadn't known was there, a truth her subconscious had buried so deeply that only a fear like this could free it and bring it to the surface where it floated, pure and bright and shining.

She loved Jerrel.

It was that simple.

It wasn't lust or loneliness or a longing for a companion that had made her thoughts turn toward him so often, driven her to him time and time again.

It was love.

With that knowledge came a fierce determination that forced out the fear. He wasn't going to die. She wouldn't let him.

Quickly Nareen surveyed what she could see of Jerrel's injuries. The arrow in his thigh could wait. The cut along his right side wasn't deep but it was bleeding freely and would have to be stanched. It was the wounds on his left shoulder and side that worried her the most. They were deep and far too close to vital organs.

Nareen tugged at the lacings of Jerrel's tunic. Her first priority was to stop the bleeding or he would die of blood loss alone.

At her touch, Jerrel sighed; then his eyes fluttered open.

"It's all right . . ." His voice was little more than a hoarse, faltering whisper. He brought his hand up to touch her arm. His fingers trembled with the effort. "Should have told you . . . should have explained . . ."

"Don't talk." Nareen captured his hand in hers. His skin was cold—too cold. Fear for him edged back, threatening her ability to think clearly. With an effort, she pushed it down.

"No time . . . need time . . ." Jerrel clutched at her hand as though she might somehow replace the strength so rapidly ebbing from him. "Don't worry . . ."

His voice faded, his eyelids drooped. For an instant, Nareen panicked. But Jerrel was neither dead nor unconscious. He was weakening fast, however, and Nareen knew that allowing her fear to paralyze her wouldn't help him.

Releasing Jerrel's hand, Nareen turned her attention back to the lacings. As they came free, she pushed aside the bloodstained leather and coarse cloth, exposing the heavily muscled expanse of his chest.

The ragged, gaping wound low on his left shoulder was frightening. Bright red blood oozed from the torn flesh, further staining his skin.

Hesitantly, Nareen touched the edge of the wound, uncertain what to do next. The injury was far more extensive than any she'd been taught to deal with.

Her touch must have hurt him, for Jerrel

moaned, then twisted away from her. The movement caused the heavy gold chain he wore to slide around where it would be in her way. She started to flick the chain and the ring strung on it to one side, then froze.

Only once had she held the ring that Advisor Danet had entrusted to her. But there was no mistaking the unusual stone. Nareen brushed the tip of her finger along the inside of the ring under the stone. The strange ridge was there, exactly where she'd expected to find it.

Nareen's grip on the ring tightened until the ridge dug into her fingertip. Doubt, uncertainty, and anger washed through her. Why had Jerrel lied? Why steal the ring? Why . . . ?

As though evading her questions, Jerrel moaned once, softly, and slid into unconsciousness.

A soft cry of protest escaped Nareen's lips, but the cry changed to a choked scream as Jerrel's body began to fade like mist evaporating at the touch of sunlight. She reached for him, as if she might somehow prevent his disappearance. Her own body refused to respond. It, too, was disappearing. Before she could cry out again, Nareen followed Jerrel into nothingness.

Chapter 16

Just as suddenly as he'd disappeared, Jerrel was back lying on the ground in front of her. No, ground wasn't the right word—it was the floor. He was lying on the floor.

This wasn't real. Couldn't be real. Nareen dropped the ring and crouched protectively above Jerrel, all the while twisting her head first to one side, then the other, as she tried to take in this madness that her senses declared was real.

The ground had been transformed into a hard, gray substance that was neither stone nor metal. Instead of stone cliffs rising around them, there were pale gray walls that curved inward to form a small chamber. A soft, silver glow pervaded the chamber, but Nareen could detect no candles or lamps, no windows, and no doors.

Even as she clutched at Jerrel's jerkin and

crouched lower, so that her body shielded his more completely, Nareen knew she must be dreaming—or mad. But how to tell which?

Suddenly an opening appeared in a seamless wall in front of them. Through the opening Nareen could see what looked like a corridor, but she was allowed only a glimpse before her view was blocked by four featureless black boxes, each about three feet high, that floated into the chamber two by two.

The boxes came to rest surrounding Jerrel's body, two at either side of his head and feet. A beam of red light shot out from each box, aimed at the light from the box diagonally opposite. The four beams seemed to lock together at the center, then slowly sank toward Jerrel.

The threat to Jerrel broke through Nareen's stupor. She pulled her dagger from her belt and flung herself on the nearest box.

The box paid no attention to her first attack. Without thinking, Nareen shifted the dagger in her hand so she could use the weighted haft, and struck again. This time the box gave a whirring noise. The beam of red light wavered, then disappeared. The box faltered, turning first toward her, then back toward Jerrel, then back to her. Nareen pressed her advantage, raining down blows that at least confused the box, even if they didn't dent it.

At her first attack, the other boxes appeared oblivious to the plight of their companion. But as the attacks continued, the other three abandoned their posts and came to the aid of the beleaguered box.

Nareen spun to meet this new threat, but before she could strike the second box, a woman's voice sounded in the chamber. The voice was surprisingly low and sultry and spoke in a language Nareen didn't recognize.

Startled, Nareen whirled around, trying to locate the source of the voice. No one was there. Even the opening to the corridor had closed.

The voice spoke again, in a different but still unintelligible language.

"Who are you? What do you want?" Nareen demanded. When no answer came, she shouted, "We need help. Take your boxes away and send someone who can tend to Jerrel."

There was an instant of silence; then the voice said, "There has been a regrettable mistake. I'm not sure the boss is going to like this when he finds out, but it's too late to do anything else now. If you would please let the medbots take him without further delay, then I can explain everything."

The boxes, as though on command, turned away from Nareen and back to Jerrel.

For a moment Nareen remained motionless, uncertain what to do. Who was speaking, and where was her voice coming from? What was a medbot? Who was the boss? All this couldn't be a dream. It was strange, but too real. But if it wasn't a dream, what was it?

The boxes turned their light beams on again. Instantly Nareen sprang to Jerrel's defense. "No!" she cried, desperately hammering on the box nearest her.

"Please," said the voice. "If you would only . . ."

Nareen ignored the plea. The box she was attacking wobbled, its beam faded. She leaped at the second box.

"Oh, dear," said the voice.

The second box turned toward Nareen. This time, rather than pounding on its top, Nareen aimed her blows at the side that had emitted the light beam.

That was a mistake. From the top of the box an intense green light shot out, aimed at Nareen's face. She tried to twist away, but it followed her mercilessly.

Blackness loomed up to swallow her. Nareen tried to fight free, but the blackness grew. Jerrel. She had to reach Jerrel. But where was he? She couldn't see and she was falling. Just before the blackness consumed her utterly, she heard the woman's voice one last time.

"Oh, dear," it said. "The boss isn't going to like this at all."

Jerrel opened his eyes. He felt warm, comfortable, very hungry, and only slightly tired—the usual reaction to a stay in the medbox.

Just as he'd expected, his ship had transported him up the minute he'd lost consciousness, then immediately transferred him to the medbox for healing. It was an automatic protective measure that had saved his life more than once.

He was safe, but what of Nareen? He blinked, remembering her bending over him, eyes wide with fear—not for herself, but for him. He could almost feel her presence, so intense was his memory of her beside him.

What had she thought when he'd disappeared? Was she all right? Though he'd had no choice, he'd left her alone on a mountain with only dead men and murderous beasts around her. Left her in a way guaranteed to make her wonder about black magic, or doubt her sanity, or both.

Jerrel's jaw clenched. It was too late now for regrets or guilt, but both emotions tore at him. Too late . . .

Jerrel stabbed at the glowing green light on the panel at one side of the medbox. Instantly, the protective energy shell that had surrounded him disappeared. He sat up.

"Hello, boss." The computer's voice was seductive and very female.

"Hello, CeeCee." He stretched. "How long have I been in the medbox?"

"Nine days."

"Nine . . . ! I must have been in worse shape than I'd thought." Slowly Jerrel slid off the medbox shelf and stood up. He was completely naked, but other than several new scars on his shoulder and sides, there was no sign of the wounds the beastmen had inflicted on him.

Behind him, the medbox automatically closed its energy shell, making it look like nothing more than a display box set in a wall.

Jerrel crossed to a table where fresh clothes had been placed for him by one of the ship bots, simple robots that did the cleaning and general errands under the direction of the ship's computer.

"Any word from Norvag?" Jerrel asked as he pulled on the shining black skin suit.

"Not for several days," said the computer. "Danet is back in Matcassen, but he didn't have any further information for you. It seems your brother has disappeared."

Disappeared. Just as Jerrel himself had disappeared for Nareen. He ran his hand up the side of the suit, sealing it so it hugged him like a second skin.

"Did you have any luck in tracing Santar?" CeeCee asked. "I tracked your movements, of course, and Norvag explained that you'd hoped to get information from this Xyanth woman." The computer, which was programmed to have a range of human emotions, pronounced Xyanth's name with a distinct flavor of disapproval.

Jerrel frowned. "No. No luck." The truth was, he'd bungled it from first to last. If what Xyanth had said was true, however, if Santar really was dead, there wasn't much he could have done, anyway.

Suddenly Jerrel felt more tired than even his time in the medbox would warrant. With Santar dead, he was the only one of his family left.

Yet, something within him—something irrational, perhaps, but nonetheless convincing—insisted that Santar wasn't dead, that he, Jerrel, would know if he was.

But what should he do now? If Santar was alive, how was he going to find him? He'd tried everything he could think of, and nothing had led him to his missing brother.

And what about Nareen? Somehow, some way, he had to find out if she was safe.

Jerrel moved toward the door of the med chamber. "I'm hungry," he announced. "First I'm going to have something to eat, then I'm going to think about what to do next."

The door dilated to let him out, then silently closed behind him. Jerrel turned and headed toward his private quarters. The ship was big—far bigger than one or two men really needed—but he liked having the room. If you spent weeks and sometimes months in space, a small ship quickly became unpleasantly confining.

"Boss?" The computer sounded uncharacteristically hesitant.

"Yes?" Jerrel was only half listening. Perhaps he could have CeeCee . . . No, he couldn't find Nareen that way. What about . . . ?

"There was a little problem when I transported you back on board." CeeCee was speaking slowly, as if forced to mention a matter it would prefer to ignore.

"What kind of problem?" Jerrel wasn't in the mood to hear another of CeeCee's complaints about equipment that needed to be replaced. When the computer didn't answer, he demanded impatiently, "Well? What's the problem?"

This time the reluctance in CeeCee's voice was unmistakable. "I think you'd better come to the study area and see for yourself," it said.

Irritated at CeeCee's deliberate evasion, Jerrel debated ignoring the computer's suggestion. The study area was nothing more than a classroom with large viewscreens and several computer control panels that allowed access to CeeCee's extensive data banks. Jerrel often worked there himself, as did the passengers he sometimes carried. What problem could possibly be located there that would worry CeeCee?

But it wasn't like CeeCee to hesitate. Jerrel took a left turn at the next cross corridor, then a right turn that led him directly to the study area's door. The door dilated to admit him and he stepped through, only to draw up short in astonishment.

Across the slightly darkened room, the main viewer was active. On its screen was a constantly changing panoply of scenes from his home world of Arcana: the Palace of the Governors, the ruins of Tashnar, the artists' school at Crimethea.

Seated before a computer control panel, back turned toward him, was a slight figure whose attention was fixed on the screen before him—or her. The unknown visitor had short, black hair and was dressed, from what little Jerrel could see, in an iridescent green skin suit that glittered even in the room's low light.

"What the . . . ? Who are you?" Jerrel demanded. The figure whirled around, obviously startled, then flung itself out of its chair and across the room at him.

"You're all right! You're alive!"

It took Jerrel's dazed mind a moment to recognize the woman who was clinging to him, laughing and crying at the same time. "Nareen!" This was impossible. How could she be on the ship?

Yet while his mind struggled with the implications of her presence, a part of him exulted at the strange twist of fate that had brought her here. Without thinking, he wrapped his arms around her and hugged her close.

"It isn't my fault she's here, boss. When I beamed you up, she was touching the neurotransmitter in the ring on the chain you were wearing. There wasn't anything I could do about it." CeeCee sounded aggrieved.

"I thought I was dreaming, that I'd gone mad," Nareen said, gripping his arms and looking up at him. Tears glittered on her cheeks, but her lips were lifted in a shy smile. "Then those boxes came. I didn't know what they were doing, that they were trying to help. I'm sorry I broke one, but—"

"Wait a minute. Slow down." Jerrel slid his hands down her back, drawing her closer. She was so warm and real, so good to touch and hold. Yet she shouldn't be here. His reeling mind struggled to reconcile that fact with her presence. "What box are you talking about, and how did you break it?"

"The black box, the . . ." she hesitated over the strange word, " . . . the medbot. It hasn't worked properly since I pounded on it."

"Why were you . . . No, wait. Don't tell me yet." Jerrel looked down at her, then toward the screen where scenes of Arcana were still flashing.

It was incredible that Nareen could be here on his ship, dressed in the form-revealing skin suit, watching pictures from his home planet and wearing a com monitor in one ear so she could hear the computer's explanation of what she was seeing. It was even more incredible that she seemed so comfortable with this new world— a world she couldn't even have conceived of two weeks before.

He led Nareen over to a table with chairs for two, then sat down, slowly, unable to take his eyes from her. He shook his head. "It's all so incredible. You here . . ."

Nareen sat down, just as slowly and hesitantly. Now that the initial excitement of his appearance had worn off, she seemed strangely shy.

"It's hard to believe . . ." she murmured, studying him wide-eyed. "CeeCee said you'd be all right, but . . . there was so much blood, and the wound on your shoulder was so bad . . ." She blinked, and her lower lip trembled. "I visited you but I couldn't touch you or talk to you. You just lay in that box, not moving and with nobody to tend you, just that strange light . . ."

Jerrel started to reach across the table to her, then stopped. It was difficult enough for him to handle his discovery of her here on his ship. It must have been—must still be—a thousand times more difficult for her. Yet she had coped without his help or advice, knowing that he was not what he had pretended to be.

She bit on her lower lip to stop its trembling. "At first, I thought it was a dream." She glanced across the table at him, then to the screen where scenes of Arcana were still flashing. Her gaze fixed on the screen, she said, "But I wasn't dreaming, was I? CeeCee, please end the pictures."

With the screen shut down, the room seemed darker, colder. "How did you . . . ? How was it possible . . . ?" Jerrel groped for words which would allow him to ask how she had managed to adapt while at the same time avoiding any intimation that he hadn't been completely honest with her. There weren't any.

"CeeCee helped me," Nareen said, still not looking directly at him. "Once she determined what language to use, she explained what happened. When she was sure I wasn't going to destroy anything, she let me explore some of your ship. At first, I was convinced I'd gone mad. Sometimes I still think I am."

Nareen pulled the com monitor from her ear, then sat frowning down at it in her hand. "She's been teaching me what to do, how things work, helping me study about your world, about some of the places you've been." She looked up quickly, an uncertain smile on her lips, then fixed her eyes once more on the monitor she held. "It's rather . . . overwhelming. I hadn't realized . . . It explains a lot."

Jerrel wasn't sure exactly what explained what. He tried to imagine his reaction had he been suddenly thrust into a situation like Nareen's, surrounded by a technology he didn't understand, trying to comprehend a society, a world he'd never known existed. What must it have been like to try to deal with all that alone?

"I'm sorry you were dragged into this," Jerrel said slowly. "I never intended . . ." His words trailed off. What he was telling her was that no matter what lay between them, he hadn't been willing to be completely honest with her. She was intelligent enough to understand many of his reasons for that reticence, but understanding wouldn't take the sting out of knowing.

"You know what's strange?" Nareen asked, almost as if speaking to herself. "I was carrying the ring to you." She smiled wistfully at his surprise. "Advisor Danet gave it to me for a man named bn'Hadar. We don't have—what do you call them? surnames?—on Errandane. You must have wondered where the ring came from, where I was taking it. And all the time . . ."

Jerrel was saved from having to respond by the appearance of a silver ship bot that floated into the room bearing a tray loaded with plates of food encased in an energy shell that kept everything warm.

"I thought you might want something to eat, boss," CeeCee purred. The voice turned colder. "There's enough for your visitor, too."

Grateful for the interruption, Jerrel took the tray from the top of the bot and put it on the table. "If you don't like this, just say so. The food generator can produce anything you want."

"I know." Nareen barely glanced at the tray. "CeeCee explained how it worked. I've been trying some of the foods from your world." She was silent for a moment, then said impulsively, "What does she look like?"

"Who?" Jerrel's attention was concentrated on the steaming plates of food before him. He hadn't realized how hungry he really was. And eating would provide a welcome distraction from having to consider Nareen's situation and the predicament it put him in.

"CeeCee."

"CeeCee? It's a computer, not a person."

"But isn't that like another kind of person? There's her voice, and sometimes she . . . well, she gets irritated with me, I think. Just like a person." Nareen glanced toward the computer control panel. "What does *CeeCee* mean, anyway? Is it a woman's name on your world?"

Jerrel caught himself just before he started to laugh. He'd owned the ship for years, and CeeCee was, to him, simply a part of the machinery, despite its seductive voice. Personalities were deliberately assigned to ship computers as a way of providing some semblance of companionship to people who might have to spend months alone in their travels in space. Only a few very lonely souls ever began to think of the computers as real people.

"CeeCee is nothing more than the first letters of the words Command Computer," he said, "which is the official designation for the central computer that controls all operations on the ship."

Nareen glanced at the computer control panel again, but this time she was frowning. "Is she from some other world, then? Does she—it—live on the ship all the time? How old is it?"

"It's not . . ." Jerrel stopped. Nareen had adapted so easily and so quickly to the ship and to using its services, such as the meal generator and the study area, that it hadn't occurred to him how little she could really yet understand. Machines and concepts he'd known since he was a child were totally foreign to her. Since she came from a world where only humans were capable of remembering, commanding, and learning, it would undoubtedly take time for her to fully grasp the concept of a machine that could do those tasks as well.

"I'll explain all that later," he said. *As soon as I figure out what to do about you being here in the first place,* he silently added to himself.

Yet even as that thought flitted through his consciousness, he found a sudden surge of hope rising within him.

Jerrel opened his eyes, then quickly tossed back the light bed covering and sat up. As usual, a good meal and several hours' sleep had completed the restorative work of the medbox. But this time energy flowed through him, energy that had nothing to do with his healing and everything to do with the presence on board of one small female who should never have known his ship even existed.

They'd spent several hours talking. Or rather, she'd asked questions, one right after the other, and he'd answered them as best he could.

He'd eventually pleaded exhaustion and retreated to his quarters, but he hadn't been able to sleep.

Somewhere during their conversation, the realization finally dawned that here, by chance, was the solution to his problems—at least so far as they concerned Nareen.

He didn't have to give her up after all. The words were an exultant refrain that repeated itself, over and over, in his brain.

She was here, on his ship. Despite his fears, she had learned to adapt to the strange world she'd been thrust into so abruptly. From what she'd told him, she had little to go back for, either. Her efforts to protect her city had cost her everything she'd valued.

He felt a stab of regret at her loss, but his regret paled beside his exultant realization that the last of his doubts about taking her with him had been erased. Silently he vowed that, somehow, he would make it up to her.

Now that she was here, he didn't intend to let her go. Ever.

Refreshed by sleep and urged on by a sudden need to see Nareen, to talk with her, Jerrel swung out of bed.

Nareen would need time to accept the idea that she could never go home, time to accept the idea of joining with him. And time she would have. No matter what the temptation, no matter how much he wanted her, Jerrel was resolved not to touch her until he was sure she had fully accepted her fate.

The door to her quarters dilated open automatically, and Jerrel walked through without thinking to announce himself. An instant later he found himself incapable of coherent thought or of further forward motion, brought up short by the sight of Nareen standing across the room from him taking a sponge bath.

She was naked and her skin glistened, as if inviting his touch. At sight of him, she blushed. Jerrel was fascinated to note that a blush, at least on Nareen, was not confined solely to her face and throat, but tinged even her white breasts a delicate pink.

In her situation, most women he had known would have grabbed a towel or their clothes in a vain attempt to hide. Some, the more blatant, would have moved so their pose was even more seductive.

But Nareen was too proud to adopt either approach. Her chin came up a fraction, but that was all. "Do you," she asked with chill disapproval, "make a habit of entering private rooms without knocking?"

"You, uh, you can't knock on these doors." It was, he knew, an inane response, but he was incapable of thinking of anything more intelligent to say.

He turned to the side, looking away from her, but his choice of direction wasn't the best. The chamber's broad bed was at that side of the room. Its rumpled cover and soft pillows still showed the marks of her body.

"Besides, what are you doing, anyway?" His voice was sharper than he'd intended, but he wasn't accustomed to being so much at a disadvantage. "There's a perfectly good shower and bath unit in these quarters. You don't have to bathe out of a bowl of water."

"I don't know how . . . I prefer to bathe this way, thank you," Nareen said. "It works just fine for us on Errandane."

Jerrel heard the rustle of cloth, then her soft footsteps crossing the room toward him. He turned to find she'd pulled on a robe of some silken fabric the deep green color of a shadowed forest. The rich hue, contrasted with her fair skin and dark hair, made the green of her eyes all the more brilliant.

His approval must have shown in his eyes because Nareen smiled shyly, forgetting her indignation at his unannounced entrance. With the wondering air of a child who has discovered something marvelous, she ran her hand over the heavy folds of fabric covering her arm. "I've never worn anything like this," she said softly. "Only the Masters and the very richest merchants would be able to afford it. And even then I'm not sure they could find anything this beautiful in all of Errandane."

Her head came up suddenly, her eyes dark with worry. "It's all right, isn't it? That I asked CeeCee to make this for me? She was explaining how the generators work, how they can make almost anything we want . . ."

"It's perfectly all right," Jerrel soothed, fighting down the urge to pull the robe from her body and take her in his arms. "That color becomes you." There was a slight catch in his voice.

Nareen smiled, blossoming under the warmth of his approval. "I worried that you would think I was being greedy by asking for something this valuable instead of some simple clothes. But when CeeCee showed me the picture and said she could make it . . ."

Jerrel smiled in return, pleased at her obvious delight. He wouldn't diminish her pleasure by explaining it was no more difficult for the generators to produce the gown she wore than to provide clothes she was more accustomed to. Besides, even if he'd had to pay a fortune, the cost would have been worth the delight she took in the simple garment.

The thought of her not completely understanding the principles of the generator brought another thought.

"Did CeeCee explain how some of the other things in your room work?" he asked casually. "Things like the lights and the com panel and the shower and what not?"

"I understand the lights, and I'm beginning to understand some of the things the com panel does—"

"But she refuses to learn how to use the shower, boss," CeeCee's sultry voice interrupted them. "I've tried and I've tried to explain it to her, but she just can't seem to understand."

Jerrel could have sworn he heard a spiteful note in the computer's voice.

"Makes a lot of extra work for the ship bots and me," CeeCee continued. "We're always having to go in and tidy up the puddles she leaves."

"CeeCee, you know very well it doesn't matter—" Jerrel started to say.

"Oh, I didn't realize!" Nareen's eyes were wide with embarrassment. "It's just . . ."

"She's quick enough on some things, boss— for a primitive—but the idea of taking a shower seems to be beyond her." CeeCee was employing her capability of sarcasm to the maximum.

Jerrel frowned, irritated at the computer. "It's not important. Shut off, CeeCee."

"Boss—"

"Shut off."

The computer went silent. If he hadn't known better, Jerrel could have sworn the computer was still present, but sulking.

"I'm sorry if I caused any—" Nareen started to say.

"Just ignore CeeCee, or tell it to shut off," Jerrel interrupted, trying to ease her embarrassment. "And take a bath any way you want to. It's no problem for the ship bots. Absolutely none."

"I did try to learn how to use the . . . shower," Nareen faltered. "It's just that . . . Well, it's so different . . . and . . ."

"Quite all right." Now Jerrel's cheeks were beginning to feel warm. He tried to divert the conversation. "Have you had a chance to visit the navigation center? It's—"

"Would you show me how to use it?"

" . . . a fascinating place, and . . . Would I what?"

"Show me how to use the shower?"

"I . . ."

"I want to learn everything I can. It's just that . . . well, this was . . . Would you?"

Had he been wearing anything but the skin suit, Nareen would have been tugging on his sleeve. As it was, she was clutching his arm and gazing up at him with a wide-eyed, pleading expression Jerrel found impossible to resist.

"Uh, sure. Of course! I'd be glad to," Jerrel added with feigned enthusiasm. The thought of Nareen in the shower, naked, with the warm jets of water playing across her body, was not conducive to calm self-control.

"Would you show me now?"

"Now?" Jerrel swallowed. Hard.

"I didn't have a chance to finish . . . That is, you came in before . . . I want to learn . . ." Nareen's voice trailed away.

Understanding dawned for Jerrel, and with it, a vague sense of guilt. While he was indulging in vivid fantasies, Nareen was struggling to deal with yet one more strange and probably frightening aspect of this newfound world.

"Of course." Jerrel was suddenly very brisk and businesslike. "It's easy. I'll just show you how to operate the mechanism." He led the way to the personal chamber at one side of the room.

The chamber was small. An opening to the left led to the privacy facilities, another opening on the right led to the shower.

"Did CeeCee explain about the—" Jerrel gestured to the left. If he was going to serve as instructor, he decided, he might as well be thorough.

"CeeCee explained everything," Nareen interrupted hastily. "She even explained the shower— a couple of times. It's just . . ." Her voice died away uncomfortably.

Jerrel glanced at her. She was staring at the opening to the shower, an expression of grim determination on her face. Her distrust of the shower was intriguing. In the space of a few days she'd adapted quickly enough to use the study area and a com monitor, to order clothes and meals from the generator, and to find her way around the ship. Yet a simple shower seemed almost to frighten her.

Shrugging off his puzzlement, Jerrel strode through the opening into the dressing area that was part of the shower room.

"It's really very simple. You can leave your robe on the bench here. If you want new clothes, just order some and the ship bots will have them waiting for you when you finish." He threw open the door leading to the shower itself. "You can just walk in and have a standard shower, or you can ask for any special temperature, time, type of spray, whatever. The shower stops the minute you tell it to."

"The shower part is all that water coming out of the wall?" Nareen peered around the edge of the open shower door with suspicion.

"That's right." Jerrel silently chided himself for not being clearer. He'd never before realized how many things he took for granted, without stopping to think about what they were or how they worked.

"And when I tell it to stop, it stops? That's it?" Nareen was studying the shower as if she expected some particularly repugnant creature to appear suddenly.

"That's it. Why don't you try it? I'll stay in the room in case you have any questions."

"I've tried it before, but . . ." She squared her shoulders. "I just walk in?"

"That's right."

Without giving her a chance to answer, Jerrel retreated to the main room. What was it about the shower that bothered her so much? Whatever it was, he hoped his brief explanation would alleviate her distrust of the mechanism.

He settled on a chair. Behind him he could hear the sound of the shower spray starting up. That's all Nareen had needed, he realized somewhat smugly—the human touch, as opposed to an impersonal explanation from a computer.

In that instant a cry of mingled rage and disgust came from the shower room, closely followed by the sound of the shower door banging violently open.

Chapter 17

In an instant Jerrel was out of his chair and in the dressing area.

But instead of some unknown monster, all he found was a very wet and highly indignant Nareen standing outside the shower, naked and coated with the liquid soap that was automatically sprayed after the shower's occupant was sufficiently damp.

"It did it again!" she raged, brushing at her arm with distaste. "It covered me with this slime, just like it did every other time I tried to do this shower thing!"

Understanding dawned. "That's soap!"

Nareen's hand froze in the process of trying to scrape the offensive goo off her skin. "Soap?"

Jerrel nodded solemnly. "That's right."

"But it came out of the wall, along with the water!"

"It's supposed to do that."

"Soap." This time she said the word with an air of wonder, rather than disgust. Tentatively she raised her hand to her nose and sniffed at the thin film of soap that still clung to her skin. "It smells good."

"It's supposed to do that, too."

"I've never seen soap that wasn't in a big lump."

With an effort, Jerrel tore his gaze away from her and fixed it on a point on the opposite wall. She was totally oblivious of her nudity, too entranced by this newest marvel to realize the effect she was having on him.

But he was *not* oblivious, and he was finding it impossible to ignore her, or to ignore the motion of her hands along her sides and across her breasts and belly as she explored the wonder of this new sensation.

The sooner he could get her rinsed, dried, and clothed again, the easier it would be to stick to his unspoken promise not to let his need for her complicate the situation. "Look, it's not that hard. If you can learn to use a com panel, you can learn to take a shower."

"I never imagined it was soap!" Nareen looked up at him, her face alight with the joy of discovery.

Jerrel looked down, but he couldn't look just at her eyes or her mouth or her chin. His gaze slid down to her breasts—small and firm and glistening with a sheen of soap—down her sides, down her belly . . .

"Damn it!" he snapped, goaded beyond endurance. He grabbed her hand and dragged her back into the shower. "The shower turns on when you

Anne Avery

walk in. You just tell it what you want and that's it."

Immediately a fine mist of warm water began spraying from rows of vertical black strips placed at intervals along three walls.

Nareen jumped. "How does the water come out of those things?" she demanded. "Where does the soap come from? How do you tell it to change? What . . ."

Soap sprayed out of the strips, along with the water. Added to the layer of soap already coating Nareen, it created a foamy covering that slid easily over her skin, rinsing down the length of her body under the warm, steady pulse of the water.

"Won't this hurt your clothes?" Nareen asked, wide-eyed. She ran her fingers over his chest as if she expected the black skin suit to dissolve.

"It's waterproof." The words weren't easy to say between clenched teeth. "Turn around," Jerrel commanded. To make sure she did, he placed his hand on her shoulder and tugged her around.

What momentary insanity had gotten him into this? Another minute facing her, another soft brush of her hand against him, and he wouldn't be able to control himself. As it was, his skin suit was already stretching to accommodate his growing arousal. Thank the stars she hadn't noticed just how adjustable the damn suits were!

But an instant later he realized he hadn't improved matters. Not one whit. Under his hand her skin was warm and wet, the flesh beneath firm, yet yielding to his touch.

As if of its own volition, his hand slid across her shoulder blade and the curve of her spine to her other shoulder. The slight friction of his touch created a froth of soap bubbles.

She was so warm and real and so very, very desirable.

Unable to resist, Jerrel brought his left hand up and with his fingers began a gentle, probing exploration of her shoulders, the length of her back, the swelling curve of her buttocks, then up again. With each stroke, each sweep of his hands, his breathing became faster, deeper, more unsteady.

At his touch, Nareen arched back into his hands. Such a simple movement, yet he could feel the way her bones shifted, the smooth play of muscles under her skin.

Her movements, her response to his touch, were like a potent drug, weakening his control, heightening his senses. He splayed his hands across her shoulder blades, then began rubbing his palms in gentle, ever-widening circles as she rolled her shoulders, leaning into the pressure of his hands.

With his thumbs, Jerrel slid around the edge of her shoulder blades, digging into the muscles underneath, then slowly worked his way up the smooth arc of her spine, probing, squeezing, rubbing. The fire swirling through his veins was urging him forward, faster, faster, and yet he wanted this gentle, wondering exploration to last forever.

His fingers moved up under the wet, silken curtain of her hair, gently exploring the nape of her neck, the hollow behind her ear, the line of her jaw, until her head was cupped between his hands.

Nareen released a slow, shuddering breath. Eyes closed, she let her head fall. Her hands came up to cover his; then, slowly, she brushed the tips of her fingers along his fingers, across the backs of his hands. The motion was so gentle, so delicate, he wasn't even sure she touched him. Yet it was enough. His palms burned, his breath caught in his throat, and somewhere deep within him the fire she had ignited raged up, threatening to consume him in its intensity.

With a choked cry he pulled away from her. But he couldn't let Nareen go, couldn't free himself from his need for her. Jerrel ran his hands down her back, along the curve of her waist, around to smooth across her breasts. The small mounds shifted under his touch, soft and yielding, but the hard, pointed nipples dug into his palms, cutting a trail of fiery sensation into his flesh.

Beside his massive body she seemed impossibly fragile. Yet within that small frame was enough passion and fire, enough vibrant life to fill even the blackest depths of heaven. With her, and her alone, he felt whole. No matter what lay ahead of them she was his, forever.

For an instant that realization held him still, caught in wonder that it could be so simple, so right.

Then the gentle mist of the shower changed automatically to hard, pounding jets that thudded against his skin with insistent force. Nareen turned to face him, arms raised—demanding, promising—and all Jerrel's thoughts coalesced into the certainty that she was his to love, and to make love to.

With sudden, desperate urgency he drew her to him. Their lips met. Jerrel groaned, then opened his mouth wider, as if in his hunger for her he might devour her whole.

An instant later she pulled back. She was panting—short, quick bursts of breath that seemed to catch somewhere in her throat. Her lips trembled, her eyes were heavy-lidded, half hidden. Her fingers fumbled at the collar of his skin suit.

"Your suit, take it off," she insisted. Her voice was low, roughened by desire.

An instant later the suit lay on the floor of the shower, forgotten. The emotional barriers between them had already fallen. With the suit, the last physical barrier was gone as well.

It was as if he had suddenly been given wings.

Jerrel found himself soaring, unfettered by the doubts and uncertainties that had weighed him down for so long. And Nareen was soaring with him, sharing the ecstasy, driving him higher, then higher still.

But it wasn't enough to touch, to kiss, to explore, not enough to feel the quivering response of the other. They were still two bodies, two souls aching to be made one.

Driven by an urgency he had never known, Jerrel swung Nareen off the floor, holding her warm, wet body closely pressed against his.

There was no need for words. Nareen understood. She wrapped her legs around him, clinging with a desperation born of her own driving need.

One step, then Jerrel pinned her against the wall that had no shower strips, his broad back shielding her from the pulsing water.

For an instant it seemed they hung suspended, as if they could soar no higher. Then Nareen looked up at him and in her eyes shone the promise of a love Jerrel had never imagined possible.

With a cry of joy he joined with her, and their bodies, their very beings, united in an ageless rhythm while the warm, pounding water cascaded over them.

When Nareen awoke, the bedclothes were tangled around her legs and Jerrel's head was pillowed on her breast, his arm protectively wrapped about her waist. She could feel the steady rise and fall of his chest as he slept and the warm caress of his breath on her skin.

Carefully, so as not to disturb him, she brought her hand up to rearrange his tangled chestnut curls. His hair was still damp.

With the tip of one finger she traced the curve of a particularly shaggy lock.

He loved her.

He really loved her.

The unspoken words were sweet and tinged with wonder.

Yet even as the knowledge of his love warmed her, there was a chilling touch of sadness, too. Jerrel could not live on her world. It had been difficult enough for him, in the short time they'd known each other, to hide who and what he was from her. He couldn't live his life like that. She knew it without trying to analyze how or why she could be so sure.

If they were to be together, then she was the one who would have to adapt. Loving him meant leaving behind everything she had ever known—her friends, her work, her city. Her world.

It was a high price to pay for love, but it was a price she would pay gladly if only she could be sure that Kalinden and its people were safe.

Almost two weeks had passed since she'd accidentally been beamed up with Jerrel. Two weeks of fear and wonder and discovery. Two weeks when she'd been so engrossed in the effort to learn everything she could about Jerrel and his ship that she'd almost forgotten the struggle on the planet below them.

In that time anything could have happened on Errandane. Kalinden's troops might have vanquished the beastmen, or they might be engaged in a full-scale battle with the creatures, desperately holding out in hopes of assistance that would never come.

There was little she could do against the beastmen, but they weren't the only danger Kalinden faced. And though Nareen wasn't sure she could do anything about Xyanth's machinations, either, she was very, very sure she had to try.

Moving cautiously so as not to waken Jerrel, Nareen slid out of bed. For a moment she stood looking down at him as he lay sleeping, overcome by her love for him and the wonder that he loved her in return.

Then she gathered up the silken green gown from the bench outside the shower and quietly left the room.

She was in the study area when Jerrel found her more than an hour later.

CeeCee had been unable to provide any information on conditions in Kalinden, but the computer—grudgingly, it seemed to Nareen—had offered to display the pictures taken by the first Rediscovery Service mission to Errandane several years before.

Images of Anweigh and Margash, of the farms in the central plains and of the empty reaches of the southern mountains flashed across the big viewscreen, illuminating the darkened room. This was her world, seen through the eyes of a reconnaissance probe. Cities she'd never known, people she'd never met passed before her and were gone.

It was, Nareen thought sadly, like looking at the carved image of loved ones long after they were dead—something to remember them by in the lonely hours of the night.

Though the door to the study area was open and Jerrel's footsteps made no sound in the deep carpeting, Nareen knew when he entered and crossed the room to her. Her eyes never wavered from the viewscreen.

For a moment Jerrel said nothing, just watched the images on the screen with a sick feeling of fear knotting in his belly.

Had he lost her? He'd fallen asleep in Nareen's arms, secure in the knowledge that she loved him. He'd awakened to find her gone.

Now she sat, still and unspeaking, studying these pictures of her world—her home—as if trying to come to a decision.

"I can't let you go back," Jerrel said, hesitantly placing his hands on her shoulders. He could feel the tension in her muscles. His fingers tightened. "I love you. I can't let you go. Not now."

Slowly she shook her head. The motion made her hair brush across the backs of his fingers, back and forth, tormenting him with the silken touch. From this angle, standing behind and slightly to her side, he could see the corner of her mouth turn down in a slight frown.

"I have to return."

Jerrel had to bend forward to catch her words.

"I'm needed there," she said, her voice stronger, firmer.

"You *can't*." His fingers gripped her even more tightly, desperately. Only when she flinched did

324

he ease his hold. "They haven't listened to you before. What makes you think they'll listen now? What can you do that could possibly make a difference?"

Nareen rose to her feet, then turned to face him, sliding out from under his hands. Her chin came up. "I don't know what I can do. I don't even know where to start. But I have to go." Her green eyes searched his. "Will you give up your search for your brother just because you haven't been able to find him yet?"

"That's different!" Jerrel snapped, then wished he hadn't. She was right. It was his need for her, his fear that he would lose her, that made him deny her a right he claimed for himself.

Slowly he shook his head, his lips twisting in a sad, rueful smile. "No, it's not different. You're right. I can't ask you to abandon your city any more than I can abandon my brother." He drew a deep, steadying breath. "So what now?"

Nareen raised her hand to touch his cheek. "I don't know. I've been trying to think, trying to come up with some sort of plan, but . . ." Her voice trailed away.

Without speaking, she sought the comfort of his embrace. In his arms life seemed so much simpler.

"Tell me about Santar," she said after a moment. Jerrel held her so tightly against him, her voice was slightly muffled.

"What do you want to know?" Jerrel ran his hand up and down her back, slowly, soothingly.

With the gentle motion, Nareen began to relax. She could feel the tension easing from his body, too.

"What kind of man is he? Serious? Easygoing? What does he look like?"

For a moment Jerrel didn't say anything, just continued to run his hand along her back. Then, "He's younger than I am. A lot younger. Gentler, more idealistic. A much better human being, in many ways, than I'll ever be."

Jerrel made a sound, something halfway between a laugh and a sigh. Nareen could feel it rumbling in his chest, like a pain that could never quite be eased.

"It's hard for brothers to understand each other at the best of times," he continued at last. "I'm not sure we ever managed even that well. I was a young man when our father died; he was still a boy. I left Arcana and he stayed, trying to find a place for himself in a society that just wanted to forget our family ever existed. I managed to go back on occasion, just for a few days at a time. The last time I saw him was when he graduated from training for the Rediscovery Service."

Jerrel's words were heavily laced with regret for what he and his brother had never had. Nareen clung to him, silently offering the little comfort that was hers to give. When he didn't say anything more, she asked, "Does he look like you?"

This time Jerrel did laugh. "No, not really. Santar's shorter than I am, finer boned. His hair is just as curly as mine, though the color is a little darker. Our eyes are the same shade of blue. Norvag swears we look more alike than we realize, but other than our eyes and our curls, I never saw that much resemblance."

He shifted slightly and leaned past Nareen to punch some controls on the com panel she'd been using to view the scenes from Errandane. "Santar sent me a picture of himself. It was taken on Arcana, just before he was assigned here."

The pictures of Errandane disappeared and were replaced by the still image of a slender young man dressed in a tightly fitted garment that appeared to be some sort of uniform. He was looking straight ahead with a gentle, dreamy expression on his delicate features. His hair was dark and very curly, and his eyes were the same intense shade of blue as Jerrel's.

For an instant shock held Nareen frozen. It couldn't be possible . . . The eyes were different and yet . . .

"I've met him!" she exclaimed, pulling out of Jerrel's arms so she, too, could reach the com panel. She fumbled with the still-unfamiliar controls but succeeded in enlarging the image so Santar's face occupied most of the screen. "That's the healer! That is, the healer's eyes were brown, not blue, but I'd swear they're the same man. I'd swear it!"

"What are you talking about?" Jerrel demanded, obviously confused by her sudden excitement.

"The healer I told you about who was taking care of the injured after the beastmen attacked the camp. Except for the eyes, Santar looks exactly like him!"

Jerrel was staring at her eagerly, as if he wanted desperately to believe her but was afraid. "You're sure?"

Nareen nodded. "Except for the eyes . . ."

"It's possible." Jerrel stared at the screen. "There were no records on Santar's ship to say he did anything like that, but it's still possible. He could have changed his eye color, erased the computer's memory of the treatment . . ."

Jerrel was talking to himself, not to her, but Nareen didn't mind. If it was true, if the healer really was Santar . . .

"If we went back, could you help me find this healer?" Jerrel demanded. "Could we trace him somehow?"

Nareen nodded. For a runner, that wouldn't be hard at all.

Two hours later Nareen found herself nervously adjusting the loose tunic and baggy pants CeeCee had made for her through the generator. She'd never worn the clothes of a holding wife before, and the garments seemed stranger even than her first skin suit.

She and Jerrel had agreed it made the best sense to return to Kalinden first. The attack by the beastmen had occurred almost two weeks before. That was more than enough time for the decimated army to return to the city in search of reinforcements and proper care for the wounded. Even if the army wasn't in Kalinden, it wouldn't take long to find out where it was and, with luck, where the healer was, too.

Nareen had chosen her disguise with care. Dressed as a runner, she would have been arrested the instant she tried to enter the gates of the city—Gasperian would not forgive her for having ignored his orders a second time. No one would expect to see her in the coarse clothes of a holding woman. So many people had fled to Kalinden for safety that she should be able to hide in the crowds, and her apparent status as a refugee would make it easy to ask questions without arousing suspicion.

Jerrel was a little more difficult. He was too big and his eye color too noticeable for him to blend into the background. She'd decided he should wear the same type of clothes he'd worn before; only this time they would be a little more tattered and stained. If they encountered anyone who knew him, he would explain that he'd become separated from the others during the night and had lost his way in the mountains. As a stranger to Kalinden, few would question his explanation.

She hoped.

"How do I look?" Once again, Jerrel entered her room without giving her advance warning.

Nareen could have sworn the clothes he wore were the same as those he'd worn before he'd been wounded by the beastmen. The major difference was these garments carried two weeks' more dirt on them. His tunic and leggings had the greasy shine of leather that has been worn too long without cleaning, the sleeves of his shirt were torn in several places, and the soles of his boots were almost worn through. Even his hair looked as if it hadn't been washed for days. Only his face and hands were clean—since Jerrel couldn't produce a two-weeks' growth of beard in two hours, they'd decided it would be better if he appeared to have managed to clean up around the edges and no more.

"Those clothes are disgusting, boss," CeeCee said. "I hope you're not planning on making a habit of asking for such filthy things, because I won't make them for you."

Nareen couldn't help smiling. "If I didn't know better, I'd say you'd been on the trail for weeks," she said, studying him in amazement.

329

He grinned, appraising her own crude costume. "In those baggy clothes and with a shawl over your head, no one will recognize you as the Sixth Runner for Kalinden, either."

Nareen flinched. She'd worked so hard and so long to become a runner, and now the leaders for whom she would have given her life considered her a demented fool at best, a traitor at worst. But it was too late for regrets.

"I brought you this," Jerrel said, extending a small silver box strung on a silver chain. "It's a portable com link. In case we're separated, you can return to the ship if you need to. It's strictly forbidden to give a link to someone who's not a citizen, but your safety means far more to me than the laws of the Empire."

Nareen turned the box over in her hands, frowning. It seemed strange to think of this ship as refuge. "How does it work?"

"Press your thumb there." Jerrel pointed to an oval indentation on one side. "CeeCee has programmed the link to respond to your print. No one else can use it."

The computer gave the equivalent of a sniff. "I certainly hope not. One primitive on board is more than enough."

"Cut it out, CeeCee," Jerrel said, keeping his gaze fixed on Nareen.

Nareen's eyes were fixed on the silver box, her thoughts racing. What if . . . ? She glanced up at Jerrel. "Is it possible to make a link that would work for anyone, even someone you don't know?"

Jerrel frowned slightly. "It's possible, but for security reasons not very practical. Without some way of identifying the person using it, anyone could come on board." The edge of his mouth quirked. "Like you, for instance."

"If you wanted to bring somebody up who didn't want to come, what would you do?"

"That's easy. All you have to . . . Now wait a minute! Just what are you planning?" Jerrel demanded, his eyes dark with suspicion.

"If we could bring up the Lady Xyanth, then she wouldn't be able to harm Kalinden any further." As a plan began to take shape in her mind, a growing enthusiasm crept into Nareen's voice. "We could take her to your world, or send her to another town on the farthest side of Errandane. Or we could—"

"Or we could forget the whole thing," Jerrel interjected hastily. "It was a good try, but there *is* a limit to the number of laws I'm going to break. Giving you the com link was it. I'm not going to interfere in Errandane politics to the extent of kidnapping your Lady Xyanth."

He paused, left eyebrow arched in amusement at the stubborn set of Nareen's jaw. "Have you considered," he continued softly, "that she couldn't have done as much as she has without the support of at least some of her men? Removing her wouldn't mean you've stopped them, too. They might even use her disappearance as the excuse to attack Kalinden, accuse your city of kidnapping or murdering her. How much support would your people have from other cities in that case?"

Nareen's shoulders drooped. It had seemed like such a good idea.

Without speaking, she followed Jerrel out of the room. She was suddenly very nervous. It was one thing to have come on the ship when she wasn't expecting it, quite another deliberately to plan on letting a machine make her disappear, then reappear somewhere else. She still didn't say anything when they stopped before the seemingly blank wall that led to what she'd learned was called the transport chamber. The wall opened, and Jerrel stepped into the room beyond. After a moment's hesitation, so did she.

For the first time since she'd arrived on the ship, Nareen found herself in the empty gray chamber with the curving walls. She tensed, remembering the horror of that moment. She'd learned a lot since then, but that didn't make it any easier.

"It's all right." Jerrel was beside her, smiling down at her in encouragement. He wrapped an arm around her shoulders, drawing her against him, then said to the empty room, "Okay, CeeCee, let's go."

For a moment it seemed nothing was happening. Then Jerrel seemed to fade. Nareen tried to reach for him but he wasn't there. Neither was her hand or her arm or . . .

She screamed. Instead of echoing in a closed chamber, the scream was torn from her lips by a cold, biting wind that cut at her savagely.

Now both Jerrel's arms were around her, once more warm and comforting and undeniably real. "Are you all right?" he asked, bending his head so she could hear him clearly in the wind.

Nareen nodded. The nod was a little shaky, just like she was. "Of course."

Jerrel gave her a hug, then released her. "Do you know where we are?"

The wind felt much colder when he wasn't holding her. Nareen felt disoriented and uncertain but was loath to let Jerrel know just how terrified she'd been. With an effort she focused on the barren hillside they stood on.

When they were making their plans, Jerrel had explained that CeeCee could put them down close to Kalinden, but it had to be someplace where they wouldn't be seen. Nareen had suggested several sites; then Jerrel had left it up to CeeCee to select the one nearest to Kalinden that was safe.

Looking around her now, Nareen realized the computer had chosen a location only fifteen minutes from a side gate in the city walls. After a quick adjustment to the belt of her tunic—it seemed strange not to have her runner's belt— she led the way toward the city.

Chapter 18

Three heavily laden carts guarded by a dozen armed Matcassen troops were just starting to pass through the side gate when Nareen and Jerrel arrived. Careful to keep her eyes downcast like any proper holding woman, Nareen skirted the wagons and tried to slip through the gate. She was brought up short by the man guarding the gate, who swung his spear down to bar her way.

"Ho, there, woman! What do ye mean, sneakin' past like that?"

Nareen brought her head up with a snap. "Sir?"

"Ye're not allowed in the gates."

"Not allowed . . . ! What do you mean, not allowed?"

"Jus' that. Not allowed. Too many people in t'city already. Don't need no more."

"Don't need any more!" Nareen stiffened in outrage, forgetting her role. "You've no right—" A hand clamped on her shoulder, interrupting her indignant words.

"What's this all about?" Jerrel demanded in a tone carefully calculated to assert his authority without raising the guard's hackles. "Why are we denied entrance?"

The surly guard shifted nervously, clearly uncomfortable beside Jerrel's much greater bulk. He glanced at the men accompanying the wagons, two of whom detached themselves from the rest and strode toward them, swords in hand. Emboldened by this backup, the guard thrust his chin out in surly defiance of Jerrel.

"T'city's closed. No one allowed in 'ceptin' provision wagons. Them's me orders, and I follows orders," he declared truculently.

"Who are you?" Nareen demanded. "I don't remember—" Jerrel tightened his grip on her shoulder, warning her to silence.

"A man has to follow orders, that's true," Jerrel agreed pleasantly, his eyes on the two soldiers who now stood on either side of the guard. "But surely those orders don't include us. The woman here has been separated from her family and she's nowhere else to go. I've been hired to—"

"No one allowed in," declared one of the soldiers.

"'At's right. No one," the second agreed.

"You can't mean to leave us out here!" Nareen protested.

By now all three wagons had passed inside the walls and the soldiers were pulling the massive wooden doors shut. The guard and the two soldiers at his sides backed toward the gate, eyes fixed on Nareen and Jerrel, their weapons in their hands. All three had the air of men who expected a fight and were ready for it.

First the soldiers, then the guard slipped through the narrow aperture remaining. "T'Lady ain't allowin' nobody in," he said, brandishing his spear. Then he pulled his spear inside, and the gates shut with a hollow, resounding thud.

For a moment, Nareen and Jerrel stood staring dumbfounded at the blank wall of wood before them. Then Nareen lifted her head to study the massive gray stone walls above, searching for some sign of the Kalinden guards who should be watching the entrance. She saw no one. Nothing moved.

A particularly icy blast of wind struck her, making her shiver. "Xyanth controls Kalinden," she said. Even to her own ears her voice sounded hollow.

Jerrel's expression was grim. "So it would seem."

"I should have been here, should have helped . . ."

"You couldn't have done anything to stop her. You tried, remember?"

"Yes, but—"

Jerrel took her arm and drew her back down the trail they'd come on. "Staring at a blank wall isn't going to gain us anything." Despite her protests, he didn't stop and didn't release her until they were out of sight of the city walls.

Drawing her into the protected lee of some rocks, he added, "We'll beam into the city. Someplace where there's little chance of us being spotted but where we can get more information."

Nareen chewed her lower lip, trying to think. "There's a small storeroom connected to an inn I know. The inn's popular and not far from the

Great Hall so a lot of people are always around. Or we could try the shops run by people I know we can trust. There are any number of rooms in the Hall and—"

Jerrel shook his head. "The Hall's out. That's the first place Xyanth would have made sure to control. The shops . . ." He frowned. "Not the shops. Let's try the storeroom. Even if the inn's closed, there are bound to be a number of ways for us to get out."

Under Jerrel's instructions, Nareen pulled out the com link on its chain around her neck, pressed her thumb to the slight depression on one side, and instantly found herself communicating mentally with CeeCee. It took a moment for her to overcome the disorientation of having a voice speaking in her head before she could give the computer directions for the storeroom she sought.

For a few seconds, nothing happened; then Jerrel disappeared in front of her eyes only to reappear in a crowded room heaped to the ceiling with boxes and bales. One small, dirty window admitted just enough light for Nareen to discern the narrow door half hidden behind a stack of wooden crates. Without hesitation, she headed for the door.

"Wait." Jerrel's voice was pitched low and carried an unmistakable note of command.

Nareen bristled, unwilling to waste even a minute.

"We need more information before we go rushing out of this room," Jerrel said, correctly interpreting the stubborn set of her jaw. "CeeCee, how many people are in the building and where are they?"

"Six in the hallways, twenty-three in a large room at the front, five in what seems to be a kitchen at the back, fourteen in various rooms throughout the rest of the building."

Nareen gaped. She wasn't sure whether she'd actually heard the computer's voice or if the words had just formed in her mind. "What are the people doing?" she demanded. "What are they saying? What's happening? What—"

"I can't answer those questions." CeeCee might almost have sniffed in disdain, so scornful was the inflection in its voice.

"Sit down," Jerrel said gently, drawing Nareen with him to the floor. "All CeeCee can distinguish is human life forms. It can't help us any more than that."

"Then we need to find out what's going on," Nareen insisted. "We can't do anything just hiding here." She started to rise to her feet again but Jerrel pulled her back.

"Sit. We'll leave in a few minutes, but first I'll try again to contact Norvag. He might have heard something, know something we don't."

Reluctantly, Nareen agreed.

Seemingly satisfied she wouldn't do anything rash, Jerrel leaned back against the bales behind him and closed his eyes. Nareen watched, fascinated, as all expression, all vitality slowly drained from his face. His features went slack, his body limp, and he sagged against the supporting bales.

Nareen wasn't sure how many minutes passed before Jerrel slowly roused from his stupor. His eyes, intensely blue even in the dim light, blinked once, twice. He straightened, then shook his head to clear it.

"Well?" Nareen demanded when he didn't

speak. "Did you reach Norvag? What did he say?"

Jerrel sighed. "I reached him." A muscle twitched in his jaw. "Matcassen is in revolt. A week ago, Lindaz announced he would lead more troops to Kalinden. The people of Matcassen didn't approve and decided they'd had enough. According to Norvag, there's been fierce fighting in the streets for the past four days, but the people are winning. Lindaz is holed up in his Hall, and the rebels control most of the city."

Nareen could feel a tentative smile beginning to form on her lips. A dozen questions danced in her head. "Who's leading the revolt?"

The corner of Jerrel's mouth inched upward. "A captain of the guards named Faldoc, but it seems one of his chief lieutenants is your friend Tork."

"Tork!" Nareen jerked upright in amazement. "But he's a runner!"

Jerrel's smile widened. "So are you, my love, but that hasn't stopped you from doing what you thought was right instead of what you were expected to do."

Nareen started to protest. "But Tork . . ." The words died on her lips. *My love.* Jerrel had called her his love. It was the first time he'd spoken those precious words. The breath caught in her throat. Her mouth dropped open, and that was all the invitation Jerrel needed.

He leaned forward and covered her lips with his, then thrust his tongue into her mouth, hungrily probing, inviting her response. Nareen needed no second invitation. She swayed toward him, eagerly meeting his advances, demanding even more.

For a moment, all thought of Kalinden and its

plight, all care for her friends and their unknown fate faded before the heated need his touch roused in her. Nareen was only recalled to the present by the sound of angry voices coming from somewhere within the building. Startled, she jerked away from Jerrel and turned toward the door to the storeroom, half expecting to see someone come bursting in.

Although the door remained shut, the voices could be heard clearly. With a muttered oath, Jerrel climbed to his feet, his sword ready, but the voices grew softer as the disputants moved away. He glanced ruefully down at Nareen, who was on her feet beside him.

"I suppose we should be grateful to whoever they are for reminding us of why we're here," he said, arching an eyebrow in resigned irony. "Unfortunately, I was beginning to enjoy myself."

Nareen nodded briefly, uncertain what to say. She shouldn't have let her emotions get the better of her, yet she couldn't regret that brief, passionate kiss. The words *my love* still rang too clearly in her heart.

Jerrel crossed to the door and pressed his ear against the wood, straining to hear any sound from the hallway beyond. Satisfied, he said, "I suppose this inn has a tavern. That must be where those twenty-three people are. If we can find a seat where we could listen without drawing attention to ourselves, we might be able to learn something about what's going on."

Unable to suggest any better plan, Nareen cautiously led Jerrel out into the dark, narrow hallway, past several closed doors, then down a flight of stairs to the ground floor. They'd almost reached the entrance to the tavern when a couple of holding men, reeling from too liberal a dip into the tavern's alcoholic offerings, staggered around a corner and almost careened into them.

Hastily Jerrel drew Nareen against him. Other than offering a few ribald comments about Jerrel's choice of a holding woman for his entertainment, the men didn't bother them but instead staggered past and on up the stairs.

The tavern was dark and so crowded they attracted little notice. Their luck held. The one empty table gave them a good view of the room, the main door, and the street outside.

As she sipped the strong ale the barman brought, Nareen strained to make sense of the snippets of conversation she could catch. Despite the drunken jests and harsh laughter, there was an underlying anger beneath the surface, like tinder beneath wood. It awaited only a spark to ignite the fire.

"Fourteen soldiers on the gate . . ."

" . . . killed trying to get word out . . ."

"The announcement said Gasperian was mad . . ."

"They're not helpin' us. Said so all along."

" . . . bodies hangin' in the square. Can't go out at night, can't talk . . ."

"It's a wonder they're still lettin' the taverns keep open . . ."

With each word, each angry phrase, Nareen's own anger grew. Matcassen held her city in a remorseless grip, and those who dared protest paid with their lives.

A hundred plans flitted through her head, only to be discarded. What could two people do against hundreds of armed troops ready to kill at the slightest provocation?

Nareen shifted impatiently on her chair, then turned to stare out at the street. Dozens of people passed, their expressions shuttered and unreadable. Surely among so many there must be some willing to fight. These were shopkeepers, merchants, holding men—people who had much to lose if Matcassen conquered Kalinden.

A disturbance farther down the street drew the attention of the passersby, who shrank back against the buildings lining the streets, clearly anxious not to be involved.

Nareen craned forward, trying to see what was happening. Her movement attracted Jerrel's attention and he twisted around in his chair and peered out, as well.

Suddenly about a dozen Matcassen soldiers marched into view, their weapons drawn and ready. At their head was a guardsman whose face looked familiar. Nareen blinked, then shrank back, away from the window. It was too late. The guardsman had spotted them.

"There's a back way, an alley," Nareen said to Jerrel between stiff lips. He was already halfway out of his chair, one eyebrow arched in an unspoken query. He'd recognized the guardsman, too.

They were scarcely free of the table when the door burst open and the Matcassen troops rushed in. Their entrance was so abrupt and unexpected, no one but Nareen, Jerrel, and a kitchen boy who'd been sent to collect dirty dishes were on their feet. The boy froze, eyes wide with fright, and dropped the stack of dishes he held. The sound of the plates shattering on the stone floor rang loudly in the tense silence.

"Well, warrior," said the guardsman, his eyes

fixed on Jerrel. "It seems you avoided the beast-men, after all."

"You expected them to do your dirty work for you, is that right, Pardraik?"

Pardraik's head cocked to one side. His face was completely expressionless except for his dark, glittering eyes. "Let's just say the attack resolved a little problem for me," he said.

Jerrel's hand edged almost imperceptibly toward his sword. Pardraik reached out and grabbed the arm of the terrified kitchen boy, almost jerking him off his feet. "I wouldn't start a fight in here if I were you, warrior. The boy here might get hurt in the scuffle. In fact, if you don't come peaceably, I might just decide to bring the boy along as hostage when we do drag you out of here."

Nareen tried to cry out a warning, but Jerrel was already holding up his hands, palms out and far from his weapons.

Pardraik grinned, a tight, humorless expression that did nothing to soften the hardness in his eyes. "That was wise." With a quick flick of his head he motioned his men to surround Nareen and Jerrel.

The boy was released once they were Pardraik's prisoners. He immediately fled to the safety of the kitchen. Only a few of the tavern customers tried to come to their rescue, and they were stopped by the extremely persuasive argument of a sword at their throats.

In minutes, Nareen was standing in the street beside Jerrel, her hands bound behind her back just as his were. Her knife had been taken from her, and one of the Matcassen troops now held Jerrel's sword.

"How dare you!" Nareen raged when Pardraik stopped in front of her. "I wouldn't have believed—"

"I dare many things when Matcassen rules Kalinden, runner," Pardraik said coldly. "Believe what you like. You'll soon have some of the answers you seek." Without another word, he set off down the street.

His men, tense and alert to any threat from their prisoners or the passersby, fell into step behind Pardraik. They surrounded Nareen and Jerrel, effectively cutting off any chance of escape. To Nareen's surprise, instead of heading toward the Great Hall Pardraik led them toward the far west wall of the city.

The expressions on the faces of the people they passed ranged from sullen anger to apathetic fear. No one made any effort to detain them, and most shrank back against the buildings or into shop doorways to give them as wide a berth as possible.

Pardraik stopped at last before an old warehouse on a dark side street. Matcassen troops stood guard at the door and at points all along the street. With only a curt nod to the guards, he led the way into the building and down a shadowed inner hallway until they reached a large room at the back. He posted two guards at the door, then dismissed the rest of the soldiers.

There were three men in the room gathered around a table and bent over a map spread out before them. At Pardraik's entrance, their heads came up and turned toward the door.

Nareen halted in amazement. "Gravnar! Teacher! What . . . ?"

Gravnar straightened, an expression of mingled amazement and delight brightening his old features. "Sixth Runner!" He crossed the room to her, arms extended in welcome. Before Nareen could respond, he enfolded her in a hug that threatened to crush her ribs and rob her of all capacity for breathing.

At last he stepped back, his hands on her shoulders. To Nareen's amazement, tears glittered in his eyes.

"Nareen," he whispered, and his voice cracked a little. He blinked, then said more firmly, "We thought you were dead. It had been so long . . ."

"Jerrel was injured," Nareen faltered. "We just returned. But I don't understand. You. These troops. I thought—"

"These men are helping us," Gravnar said. His fingers tightened on her shoulders. "Thanks to you, to your warnings, we have a chance we would not otherwise have had. And Pardraik and his friends give us an additional advantage we hadn't expected."

Nareen glanced at Pardraik, who stood watching her, his eyes shadowed, his mouth twisted in a wry grimace.

"I'm loyal to my city, runner, but not to those who would destroy her," he said. "Too many have already died to feed the hunger for power that consumes Master Lindaz and his Lady. Regardless of our oaths of loyalty, many of us have chosen to fight on the side of Kalinden."

"Then what about these cords around our wrists?" Jerrel demanded, glaring at the guardsman.

This time the corner of Pardraik's mouth twitched in real amusement. "I couldn't risk leaving you free until I'd had a chance to explain, could I?" He drew a dagger from his belt and

345

sliced through Jerrel's bonds, then Nareen's.

Jerrel rubbed his wrists, staring at Pardraik thoughtfully. "Back in camp, when Xyanth told you to kill me, would you have done it?"

"Of course not. Why do you think I concocted that excuse about not wanting to draw the carrion eaters? We were going to stage your escape, but the beastmen took that little problem out of our hands."

Jerrel nodded slowly, his eyes fixed on Pardraik's face. "So what now?"

Pardraik glanced at the two men who had returned to their studies of the maps before them. "Your people and mine are meeting here in about an hour. We may move against Xyanth tonight but we need more information to make our final decisions. Until then . . ." His gaze returned to Jerrel, frankly curious. "There's a man with us, a healer, who's asked about you ever since the runner came through camp searching for you. Do you know him?"

"I might." Jerrel's voice conveyed no hint of the tension Nareen sensed below the surface. "Perhaps we could meet him."

"Of course." Pardraik opened the door and asked one of the guards outside to come in. "Beck will take you to him. You can't go back on the street. My men and I are supposed to hold an outpost at this side of town, but there are more of us located in a number of old buildings joined to this one by tunnels. I don't want anyone to guess that what remains of your Kalinden troops are housed here, as well."

As Nareen turned to follow Jerrel and the guard, Gravnar restrained her with a brief touch on her arm.

"I rejoice that you've returned, Sixth . . . Nareen," he said. His eyes dropped from hers. "I was a fool," he added bitterly. "I should have realized . . . should have known . . ."

"It doesn't matter," Nareen muttered, uncomfortable with her teacher's self-reproach. "You did what you had to. Gasperian wouldn't have been any more willing to believe you."

"Perhaps, but that doesn't—"

"What's important is that you believed me eventually."

Gravnar's head came up sharply. The shame Nareen saw in his faded eyes stabbed at her like a beastman's lance.

"It was Tisnerl who made me see what a fool I was," the old man admitted. "Only you and he had the wisdom and the courage to act, in spite of everything."

"Teacher . . ."

"Go now. Your friend is waiting, and Pardraik and I have matters to discuss." Gravnar squared his shoulders, forcing all hint of emotion from his expression.

"I . . ."

"Go."

With tears stinging her eyes, Nareen started to turn away when Gravnar once more stopped her.

"I'm glad you've returned safely, sixth runner," he said, very softly.

Nareen could only nod. Before she could embarrass them both, she spun about and headed toward the door where Jerrel waited for her.

Jerrel followed Beck through the narrow, twisting passageways without speaking. He was aware of Nareen behind him and grateful for her presence, but his thoughts were concentrated on the nameless healer he would soon meet, the man he hoped might be his brother.

He shoved his hand in his tunic pocket where he'd put Santar's recorder ring. The ring was cold to the touch, yet solid and somehow reassuring. He'd decided at the last minute to bring it, as a talisman more than for any practical purpose.

Beck stopped at last at an open doorway in an old warehouse. The room beyond normally would have held bales of hides or sacks of grain. Now it was crowded with perhaps forty makeshift beds, most of them occupied by men who lay ominously quiet or tossed about in the throes of fever and pain.

"The healer is usually here," the young man said. "I have other duties so I'll leave you now. There are several people assigned to help the healer who can lead you back to the main building if you can't find the way yourself."

Jerrel only nodded in dismissal, his attention focused on the room before him. The makeshift hospital was well organized, but the pervasive smell of unwashed bodies, blood, and disease turned his stomach. It was hard to imagine his once fastidious brother in a place like this.

Jerrel stopped a grizzled soldier on crutches who was hobbling past. "Is there a man here, a healer, with curly hair and brown eyes?" he asked.

At Jerrel's description, a look of respect illuminated the man's plain features. "You mean the healer from Elsin," the soldier said. "He's a good man. Been teachin' our own healers a thing or

two, he has. Saved m'leg when the others wanted
to cut it off."

The man would have rattled on, but Jerrel cut
him short and demanded to know where this healer could be found.

"Back in the corner," the soldier said, pointing.
"That's where the worst ones are, the ones who
woulda died days ago if the healer hadn't been
carin' for 'em."

With a curt thanks to the soldier, Jerrel made
his way toward the corner indicated, Nareen trailing silently in his wake. The going was slow. There
was little space between the rows of beds, and that
was frequently filled by patients or by attendants
caring for those not yet able to get up.

In the dim light filtering through the small,
dusty windows set high in the walls, it was difficult to see clearly. Jerrel was more than halfway
down the room before he spotted a slender, curly-
haired man bent over a bed where a soldier lay
thrashing in the grip of fever.

Jerrel stopped, his heart suddenly hammering
in his chest. It was so hard to tell. The man's
face was turned from him. He seemed the right
height, the right build. Even the hair that curled
about the collar of his long, coarse tunic seemed
the right shade of deep brown.

The man didn't look up but kept his attention
fixed on the soldier he was tending. At last the
soldier quieted and the man straightened, then
stretched to ease cramped muscles. He turned,
scanning the room as though trying to decide
where his services were needed most. His gaze
swept past Jerrel, then swung back abruptly. For
an instant he stood motionless, his dark eyes
locked with Jerrel's. Then he moved around the

end of the bed and came striding up the aisle.

Jerrel remained rooted where he stood. The man was his brother, of that he had no doubt. But this was not the eager, starry-eyed youth whose first months on Errandane Jerrel had shared through means of the recorder ring. This was a man who knew the meaning of loneliness and shame and suffering. In the brown eyes that met his so directly, Jerrel saw sadness, wisdom hard bought through experience, and a gentle dignity tempered by pain.

Santar came to a halt in front of Jerrel. For a moment neither spoke. Then a smile warmed the younger man's face, making it beautiful. "Welcome, brother," he said softly. "When the runner came through camp in search of a man named Jerrel, I wondered. She was looking for you, wasn't she?"

Jerrel smiled in return. "If it hadn't been for her, I might never have found you." He stepped to the side, expecting to find Nareen right behind him. She'd stopped a dozen paces back, and he motioned her forward. "Her name is Nareen. She is a runner from Kalinden and I owe her my life."

"From Kalinden!" Santar glanced at Nareen. A shadow passed across his face. "Though I'm glad to see you, I could almost wish she hadn't led you to me." When Nareen came up to them he added stiffly, "Greetings, runner."

Nareen's gaze shifted from Santar's face to Jerrel's, then back again. "Greetings, healer," she said. Then, more softly, "Or should I say, Santar?"

Santar flinched. It took a moment for the significance of her remark to penetrate. His eyes

grew round and he turned to Jerrel questioning-
ly.

Jerrel nodded. "She knows. She's even been on
my ship."

"But why? How?"

Without speaking, Jerrel reached into his
pocket and retrieved the recorder ring, then
offered it to his brother on the palm of his
hand.

Hesitantly, as if he thought his eyes might
have betrayed him, Santar picked up the ring
and turned it over in his fingers. "My ring." His
words were scarcely above a whisper. He looked
up to meet Jerrel's steady gaze, his voice suddenly
sharp. "Have you reviewed its contents?"

Jerrel nodded and said, "Yes."

"Then you know some of the mistakes I've
made, the blunders I've committed."

This time Jerrel only nodded. It hurt to hear the
shame and self-accusation in his brother's voice.

Santar turned to study the room around them,
his gaze sliding quickly over the long rows of
beds occupied by the wounded. "You don't know
everything." Taking Jerrel's arm, he said, "Come.
Let's find a quiet place where we can talk." When
Nareen hesitated, he added, "You should hear
this, too, runner. In a way, it affects you far more
than it does me."

They found two empty beds pushed against the
far wall. Jerrel sat on the edge of one bed; Nareen
chose to stand in the aisle. Without taking his eyes
from his brother, Jerrel reached up to squeeze
Nareen's hand where it rested protectively on his
shoulder. Her presence, the gentle pressure of her
hand, were strangely comforting.

"I should have realized you'd come." Santar sat

on the edge of the bed, facing Jerrel. "Have you seen Danet? Spoken with him? Is he all right?"

Jerrel nodded. "He's fine. He's been helping us search for you. Your disappearance worried him—a lot."

The reproach brought a swift flush to Santar's cheeks. "I couldn't tell him. I didn't want him to know what a fool I'd been, what mistakes I'd made. I . . . The records on the ring aren't complete, you know. Sometimes I took the ring off."

A muscle in his jaw jumped. "I was so young and arrogant, so sure . . . I didn't realize there really is evil in the universe." He brought his eyes up to meet Jerrel's. "Most of the time they thought I was mad. I thought I could tempt them with some of our knowledge in exchange for their ruling more justly and humanely."

"You're not the first to make that kind of mistake, you know," Jerrel said softly.

The corner of Santar's mouth twisted in a wry smile. "I know, but I don't think many have created the disaster that I'm responsible for."

"What do you mean?" Jerrel asked, puzzled.

"I mean this suffering," Santar said, gesturing at the room. "I'm the reason the beastmen have attacked human settlements for the first time in over a century."

"You!" Jerrel stiffened in surprise, then flinched as Nareen's fingers dug into the muscles of his shoulder.

"That's right. Indirectly, at least." Santar's expression was bleak. "A month before I arrived in Matcassen, a border patrol captured two beastmen foraging a long way from their usual territory. Only one of the beasts was still alive by the time I found out. No one tried to communicate with it. They just kept it in a filthy cage and tormented it whenever they got bored.

"And you set it free," Jerrel guessed.

Santar shook his head. "I used my ship's translator to help me learn its language; then I taught some of the guardsmen to communicate with it, too."

"You what?" Jerrel had the sickening feeling he knew where Santar's tale was leading.

His brother winced. "I thought it would help the two races begin to understand each other. I never dreamed Xyanth would take that knowledge and twist it for her own ambitious ends."

Jerrel could feel Nareen tense beside him. "She sent those guardsmen to prod the creatures into attacking Kalinden." It wasn't a question. He knew.

"They took the captured beast back as a bargaining tool," Santar agreed. "The creatures aren't as intelligent as we are. Their language is crude and they're incapable of subtle thought. But they didn't have any problems understanding Xyanth's proposal. Or in carrying it out."

Santar's gaze dropped to the ring he held. He frowned, then slowly slid the ring over the middle finger of his right hand. "I should never have taken it off."

Neither spoke. From a bed not far away came the sounds of someone mumbling and moaning in a fevered sleep. Santar watched until the man quieted; then he turned back to face Jerrel.

"There isn't much more to tell you. You know I allowed Xyanth to seduce me. She was so . . . beautiful, so . . ." Santar's jaw worked as he tried to control the anguish that suddenly threatened

353

to overwhelm him. "I didn't know about the beastmen. Not then. She drugged me; then she and Lindaz had me tortured, trying to force me to reveal more than I already had. At some point I passed out, my ship beamed me up automatically, and I . . . disappeared."

Jerrel could feel Santar's pain, the guilt eating at his brother's heart and soul like some corrosive acid. There were no words he could offer to ease that pain, no comfort he could give.

"If I ever see her again, ever have the chance . . ." Santar's features convulsed in sudden rage. His shoulders hunched and his hands twisted into claws. They trembled slightly, his fingers flexing as though wrapped around Xyanth's throat, throttling her. With an obvious effort, he forced his hands to uncurl.

"I can't undo the damage I've done," Santar continued at last in a low voice, "but I've tried to make amends. I used my ship's computer to analyze the plants of Errandane and identify those that could be used to manufacture medicines. I changed the color of my eyes to brown, then came back here to serve as an itinerant healer. I teach anyone who's interested as much as I can."

Santar sighed, then straightened, forcing his shoulders back, his head up. "At least this way many who would have died from their injuries will live, and many who would have been crippled will walk or have the use of both arms. My medicines ease their pain, cool their fevers, heal their wounds. It's the best I can do."

Jerrel thought of the soldier in the entrance, the one who had spoken of the healer with awe and respect. Before he could say anything, Nareen, with a hiss of sharply expelled breath, turned and stalked off.

Startled, Jerrel jerked around. He opened his mouth, ready to call out to her, then shut it with a snap. He hadn't stopped to think how horrifying his brother's revelations must be to her, but there was no sense in trying to talk to her yet. Nothing he could say would make Santar's role in her city's suffering any less. Nothing he could do, nothing Santar could do, would erase the damage that had already been done.

Jerrel turned back to his brother only to find Santar watching Nareen's retreating form. For an instant Jerrel was tempted to assume the role of wise older brother, to tell Santar he'd done enough, that he'd paid for his mistakes. He started to speak, but something in those dark eyes stopped him. Santar's mouth softened in a sad, gentle smile. Jerrel had the impression his brother knew what he'd been thinking.

"Enough of me," Santar said. "I can't spare much more time, and you haven't told me anything of your adventures." His eyes flicked to the door where Nareen had disappeared, then back to Jerrel. He said nothing, but his unspoken questions hung in the air between them.

As briefly as he could, Jerrel recounted the events of the past weeks. As he spoke, his concerns for Nareen came flooding back. Like his brother, she'd chosen a difficult path and would not deviate from it until she'd finished. And her path might prove to be far more dangerous.

"So, now that you know I'm all right, you're going to help her," Santar said when he'd finished. It wasn't a question. "And then?"

Jerrel couldn't help grinning. "And then I'll show her the universe. I think she'll like it."

Santar grinned back. "The Service and Imperial laws frown on that, you know."

"I know." Jerrel rose to his feet. His grin faded. "We have other problems to deal with first, however."

Santar stood too, his mood somber again. "Whatever I can do . . . Seeing you here, knowing what's happened . . ." His jaw firmed. "I think it's time I did more than brew medicinal teas."

Jerrel was on the point of refusing his brother's offer when he realized there was no one except Nareen he would rather rely on in whatever lay ahead. And Santar had as much reason to want to stop Xyanth as Nareen did.

"I would be glad of whatever help you can give us," Jerrel said, firmly clasping his brother's hand. He was, he realized suddenly, very proud of the man Santar had become.

Chapter 19

In her haste to get away, to put some distance between her and the man who was partly responsible for so much of her people's suffering, Nareen stumbled twice over the uneven old floor.

How could Santar have been so stupid? So blindly, trustingly naïve? What, by all the gods, had he been thinking of to have tried to make friends with the murdering beastmen? Why had he thought he could trust that witch, Xyanth? Why? Why? Why?

Driven by frustration and anger, Nareen only stopped when she reached the stairs to the barred and locked front door of the warehouse. Fresh air and the cold wind would feel good right now, but she couldn't risk going out in the street.

Briefly she considered going back, then discarded the idea. Gravnar and Pardraik had other duties and little time to spare for her. She would gladly volunteer her services, but what use did they have of a runner now?

Morosely, Nareen hunched down on the floor, her back propped against the wall behind her. What were Gravnar and Pardraik and Tisnerl and the others planning? What resources did they have? How many men? If they didn't act tonight, how long could they stay in hiding without being discovered?

Nareen sighed, thinking of all the additional lives that might be lost in the effort to regain Kalinden. Without understanding the forces he was playing with and against the rules of his own people, Santar had loosed a devil upon her people.

Her hands clenched in hopeless anger. If only it were possible to make him pay for the harm he'd done.

It wasn't.

His efforts to make amends were well-intentioned, and futile. Nothing and no one could bring back the dead.

She supposed she ought at least to feel pleased Jerrel had found his brother, but she couldn't manage even that. And if she couldn't share his happiness, couldn't bear to face his brother, what did that bode for the future?

Pardraik found her a little while later, still slumped against the wall. At the sight of him, Nareen scrambled to her feet, glad for the distraction, for the chance to do something—*anything* rather than indulge in fruitless worries that went nowhere. "Is everyone here?" she demanded. "Are you ready—"

"Everyone's here, but there's no need to discuss anything," Pardraik replied harshly. "The decision's made. We move against Xyanth tonight."

"You're sure—"

"Why tonight?" The question made both Pardraik and Nareen whirl about.

Santar, his expression drawn, stood on the steps from the upper floor. Jerrel paused half a pace behind him. When Pardraik didn't answer, Santar asked again, "Why tonight?"

"Because we've no choice. Xyanth intends to force Gasperian to abdicate tonight," the guardsman replied at last. "If Gasperian refuses, his life will be forfeit."

Nareen's slight cry of protest was the only audible response to the news. When not one of his three listeners moved or said anything more, Pardraik added, "Runner, you and your warrior friend will come with me. We meet in a few minutes to discuss our plan of attack; then you need adequate weapons."

Jerrel nodded in acknowledgment and stepped forward, but Santar was ahead of him. "I'm coming too."

"You, healer?" Pardraik's mouth opened in surprise. "But—"

"I have my reasons, guardsman, and I know more of fighting than you might suppose."

Even without knowing anything of Santar's motives, Pardraik understood men well enough not to argue with one so clearly determined to have his way. His mouth snapped shut. "Very well, then, let's go."

Their return to the room where they'd met Gravnar seemed interminable. Nareen's thoughts were a hectic jumble of vague plans, useless speculation, and sharp fears that not even her runner's training could repress. Several times she felt Jerrel's sympathetic gaze, and twice he touched her, briefly, in reassurance. She moved closer to him, grateful for his presence and glad he would be fighting for Kalinden. Yet even that was small comfort when weighed against what lay ahead. If they failed . . . Nareen forced that thought out of her mind. They wouldn't fail. They *couldn't*.

The room was packed with angry, grim-faced men and women in the uniforms of both Kalinden and Matcassen. Nareen stopped on the threshold, surprised at the number of Matcassen officers who had joined in the fight against Xyanth. Since they, like Pardraik, would be playing a double role, their presence meant Matcassen's forces were weaker than she'd expected. It was small satisfaction, but satisfaction nonetheless.

With Jerrel's hand on her back pushing her forward, Nareen wormed her way through the crowd until she'd found a spot near the front of the circle from which she could see and hear what went on. Jerrel and Santar took positions on either side of her. Because of his size, Jerrel drew a few protests for blocking the view of those behind him. One frowning glance from him was enough, however, to quell the complaints.

The seven men seated around the table in the center of the circle were advisors and military leaders from both cities. Tisnerl sat at the far side, facing her. He was the only advisor from Kalinden. As if drawn by the intensity of Nareen's gaze, he looked up and smiled at her. Was he, she wondered, the only advisor who had believed her? Or the only one to escape Xyanth's trap?

It took less than a half hour for the group to make the final decisions regarding the planned attack. Watching them, Nareen was amazed at the willingness of both sides to work together. The Matcassen troops would be fighting their comrades, friends, and, perhaps, relatives. The Kalinden troops had little reason to trust anyone from Matcassen, yet trust there was. If all went well and Gasperian was restored to power, the cooperation evident in this room boded well for future relations between the cities.

As though he'd read her thoughts, Tisnerl sounded a word of warning. "We have worked well together in these past few days, despite our different loyalties," he said. "But we must not let that fact blind us to reality.

"All the Kalinden forces in the city who aren't dead or imprisoned by Xyanth are with us. They are very few. Many from Matcassen, sickened by the senseless killing and the injustice, have chosen to rebel against the Lady Xyanth. Yours was a difficult decision, and we of Kalinden honor you for it. But you are far outnumbered by those who chose to remain. The soldiers who still fight under Xyanth's banner are wary, well armed, and aware that they have much to lose if their attempt at conquest fails."

Tisnerl paused and his gaze swept the silent crowd around him. "Even if we succeed tonight, Lindaz will surely lead more troops against us to revenge his Lady. We can take nothing for granted."

Nareen opened her mouth, ready to tell the group of the information Norvag had given them. Before she could speak, Jerrel cleared his throat, making her jump.

"As to that, Advisor," Jerrel said, "you can forget the threat of Lindaz attacking any time soon. I've heard the people of Matcassen have risen up against him. He's probably far too occupied with saving his own city to worry about attacking Kalinden."

At first, surprise held everyone quiet. As understanding began to replace surprise, pandemonium broke out. The people of Kalinden were suddenly laughing, shouting, and slapping each other on the backs in enthusiastic glee. The people of Matcassen either remained where they were, frozen with shock, or moved about in a stunned daze. It was one thing not to support a murderous woman intent on power and personal gain, quite another to think of their city in the throes of what might well be a bloody rebellion.

"You're sure of this, warrior?" Tisnerl demanded above the din. "How did you hear?"

"It doesn't matter how I heard, advisor. I'm sure the information is accurate. You don't need to worry about another attack from Matcassen any time soon."

How many of his own world's rules was Jerrel breaking to reveal the information he'd gained from Norvag? Nareen wondered. Yet, knowing the value of that information to her people, he hadn't hesitated.

In the confusion of noise and milling people, Nareen tugged on Jerrel's sleeve, anxious to express her gratitude. He glanced down at her, driving out the words on her lips. The gentle smile on his lips and the warmth in his eyes made her thanks unnecessary. He understood her thoughts without her having to say a word.

"Let's find Pardraik," he said, putting his arm around her shoulders and drawing her close. "He's promised us weapons, and since his group is one of those attacking the Great Hall, I assume you'll insist on being included."

"You're not going to try to convince me to stay here?" Nareen demanded, sure she already knew the answer.

The corner of Jerrel's mouth twisted with wry awareness. "I only fight battles I have a chance of winning."

With Santar close behind them, they pushed their way out the door and into the hall. They found Pardraik in a small room not far away, thoughtfully studying a number of swords laid out on a table before him. At their entrance, he looked up briefly, then turned his attention back to the weapons. Even from across the room, Nareen sensed an anger in him that hadn't been there before.

He chose one heavy blade and swung it from side to side, judging its balance and weight, then lunged forward against an invisible enemy. Straightening, his eyes still on the sword he held, he said, "I was sixteen when I entered Matcassen's army. Lindaz was only thirty-two or three at that time, yet he'd already been Master for seven years and had made us one of the strongest cities in the west of Errandane. I was proud to serve him, proud of what he'd accomplished."

The guardsman met their questioning gazes directly, his mouth hard with repressed anger. "He married Xyanth when he was almost forty, and attacked and conquered the city of Ravelatt when he was forty-one. She'd convinced him Matcassen couldn't tolerate the insults and thieving raids of a petty little neighbor."

He glared at them, challenging them to respond. "After Ravelatt, Lindaz followed his Lady's suggestions. I fought in three campaigns against other cities, every one of them successful. I couldn't stomach the thought of another, especially one that Xyanth was leading."

When no one said anything, Pardraik shrugged, then turned to place the sword on the table. "However much I hate his wife, I would never have rebelled against the Master of my city. Never."

The silence stretched between them, taut as a rope pulled tight between two poles. At last, Nareen crossed to Pardraik's side. "You're leading a group of men into the Great Hall," she said softly. "I will guide you."

Pardraik met her steady gaze, obviously uncertain how to respond.

"And Sa . . . the healer and I will accompany you, as well," Jerrel added, stepping into the room. Santar remained standing in the doorway, silent and watchful.

"Your help would be welcome, runner," Pardraik said at last. "Gravnar will accompany another group, and we have need of someone who knows the Hall well."

Pardraik's gaze flicked from Nareen to Jerrel and back. His hand dropped to caress the swords on the table. "We leave for the Great Hall in four hours," he said.

The wind had, if anything, become even fiercer and more piercing. Nareen scarcely noticed. Her attention was focused on the doorway where Pardraik and five of his men had disappeared. There was no sign of them, which meant they hadn't yet reached the secret tunnel that would take them into the Great Hall.

She tugged at the green armband that identified her as one of the rebels. It was too tight, but there was no time to retie it. She glanced up at the star-filled night sky above them. The brilliant guide star had not yet swung into position beside the polestar, the signal for the groups now fanning out across the city to begin their attack. They had perhaps twenty minutes more.

Nareen glanced back at Jerrel and Santar and the two remaining soldiers. Jerrel was the only one not watching the street.

He was turned toward her, his face a dark mass in the darker night. Nareen couldn't see his features, but she could sense his concern. Silently she reached out to him, wanting to draw what reassurance she might from the feel of him, from his warmth and strength and quiet power.

At her touch, Jerrel covered her small hand with his. Her fingers were cold and he could feel her shivering slightly in the unrelenting wind. Gently he rubbed the top of her hand with his palm, seeking to warm her.

For the first time in years he knew what fear tasted like. Not fear for himself, but for her. She carried no weapon except the runner's knife that Gravnar had given her. All too soon they would face heavily armed, well-trained soldiers who wouldn't hesitate to cut her down as they would any other attacker.

Despite the need to remain silent, Jerrel almost blurted out the words of warning and of love that hovered on his tongue. Only Pardraik's scarcely audible whistle, signaling them to move forward, stopped him.

The five of them scuttled across the empty street and into the relative safety of the building opposite, then, without speaking, followed Pardraik through the cluttered shop of a rug merchant to the storeroom behind.

A candle held by one of the men provided just enough light for Jerrel to distinguish the piles of rugs carelessly heaped on either side of an open trap door set in the floor. Before he started down the crude steps, he made sure Nareen was right behind him, her dagger in her hand.

Navigating the cramped underground passageway proved no problem. The difficulty lay in getting through the heavy wood door at the far side.

"It won't budge," puffed one of the Kalinden soldiers after several minutes of futile shoving. "It's barred or blocked or both. We can't get through."

"We have to," Nareen insisted, trying to see around a Matcassen soldier who was blocking her view. "There's no time to go back."

"Then how're we t'manage?" growled a third man who'd also tried to force the door.

"Let me try."

Nareen twisted to look behind her, uncertain who had spoken. It was Santar. In the dim light of the flickering candle, his face looked frighteningly gaunt.

He didn't wait for permission, just shoved his way to the door and immediately began hacking at the obdurate wood with his short broadsword.

Under his attack, the door shook, then shattered. Santar reached through and pushed aside the heavy crossbars that had blocked the entrance. Even then, boxes and bales stacked on the other side prevented them from pushing open what remained of the door.

Santar, aided by Jerrel, had to shove and strain to force the door open wide enough for them to slip through. He went first, followed by the two soldiers. Nareen would have gone next, but Jerrel squeezed through the opening ahead of her.

From the dark beyond the door Nareen heard curses, then a horrifying crash as whatever had been stacked in the room was pushed down. Pardraik swore, then forced his way past, the candle in one hand, his sword in the other. Before anyone else could shove her aside, Nareen leaped through the opening.

Even though Pardraik had climbed on a pile of hides in an effort to provide more light from the candle, the twisting shadows and treacherously tumbled bales and boxes made the storeroom a dangerous obstacle course. With the remainder of their small band crowding through the shattered door behind her, Nareen had no choice but to scramble over and around obstructions as best she could.

She found Santar and Jerrel on the other side of the room forcing open the door to the outer hallway. They burst through, their swords ready in their hands in case of resistance. There was no one on the other side. From an intersecting hallway to the left, the dim light of a torch mounted in a wall bracket provided a beacon toward the stairway that would lead them to the upper floors.

"Runner!" Pardraik gestured toward the stairs. "Where are they likely to be holding Gasperian? Can we get farther into the Hall without being spotted?"

Swiftly Nareen considered the options, then shook her head, frustrated. "It could be anywhere. His quarters, the cells on the lowest level . . . It's a big Hall."

Pardraik only hesitated for a second. "Right. Then lead us to his quarters. We'll start there."

Nareen nodded and led the way toward the stairs. They were only halfway to the next floor when the noise of distant fighting suddenly reached them. She hesitated, trying to judge the location of the fighting based on the muffled sounds from above.

"The fighting's on the main floor. I'm almost sure of it!" she cried.

"It doesn't matter." Pardraik waved her on. "We have to find Xyanth first, and chances are she'll be as far from danger as she can get."

Nareen glanced at the guardsman doubtfully, then nodded and set off at an even faster pace than before. With each step she was aware of Jerrel behind her, as close as her own shadow and far more welcome.

And with each step, her tension grew until every nerve in her body quivered. Xyanth held Gasperian. She undoubtedly knew of the attack against her. There was nothing to stop her from murdering the Master of Kalinden, especially if her own safety was threatened. But where in this immense Hall would she have gone?

Nareen skidded to a halt, struck by a sudden thought. What was it Xyanth craved most? Power! And where was the center of power in a Great Hall if not in the main reception hall? It was there the Master's chair stood, a physical symbol of the power and influence that Xyanth so desperately sought.

"I know where Xyanth and Gasperian are!" she cried, wheeling about suddenly.

"But . . . !"

"How could you . . . ?"

Nareen ignored Jerrel's and Pardraik's startled questions and the confused mutterings of the others. "Follow me!" Without checking to see if they did, she raced back the way they'd come, the runner's dagger ready in her hand.

A half flight of stairs. A short hall, another flight of stairs, this time broader and better lit. Then an open landing and to the left, toward the main hall, more sounds of fighting.

Nareen took two steps toward the left and was pulled up short by Jerrel. "Where are you going?" he demanded harshly.

"The main hall!" Nareen struggled, and failed, to get free of his grip on her shoulder. "That's where she'll take him. She wants power, and her takeover of Kalinden will seem more legal if Gasperian gives her the Master's ring there in the main hall."

"But the hall isn't easy to defend and it's already under attack," Jerrel protested.

"She's right!" Pardraik's sudden grin was frightening in its ferocity. "Xyanth won't care if a hundred men die protecting her so long as she's got what she wants!"

"There's a side door. It's hidden behind a tapestry, almost never used . . ." Nareen was panting in her eagerness to get moving.

"How do we get there?" Jerrel seemed willing to believe her but he still wasn't ready to let her go.

"Through a private audience room behind the main hall. But we have to go that way." Nareen

369

gestured toward the left, where the sounds of fighting were the loudest.

Jerrel and Pardraik exchanged glances, then nodded. As Pardraik started forward, Jerrel pulled Nareen to the side, out of the way of the eager men rushing past them to follow the guardsman.

"You stay behind me, do you hear?" Jerrel demanded fiercely, giving Nareen a warning shake.

"It's my city!"

Jerrel groaned, then jerked her against him. "And you're my life," he said, just before he brought his mouth down on hers in an angry kiss.

"I couldn't bear it if anything happened to you now," he added an instant later as he broke away. "Get behind me, where I can protect you. Do you understand?"

Nareen could only nod, but the gesture was wasted. Jerrel was already racing toward the battle ahead.

The wide corridor seemed filled with men, each desperately trying to kill his opponent before his opponent could kill him. Nareen halted, shocked into immobility by the scene before her. Jerrel? Where was Jerrel? For an instant, panic gripped her. Pardraik's band were already so caught up in the fray it was almost impossible to pick them out. From the number of men who wore the green armbands of the rebellion, it was clear that at least two if not three other groups had managed to break into the Hall.

Nareen spotted Jerrel and Pardraik at the edge of the fighting. Both fought with a savage brilliance that kept forcing their opponents back, into the melee where there was less room to maneuver. Santar was on the other side of Jerrel, fighting with equal determination if considerably less skill.

Unfortunately, Xyanth had kept her guardsmen, her best fighters, around her. There was no way to tell which side was winning—the faces of the Matcassen troops showed the same grim determination as did those of the attackers.

It took a moment for Nareen to realize the struggling mass of men was slowly moving down the corridor, back toward the main doors of the reception hall. If she'd needed any further proof that Xyanth was in the main hall, the Matcassen guards' defense of that door was it. The combatants had only to move a few feet farther and they would clear the door of the room she was aiming for. She needed to tell Jerrel or Pardraik, warn them . . .

Without stopping to consider the danger, Nareen thrust the runner's knife into her belt and picked up a short sword still clasped in the hand of a fallen Kalinden soldier. The grip was too large for her hand and slick with the dead man's blood. Pausing only a moment to wipe the hilt on her tunic, Nareen rushed forward, the sword firmly gripped in both hands in front of her.

She'd almost reached Jerrel when a burly Matcassen guard without a green armband burst out of the fray and straight at her, sword raised. His swing was uncoordinated, powerful, and it barely missed. Nareen could feel the brief rush of air as the sword passed her, scarce inches from her face.

She twisted, bringing her own sword up to parry his next swing. The shock of metal on metal drove her backwards, the force of the blow causing a sudden spike of pain through her wrists,

371

arms, and shoulders. Her hold on the still bloody hilt slipped and the useless weapon went spinning out of her hands.

Nareen leapt sideways, away from the guard's next thrust. If she could get Jerrel's attention, tell him about the door . . .

The next thrust never came. With a sharp cry, Santar was suddenly beside her, parrying the blow intended for her. He was neither as skilled nor as powerful a swordsman as his brother, but he fought with a single-mindedness that allowed him to ignore a slicing cut to his left arm and overcome the Matcassen guard.

For a moment he stared at his fallen enemy with a shocked expression, as though he was only just beginning to realize the fighting was real and death an always possible outcome. That pause almost cost him his life.

Nareen's shouted warning came too late to stop the lethal blow aimed at him by another guard, but Santar managed to dodge so that the edge of the blade came down on his leg and not his head. He gasped, staggered, and fell to one knee, dazed by the rush of blood from the gaping wound in his thigh.

The guard's second blow should have been fatal. It would have been if Jerrel hadn't swung around and driven the man back with a vicious, arcing swing that just barely missed decapitating him. The man stumbled, then recovered and raised his sword for another attack.

Jerrel swung again, over Santar's head, then turned to fend off an attack by the man he'd been fighting a moment before. Before the first guard could take advantage of the distraction, Nareen grabbed Santar's sword from his unresisting hand

and flung it at the guard's legs. The man howled in pain as the sharp edge sliced through the muscles of his thigh. He collapsed less than a foot away from them.

"The door!" Nareen shouted to Jerrel, trying to drag Santar to his feet with one hand and point at the door with the other.

Jerrel glanced briefly in the direction Nareen indicated, nodded once, then lunged to the side to counter another deadly thrust.

By this time Santar was on his feet, unsteady and clutching his arm but able to move on his own. Nareen pulled his uninjured arm over her shoulders and, half supporting him, half dragging him, led him toward the door.

Under pressure from Jerrel, Pardraik, and the others on the fringe, the Matcassen troops were continuing to retreat. That retreat gave Nareen the precious time she needed to fumble with the heavy latch, then push the door open and help Santar cross the room to a chair. Enough light came through the tall windows from the rising moon for her to see the way.

As she eased Santar into the chair, Jerrel sprang through the door and slammed it in the face of the pursuing Matcassen guard. In seconds he locked the door, then slid a heavy chest in front of it.

"Will that hold?" Nareen asked.

"Long enough." Jerrel crossed the room to them in a few strides. His gaze flicked from her to Santar, then to Santar's bloody arm. "How bad is it?"

"Bad, but not fatal."

"I'll live." Despite his obvious pain, Santar's mouth twisted in angry self-mockery. "I've seen enough wounds like this lately to know."

Jerrel bent over his brother. "You have the ring. We'll beam up, get you in the med—"

"No!" Santar started to rise from the chair, then bit his lip at the pain and sank back, shaking his head. "No. You've other matters. Xyanth . . ." He was panting now from the effort of speaking. "I'll be all right. You can come back . . ."

Jerrel hesitated, uncertain, and Nareen had to bite her own lip to keep from protesting. *He'll live!* she wanted to shout. They were only a few hundred yards from the dais in the main hall. Gasperian could be murdered in the time spent tending to Santar—if he wasn't already dead.

"Go. Now." Santar's voice was weak, but there was an unmistakable note of command.

Jerrel hesitated for an instant before nodding in acknowledgment. He quickly untied Santar's green armband, then his own. "Here, you can use these to stop the bleeding."

Santar gave a weak laugh. "Who's the healer here?"

Unable to tolerate further delay, Nareen turned and crossed to the huge tapestry that hung to the floor on an opposite wall. She lifted the corner of the heavy weaving, then forced her way along the wall in the dark until her groping hand encountered the hidden door.

She was still fumbling with the bolts when Jerrel joined her. "The door opens behind another tapestry in the hall," she said. "The dais will be about a hundred yards to our right. That's where I expect them to be."

"All right. I'll follow you."

"Agreed." Nareen hoped her voice carried more confidence than she felt. What if there were a dozen guardsmen in the hall? What if Gasperian was already dead? What if Pardraik's men and the other attackers failed? What if . . . ?

She pushed down the frightening thoughts. It was far too late for what ifs. "I'll leave this door ajar in case we need an escape route."

Nareen slowly pulled the door open, careful to make no sound. The tapestry would muffle most of the little noise they'd make, but who knew how close a guard might be standing on the other side?

Cautiously, Nareen slid through the narrow opening. To her relief, the tapestry in the hall hung farther from the wall than she'd thought, which meant there was more space and less chance of their movements being detected.

A pale glow shone around the edges of the weaving. Xyanth probably hadn't thought it necessary to provide much light. The shadows would serve them well.

Nareen edged along the wall. Jerrel's hand brushed once, briefly, across hers, a welcome reassurance.

For a moment she couldn't hear anything, then caught the confused sound of scuffling feet, the grating noise of wood scraping over stone, and a cruel female voice that made Nareen freeze.

"Well, Gasperian," Xyanth said, "can you still refuse me when there's a knife at your throat? Hmmm?"

Chapter 20

Only Jerrel's hand digging into her arm stopped Nareen from rushing forward. She tried to jerk free but his grip tightened. Not until she stopped straining against him did he release her, and then only to reach past and cautiously lift the edge of the tapestry so they could peer out.

Their range of view was restricted, but it was enough.

Xyanth stood on the dais in front of the Master's chair, her back to them. The wavering light of a lamp on the wall behind her reflected off the rich gold and silver embroidery of her robe, providing the only brightness in an otherwise grim and shadowed tableau.

Gasperian knelt before her, his hands bound behind his back, his arms held by two burly Matcassen guards. The lamplight cast dark shadows in the hollows of his gaunt face, burying his eyes in their deep sockets. Xyanth's dagger was at his throat, forcing his head back.

"You can kill me, but you'll have the Master's ring only when you take it from my dead body." Gasperian's voice grated. He sounded old, tired.

"That's easily arranged!" Rage distorted Xyanth's features. She forced his head back even further. "I tire of these games, Gasperian. You have no choice. Why struggle against the inevitable?"

"What good will the ring do you if I'm dead and there was no legal transfer?"

"I have your city. I'll have the ring, one way or another."

"A knife will provide a fitting end for a fool like me, who once loved you." Gasperian lifted his chin a fraction higher, clearly exposing the vulnerable juncture between his jaw and throat. "Kill me and have done with it!"

Even in the dim light Nareen could see Xyanth's grip on the dagger tighten. For an instant Lindaz' Lady hesitated. Her hand trembled and her body tensed under the ornate robe.

"What? Never had to do your own killing before?" Gasperian taunted, his lips drawn back from his teeth in a frightening mockery of a grin.

Xyanth's response was closer to the snarl of a feral cat than to any human sound. She drew her hand back. The blade of the dagger flashed in the lamplight.

Nareen leapt from behind the tapestry, the runner's knife in her hand. "No! Drop the dagger!"

Startled, Xyanth whirled about, her weapon raised high. "You!"

"There are men behind the tapestries, and more

in the hallway, my Lady," Nareen said in the boldest tones she could muster. "It will gain you nothing to murder Master Gasperian now."

Even as she spoke, Nareen's heart thudded in her ears and she cursed silently. When she'd peered out from behind the tapestry, she hadn't seen the two additional guards at the foot of the dais. Her sudden appearance had startled them, but not enough to make them drop the swords they'd drawn. And where, she wondered desperately, was Jerrel? She'd been sure he'd follow her.

For an instant, Xyanth stared wildly around her, trying to spot the hidden men Nareen spoke of. When not one tapestry stirred and no door burst open to admit armed men, her delicate features distorted with rage.

"Seize her!" she screeched, pointing a long, sharp finger at Nareen.

The two soldiers holding Gasperian on the dais hesitated, uncertain. As their grip loosened, Gasperian struggled to regain his feet. He didn't succeed, but his efforts ensured that his guards remained on the dais. The other two soldiers advanced on Nareen, swords raised.

The one on the right grinned in anticipation. His grin didn't last long—it was obliterated in a gurgling rush of blood as Jerrel's dagger buried itself hilt-deep in his throat. The man scrabbled vainly at his neck, dead before he toppled to the floor.

His companion froze, disoriented. The momentary hesitation cost him his life as another dagger thudded into his chest. Nareen wasn't sure the man had even seen his slayer.

Jerrel stepped from the shadows. At the sound

of his footsteps, Xyanth tore her gaze from the two dead guardsman and spun around to face this new threat.

"You!" Her single word carried a venomous loathing. "You're dead!"

"Are you sure?" Jerrel's tone was deliberately tormenting, provoking her to even greater rage.

"Kill him!" Xyanth shrieked.

Gasperian's two guards, relieved at having a clear order and a visible enemy, abandoned their prisoner and charged Jerrel.

Their attack held Xyanth's attention, allowing Nareen to gain the dais. Gasperian's bonds were cruelly tight, and she had to take care not to cut him as she sawed at the ropes. She stepped back at last, tossing the severed remnants of cord to the side.

Gasperian massaged his lacerated wrists. "Sixth Runner . . ."

"We're regaining the city, Master," Nareen interrupted. "For now, the Lady Xyanth . . ."

Shaken by the shame and anguish that showed so clearly in Gasperian's dark eyes, Nareen could say no more. Wordlessly she extended the runner's dagger.

Gasperian hesitated for a fraction of a second, then accepted the dagger with a nod of thanks and turned back to face his former captor.

Xyanth, the skirts of her robe clutched in her hands, hovered on the edge of the dais, poised for flight. Her eyes darted from the tapestry covering the hidden door to Jerrel and the two guardsmen, then to the main door where the sounds of fighting in the corridor came through clearly. The nearness of the battle seemed to make up her mind. She took a half step forward, ready to leap from the platform, when Gasperian's harsh voice stopped her abruptly.

"Where were you thinking of going, my Lady? Surely you're not leaving so soon?"

Xyanth whirled with a hiss of rage. She dropped her skirts and crouched, prepared to defend herself against Gasperian's attack. Her left hand curled into a claw, each sharp nail a dangerous weapon. Her right hand still clutched the dagger she'd held against Gasperian's throat only moments before.

"Come, my Lady." Gasperian extended his hand toward Xyanth. "Your game is ended and you've lost. Give up now, before any more lives are sacrificed."

"Never!" she spat, circling backwards, away from him. "I'll not surrender to you nor to any man."

A choked cry of agony diverted Nareen's attention. She'd almost forgotten Jerrel's struggle. He now faced only one guard. The sense of relief that flooded her lasted only a moment, until the main doors of the hall crashed open to admit a dozen armed Matcassen soldiers.

They were bloodied and bedraggled but clearly in charge—and they did not wear the green armband that signified they'd fought on the side of Kalinden.

Even as she felt her heart constrict with despair, Nareen strained to catch the sound of fighting, some indication that there was still a chance Matcassen did not control the Great Hall.

The corridor outside was still and empty, totally silent.

As the soldiers advanced warily, their weapons ready, Nareen glanced back at Gasperian and

Xyanth. The two stood motionless, their eyes fixed on the approaching soldiers. In one face was the bleak recognition of defeat, in the other a gloating triumph that made Nareen's blood rage. She glanced to the side and found Jerrel, his sword still raised, cautiously backing toward the dais as he watched both his opponent and the soldiers.

At that moment, he glanced up. Their eyes met. Jerrel jerked his head backward, ever so slightly, and rolled his eyes toward the ceiling.

Nareen bit her lip. Of course! Once again, she'd forgotten the com link on the chain around her neck. But how to take Gasperian with them? If only she'd thought to ask while she still had the chance!

"You've done well, men," Xyanth crowed, coming forward. She stopped only inches away from Nareen, the dagger still in her hand but her attention fixed on the soldiers. "You'll be well rewarded for your loyalty."

"I wouldn't speak quite so soon, my Lady." The shadowed figure that had suddenly appeared in the doorway stepped into the vague light of the lamps.

"Pardraik! Guardsman!"

For the first time, Nareen heard a note of uncertainty in Xyanth's voice. A knotted strip of green cloth showed clearly on Pardraik's upper arm, and the soldiers, without speaking, were stepping aside to let him through.

They're on our side! Nareen realized exultantly. *We've won!*

"The fight is over, my Lady, but it is you who has lost," Pardraik added, stopping several feet from the dais to stare at Xyanth.

"But you're from Matcassen!" Xyanth protested, clearly stunned.

"We wear the uniforms of Matcassen because we're loyal to our city, not because we support your personal ambitions." Pardraik gestured at the men behind him. "It's one thing to follow a warrior who fights for the glory of his people, quite another to die because of his wife's greed and hunger for power."

"Lindaz will kill you for this!" The last word ended with a spitting hiss.

Pardraik shrugged. "I think not. All of Matcassen is in rebellion. By now, it's quite possible your husband is a prisoner." He paused, his eyes fixed on Xyanth. "Or dead."

"Dead?" Xyanth stared wild-eyed at Pardraik. "Dead!"

The guardsman didn't answer. He moved to the steps leading to the dais. Without taking his eyes from Xyanth, he gestured to the soldiers to surround the platform. They'd already taken Jerrel's remaining opponent prisoner.

Nareen briefly turned her attention from Xyanth to Gasperian. The Master of Kalinden hadn't spoken a word since the soldiers first entered.

Her momentary inattention was a mistake. Without warning, Xyanth grabbed her from behind and pressed the point of the dagger she held to Nareen's throat.

"The blade is poisoned!" Xyanth cried, pressing the tip even more firmly against Nareen's flesh.

Nareen froze. She was stronger and faster. Despite Xyanth's greater height, she could easily get away. But she couldn't be sure she'd get free before Xyanth drew blood, and poison required neither strength nor speed to kill.

Knowing Xyanth, Nareen had no doubt the poison would be one that was both painful and slow-acting. The woman enjoyed seeing her victims' pain too much not to prefer a cruel death to a quick one.

"The link! Use the com link!" Jerrel's voice sounded strained and far away.

Nareen tried to turn her head toward him, but the pressure of Xyanth's dagger against her throat prevented her. From the corner of her eye, she caught movement at the edge of the dais. One of the soldiers maneuvering for position, perhaps. It wouldn't work.

Jerrel was right; her best chance of escape was through the com link. Even with Xyanth's poisoned weapon almost pricking her skin and the sound of the woman's ragged breathing in her ear, Nareen couldn't help wondering what the reaction to her sudden disappearance would be.

"I'm leaving and the runner will come with me." Xyanth's voice echoed in the huge chamber. She moved back toward the hidden door, dragging Nareen with her.

With each step, Nareen cautiously inched her hand toward the collar of her tunic and the chain that lay against her skin. If she could . . .

"There's no way out in this direction, my Lady."

The words came from behind them. They were softly spoken and it took a moment for Nareen to identify the speaker. Santar!

Xyanth froze, as though she recognized the voice but couldn't trust her senses. Nareen used that momentary inattention to wrench free. The woman hardly noticed. Slowly she pivoted to face the man who spoke, her face rigid with shock.

Santar stood only three feet from her. His left arm hung useless at his side and he swayed slightly as he tried not to put any weight on his injured leg. The temporary bandages he'd rigged were already crusted with dried blood. In his right hand he clutched a heavy soldier's knife, but the tip of the weapon pointed toward the floor. His eyes were dark with pain and he drooped with weariness.

Xyanth's eyes widened in disbelief and fear. "You're dead." The words were little more than a whisper.

"Not yet, though that's no thanks to you or your distinguished husband." The bitterness that laced Santar's words, as much as the meaning, roused Xyanth from her stupor.

"You're dead!" With a screech she threw herself on him.

Santar tried to dodge but his injured leg crumpled as he put his weight on it. Off balance and falling, he instinctively raised his right hand to fend off his attacker.

To no avail. In her blind rage, Xyanth either couldn't or wouldn't stop. Her momentum carried her down with him, impaling her on the knife in Santar's hand.

There was a muffled gasp, then a thud as their bodies hit the floor together.

For an instant Nareen stood motionless, too stunned by the sudden violence to react. It was Jerrel vaulting onto the dais that finally roused her to approach the crumpled bodies lying half hidden in the shadows.

Xyanth's hair streamed about her, and her heavy robes covered them both, like a blanket over a pair of lovers. The fabric's metallic embroidery glinted dully in the light.

"Damn the witch," Jerrel cursed under his breath. He stooped and unceremoniously tugged Xyanth's limp body to one side, then knelt beside his brother.

Santar lay on his back, his head turned to one side, his eyes closed, his features distorted by pain. His injured left arm was twisted under him at an awkward angle, broken in his fall. A deep new gash across his cheek oozed blood. Xyanth's dagger lay on the floor only inches from his head, its tip stained with blood.

Nareen scooped up the dagger, horrified. "It was poisoned, Jerrel!"

"I know. I have to get him to the ship. He disabled his own com link, the fool!" Jerrel spoke between clenched teeth. He indicated the heavy ring on Santar's right hand. "At least he had the sense to wear the recorder."

"He is dead?" The words were softly spoken, heavy with regret.

Nareen turned to find Gasperian standing behind her, his gaze fixed on Santar and Xyanth. He looked old, bowed by the horror of what had happened and by his failure to prevent it.

"Not dead, but badly injured." Jerrel picked Santar up in his arms, then stood. The younger man's head fell back. His right arm dangled limply. "I need to get help."

"Of course. My . . . these men can help. My personal surgeon is in the Hall . . ."

Gasperian's voice faded. His eyes dropped. Nareen could scarcely hear his final words.

"That is," Gasperian whispered, almost to himself, "if he's not already dead like so many others."

"Not them. I know another . . ." Jerrel glanced at Nareen, one eyebrow raised in a question.

She shook her head, understanding what he could not ask. Now that Kalinden was safe, she felt suddenly drained, exhausted. Jerrel would come back, but for now she had her own work. Somehow, she would have to find the strength to get through the next few hours. The future would have to take care of itself.

"Jerrel will manage well enough, Master," she said, drawing Gasperian away. "You have more important matters to attend to now." From the corner of her eye she saw Jerrel disappear behind the tapestry that one of the soldiers held to one side for him.

"I . . ." Gasperian hesitated, glanced back at Xyanth's still body. "I wanted her, you know. I offered for her years ago. Perhaps . . . if I had only . . ."

"She's dead, Master. Let her go." Nareen knew she should be shocked at the lack of respect in her voice. Right now, she didn't care.

"Come," she said, leading Gasperian toward the waiting Pardraik and his soldiers. "There's still a city to protect and the beastmen to fight."

Jerrel pushed the heavy door open and stepped out onto the roof of the Great Hall. Though there was a faint tinge of gray in the eastern sky, the night still held reign under a glittering canopy of stars and the fading light of a full moon.

It took a moment for him to locate Nareen, standing at the wall surrounding the edge of the roof.

She must have heard him coming—he made no effort to walk softly or disguise the sound of his footsteps on the stone—but she neither turned to him nor spoke, just stood there, huddled in a borrowed cloak, looking out over the rooftops of Kalinden.

Jerrel stopped just inches from her. He didn't try to touch her, but his hands, his very being, ached with the wanting to. Her only response to his nearness was to draw the cloak more closely about her.

Anxiety and fear suddenly twisted his insides. He was losing her.

When she'd agreed to join him, she'd been an exile from her city, disgraced and dishonored. Now, all that had changed. He'd had no problems finding her—even amid the confusion reigning in the hall below, people had known where the Sixth Runner was. They'd seemed almost awed by her efforts to save Kalinden. Already the tales of her exploits threatened to assume near mythic proportions.

"In all your travels, have you ever seen a city as beautiful as Kalinden?" Nareen's voice was low, barely above a whisper, but each word came to his ears as painfully as if she'd shouted.

Jerrel stared out at the shadowy, silvered outlines of Kalinden. Even softened by moonlight and dark, the city was stark, harsh—a creation to match the mountains that surrounded it.

And yet, he couldn't deny there was a fierce beauty to the scene. If this were all he'd ever known, all he'd ever loved . . .

"You love this city," he said. It wasn't a question.

Nareen nodded slowly, her gaze still fixed on the scene before her. "Yes. Yes I do. It's my home."

If only he could see her face, know what she

was thinking. He could force her around. All he'd have to do was put his hands on her shoulders . . .

He couldn't touch her. Didn't dare, because he wanted to so much.

"How is your brother?" There was no inflection, no key to her thoughts in her voice.

"He'll live, but he'll need a few more days in the med box. The poison was slow-acting but deadly."

Silence stretched between them, a tangible thing.

Was his brother part of the reason she was so distant? Would Santar's mistakes, the harm he'd inadvertently caused her people, come between them like an invisible wall?

"I'm glad. That he'll live, I mean," she said at last.

She turned slowly to face him, her face uplifted to his in the waning moonlight. Even by that pale radiance he could see the stern set of her jaw.

"What he did was wrong. He had responsibilities, duties and obligations that he chose to ignore. A lot of people have suffered because of him."

Jerrel hesitated, uncertain. Nareen's words were hard, uncompromising, yet he could swear he detected unspoken doubts behind them, questions that had nothing to do with Santar.

"Though it doesn't excuse him, his intentions were good," Jerrel offered cautiously. "Should he have ignored his own heart, his own belief that there were better ways to do things, other ways to live?"

Again the silence stretched.

"Gravnar's dead," Nareen said at last. The words sounded as if they'd been pulled out of her by force. Her lips tightened and she swallowed uncomfortably. "He died in the attack against the Hall."

"I'm sorry." It was inadequate, but what else could he say? Without thinking, Jerrel raised his hand to caress her cheek in a futile gesture of comfort. A tear, invisible in the silver darkness, stung his skin. He gently brushed it away with his thumb.

"He was my teacher, my guide," she said. This time she made no attempt to stifle the quaver in her voice. "He was my friend, the father I never knew. I . . . I can't imagine the world without him."

Jerrel would have drawn her into his arms, offered what small physical comfort he might, but she remained stiff and unbending, her pain her own.

"Gasperian offered me the position of Chief Runner."

Though he tried, Jerrel could detect no trace of a question in her words. She wasn't asking his advice, she was telling him what had transpired.

"I see." Jerrel let his hand fall away from her.

"I'd hoped, someday, to earn the right to be Chief Runner. It's all I've ever wanted since Gravnar began teaching me. Me, a homeless orphan with no claim on his time or affections."

Nareen turned away from him to look out over the city, her hands braced against the parapet as though she feared to lose touch with the stones of the city she knew so well.

"There were people who depended on your brother, and he failed them. There are people who depend on me, people to whom I owe everything I am, everything I hoped to be, and yet . . ."

She lifted her gaze to the stars overhead. "You've shown me worlds I never knew existed, offered me a chance to see and feel and do things I never dreamed of. I want . . ."

Abruptly she whirled back around and clutched his jerkin, grabbing the leather in her fists as though she feared he might disappear. Her face was raised to his, her eyes dark wells whose depths glittered in the insubstantial light.

"Take me with you," she said fiercely. "Now, before I'm too afraid, before I think of another reason I can't leave, another thing I *ought* to do."

At her first, frantic tugging on his tunic, Jerrel had wrapped his hands over hers in an awkward gesture of comfort. Now his own hands tightened, crushing hers.

"You'd leave Kalinden, everything you've known, to come with me?" Jerrel struggled to speak, unsure he'd actually heard her correctly. He couldn't have been more confused if the Great Hall itself had suddenly shifted under his feet. "Why?"

"Why?" The word was almost a sob. "Because I love you. Because I can't bear to live without you. Because I can't, I *won't* ask you to give up everything you've known to remain here, knowing the sacrifice that would mean."

She loved him! He hadn't lost her! She would come with him and . . . The exultation that surged through Jerrel fled even more quickly than it had come.

She would come with him, but at what sacrifice? Years of regret and shame that she'd abandoned her city when she was needed most? Endless nights of lying beside him, knowing she'd given up everything for him while he had given her nothing but a rootless, uncertain existence?

But what was the alternative? Remain here? On this backward world of warring city states? On this lost remnant of an Empire that stretched across a thousand, a hundred thousand stars? Here? Forever?

Unable to face the uncertain, tremulous expectancy he saw in Nareen's eyes, Jerrel lifted his gaze to where dawn was staining the horizon with hues of pink and lavender and rose.

The moon had almost disappeared behind the western mountains and the stars were retreating, their light dimming against the still tentative brush of day.

That was his home, his life. He belonged out there in the empty vastness of space, not bound within the narrow confines of a world that had forgotten its past. The limitless universe was his. What could possibly compare to that kind of freedom? What could tempt him to forgo it?

It was Nareen's insistent attempts to free her hands from his that made him turn his gaze from the fading stars back to her. Reluctantly, he released her, then clenched his hands against the sudden chill when the warmth of her was gone.

"No," Jerrel said, very softly.

"No?"

"No, I won't take you with me, because I'm going to stay here with you. I can't do anything else." He raised his hands, palms out, empty. "I love you. I can't ask you to sacrifice everything for me, and yet without you . . ." Jerrel paused, willing the unsteadiness out of his voice.

"I can't live without you," he said, very simply.

The spreading dawn touched her face with a

roseate glow that softened the lines of strain in her delicate features but did nothing to lighten the shadowed depths of her eyes. Those dark orbs, all trace of their normal brilliant color lost in the emotions that gripped her, were fixed on his face with an intensity that was almost physical.

"But you can't . . . I can't ask you to . . ." Nareen sputtered, almost choking on her words. "It's ridiculous for you . . ."

Her protests halted abruptly. Her eyes grew round and her mouth gaped, as though an unexpected thought had suddenly robbed her of the power of speech.

Ignoring his questioning gaze, Nareen fumbled at the collar of her tunic, then, with a quick duck of her head, pulled the chain with the com link from around her neck.

"I've been a fool," she murmured, her eyes, like his, fixed on the silver box in the palm of her hand. "But it doesn't . . . We don't . . ."

Her tongue flicked out to lick her lips in a nervous gesture that roused a sudden, aching heat within him. She turned to look out over the rooftops of Kalinden, awash now in a flood of color that softened the harsh lines and gray stones of the buildings, transforming them. The movement brought her closer to Jerrel, so close he could easily have gathered her in the curve of his arms. He settled for letting his hands rest on her shoulders.

Even under the heavy folds of the cloak he could feel the energy that surged through her. She laughed suddenly and Jerrel could resist no longer. With a groan he pulled her against him.

As he drew her to him, she twisted in his embrace, her face raised to his. She still clutched the silver com link in her hand, but Jerrel scarcely heeded it for her arms were wrapping about his neck, pulling his head down toward her, toward her lips that parted in an open invitation.

"I love you," she said fiercely, exultantly, her breath warm on his face.

Jerrel's mouth was scant inches from hers when her next words brought his head back up with a jerk.

"Will you show me the dawn on your world?" she said.

"My . . . But . . ."

"I love you, Jerrel bn' Hadar. Too much to chain you here when you've known the stars."

"But Kalinden . . . your people . . ." Jerrel faltered. He scanned her face, searching for some clue he must be missing. Tears swam in her eyes, dimming the intense green he could now see clearly—but they were tears of joy, not sacrifice, and her smile was more radiant than the dawn itself.

"We're two people from two different worlds," she said, ignoring the crystal drop that overflowed and trickled down her cheek. "I just realized . . . We made the mistake . . . *I* made the mistake of thinking that it had to be one or the other, my world or yours. I can't abandon my city, my people, yet you've shown me the stars and I can never be content with anything less."

"I don't understand. What . . . ?"

"We can have both!" Nareen was laughing again, this time through a cascade of tears. "Don't you see? Once the beastmen are driven back, Kalinden will go on as it always has. I'm needed here, but I don't have to be Chief Runner, I don't have to spend all my time on Errandane.

If I said I was going to accompany you on your trading . . . We could work something out so we could spend time here, then be free. . . . Jerrel, it's so simple! Why didn't I realize before that it could be so blessedly simple?"

For an instant, Jerrel couldn't move; then, with a choked sound compounded of laughter and amazed comprehension, he crushed Nareen against him, claiming her mouth in a kiss that was fire and storm and all the hungry need of a life lived too long alone, but that would never be lonely again.

With Nareen in his arms, her lips against his, the world disappeared and Jerrel never noticed until an embarrassed cough and mumbled, "Sorry . . . Didn't realize . . . I'll come back later," intruded into his consciousness.

Jerrel raised his head. Nareen was still in his arms, warm and real and pressed tightly against him. Everything else about him had changed, however.

Dazed, Jerrel looked around him, blinking. It took a moment for him to identify the curved gray walls of the transport chamber and the old man standing in front of the open doorway.

"Norvag?"

"If you have to ask, your condition's even worse than it looked," Norvag said, grinning at them both with smug approval. "CeeCee said Nareen was beaming you back on board. I thought you might . . ." His grin stretched even wider, if that was possible, and he rubbed his hands together in satisfaction. "However, I see I was wrong."

"Uhmm . . ." Not one intelligent comment came to mind, but at least Nareen was still clinging to him. Jerrel drew her closer in a protective gesture that seemed to meet with Norvag's full approval.

"Well, I've some chores to attend to," the old man said, backing toward the corridor. "Just got back, you know. Lots of things been put off." He got as far as the door, then just stood there, still grinning. "Danet's decided to stay in Matcassen, keep on with his observations. Santar's doing just fine. Be out of the med box sooner than we expected. I shouldn't wonder if—"

"Norvag." Jerrel wasn't sure he could manage a more coherent statement, but Norvag obviously heard the threat in his tone.

"Right. Best get busy." This time Norvag made it all the way out of the chamber. Before the door could shut, he put his hand on the edge of the opening and turned back to face them.

If Jerrel hadn't known that Norvag never cried, he would have sworn that it was a tear he saw glinting in the corner of the old man's eye.

"I just wanted to say . . ." Norvag hesitated, then added softly, "Long life and happiness. To both of you."

An instant later he was gone and the door had shut, leaving them alone in the center of the chamber.

"Norvag always was an optimist," Jerrel said at last, breaking the silence. He glanced down at Nareen, smiling. "If these last few weeks with you are any indication of what's ahead, I'm not too sure about our prospects for a long life."

He drew her closer and was just bending his head to claim a kiss when CeeCee interrupted.

"I thought you were going to leave that primitive on the planet, boss. You know the law frowns on bringing primitives aboard and—"

"CeeCee," Nareen interrupted, "shut off."

"You're not the boss here!" CeeCee squawked. "It's one thing to try to educate a creature like you, but to have you tell me to shut off is quite another! You're not even supposed to be here so if you think—"

"CeeCee, shut off." There was no ignoring the anger in Jerrel's sharp command.

CeeCee shut off.

Jerrel waited a moment, wondering if the computer was going to interrupt again. When it didn't, he turned his attention back to Nareen and found her gazing up at him.

As she stretched up to claim the kiss he was only too willing to offer, she said with a soft laugh, "I don't know about the long life part, but I think I can just about guarantee the happiness if you'll only get rid of that damn computer!"

UNRAVELED

C.J. BARRY

To continue her father's life's quest, Tru Van Dye has to leave the insular colony of Majj scientists where she was raised and find Rayce Coburne. Yet the virtual-reality program she acquires to gird herself against the man's touch is for naught—his presence overwhelms her. Tru's clever plans, her control, everything is coming unraveled.

Rayce Coburne tried to give up treasure acquisition. He despises dealing with icy customers. And Tru Van Dye is worse than usual—a prissy woman who will blackmail him with all his hopes and dreams. Still, there is a way he can fight back: A kiss a day is the perfect strategy. Unless the spinning he feels inside is Tru unwrapping his heart.

SUSAN GRANT
THE STAR PRINCESS

Ilana Hamilton isn't an adventurer like her pilot mother, or a diplomat like her do-right brother; she's a brash, fun-loving filmmaker who'd rather work behind the camera than be a "Star Princess" in front of it. Heiress or not, she's a perfectly normal, single woman . . . until Prince Ché Vedla crashes into her life.

With six months to choose a bride, the sexy royal wants to sow his wild oats. Ilana can't blame him—but fall for the guy herself? Hotshot pilot or no, Ché is too arrogant and too old-fashioned. But when he sweeps her off her feet Ilana sees stars, and the higher he takes her the more she loves to fly. Only her heart asks where she will land.